A Corner House in Moscow

Title page illustration: Northern Swallow, Wikimedia

A Corner House in Moscow

Mikhail Osorgin

ZEPHYR BOOKS
Ashgrove Publishing
London

LIST OF MAIN CHARACTERS

AT THE CORNER HOUSE IN SIVTZEV VRAZHEK

Grandfather – retired professor of ornithology; [Ivan Alexandrovitch]
Grandmother – [Aglaya Dmitrevna]
Tanyusha – granddaughter; [Tatyana Mihailovna]
Dunyasha Kolchagin – maid
Nicolai – dvornik (caretaker)

VISITORS TO THE HOUSE (IN ALPHABETICAL ORDER)

Andrey – Dunyasha's soldier brother; [Andryusha Kolchagin]
Astafiev – lecturer in philosophy; [Alexey Dmitrievitch]
Ehrberg – student intending to study law
Lenotchka – Uncle Borya's wife
Lvovitch, Edward – Tanusha'a music master; professor, pianist and composer
Poplavsky – professor of physics
Stolnikov, Sasha – army officer; [Alexander Ignatievitch]
Uncle Borya – Grandfather's son; engineer; [Boris Ivanovitch]
Vassya Boltanovsky – student of natural science; Tanyusha's close friend

OTHER CHARACTERS (IN ALPHABETICAL ORDER)

Alyonushka – assistant to Dr Kuporrossov; nurse to Vassya [Elena Ivanovna]
Anna Klimovna – Zavalishin's common-law wife
Brickmann – examining magistrate
Denissov – chairman of the House Committee in the block where Astafiev lives
Fyodor Ignatyitch – greengrocer; friend of Nicolai
Grigory – Stolnikov's batman
Kashtanov – former army lieutenant; friend of Stolnikov
Marya Savishna – Vassya's landlady
Protassov – engineer; friend of Vassya; [Pyotr Pavlovitch]
Smehatchev – Astafiev's stage name
Zavalishin – close neighbour of Astafiev's; executioner for the Tcheka

CONTENTS

PART I

I – The Ornithologist – 9
II – A Wonderful Day – 12
III – The Cemetery – 14
IV – *The Cosmos* – 17
V – Tanyusha – 21
VI – Lasius Flavus – 23
VII – Plan – 25
VIII – Time – 27
IX – Soldiers – 30
X – Tanyusha's Birthday Party – 33
XI – The Hired Musician – 36
XII – Visions – 39
XIII – *De Profundis* – 42
XIV – The Return Flight – 45
XV – The Passing of a Human Being – 48
XVI – The Most Irrational Little Creature in the World – 49
XVII – What Happened to the Clock – 52
XVIII – Uncle Borya – 54
XIX – The Scratch – 57
XX – Behind the Blinds – 61
XXI – The Fifth Card – 65
XXII – The Moment – 68
XXIII – Death – 71
XXIV – Night – 72
XXV – A Pair of Boots – 75
XXVI – 'Fire' – 78

CONTENTS

XXVII – The 'Miracle' – 82
XXVIII – Back from the Front – 86
XXIX – At the Memorial – 89
XXX – The Dvornik – 91
XXXI – Envy – 94
XXXII – October – 97
XXXIII – Between Two Windows – 101
XXXIV – The Bullet – 105
XXXV – Kolchagin's Career – 107
XXXVI – The Trunk's Nights – 111
XXXVII – The Little City of Monkeys – 115
XXXVIII – The Disabled – 118
XXXIX – The Circle Closes In – 121
XL – A Thing – 125
XLI – The Little Brown Sphere – 129
XLII – The Visit – 132
XLIII – The Concert – 136
XLIV – The First Kiss – 140
XLV – 'Ira' – 143
XLVI – With Care – 146
XLVII – *Axios* – 149
XLVIII – The Pilgrimage – 151

PART II

XLIX – Spring – 155
L – Books – 161
LI – Strangers – 164
LII – Twilight – 167
LIII – The White Frock – 170
LIV – A Declaration of Love – 174
LV – In the Thicket – 179

CONTENTS

LVI – A Second Chat – 185
LVII – Bagman – 189
LVIII – 'Stiffeys' – 194
LIX – I Know – 200
LX – The Man in the Yellow Gaiters – 205
LXI – The Trusty Knight – 212
LXII – Conversations – 217
LXIII – Sister Alyonushka – 221
LXIV – The Fifth Truth – 226
LXV – Comrade Brickmann – 230
LXVI – At His Bedside – 235
LXVII – The Traitors – 239
LXVIII – He Who Came – 243
LXIX – Moscow, 1919 – 246
LXX – In the Cell – 251
LXXI – Among the Influential – 255
LXXII – The Wolf Prowls – 260
LXXIII – Friends of Childhood – 263
LXXIV – The Two Sides – 269
LXXV – Zavalishin's Domain – 271
LXXVI – An Interview with a Dignitary – 275
LXXVII – The Little Pig – 278
LXXVIII – Vassya's Unfaithfulness – 283
LXXIX – The Explosion – 287
LXXX – Emptiness – 291
LXXXI – The Meeting – 296
LXXXII – Opus 37 – 299
LXXXIII – The Cuckoo Clock – 302
LXXXIV – A Surgical Case – 306
LXXXV – The Sivtsev Vrazhek Party – 310
LXXXVI – When the Swallows Come Back – 314

PART I

– I –

THE ORNITHOLOGIST

In the immensity of the universe, in the solar system, on the earth, in Russia, in Moscow, in the corner house of Sivtsev Vrazhek, in his study, in his armchair, sat the learned ornithologist, Ivan Alexandrovitch. Confined by the lampshade, the light fell on a book and struck the corner of the inkstand, the calendar and a pile of papers. The scholar, however, saw only that part of a page where there was a coloured picture of a cuckoo.

They were not learned thoughts that strayed through his mind, but simple, homely thoughts about the number of years that lay before him. They bore him away to the depths of a forest where a cuckoo was calling – the number of times it calls being the number of years one still has before one. Such was the popular belief, no more foolish than any other way of tailing the future. The cuckoo makes mistakes, just as doctors do; and not a single doctor can foretell when a man is going to be run over by a tram.

The grey-bearded, broad-faced, typically Russian professor did not want to die; and was unafraid of death only because he had been a man, and a wise man, both in his youth and in his old age. He was famous in the world of learning, and had a very special love for his own science; for there was beauty in it – hues of feathers, songs, nature, birth of spring and farewell to summer. There was poetry in his science. Every little bird was known to him, and, because of that knowledge, was dear. And the professor of ornithology did not want to die: he wanted to go on living. But how many years was the solitary, careless bird promising him?

The cuckoo called three times. The professor smiled, for he was not superstitious; besides, he was used to his clock. He closed the book and placed a slip of paper as a mark in it. He yawned – a good sign. In his old age he suffered from insomnia. Then he rose, fingered his waist, blew out the lamp and entered the bedroom.

An hour later, when the house was wrapped in silence and the cuckoo had called four times, a mouse crept from beneath a bookcase and listened attentively. Everything, it seemed, was as it should be – all asleep and no sign of the cat's eyes. The mouse flicked its tail, twitched its nostrils and set out.

Its way lay through the professor's bedroom, under the door of the other bedroom and into the dining room. Such a tiny expedition was only for crumbs. A longer journey was the one to the kitchen; but that was very dangerous (the cat). And it was best to start from a different point – from beneath the trunk in the passage. There, too, there was a hole in the floor.

The mouse saw only the bit of the floor nearest to it and the outlines of more distant objects, just enough for it not to lose its way. If only it could see like the cat!

When it had run to the door it slipped its plump little body through a chink and made sure with the end of its tail that it had indeed crept through. Another pause: a slight disturbance. The ornithologist slept as old men do, restlessly. And in his sleep he was saying: 'What? Why? Oh, what does it matter?' But now he was breathing regularly again, asleep.

The entire life of the professor had been devoted to his science. He could recognize birds at a distance by their feathers, forms and soft twitterings. But was he able to recognize people with the same ease? It was because of the twitter in her voice that he had fallen in love with his life's companion. Fledglings had hatched – three of them. Feathers had come; and they had grown and flown away. And now there, on the other side of the wall, lay his granddaughter, left fatherless and motherless.

The old lady, herself a songster, was still alive after all those forty years spent at the bird-scholar's side. A bird could not be chosen as he had chosen a human being! But there were, of course, all kinds of things in life, especially in one's youth.

Again the old man stirred in his sleep, and the grey ball vanished beneath the door into the adjacent bedroom.

It was stuffy in here. The bed stood enormous, with pillows all over it and a corner of the blanket hanging down. In the bed, curled up like a child, slept a little grey old lady, the professor's wife. On the table by the bed stood a glass of water, some powders, and sweets in a paper bag. And the armchair stood quietly by, its seat sunk from having been much sat upon. It smelled of lavender in here, and bygone days.

It was so unalarming in this room that the mouse crossed the carpet in a leisurely way, stopped, sat down and grew thoughtful. It was peaceful here as nowhere else, and like nowhere else – safe. The old lady was breathing inaudibly and dreaming simple, uninteresting dreams, sleeping with lips tightly pressed, her teeth in a glass of water.

Farther on, however, was a room which it was best to cross quickly without a pause; an alarming room, untenanted, resounding. There is something peaceful and homely about the odour of bedrooms; but the drawing-room, with its big windows and distant outlines, was very frightening indeed.

Something within the mouse's field of vision glittered, and it sprang back, nostrils and whiskers quivering on its sharp little muzzle. There was nothing to be frightened about, after all; it was only the grand piano's glass supports. But, heavens! in such an enormous world everything strikes a defenceless grey mouse as alarming.

The little mouse and the huge grand piano, capable of bursting into sound with all its strings and deafening it... That grand piano was the master of the house. The professor played – 'Now, if you like, I will imitate the nightingale. It begins like this – *fu-ee, fu-ee*, then low; *foor-r-r* and a trill, and then it warbles – quite impossible to imitate!' His wife, the old lady, Aglaya Dmitrevna, played very well indeed, but it was very difficult to get her to do so – 'Well, but my hands are old; they can hardly move.' Tanyusha was a pianist of the future; she had power, ability and a love of music. Tanyusha studied at the Conservatoire and played at small concerts without being nervous. But the grand piano only lived to the full when Tanyusha's music master, Edward Lvovitch, came in the evenings. Then, indeed, it lived. And that happened nearly every Sunday. It was a long time before the mice in the basement could get to sleep on those evenings; and on those nights they did not venture forth to explore.

Edward Lvovitch was a plain, elderly man, no conversationalist, but a wonderful pianist, and a composer, too. He was fond of sweet rusks with his tea, and had never in all his life tasted vodka. A somewhat curious individual.

Meanwhile, the mouse was already returning from the dining room, having found quite a quantity of crumbs, and was about to peep into the passage when there came a thud, and it had to run away. It had ransacked everything in the dining room; then it had gone back again through the drawing room and the bedrooms, back into the little hole and home. It was already growing light. The dark was alarming enough, but the light was even more so. It was always alarming.

Eternal fear ran in the shape of a little grey ball through the professor's house, and nobody noticed it. Nobody knew that a whole family of mice was helping the worm to gnaw away the wooden supports of the floor and the solid, though not everlasting, walls. The earth is getting cooler; mountains are crumbling; rivers are becoming more peaceful and shallower; everything is tending to reach one level; and the energy of the world is slowly failing. But the end is still far off.

For a second the mouse's tail lingered outside the hole, then vanished.

The cuckoo called six times. The professor stirred and his bed creaked. Sunshine touched the window curtain, and together with the sun there flew to the window a swallow that had arrived that day from Central Africa.

– II –

A WONDERFUL DAY

Morning was born – a rosy morn in a snowy robe. It beat at the panes with milky wings; then the casement-bolt clicked and the window flew open. Blinking, Tanyusha came face to face with the morning, and a chilly breath of air crept between her nightgown and her skin. On tiptoe, with light springing step, she ran back to her bed to snuggle in it a little longer, glad that the day was going to be fine.

What are the thoughts of a girl of sixteen in the early morning, with the window wide open? Her first thought is that it's a fine day; her second, that today is Sunday; instead of a third – a smile without a cause. Then daily duties and cares: Lenotchka had to be rung up to be told to be sure to come that evening. It was nice to be enjoying the cosiness of bed, but drawing her was the impulse to go and pour cold water over herself, and try over some new music after coffee. In the evening, dear, funny Edward Lvovitch would play.

Like the true grandchild of her 'bird professor' grandfather that she was, Tanyusha noticed at once that the swallow had come. She must be sure to tell grandfather about it. Yesterday there hadn't been one; so this then was the first day of real spring.

Bells, bells, din of the awakened street and the swallows' *chir-r-r*. Life before her stretched so far. With her slender fingers – nails cut short like a musician's – she stroked the already rounding curve of her shoulder from which her nightgown had slipped. Then all of a sudden, feet on the strip of carpet, she ran to the glass to look at her face, and 'I'm not at all so bad-looking!'

At sixteen a girl knows what her eyes are like, and makes a contemptuous grimace at herself. But the glass does not yet tell her about the secret of the little bare shoulder. A moment later the mirror was coldly reflecting the arm that raised the jug and the water streaming over her body; mirroring coldly, for nobody's benefit (surely not for swallows that flew past the window?); then briskly, firmly, the rough towel did its work, and Tanyusha was ready.

On the wall hung the photograph of a picture, a picture of people sitting on a sofa listening to music.

By the time a button had been sewn on, it was already nine o'clock. To waken grandfather was Tanyusha's privilege. She tapped at his door.

'Grandfather, get up! It's a glorious day. And, news – the swallows have arrived!'

'Hullo, Tanyusha, I am getting up, I am getting up.'

'How did you sleep?'

'Very well, and you?'

'I, too. Oh, grandfather, what a glorious day! I'm going to order coffee.'

The windows of many Moscow homes were opened wide that morning; and out of them glanced young faces and old, fresh faces and sleepy faces, blinking and listening to the long-drawn Sunday peal of bells. The old hardened putty, with cotton wool sticking to it, crumbled to bits; the little glasses were taken out from between the double windows and die acid poured away. Then the window-sills were swept clean, bits of refuse fa lling out of the windows. Sun, air and chimes swept into the upper rooms in heavy waves that broke against the walls, the furniture and stoves. Easter joy was in the believers' souls, and to those who had no faith spring brought in its place an animal gladness.

Carpets were being beaten in the yards; and on the kitchen windowsill the cook placed a box of earth into which she stuck some onions.

Pressing to his side loose sheets of Roman law, a student stopped on his way home to the students' quarters to buy some pickled apples at the corner of the Malaya Bronnaya; while beneath the Stone Bridge a boy flung out a thread with a pin, curling his tongue round the corner of his mouth and thinking how a 'big one' would suddenly snap at it.

A tram rang its bell frantically and unnecessarily, while a policeman controlled with a white cotton glove the movements of two carriages and a dray.

That day a seminarist who had been thinking of suicide for months decided to put it off once more; and a plain and lonely woman doctor who, with flushed face, had bought an inexpensive hat – the first that came to hand – put it aside and went out in her old one: she had been training her will since girlhood.

The Réaumur thermometer was gambling gaily on a rise.

Altogether it was a wonderful day.

– III –

THE CEMETERY

There are, however, windows that are never opened; others that open behind gratings, like prison windows. A dim light falls through the ever-dusty panes upon cupboards and registers stuffed full of documents.

In Paris, in Berlin and London, where spring came earlier, it skirted old buildings warily, without casting one ray of sunshine into the windows of the diplomatic archives. The men who guarded these cemeteries of plans, negatives and papers covered with writing were men able to think in figures, polyglots, clever men.

The sun thought that it alone controlled all life on earth. The whole of human life appeared to it only as an incarnation of the energy of its own rays. It had peopled the North Pole with the highest forms of the organic world and, when the time came, brought about the dreadful cataclysm of the living, destroyed the high culture of the poles, and developed the backward Equator till it reached the utmost perfection of form. It laughed at the efforts of earth's organisms to adapt themselves, and at their struggle for existence that contributed so little towards making life easier and improving the race. All that polypus or man ever did was its doing – the sun's – was its own transmuted ray. Intelligence, knowledge, experience, faith, no less than body, food and death, were nothing but transformations of its own light's energy.

But the little man sewn into buttoned-up strips of material, who suffered from colds in the head and protected himself from the sun behind walls, letting in by means of a wire no more than the indispensable globe of light in a sealed glass, tried to arrange his life according to his own ideas. He dipped his pen into the inkpot and wrote, muttered under his breath and gave orders.

Hecatombs were formed by the piles of paper.

Truth and falsehood, which kneaded and baked together created motive, cause and fact, flew along wires. Striving to subdue all life to his own inanimate will, man's brain warred with the sun. Man fenced in a bit of land, walled round a town, set frontiers about a state, limited race by colour, nationality by tradition, contemporary affairs by history and existence itself by politics. His cunning and inquisitive brain built up a pyramid of the living and dead, climbed to its summit – and was overthrown with it.

The sun laughed at him, and he laughed at the sun. But it was always the sun that laughed last. With a force beyond man's comprehension, the sun cast upon earth sheaves of energy that had come to life in the electro-magnetic whirl. Like battering rams, its rays fell upon earth, and everything that man had considered to be the creation of his own intellect was destroyed, whereas all that the sun created lived.

Taciturn and self-sufficient, an official deciphered a letter word by word, and translated it into a German prose that was jerky and literal. The ambassador read it through, smiled and approved: he had been commended in the letter.

The ambassador thought he knew everything that was known in the highest circles in Berlin, but in reality he knew only a considerable part. The highest circles in Berlin knew all there was to know, save what the little Serbian schoolboy knew. The schoolboy knew very little, of course – almost nothing. Impetuous, sincere, with a strong sense of honour and exceedingly highly-strung, he had been tainted by a drop of national poison. He had learned to shoot at a target drawn upon the outer wall of a hen house, which might have been hard on the speckled hens and their vociferous pasha had not lucky chance saved them from every bullet he fired.

When the little Serbian had learned to shoot, he made up his mind to become a national hero. For that, it was necessary to slay a national foe – no other way of becoming a hero having been thought of. And as there were quite a lot of little Serbians learning to shoot at targets on hen-house walls, fate was bound to send to one or other of them a novel target – the breast of the Austrian archduke.

That might not have happened, of course. But if it had not, something else would. To whatever happened there was an answer ready behind the dusty panes of the archives. The sun made history; and man wrote commentaries on it, looking upon himself as its maker. That was the reason why he shut himself in by walls and did not open the windows in spring. The cemetery of papers and secrets which he had obtained through friendships and spying he considered to be the world's signalling station and the country's very pulse.

There were a number of such cemeteries, both big and small, and their countries, potentates and peoples were very proud of them.

Although in the passage of centuries and the whirling of nebulae the united strength of all those cemeteries amounted to no more than 'Will Lenotchka come this evening to listen to the music?' the paper cemeteries played a tremendous and decisive part both in Lenotchka's life and Sivtzev Vrazhek's, as well as in the lives of all who plough and write, sow and love, lived yesterday and will live tomorrow.

And at that moment when the sixteen-year-old girl flung wide her window and saw the first swallow, a spark from a wireless station went crackling through the air; a thought wormed and twisted its wily way through the diplomat's brain; a hen, chancing to bend her head, avoided the schoolboy's bullet; and the pen of the third-rate journalist swelled the bubble of national pride.

Driving its hoofs deep into the rich, damp soil, a horse was drawing a plough.

Into a mould ran scoopfuls of molten metal thrown in at the slight touch of a workman's lever.

The buds of a young birch were swelling; the grass was putting forth green blades.

But the man who was following the plough did not yet know that it was on that little green meadow near the birch, doomed to be shattered by a shell, that he, too, would fall, riven in two and deafened by that metal – cooled and heated again. Nobody knew of it. It was of little consequence and left no trace.

In the paper cemeteries figures took the place of gravestones and crosses. Surplus units vanished in round numbers. The man behind the plough did not exist – could not exist; nor the workman either, nor the birch, nor the shell that felled it.

The living disappeared in the rounding off of figures.

– IV –

THE COSMOS

That evening the windows of the little house in Sivtzev Vrazhek were lit up with a welcoming brilliance.

As he approached the front door, Edward Lvovitch raised his head and saw the red curtains of the drawing room. The sight of them gave him a sensation of warmth and well-being. Mobility and blood returned to the musical fingers, numbed with cold in the pockets of his light coat. He was a trifle late that evening, and found them all assembled drinking tea.

Aglaya Dmitrevna, wearing spectacles and a large ancient brooch, was presiding at the samovar. The old professor was arguing with a young friend, Poplavsky, a professor of physics. Tanyusha and Lenotchka were listening.

Lenotchka's eyes were round in a round, rosy face. When she listened, Lenotchka was always surprised, and when she was surprised her eyebrows rose and her small button-like mouth opened. Tanyusha knew how to listen, and was able at the same time to watch the speaker and think not only about him and his interlocutor, but about herself and Lenotchka's funny look of surprise, and about the amount one ought and wants to know.

There were other guests besides: Ehrberg, the highly respected and disagreeably clever student; Uncle Borya, the eldest son of the ornithologist, and his wife – both of them inconspicuous people.

Edward Lvovitch entered, rubbing his hands. His usual place on

Aglaya Dmitrevna's left was waiting for him. Everything was as it should be, following the tradition of an acquaintance of two or three years.

They drank tea. The professor of physics, Poplavsky, was discussing the experiments of Michelson and Morlay and the motion of light-waves with the old professor. The latter expressed a doubt: weren't physics impotent?

'Your light-bearing ether is somewhat open to suspicion. Too much has to be adapted and made to fit. You physicists are in an impasse.'

Poplavsky did not deny the impasse; but did that undermine the science? Wait till tomorrow!

After tea everybody went into the drawing room. The professor, Tanyusha and Uncle Borya settled themselves on the spacious divan; Aglaya Dmitrevna, with her knitting, in her easy chair in the lamp-light; Lenotchka on a chair, still looking surprised; Poplavsky in the darkest corner; Uncle Borya's wife somewhere inconspicuous.

Edward Lvovitch played daily at various places, but his favourite day was Sunday, spent at the ornithologist's house. And, curiously enough, he was nervous. Though not old, he looked like an old man, with his bald head and long unkempt locks on the nape of his neck and his temples. The sight of one of his eyes was poor and his back very bent. Edward Lvovitch's ugliness caused him a good deal of discomfort, and he had a trick of rubbing his hands together.

He sat down at the piano, but immediately leapt up to regulate the height of the stool, setting it at length at the right distance from the keyboard. He struck a chord and ran his fingers up and down the keys. Then he grew uneasy again and glanced first at the top of the piano, then under it. Tanyusha grew uneasy, too, and ran up to help him. It appeared that the edge of the carpet had got beneath one of the legs. With Uncle Borya's aid it was pulled out. Another chord – all right.

'I would rike to try over something.' Instead of 'l', Edward Lvovitch pronounced a slurred 'r' 'Onry if you would care to hear, of course... I could pray something erse.'

Tanyusha understood.

'Do play your own thing, Edward Lvovitch. The one you were talking about, then. Is it finished?'

'Is it finished?... How sharr I say?... I know it by heart, though it's armost an improvisation. Its titre is... it might be named *The Cosmos*.'

'Cosmos... that's interesting,' observed the professor of physics. 'Only music could fully...'

Lenotchka sat looking surprised.

'Perhaps the room might be somewhat darkened,' Edward Lvovitch ventured to ask with embarrassment.

Tanyusha turned down the lights, and there remained only the lamplight by which the old lady was working.

And Edward Lvovitch played.

Lenotchka's surprised eyes followed the composer's fingers flashing over the keys in the semi-darkness, and watched his head one moment flung back, the next bent forward over his hands. Lenotchka listened to the sounds, to single notes and harmonies, thinking how unlike melody or dance music or opera overture it was. Then she remembered that Edward Lvovitch was called a genius, and that his left eye squinted, and that here she was listening to a genius playing. It was beyond Lenotchka's powers to collect and arrange her thoughts into one whole, and her eyebrows lifted in surprise.

Uncle Borya sat on gloomily. He was an engineer, but had not been successful in his profession. He had a plain wife who looked old. Then there were many things of which he knew absolutely nothing, among them – music. Beethoven, Grieg – he had heard all that. Just names. But how is one to make out which is which? Scriabin... dissonances. Why is the thing Edward Lvovitch is playing called *The Cosmos*? The cosmos has something to do with astronomy... How nice it would be if everything above his head turned out to be sheer nonsense, nothing more than fancy. Then he would rise in the world and become a man of importance. And why, after all, should steam boilers be on a lower level than music? What do they know about steam boilers? Nevertheless, Uncle Borya gloomily acknowledged to himself that music was indeed on a higher level than steam boilers and that this set him lower in the human scale, making him feel miserable and uninteresting.

The old ornithologist sat stretched out, with his eyes closed. The sounds floated above him, brushing him with their wings and soaring aloft. Now they came flying in a tumultuous flock with loud cackling and cawing, now singing with piercing sweetness from afar. It was not upon earth, but not far above it – no higher than the clouds or the flight of a lark. Edward Lvovitch's *Cosmos* was not in the least awe-inspiring! Nor so complex either; not even exotic. Just the Russian countryside. But how good it was! Peaceful old age, the divan, a dear little granddaughter, and the highest and best that went by the name of art within reach... I am a professor and am well known; I am old, but do not want to die, though of course I shall be ready to go quite calmly when the time comes, for I have lived and fulfilled my being, and now that the end is drawing near, feel sure of myself and confident... Sounds are like flowers, and music like bright meadows, forests and waterfalls. Edward Lvovitch is a trifle absurd, but he is a past-master of his art, and feels a great deal that others can attain only through learning, thought or old age.

In the vast expanses of the universe, in the midst of nebulae, starclouds and suns – a cooled planet, Aglaya Dmitrevna's lamp. The old lady listened, knitting on without dropping a stitch. She listened with pleasure, thinking that there was very little water left in the samovar and that the charcoal was still hot, but that Dunyasha would be sure to think of it... Edward Lvovitch is a wonderful musician and an excellent teacher. Tanyusha is sixteen; let her go on learning. Though she will marry in any case, which is of course what matters most. With her knowledge of music she will make a better match. And she may as well finish her historical studies, too, for there's no hurry. Tanyusha is an orphan, but an orphan is indeed fortunate when both grandparents are alive and things go well with them... All the same he is going on playing a very long time. And Aglaya Dmitrevna peered above her spectacles, and nearly dropped a stitch.

In the darkest corner of the room, in a soft armchair, Professor Poplavsky was thinking along his own lines. The creation of the world – how stupendous! But one should first think of the atom in order to get a true idea of it. And the atom is not the least. Edward Lvovitch strives to reach a conception of the creation through the power of music with its seven tones. But knowledge may not be converted into a musical conceit. The seven colours of the spectrum would yield a better result. And here we are weighing most accurately the fiery mass of a far-off star, defining the complicated composition of a heavenly body and determining its age! Yet music may be right, in that it follows in its conception the very same path and leads to the same illusory creation. The astronomer studies the universe. Yes – but which? It no longer exists for us as such. Our telescopes show us nebulae, stars and planets. The sun was like that – eight minutes ago; a star – a thousand years ago; some other star – tens, hundreds of thousands of years ago. A great delusion. But that Edward Lvovitch is playing wonderfully well. Music owes its greatness to its ability to do without words and figures, and to the fact that it does not need to be translated into an imperfect idiom. There may be no cosmos in those sounds of course, but translate them into the language of words and figures and you will get – geometry.

– V –

TANYUSHA

Tanyusha was sitting curled up on the divan, her head nestling against her grandfather's shoulder.

At first she drank in the sounds, then abandoned herself to the flow of harmony. A tiny, glowing point, she floated on through airless space, surrounded by the eternal and unanswerable questionings of the stars, planets and nebulae, now rising from things earthly to the universal, now dropping from the universal to life's commonplaces. She sought no cosmos in the music, but simply gathering it up into her soul lived in its orbit, at its side. Her own light body, the cosy warmth of her grandfather's shoulder, the dim light of the drawing room and the undulation of the music, all this she left entirely to the processes of her subconscious mind. She filled the spacious room with images, saw them take shape below the ceiling, and watched their choral dance around the lamp, following the haphazard figures of their dance and the rhythm of their measured movements. She flew with them beyond the confines of the walls. Then, listening intently, her lips parted, she obediently received into the storehouse of her mind new bales of unpacked thought – stores of raw material which she would set herself to work at later on with all the strength of early morning. She was not apprehensive in the least; and though she knew it would be difficult, she was both grave and glad.

The cosmos? Tanyusha could not grasp it. For was it not the whole sum of things and the crowning of all, whereas she was but on life's threshold, hardly yet beyond the confines of chaos from which she had come at her birth? So far she had only just begun to gather up the crumbs of knowledge, being still entirely in the world of problems and first perceptions – all most important, all tottering and contradictory. She strained eagerly towards what was clear – the axiom, casting theory aside, chafing at alternative solutions and experiencing no need of faith. She felt sure that everything was important – everything, down to the hair in grandfather's beard that was tickling her face. But there was so little time and so much to get done that she took a mental leap from details – these she would think of later on – to the enormous general, from the crumpled folds of the tablecloth to the sweet and terrible 'What is the meaning of Life?' and more especially 'How should one live?' She had already come to the decision that the goal of life lay in the actual process of living; but she had been afterwards disturbed by the thought: Was that true? And hadn't she been unfair to the goal? Hadn't she thereby lowered the meaning of existence? During a conversation with grandfather, Poplavsky had once said that three points in a straight line might not give a straight line at all: that it would be 'relative.' She had not quite understood, but was troubled by the idea. What, then, of all she had come to consider as certain, the things by which she tested her deductions? How could grandfather – learned grandfather – smile and be so calm? Did he by any chance know something that was beyond all that? Even Poplavsky's eyes had grown mournful when he had talked about his absurd points. But grandfather, who ought to understand, and who knew too, had been quite calm about it.

'Don't say such dreadful things in front of Tanyusha,' he had said jokingly. 'She won't be able to get to sleep.'

And it was true that it had taken her a very long time to get to sleep that night, although she had not thought about those points, but had attacked instead the general problem of living when there was nothing quite, quite certain in life.

And then, obscurely, she had guessed at the existence of two kinds of people: those who take things as they are and build their happiness upon them, and those for whom there is nothing upon which to build, since the foundations under them are always being shaken by ever-changing problems. Grandfather was one of the former; but it was possible that those people knew something higher still, something above all questioning, unshakeable. She, however, with her eager mind, belonged to the second sort of people.

And, attentively, her musical ear caressed by each minute particle of sound, blending them from time to time into one whole and visualizing them confined to the five lines of the music score – herself a pianist – Tanyusha listened to the strange and powerful improvisation of her master, thinking her own small homely thoughts, and great ones, too, to which the feeble powers of her consciousness were not yet strong enough to discover a solution. Her world as yet was only in the process of being created.

Edward Lvovitch will finish in a moment. It's almost melody now. All that he has tried to express is now reducing to a few quite simple sounds. Can it be that it's all so clear to him?

Edward Lvovitch did finish, and everybody remained silent. He got up, rubbed his hands and gazed guiltily at the lamp. And Aglaya Dmitrevna, looking up kindly above her spectacles, said:

'That was so nice; you have no idea how nice it was! I have been listening with real pleasure!'

She said it quite simply. The others tried to think of something to say, but there was nothing that could be said. And, coming to herself, Tanyusha sighed.

– VI –

LASIUS FLAVUS

One bright morning at dawn the Angel of Life cast seed upon the moist black earth that lay in readiness for it.

The sun rose, and the seed, quivering with expectation, steamed a warm haze about itself, swelled, burst, and put forth a sappy white shoot and a thread-like root.

The root worked its way downward, seeking the repletion of moisture and clinging to the rich particles of soil. The shoot put forth all its strength to straighten itself, showed a green leaf and opened out in the sunshine.

But when the sun set, the Angel of Death carried a linden basket full of weeds over the fields and threw among the new green shoots the seeds of discord and of evil. And when morning came, their deceptive green as well was warmed by the impartial sun, and man rejoiced over the abundant young growth in the fields he had sown.

That year the Almighty and Non-existent promised victory to the Angel of Death. And when the first blade of grass lengthened out and began to form an ear, up climbed hurriedly the ant Lasius Flavus. He was not a hunter of plant lice. The anthill on the skirt of the forest had a fine herd of grubs and was amply provided for by their sweet milk. Scouts had reported that all was not quiet in the neighbourhood and that the ant republic was being menaced by an attack of the tribe of hunters, Formica Fusca, which had already swarmed across the embankment of the railway that was being laid and was massing its forces at the corner of the field. It was not the fight they dreaded, but the slavery that threatened them, and that at a time, too when the winged females had just returned from their first flight, wingless, and were preparing to give birth to a new generation of workers.

It was in the sultry heat of a July day that the first battle raged. Jaws of steel cut into enemy legs and antennae, and sliced them off with a single snap; bodies coiled up into balls, and the strong gnawed right through the middles of the weak.

At the spot where the armies met, the sandy path was strewn with gnawed-off legs, bits of antenna: and wriggling balls of bodies. The plunderers were hastily dragging the pupae along the bypaths to provide for their future comfort by these slaves of tomorrow. Some famished warrior or other got into the enemy's stalls and greedily milked a fattened grub. A moment later he was squirming on the ground in deadly grips with the herdsman who had rushed to defend the property of his tribe.

The battle raged right on till sunset, when the anthill was already besieged by the reinforcements of their pale yellow field foe. But something happened then which not even the ablest among ant strategists could have foreseen.

The earth shook; noisy shadows advanced, and the anthill was suddenly swept away by a blow that came from heaven knows where. Everything on the paths was thrown into a state of confusion, and foes at grips in a struggle of unabated ardour were crushed by an unseen, unknown force.

The grass around was bruised and trampled; grains of sand were crushed into the bodies of ants, and not a trace remained of the well-ordered armies. In space, of which even the most astute ant intellect may have been ignorant and of proportions inconceivable to it, there passed, like a menace, like a world catastrophe, a godlike, irresistible and all-destroying force.

It was not only the ant armies that perished then; the crops that had been sown in strips there perished too, flattened out by soldiers' boots; little bushes of juniper that had been trampled upon drooped to earth, and myriads of creatures, both alive and preparing to live – larae:, puae, tiny beetles, plant lice, nestfuls of field birds, little cups of flowers scarce open – all perished beneath the feet of the division that skirted the forest. And when, following the machine-gun section, the weary horses drew along the guns, there remained nothing but a trampled and deep-rutted strip of earth where once a living world had been.

For a long time afterwards the ant spy of the herdsman tribe, Lasius Flavus, continued to crawl unsteadily about the wilderness into which God's live garden had by a miracle been converted. Neither friend nor foe could he find, nor could he recognize the land. He crept about bewildered and unhappy, a tiny victim of the commencing cataclysm.

The division halted in a little village, according to instructions. Dogs barked and ran away yelping; soldiers with buckets stretched down in a line to the river; a hoarse voice uttered words of command; flustered hens cackled, and night came down over the earth – not one second later than it was due.

And once again the stars lit up their ancient lamps.

– VII –

PLANS

The programme of the swallows that had flown over to Sivtzev Vrazhek from Central Africa, and that were now living above Tanyusha's window, was in the main carried out. Fledglings worked their way out of the egg, grew strong, learned to use their wings, and were now ready to live independent lives. There were, for the moment, very few cares. Their interest in life was not so overmastering yet; and the swallows and, indeed, the whole swallow tribe turned most of their attention to the problem of extra feeding, which would enable them to stand the journey back in the autumn. The only birds to give themselves whole-heartedly up to the joy of living were the young – free from passions as yet and light-hearted, ready to investigate everything, chase flies, chatter nonsense on telegraph wires, and, in the evenings, catch the rays of the setting sun on high, when dusk was already creeping below.

The life-programme of the disagreeably clever student, Ehrberg, was somewhat more complicated. He was coming to the end of his university career, but was thinking of staying on to specialize in civil law and marrying in accordance with the dictates of inclination and reason. There being no hurry, he was able to look round carefully and thoroughly before choosing a wife from among the young families of the professors. One of the candidates to that happiness was Tanyusha. That was why Ehrberg came on Sundays to see the professor of ornithology. But keeping Tanyusha in reserve, he continued to look around in a leisurely way, perfectly certain that he could make no mistake in his choice.

In July war was declared. Among the half milliard people whose everyday plans it upset was the disagreeably clever student, Ehrberg, who had just taken his final examinations. Like all the clever people who had tasted of the wisdom of state lore, he reckoned that the war could not last longer than three months. Therefore, anxious not to spoil his career by getting a civilian post behind the lines, he entered a training school for cadets. The uniform suited him, and an officer's would suit him better still. He very much needed the enforced rest from intellectual work; and military training was good for the physique. Ehrberg was not slow to learn how to plant his feet firmly in walking, how to report, keep his belt tight and fold his things neatly before going to bed. Being tall, he was put at the end of the rank during drill.

It was Dunyasha, the maid whose brother had gone to the war at its very beginning, who was more in love with Ehrberg than anyone else. Looking upon him as a future officer, it seemed to her that Ehrberg was the highest type of being, quite inaccessible – which indeed he was to Dunyasha, who would blush in patches, from her chin to the tip of her ears, when helping him out of his cadet's coat. And it was Dunyasha who was the first to notice that Lenotchka did not take her round, surprised eyes off him. It was not to be wondered at of course: he was handsome, important, and talked of military operations with the same assurance with which he had formerly discussed the Stanislavsky Theatre and the problems of international law. But in uniform he looked still nicer and younger, and not so remote from the heart of a simple girl.

Had Tanyusha known that she was one of those selected by Ehrberg she would have feared him. But Ehrberg did not in any way make a distinction between her and the others, unless it was by a gentle respectfulness and special attentions to the old lady, Aglaya Dmitrevna. This attitude pleased Tanyusha, and she was friendly with him. She neither understood his private ends nor discriminated between them. Had he not proved himself to be a man in not wanting to go and hide behind the lines like so many others? Ehrberg had enrolled himself as an ensign and everyone approved of him for having done so. And Tanyusha was glad: he was an acquaintance of hers. She was quite unaware of Lenotchka's feeling towards him, but in those days one thought and spoke so little about one's personal feelings and affairs, or even about music. The war had absorbed everyone, so that it seemed somehow strange to talk of anything else.

Ehrberg had an elderly mother whom he did not introduce to any of his acquaintances, either for want of opportunity or intentionally. His father had been a German of Riga, whereas his mother, a nonentity, came of lower middle-class Moscow people. His mother, too, had plans: that everything in life should be just as her wonderful son wished. Had not things been as his father had wished before? And no harm had come of it. Men knew more than women ever imagined. And she wore a cap, did the housekeeping and saw to the cleanliness of the strong, closely worked crotchet antimacassars that were scattered over the armchairs.

Ehrberg was in the habit of kissing his mother's hand. If it had been she who kissed his, it would have been unaffected and sincere. When he went out his mother would never ask where he was going or when he was coming home. He would tell her of his own accord if it were necessary that she should know.

In the swallows' plans there was the troublesome, trackless migration; in Ehrberg's, soundness and stability. When Ehrberg drank, the hand that set the glass of tea down on the saucer was shapely, steady and sure.

– VIII –

TIME

In the basement under the scholar-ornithologist's study, at the spot where at beam was fixed against the foundation wall, there was a greenish patch covered with white, woolly mould. On the damp stone floor a little cone-shaped heap had been formed by moist particles of lime and minute bits of wood that had fallen from the beam.

To the mouse this patch looked something like a Gobelin tapestry. Its fungus pattern was delicate, ingenious and many-tinted. Thousands of generations had worked at it. The oozing of the damp, slaked lime awakened life between the bricks and plaster. The work of destruction went on without any co-ordinated organization, as though following no plan. Microscopic creatures, with their own ways of feeding and multiplying, ploughed up and manured the fungus field. They perished, radiated heat and stirred into activity the fertile patch that was growing gradually into a dense forest of graceful palms, drooping willows and fancifully festooned lianas.

Flashing its little beady eyes and straining the muscles of its tail, the grey mouse was briskly breaking off tiny bits of the thick floorboards with its little claws and teeth. It was a work that had been begun by its forebears. An exact calculation had been made of distances and directions. The calculation was already long forgotten, but the trace of claws and teeth pointed out the way. Resting its hind legs against the rough wall and the soft mound of rubbish, the mouse did two things at a time: continued the cultural work of generations and ground off the points of its teeth that were growing too fast.

A noise from without alarmed the worker in the basement. A cart went rumbling by along the cobbled Moscow road; one or two flakes dropped from the wall, stopping up the worm's passage with refuse; a little bit of rotted wood in the beam gave way. The professor's old house shook and heeled over infinitesimally, though not even the sharp-sighted mouse was able to detect it. A drop of yesterday's rain, that had not had time to evaporate, ran in between the stones of the outer wall; on the roof a rusty nail, that held an iron plate of the roofing, broke, and a swallow fluttered out of its nest beneath the window. Poised in the air, the swallow examined the clay fastenings of its building; then, its mind at rest, returned to the eggs it had left behind. Its home was new and strong.

Needing information, the professor spent a long time looking through a fat German volume. After some considerable time, he remembered that he had already reproduced those very figures in a former work of his. He drew a case out of a register, took out a manuscript of long ago, searched through it, and was surprised at his former results. The new data would alter them considerably. The manuscript was of the same size as the one which he had but recently begun and had the very same lines. But the old paper had grown yellow with age, and the professor's writing, formerly big and bold, was now cramped and irregular, and slanting to the right. The professor did not notice this. From the wall his young wife, in a narrow-waisted dress, with shoulder-of-mutton sleeves, looked down at him and smiled; but he did not notice her either.

The old lady in the next room took her set of false teeth out of the glass and wiped it dry. Then she put the teeth into her mouth, settled them in comfortably and looked in the mirror; the hollows of the cheeks were filled in and smoothed out. She sighed and set her cap straight.

Tanyusha was not at home. She was sitting in a big, half-empty lecture theatre, listening attentively to a lecture in which the professor – carefully, afraid lest he should be too extreme – was undermining the theory of evolution. His critical mind required a periodic repetition of history. Delving deep into the centuries, he drew an attractive picture of the vanished civilizations of the East. To Tanyusha's surprise – she was but sixteen – the Mediterranean nations, whose culture she had been taught to look upon with wonder and admiration, now passed before her eyes, achieving little more than to discard or to restore fragments of a most ancient culture, evolved by nations that had come into the world before them.

There had risen from the depths of centuries a mighty religious system, whose discipline had embraced every aspect of life, permeated all the interests of the mind and all the trifling details of existence – filling man's entire life.

From beneath the strata of Greek sciences and philosophies, unexpectedly shorn of all originality, Babylon emerged, and the lofty thinking of the Egyptians, Iranians and Hindoos pierced through. The continuity of historical development was cut short by the decay of civilizations and the culmination of processes.

In the elderly lecturer's mind all this gave rise to pessimism and despondent thoughts; but the minds of the young were stirred to wonder and admiration in the presence of the past, and to a respect for those ancestors of distant ages, not merely as beings in man's image, but as thinkers, poets and mighty politicians.

A new spring of life forced its way out of the ruins of past ages and man's mind strove after yet another revival.

There were facts, however, clear to young and old alike: the wreck of those values that had claimed to be absolute, the precariousness of the edifice of present existence and the imminence of the threats that were massing over the new Babylon.

Her eyes riveted on the pince-nez that were constantly dropping off his nose, Tanyusha listened to the lecturer, looked into the past, sensed the future and grew. Rapid strokes crossed out the writing on the delicate brain – childish thoughts and simple beliefs; the untidy scrawl of a child's diary disappeared beneath the shorthand of new words, and the gall of thought dropped into the honey of the heart.

Tanyusha listened, and her lips were parted.

– IX –

SOLDIERS

Dunyasha's brother, Andryusha – Private Kolchagin, infantryman – had very little to do with the lordly little house in Sivtzev Vrazhek.

He had lived in the village until he reached the age of military service, and was twenty-three years old when war was declared. He had hardly time to look around before he found himself in the trenches. Soon, however, the trenches were abandoned and the retreat begun.

Kolchagin had no idea, for that matter, whether they were advancing or retreating. He never saw the enemy at close quarters, only heard him. He had not the faintest notion what the war was about, but carried out punctiliously whatever instructions were given him. He could stand a great deal and was quite satisfied with the food. Being single and having no household of his own, he missed the village less than the other men. When tired he slept. When he could afford it, or when anyone treated him, he had a drink. Those officers who did not fight he respected; those who did, still more, for in his opinion they were the only true officers.

There were thousands and millions of others like him – a little older, a little younger, a little duller, a little smarter. In the aggregate they were a great fighting force; individually, Ivans, Vassilis and Mikolais from Vytyazhka, a hamlet near the village of Krutoyar. At a distance of a couple of thousand miles from their hamlet were little towns with stone buildings and rich stores of manure – Blaukirchen,

Yohanniswald. The soldiers from these little towns wore brass helmets, knew how to read and write, understood more and marched better. But although a formidable army all-together, individually they were mere Hanses and Wilhelms, small farmers, journeymen, workmen. Farther west, Jeans and Basiles lived in the little towns of Massy and Bievre, and had to leave them to go to the front. Farther south, young Giuseppes and Basilios in the picturesque seaside Pieve di Castello and the hilly Rocca di Sant Antonio, from which women saw them off. The recruits made a brave show and held themselves heroically, especially in front of their womenfolk. The confusion in their minds was veiled by a vague doubt. But a number of simple, easily pronounced words and quite high-sounding turns of speech – the same in all languages – had been discovered, not only to minimize the difficulty of thought, but as actual substitutes for it. Lawyers who were trying to get into Parliament through journalism were engaged upon their discovery. That all this was right and honourable, and even wise, was sincerely believed by quite a number of good, honourable and wise people; and this lent considerable weight to patriotism and war.

Beneath the edifices of the diplomatic cemeteries drainage pipes had been laid, along which foul liquid flowed to the central sewer, thence on to irrigate some fields where grew prime cauliflowers. In this way official turpitude and lies were transformed in the last stage and by a process of sedulous cleansing into the purest tears and the beauty of valour. People of limited intelligence talked of mere cheating, which was unjust, since the deception was a most complicated and grandiose affair. People with narrow foreheads became defeatists, therefore, whilst the wise retired from active life, some for many years, others forever.

The difference between these people and the others – those of a third kind and a fourth and all the rest – was so infinitesimal, so inconspicuous, that fate decided to allot them all the same part in the war, quite indiscriminately, intent only upon avoiding all possible mistakes. Wielding the scourge, it left on every body a red, unhealing scar.

Yes; but the point is that there was something far more important than any such reasoning – nothing less than the problem of trousers and shirt. Somehow or other a sudden stoppage had come about in the delivery of army kit, and there was not a single field bath. To have one's own shirt from home was something very special – something that couldn't be explained in a word or two, but plain enough to the understanding, for all that. If a bath was nothing less than a bright Easter Day, then a shirt was a Day of Resurrection – something in the nature of air after the stuffy, mud-walled dugouts. That was why Andrey wrote Dunyasha a letter which dully passed the censor, reached the kitchen in Sivtzcv Vrazhek and found its way on to the professor's table.

The letter was read by Tanyusha and discussed by everyone. As for Dunyasha, she tried to add up how much it would come to to send her brother a shirt if she made it herself.

After dinner, Tanyusha came into the kitchen and gave her far more money than was necessary for two shirts and a pair of trousers. Tanyusha felt embarrassed, and the maid would have rejoiced had she been able to understand the reason why her masters had given her money for things her brother needed. She had been with them a long time and looked upon them as generous, for they had frequently given her presents, obviously valuing her work. But why give money for Andryusha's shirt? That wasn't at all easy to understand; she therefore accepted the money as a gift to herself.

Matters were now simplified. She bought some material of good quality, sewed in the evenings till the things were finished, and sent them off. Tanyusha found out for her how to send to Andrey at the front and wrote out everything herself. And Dunyasha found it very queer that here was a letter and a shirt going out of that kitchen straight to the front where Andryusha was shooting at the Germans.

And so it happened. A month went by, and again the postman brought tidings from the front: Andrey had received the shirt; it fitted him exactly, and 'We'll soon do for the enemy.' Hans, too, wrote home to his wife in the little town of Blaukirchen. But the best letter of all was written to his fiancée by Giovanni, the good-looking youth from Pieve di Castello. He sent her 'mille bad,' and added at the very end:

'L'amor e invincible, come la forza italiana.'

His division happened at the time to be in the neighbourhood of Verona. But what did that matter? The postcard was a bright one, with the Savoy coat of arms in the left-hand corner. Rosina showed it to her friend and both girls were delighted with it.

When she went to bed, Rosina put the letter under her pillow. And it was not before she had heaved many a long sigh that she finally got to sleep.

Rosina was thought to be the prettiest maiden in the village.

– X –

TANYUSHA'S BIRTHDAY PARTY

On Tanyusha's birthday (seventeen years old!) Sivtzev Vrazhek heard music till morning; not, however, from Edward Lvovitch, but from a musician specially hired for the occasion. For the first time, and all at once, there appeared in the professor's house – such a grave, civilian house – quite a number of young army men, mostly cadets, some officers and one volunteer, Byeloushin. Dunyasha's brother, Andrey, who was on leave after his first slight wound, helped her to wait at table.

'Call this dancing!' he said to Dunyasha. 'Down our way, at the front, they don't hop round like that, they don't, in the officers' mess. And the music there's something like, because it's the regimental band what plays. Don't think much of this!'

When handing round tea Andrey stood stiffly at attention before the officers, merely sideways to the cadets, and as for the volunteer, simply took no notice of him at all.

Among the officers the most striking was Stolnikov, who, in spite of his youth, was already a first lieutenant, having been promoted at the front. He was strong, well-built and tanned, no fool and quite a good dancer. Only Ehrberg – a cadet still, though nearing the end of his training – danced better. If Lenotchka's heart ever wavered, it was only Stolnikov who could divert its attention from its first idol. Stolnikov was more open and genuine than Ehrberg, but the latter's seriousness and inscrutability attracted her. Lenotchka enjoyed herself at the Sivtzev Vrazhek party, and her eyebrows looked a trifle less surprised than usual.

Stolnikov was due to return to the front in a day or two and was quite ready to go. He was in Moscow on business – sent north to buy horses. He felt like a visitor in town, for he was already used to the front. He was in the artillery and had got on well with his battery. It seemed to him that life at the present moment was at the front, not in Moscow; though it was good to be in Moscow, too, when things were jolly and people didn't talk a lot of rot about the war which they didn't know anything about.

Ehrberg might be sent to the front any day now. It was plain that the war was going to drag on.

There were some students too: Muhanov, a medical student; Myortvago and Trynkyn, law students; and a student of natural science, Vassya Boltanovsky. The last, a great friend of Tanyusha's, was an enthusiast and a believer, a keen playgoer, too, and a music-lover. Vassya, with whom Tanyusha could talk freely and easily, maintained that the world had gone a little off its head, but that far from being a misfortune it was thrillingly interesting.

'We shall see such things – happenings that are absolutely inconceivable at the present moment! Life is thrillingly interesting at present, Tanyusha.'

Vassya Boltanovsky was a great favourite of the old ornithologist, who had known his father when he had been just such another eager, sunny student. Vassya was the only person whom the professor, who was invariably polite to everyone in a refined, old-fashioned way, would pull affectionately by the hair and make much of in a fatherly way.

'Life, my dear boy, is always interesting, and no unusual events are required to make it so, rather the contrary. Such events only interfere with an attentive reading of the book of Nature. You, as a student of natural science, ought to realize that more clearly than the rest. War is best examined through the microscope; there is not the slightest difference. But in so far as actual living is concerned, peace is preferable.'

'Through the microscope you just get the grub,' Vassya returned, 'but here you get man. Here, professor, the whole world's standing on its head. Before the war is over such things will happen – well, quite scaring and jolly!'

'Scaring – yes, but not particularly jolly. They'll kill you, and then it won't be very jolly for your mother. One shouldn't talk like that, Vassya. You should take human life into consideration – the tremendous value of it!'

'Yes,' Vassya spoke thoughtfully, 'that's true enough. It's difficult to reconcile oneself to that. If only it weren't for blood – '

Muhanov, the medical student, who had not yet come to the end of his course in osteology, put in his weighty opinion:

'There are no operations without blood, professor.'
Whereupon he got from the professor, who did not like the medical profession:
'But there do happen to be operations without blood. If you dislocate your jawbone the doctors aren't going to cut you open. And then, you know, there is a whole world of beings that exists without operations, and certainly no worse than ours. We have nothing to boast about. And, in general, Nature will not stand the eruptions of force in the evolution of the world. She will take revenge, and a cruel revenge too!'

Tanyusha thought that her grandfather was right in so far as he was kind-hearted, and in so far as the killing of human beings was abhorrent. But then, war was not exactly just killing; and was there such a thing as a 'peaceful evolution' of Nature? There were, on the one hand, leaps and bounds; on the other, war, revolution, strife. Grandfather wanted everything to be simple, peace-full and right. But in reality things weren't like that at all.

At this point, however, began a problem to which Tanyusha could find no solution.

Dunyasha's brother, Andrey, had ideas of his own about the war. He would unfold them in the kitchen, in suchlike terms:

'There's no doubt about it; I've killed human beings – not with my own hands, of course, but with a bullet. But, if it comes to it, I'll use the bayonet all right. All the same I'm not a murderer, I'm not; I'm a fighter. We're fighting for State reasons, Dunka, and not for ourselves. I'm blowed if I care about the Germans, though really I ought to hate them, as it's along of them that I'm going through all this, because of my duty to my oath. When we get the order we go like lambs to get wounded, and even killed. But as for my wanting the war, I don't want it – in fact, I don't want it at all, I'll tell you straight. But the worst part of all is the lice! Why ought I to go and feed 'em? And that's what it comes to, you know... That takes a bit of understanding.'

To the professor's question: 'When are you going to beat the Germans?' Andrey answered briskly: 'Please, your honour, we'll finish them off soon, and no mistake, for the honour of the country. It's the only thing to be done.' And he cast a sidelong glance at the martial young officer.

The latter said: 'Well done, infantry!' And Andrey shot out: 'Glad to do our bit, your honour!'

Everyone laughed, the cadets were envious, and Lenotchka came to the definite conclusion that Stolnikov's personality was more interesting that day than Ehrberg's.

As Andrey went out into the hall, his elbow brushed against the volunteer, as though by accident. And in the kitchen he declared to Dunyasha:

'There's only one of ours there that's the right stuff. The other chaps are just bluffing – haven't smelt powder, that's what's the matter with them.'

– XI –

THE HIRED MUSICIAN

Drawing his legs up awkwardly and hunching his shoulders, Edward Lvovitch sat in a low armchair in a corner of the drawing room. Unintentionally forgotten by all the company, he was, that evening, the most uninteresting person present. As he sat there, listening to the pianist pounding away on the keys, he frowned involuntarily, and his soul suffered for the instrument.

It had been impossible for him not to come to Tanyusha's party on such a solemn occasion (seventeen years old!). Now, however, he could go without waiting for the supper; and yet he could not make up his mind to do so.

From the corner where he sat, he could catch glimpses of Tanyusha's shimmering frock and her exquisite little Russian head with its smoothly dressed hair... Tanyusha is opening out like a flower, and is bound to grow up a beautiful, well-formed woman. It is not only her youth that lends her such charm; she is truly lovely. She is as lovely as he himself is pitiful and ugly. She is young, and he on the wrong side of forty. He is gifted, but that does not give him pre-eminence over anyone. Even Vassya Boltanovsky – absurd little fellow with his turned-up nose – has more chances on his side, because he is young and daring. He has his arm around Tanyusha's waist and is whirling her round the room. And Tanyusha is breathing near him, on his cheek... The pianist is thumping on the keys – enough to drive one to distraction.

Myortvago, the slender, old-looking, clean-shaven student, entered the drawing room, accompanied by a young girl whose name Edward Lvovitch did not know, as she was simply called 'Myortvago's fiancée.' Though only one year older than Tanyusha, she looked a young lady already, composed, smartly dressed – rich, it was said. Myortvago was in his last year at the university, which meant that in a year's time he would be donning a dress-coat and saying: 'My lord and gentlemen of the jury,' and looking through case papers in the evenings. Conscription did not concern him: he was an only son. That student, Myortvago, was indeed in luck!

But Edward Lvovitch did not envy him. In fact, he was envying no one but Vassya Boltanovsky, and even Vassya only while he was dancing with Tanyusha. He was envious of Ehrberg far more frequently and more intensely. He was a trifle overawed by Ehrberg, for Ehrberg was so clever and calculating. But how curious that he was going to be an officer and going to the front. Could he have miscalculated by any chance?

The professor sought out the composer:

'It's good to see the young enjoying themselves. You ought to go and dance too.'

Edward Lvovitch rubbed his hands.

'Yes – I mean no. I've grown beyond that sort of thing. But I'm looking on with pleasure.'

'Our Tanyusha is growing up, isn't she?'

The 'our' included Edward Lvovitch in the family circle. It was not surprising, for had he not been responsible for Tanyusha's musical upbringing? Edward Lvovitch looked up, squinting at the professor's beard and beheld a broad, happy smile. It was then that he finally decided to go home; but he searched in vain for the proper words and was not at all sure that it was the right moment to speak of it, so he just rubbed his hands again. Just at that moment the pianist broke off at a glaring discord.

The professor's glance fell on the engaged couple. He went up to the fiancée, patted the student on the back, thought of nothing to say to them beyond 'Well, well, and how are things getting on? Aha! Well, well!' and made his way ponderously to the dining room, where Aglaya Dmitrevna was sternly inspecting the setting of the table, to make sure that everything was in its right place, that the numbers were right and that Tanyusha had put round the cards with the names. Tanyusha had selected Vassya and Edward Lvovitch to sit

THE HIRED MUSICIAN

beside her. The old couple were not going in to supper. Nevertheless, on reaching the table the old professor swallowed half a liqueur-glass of vodka and nibbled at a mushroom. That warmed and cheered him. A shade enviously, he gazed at the spread, then remembered his catarrh and said to his wife: 'Well, granny, you have been busy!' kissed her wasted hand and made for his study. On the threshold, however, he stopped and returned. Once more he went up to the old lady.

'I've been watching our Tanyusha, granny. Our Tanyusha is growing up, you know.'

Aglaya Dmitrevna looked at her husband, counting the while how many more forks were needed. The professor patted her cheek, and granny forgot the number.

'Seventeen,' the professor went on. 'No joke – seventeen, eh? Our Tanyusha, our little granddaughter...'

At this point, Aglaya Dmitrevna's kind face beamed. Was it that she looked back to the time when she, too, had been seventeen, or that she had remembered how many forks were still wanted? They looked at each other, those two little old people, and suddenly from the professor's eye a drop rolled on to his beard. In his haste and confusion he caught one of the buttons of his frock coat in the old lady's lace, and said: 'Dear, dear, dear, what a thing to happen!... And what do you think? I've just had a little taste of mushroom.'

And these two little old people wiped each other's eyes. Aglaya Dmitrevna's little mouth puckered, and the drop on the 'bird professor's' beard fell on to his frock coat, where granny dipped her finger into it.

Round the drawing room, keeping close to the walls, then stealthily through the dining room, Edward Lvovitch came sidling out into the hall. There, in his agitation, he sought a long time amongst the heap of army coats for his own dark fawn one with the check lining. Then he pushed open the kitchen door and asked in an undertone:

'Dunyasha, would you mind locking up after me?'

'Then you aren't going to stay to supper, sir?'

'Yes – no, thank you, no...'

To the very corner of the street the shy composer was pursued by the thumping of the hired musician.

– XII –

VISIONS

Dunyasha's soldier brother, Andrey Kolchagin, had been very slightly wounded in the war. A bullet had whistled past his head, torn off a little tuft of his crisp fair hair and had flown on – to bury itself in the earth, or may be in somebody's heart. They had been attacking the Austrian trenches at the time, and had taken them too. But Andrey Kolchagin, who had fallen from loss of blood and concussion, was picked up by the ambulance men.

The wound soon healed; but Andrey continued to lie in hospital, chiefly on account of headaches which gave him no peace. There were times when he would cry out with pain and others when he could not stir. But as soon as his headaches left him he got a month's leave. And, after a rest in Moscow, he recovered completely. He lived nowhere in particular, but slept in Dunyasha's kitchen, she sleeping in her own room. He ate from the professor's table and was extremely grateful. In so far as he was able, he helped with the housework and ran errands.

Long after his illness, however, he continued to suffer from restless sleep and occasional nightmares, especially when he had had a drop too much. As a rule, Andrey did not get drunk; only just occasionally, on holidays. Nor were there any spirits on sale, which meant he could drink only just now and again.

One night Andrey was awakened by his own words, to find himself saying, clearly and boldly: 'Yes, your honour.' And there was a rapping as of a machine-gun in his left side against the thin mattress on the floor, neither slower nor faster, and just as loud. And sleep fled at once.

He was already used to this symptom, and lay on between sleeping and waking, turning things over in his mind: he had lain just like that in hospital, next to a volunteer, a gentleman. The things that chap hadn't told him! Wonderful brain he had; knew everything! – about life and about the war; how maybe it wasn't necessary at all, and the pack of lies the men were told. And he had talked quite openly about everything. He had had his foot amputated, so it was all the same to him now; he wouldn't lose nothing by it, he wouldn't. That was why he didn't quite trust the fellow; and besides, he was a gentleman and a former schoolmaster, though that wasn't a reason for not hearing him out.

Now, lying alone, Andrey could not recall anything of those talks. One thing, however, had stuck in his memory: there was no need perhaps to have a war at all, that it was all a pack of lies, and that they were doing their best to fuddle the men's heads... The way one was eaten alive by the lice at the front was the limit! Still, it was all for the sake of the country. But why weren't there no baths? And how the machine-guns would yap away – there, just like that in his left side – *tu-tu-tu*.

Then Andrey's thoughts turned to boots – boots in general, and fine, smart ones in particular. He remembered various kinds of boots he had seen. For a pair of officer's boots, to wear behind the lines off duty, he would quite likely have given half his leave; though they were, of course, of no use whatever in the trenches.

Then his thoughts turned for a while to the kitchen in which he was lying. He thought of how the mice were running about, how Dunyasha was sniffling in her sleep, that there was a smell of fried onions about the place, and that he didn't want to get up to go out. And the machine-gun in his side went on with its song. Sweat stood out on Andrey's forehead... What a strange illness this was that it didn't pass!

For some reason or other he began to think about his company commander: how the men couldn't bear him. The other officers were all right, but that company commander was a brute and not a human being at all. Jolly brave when there was a fight on: you couldn't say nothing against him there; but at drill or other times – well, simply not a human being, just like a wolf! One of his eyes squinted, and he would roar at everyone and go for the men with his fists. You couldn't have nothing worse than an officer what hits out for nothing – nothing but spite.

At this point Andrey's nightmare began. It seemed to him that the company commander was beating him, and that he, Andrey, was hitting back. But he was striking nothing, just empty air, and couldn't manage to land his blows, try as he would. And he took fright... There was no stopping now, and, as it was sure to be the end of him, well – there might as well be a good reason for it. And there was a thumping in his chest, his rage bursting through his tunic. He thrust it back into his chest with his left hand and with his right went on hitting at the company commander – in the fellow's face, right between his squinting eyes... And every time a miss! He was going to be done in now, and all for nothing; and that was the hardest of all. If only he could get things off his chest, on to that officer's mug with its moustache! But it couldn't be done. And all the time the company commander's squinting eye went on leering; it had never done that before...

Andrey tried to wake up. Thank the Lord! It wasn't anything after all... But he was still standing, as before, in front of the company commander, and the fellow was going for his left side with a wooden spoon. The spoon was an army one and was cracked through. It wasn't that it hurt him so much as that it was insulting. And again Andrey felt rage surging up in him, and once more the company commander came up to him, and the same dirty business began all over again. Andrey gripped him by the throat, under the collar, and pounded away; but the throat was as soft as a rag, so that nothing happened. The company commander rolled his eyes and croaked: 'I'll shoot you, you son of a bitch!' and caught at the spoon with his hand and pulled it out of Andrey's side, together with some of his flesh... Andrey gave a gasp and woke up, once more covered with sweat.

He turned on to his other side... His neighbour, the volunteer, was pressing a nostril and blowing, while in a common voice he said: 'The war's all for nothing, and as for that company commander, we'll soon tear him to pieces.' He took the sheet, as if it were the company commander, and began tearing and folding, tearing and folding. And Andrey thought: 'What d'you care?' At this point there came a whistle and – whack! right at Audrey's head. He yelled out an oath and woke again; this time wide-awake.

It was light beyond the window. A large fly was buzzing against one of the panes. Andrey's head ached a little. He wetted the nape of his neck under the tap, as the assistant surgeon had advised him to do, and went out. It was six o'clock by the alarm clock, just after six. Andrey decided not to go back to bed again. He would have to get up soon anyhow. So he drew on his trousers, put on his tunic and went out of the gates, beyond which the dvornik was clearing the road with shovel and box. Andrey watched him without any particular curiosity, but with sympathy. Although he was a 'warrior',[1] he could see nothing degrading about the work of a dvornik.

---

[1] The soldiers were thus ironically called by the peasants.

Afterwards they stood about, smoking.

'You got up early today,' remarked the dvornik.

'Can't get no proper sleep after hospital.'

'How many days left?'

'Tomorrow will be the first day of the last week. Then back to feed the lice again.'

'Well, ready to go or not?'

'Why not? There are lots of fellows down there too. If only one could really know... Maybe the war's all for nothing.'

The dvornik, who had worked about the place for thirty years, thought a while, then remarked authoritatively:

'That, brother, isn't our business. We can't know that. But as the enemy's in Russia, one's got to fight.'

'It's our blood, though, isn't it?'

'And what about it – our blood? Whose d'you expect? Up with the shovel and into the box. It'll all be made out and settled in the next world.'

Andrey's head ached a little; nevertheless, he went to fetch an armful of faggots for Dunyasha's hearth.

It was Monday – a heavy day. The inhabitants of Sivtzey Vrazhek were wakening gradually.

– XIII –

DE PROFUNDIS

Steel, cast-iron, copper – such is its powerful, carefully tended body. Feet rounded into wheels; steam and oil in its veins; fire in its heart. It stands motionless.

Then it heaves a deep sigh, gives a few short, sharp coughs, then a snort, whereat the whole long chain of carriages starts, clashes and comes to life. Above them wreathes a column of smoke. Within the engine's breast its careful, parasitic nurse, the sooty, oil-smeared stoker, is shovelling busily. Still more food for the fire it breathes! Then it is off and far away.

Huge, round-chested, powerful, it changes in the distance to the head of a caterpillar, crawling along the ground. Broken-in and tamed, it is steadily drawing all that has been entrusted to its strength, hurrying, sighing, whistling, afraid of losing a moment, and meeting with a flying roar other such eternal workers! – iron slaves of men – dragging their share of the burden.

It has already borne Private Andrey Kolchagin to the front, in a van overloaded with live bodies. Now, in its carriages, it is bearing away young officers, among who is the calculating and disagreeably clever Ehrberg, in a brand-new uniform, looking grave and inscrutable as ever – in the eyes of the enamoured Lenotchka. Ehrberg is looking at the hands of his watch and counting the rhythmic beats of the train.

Two minutes a verst. How slow! The windows are flying past the posts marking the distance. One big post, then four intervening stones indicating the number of sagenes[1] passed. *Ti-ta-ta, ta-ta-ta.* And what if Ehrberg should not return? Calculating youth, do you know the fate that awaits you? The bullet knows its way, and the man goes breast forward to meet it, blind to its flight. And what if Ehrberg has seen Moscow for the last time yesterday – both the towers of the Kremlin and Sivtzev Vrazhek? *Ti-ta-ta, ta-ta-ta.* How strange! Yet quite possible! Ehrberg puts his watch back into his pocket and buttons up his 'French'.[2]

A jolt. The tamed monster stops, gulps down some water, blazes up afresh and sighs forth steam. Soldiers scramble hurriedly up into the carriages and vans, with kit bags on their backs. And in those kit bags are home-made biscuits; a leg of mutton, too, in some... But what are you in such a hurry for? You'll only be killed down there! Here is an officer travelling in one of the carriages; and down there is a field, and over the field is the sky, and on the field a body torn open by shrapnel. And that body travelled in the very same way, with the very same hopes.

Hurling his kit bag into the van, one of the soldiers clambers up with the help of his left knee, his right leg dangling, the clumsy beggar – a real mouzhik. Mind! See that you aren't late from your leave, you men! Hurry up and go on living as long as you can. Get the Cross of St. George for courage and a bucket of lime over your festering wounds; and may your mouths be stopped up, too, to prevent you from whimpering in the next world either; a mound of earth on top

---

[1] A sagene is equal to seven feet.
[2] Tunic of uniform; thus named after Lord French.

of you and, in the end, one soldier's requiem for you all. And your kit bags? What will they do with your kit bags? Make haste and tear at your legs of mutton, you men, blockheads that you are! But there's a clever man, a calculating gentleman, travelling your way too, and you and he are drawn by the very same engine. Perhaps the world has really and truly gone off its head!

Again the train gives a jolt and moves on. It bears away these men, and comes back with a fragile load – the mutilated bodies of human beings. Twenty men, and fifteen legs to go round. Enough! The man with a little hole in his back, just below the shoulder blade – the bullet had gone right through and come out beneath the nipple – is coughing, which means he is alive. And that blind man – he too, then, is alive, for there are none left upon earth that still have their sight.

Ladies with red crosses on their breasts board the train, bringing tea and shag with them, and flowers. Because of his officer's rank, his youth and his daring, the man with the little hole in his back is given a bunch of harebells. But what if he should suddenly leap up to strangle – to strangle with what remains of his strength – and beat with his crutch upon the red cross and those healthy woman's breasts, battering them flat with a wooden maul? Take that for the bunch of flowers! But there is sympathy and honey on the Sisters' lips. And they had tasted so little honey yet, those young soldiers the train was bringing back!

The train got rid of them – turned them out at the terminus – and, indefatigable, started back again. The load it drew this time was no mean one: machine-guns – to kill; gas-masks – in order not to be killed; shells – to kill; medical stores – in order not to die; mortars – to kill; ambulance wagons – for the wounded. But what else? Where are the mincing-machines to grind up Ivans' brains with Pyotrs' hearts and crush them together through an iron sieve? Where are the brimstone and pitch for the making of torches out of human carcasses, that life may be brighter? And the iron-tipped cat-o'-nine-tails to dig its claws into the sockets of the eyes and shatter the brain pan to fragments? Instead of these, bandages are brought to bind an insignificant scratch. A poor little soldier has scratched his little finger while chopping up wood. The splinter is removed; then iodine and lint, and a bandage on top. The result is a chrysalis. But supposing he frets? And you thought the soldiers would stay at the front when a breath of freshness stirred the air? Yes – the world has gone out of its mind. And it is the mind that has brought such cruel calamity upon it. Not everyone should be clever, of course, but this time it is the fool who has elected to reign supreme.

The train reached its destination with that cargo as well. On the way back it took a mail-van in which there was a letter from Mikolai to Darya, with respects to all the neighbours as well. 'I'm all right and going strong.' The letter ran on wheels, and he who had written the letter called out after it from under the ground: 'Stop, wait a moment! I'm dead!' From Mikolai there came another letter bidding Darya 'live on many years,' though, buried in his teens, Mikolai himself did not live long – not long at all.

There were a couple of letters from Ehrberg – one to his mother, the other to Sivtzev Vrazhek: 'I have not been in action yet, but there is really no need to be anxious about me. It is not so terrible as it is made out to be.' And to Tanyusha: 'My kind regards to all your people. I often remember your Sunday musical evenings. All that seems so very far away. I am hoping, however, to come to them again, many times...'

Hoping? Oh, Ehrberg! Oh, calculating Ehrberg, don't you hear that whizzing? Are you not familiar with it yet? Oh, Ehrberg, duck your head; run, Ehrberg! Throw yourself down upon the ground and dig your head into it – deeper, deeper. What is there to be ashamed of? The men all do it. Your pose may cost you your life, and you are calculating – It will not hit you? No, but here comes that whizzing sound again! Oh, Ehrberg!

That day, in the little house in Sivtzev Vrazhck, Edward Lvovitch played *De Profundis*.

– XIV –

THE RETURN FLIGHT

Not very high up in the sky, swallows were flying from Russia to Central Africa, though only to spend the winter there, to wait for the cold weather to pass and then return again.

Russia was their native land, and Russia was the land they loved. In her fields, beneath her windows, they found the best life had to give – food, shelter, love. On foreign soil there was merely rest. But during the winter months there was too little sunshine in their native land – the swallow's heart might turn to ice; whilst the scorching of the summer sun in Africa was far too deadly for its caresses not to consume. And there were other reasons, too, for the migration of the white-breasted birds; though it was not given to man to know them, not even to the old professor above whose window there lasted on a little nest of Moscow clay.

And from above, as they flew, the swallows beheld threads of rivers and cool spots of lakes in a setting of green; big and little towns like mounds of rubbish, with the forests around them less dense and the green of the meadows less lush, as though nature were shunning their grime and their smoke by going out farther afield.

They saw, too, flying low, the quiet ploughman behind his quiet horse, and the trail of the furrowed earth behind them.

They saw the rapid speeding of a train along two threads of iron and the progress of a motorcar along a grey, levelled road. But their own flight was swifter.

They saw, too, how divisions of soldiers crept like huge caterpillars from two directions to one frontier-line, where the earth was dug up and where the caterpillars hid away and vanished.

It happened once that a bird of monstrous proportions appeared in the sky, droning threateningly, powerfully, with little white-and-yellow balls leaping round it. Several swallows flew into one of those yellow balls that the wondrous bird had left behind it in the sky, and immediately folding their wings fell in little clods to earth, whilst those nearest them were dazed by the poison that man had sent forth into the sky.

All this, however, only flashed past them in their rapid flight. From high up, the earth appeared just the same as before, and the man, who was drawing straight lines along the grey and green of the fields, and marking them out into minute squares, scarce perceptible.

The swallows flew over the sea and saw from above right down to its very bottom. Like little wind-blown leaves on a pond, ships floated one after another over the sea, and their minuteness on those vast seas proclaimed, not man's might, but his nonentity. The tired swallows descended upon one of the ships. It was dark and they could no longer see.

When they rose again in the morning to continue their flight there appeared from the depths of the sea a strange, clumsy fish, which swam up to a ship, rose to the surface, spat forth and sank back. Whereupon, the air rocked with such violence that it nearly shattered the wings of the feathered voyagers. Then the ship heeled and quietly sank. All of which the swallows saw, but did not understand; nor did they even wonder, for that matter, why a fish should sink a ship that was peacefully sailing the seas full of people.

After that, the swallows flew above sands, aware that their journey's end was at hand, and counting their losses. And their losses were terrible. The leader had called to them on their way to rest upon the shores of Sicily. And at nightfall human beings had come with baskets and nets, and had begun to kill the little birds. Many had perished then. Their soft, huddled little corpses had been carried away from the beach in baskets, and many others had been trampled upon and left to blacken in the sands, when those that had escaped unharmed took flight at dawn.

To the swallows, the terrible action of man was as a hurricane or murderous frost stealing upon them unawares. Those that were saved glorified Life and sang praises to the sun.

And the first oasis gleaming in the swallows' path was hailed by their blithe *chir-r-r*!

In a strath, some distance away from the woods that the shells had hacked to stumps, a hundred versts from his frontier, though on soil that belonged to his country (as if the whole earth is not ours!) lay a badly wounded man in an ensign's uniform. A bit of shrapnel had entered his chest. Stopping up the wound was a scrap of paper, from which the blue of the stamped name 'Ehrberg' – a name now useless – had been washed out by red.

He was still alive, that human being who had been so calculating and disagreeably clever in life. But he was calculating no longer and, indeed, not far from wisdom. With his uninjured, tear-dimmed eye he stared up at the flaming skies, while the fingers of the hand that was whole dragged at the roots of the grass. His ear caught a groan quite near, familiar – his own. Then the groan turned to a rattling, and there was a gurgling in his throat, and cold – not for the first time – encompassed the body that seemed not his own.

Only he whose name had sunk into the sticky wound knew whether consciousness was there or not.

– XV –

THE PASSING OF A HUMAN BEING

When the swallows flew away from the Sicilian shores, leaving many dead and trampled companions of their tribe behind them, one of the unfortunate ones, whose wing was broken, could not follow the flock. Beating the air with its uninjured wing, it jerked its wearied body up from the ground and strained its neck in the direction of its friends' flight. Its *chir-r-r* was scarce audible, no more than a whisper; nor did its suffering add anything to the sum of the world's pain.

When the sun rose higher a blue film covered its eyes, and it began to pant in hot air. When the sun began to slant again it died. The swallow was the same one that had made a downy lining three years in succession for the old nest above the window of the Sivtzcv Vrazhek house – the one that had seen the human girl, Tanyusha, with a jug in her hands above her bare shoulders, and that had twittered more sweetly for the old professor than ever his cuckoo had called. It was the one, too, that had gobbled up the grub which was gnawing the beam beneath that very roof.

Thrusting its head out of its hole, a mouse swept round its whiskers and retired, sensing that something or other was amiss. A bird of prey, perhaps, or a hungry wolf. Neither birds nor wolves would go hungry that day.

A beetle with a gilded back, just as if he too held the rank of an officer, crawled listlessly by, bent on no particular quest. He looked about him for some place where he might hide away for the winter, thinking he could live through it; but his days, too, were numbered.

The sun rose, mounted high, looked down sullenly, and in a small, gently sloping arc went down below the earth, leaving a red trail behind it.

Ehrberg had a mother in Moscow – a humble old woman. She did not know that in an hour's time she would be a mother no longer.

It was all quite simple and ordinary, equally necessary and unnecessary. In the account of the world's expenditure it was nothing at all; in that of one being's life – everything. But everything only while the last breath still stirred the air above the dry, blue lips.

And, suddenly, from the point where live consciousness had hidden away in its struggle for self-preservation and in its desire that its lamp should not be put out, the mind flew up and rose swallow-like into the sky. Then the centre of the world ceased to be the centre, and losing its support, the world spun round and flew up after the mind. At the same time all the threads of thought, doubt and attachment suddenly snapped with the slight crepitation of an electric spark; everything grew clear and simple, and the house of cards fell, rustling softly.

Anything simpler and better than what took place then could not be conceived, not even by the wisest human mind. Nothing remained save to remove and cover up with the common pall of earth the frame of worldly arrogance, the nameless body with its painless wound and the meaningless scrap of reddish-brown paper.

A star lit up in the heavens and surveyed the earth's surface. It discovered Ehrberg's body lying outstretched, and reflected itself in his dead, open eye – wanly, reluctantly, as though performing a duty out of respect for the dead. Soon a cloud covered it up till the morrow.

– XVI –

THE MOST IRRATIONAL LITTLE CREATURE

IN THE WORLD

It is possible that the historians of the war have already established, or are in a position to establish, at whose command and by whose slight motion of the finger the first shell of the Great War rose into the air and burst.

It is possible that the first shot was the feeble one of a rifle; it may be that it was a volley. Nor is it possible to ascertain the name of the first fratricide.

And did the first bullet actually bathe in fresh blood? And did a bit of the first shell splinter a bone? Or did they, flying on steadily, bury themselves in the earth? What a sterile field for research! Yet, what would an American collector not give for those little bits of lead and cast-iron!

What was the name of the first mother to be bereaved? Is there a memorial to her, with a fountain – a fountain of tears? In whose album does the stamp of the first letter from the front display itself? Was the first groan registered for the gramophone? And was it a string that strangled or a stone that crushed the first curse openly uttered?

Henceforth, and for many a year to come, no searching thought, no descriptive pen, will till or sow the fields without the red poppy of war.

Cornflower and starwort time had receded far into the past. The earth breathed cruelty and oozed blood.

There, where the poppy did not grow, the spurred rye thrived, and the ruddy mushroom beneath the whispering aspen. Crimson sunsets over the sea; flaming rivulets of blood trickling along the pillars of the Northern Lights. And it was not the memory of the black fly that stuck in the guilty conscience, but that of the bug that had sucked its fill.

Yet it was not like that in reality: nature did not change. The day the European war began not one single blade of the field, not one white floweret blooming – why, none can tell – was troubled by the momentous nature of the hour; not one single mountain stream quickened its limpid course; not one little cloud dropped an additional tear.

'What's the matter with me?' a swelling pea said. 'Oh, how difficult!' a hunched, sappy shoot said, as it lifted a small clod of earth. 'Just look at us!' cried the white mushroom, washing in rain. 'And us too!' chimed in a pale toadstool. And once and for all the dome of heaven was pierced through with a golden dart.

The storks that could not find their old nests on houses that had been destroyed carried babies to the neighbouring villages. After reddening one of its cheeks the apple turned the other to the sun. The mole is blind; the mouse nimble; the hedgehog prickly; the bee – we know not why – knows its most direct course through the air; and the bumblebee booms on a deep bass string.

A chrysalis burst open and out crawled a butterfly with crumpled wings.

In the same street a man died and an infant was born; the man without putting off the day of his death till the conclusion of his life's events, and the infant untouched by the fear of the future. And to their families these incidents were events greater than the Great War itself.

And this, too, happened. In flowing ancient script-writing an old hag was writing down history on an enormous roll, with an enormous goose quill. At the sound of the first detonation the pen jerked and let fall a drop of blood. Like a tiny serpent a little worm of ink

THE MOST IRRATIONAL LITTLE CREATURE...

ran about, while a grey lock of the old woman's hair fell on the parchment and smeared the drop all over a whole ell of the roll.

When she noticed it, the hag caught the tuft of her hair, sucked it clean with her dry tongue and tossed it back behind her ear. But the ink-worm went on, playing antics, losing bits at the commas, winding in and out of the lines and stretching out in brackets above the ancient script-writing. And it lied: it whitened sin and blackened great deeds, mocked at things holy and diluted with crocodile tears the gall of words. Meanwhile the devil, behind the old hag's back, caught at the pen by the tip and tickled her scraggy neck, whispering childish, provocative things and disporting himself with her as though she had been a mere child.

Mouthing and waving the devil away with her free hand, the old hag wrote on, thinking the history she wrote was true – and it may be that it was.

Before morning the cock crew, the devil vanished and the hag fell asleep over the parchment roll besmirched with red.

The old hag's cat had a small grey kitten – the fruit of love on a neighbouring roof. When the hag fell asleep it jumped onto her knees, and from her knees on to the table, where a lamp was still burning by the pile of yellow old papers. Filled with surprise at the sound of the old hag's snoring, it put its little head on one side and touched her on her hairy lip with its tiny paw.

At that instant the old hag saw in her dreams a level road across which barbed wire was drawn. But she did not notice the barbed wire, and walking straight on cut her lip on it. Thereupon she waved her arms about in her sleep, and the kitten darted aside, upsetting the lamp as it did so. The oil trickled out and the parchment flared up, crackling. But not all of it was burned. Wise people and learned people, each according to his own light, will put word to word and corner to corner, each in a different way, later on. It was only the upper part of the roll which was destroyed – the part on which the old hag had traced in big letters: 'Those Who Are Guilty.' And that will be a subject of discussion for centuries to come.

As for the kitten, its fright had made it hungry. It ran to the saucer and lapped up the milk, wetting the whole of its little face in it. Then, washing itself, it sat down in the middle of the room and began to think that it was dull sometimes, even when one was young.

It was quite the most foolish little creature under the sun.

– XVII –

WHAT HAPPENED TO THE CLOCK

In the professor's beloved clock – the cuckoo clock – a little screw had long since worked itself loose. It was the little screw upon which depended the cock that supported the pendulum spring.

At two o'clock one morning, as usual, the ornithologist pulled up both weights – dark fir-cones of copper – and went to bed. The little screw slanted and waited.

When it was nearly three a scarcely perceptible turn of the cogged wheel tilted it, and it fell out. Uncontrolled by the pendulum, the wheels felt all of a sudden an unexpected freedom and started to run furiously; the hands started, too, and coursed rapidly round the face of the clock; whilst the cuckoo, finding no time to open its mouth, remained dumb from sheer fright.

While everyone slept in the house, time flew on madly. Flakes of plaster descended in a whirlwind of dust from the walls; the fastenings of the roof gave way and burst; grubs, that turned in a flash into chrysalids, then into little beetles, died and multiplied, and went on gnawing the beam. The cat, grown old, swallowed in its dreams a hundred mice that had made a dozen new passages in the floor. A swallow, no longer the same, had time to get to Central Africa and back again twice without even taking its head from under its wing.

Already a shadow in an old shroud stood at Aglaya Dmitrevna's bedside, looking askance at the ornithologist's door that had been left ajar; while, as she slept, Tanyusha's chest took on the rosy flush of young blood.

On all the fronts, lives and trenches were being swept away in a hurricane of fire. The ball of success, courage and strategy sped from foe to foe. The graves of brothers were heaped up high and the dead slumbered peacefully on the breast of the dead, whom they had killed all unwittingly the day before, without taking aim – just by a turn of the machine-gun handle.

When barrages shook the earth Hans' bones would press closer to Ivan's, and the skull would say with a grin: 'We are out of danger, aren't we, Ivan, my enemy? Our shelter's the safest.'

And Ivan would reply, with chattering teeth:

WHAT HAPPENED TO THE CLOCK

'One can only die once, Hans, my enemy!'

And both of them, in the cool of the comfortable grave, would laugh at the men in the trenches nearby, who were slowly being eaten alive by the fat grey lice.

It was all so simple for those who had taken advantage of the privilege to live no longer; and they were far from all thought of revolt. But the others watched with ever-growing horror the livid mist of the future coming down in poison gases on the earth; and hurriedly, fearing to be too late, elbowing their way roughly, they rushed at food, sought love, pressed close together and gave birth to a new generation, for the benefit of which that great human comedy was being enacted.

When the weights ran down, the cuckoo clock stopped. But it was already too late. For there is no single human being who can bring back the past. Tomorrow the old professor will get up just a little aged, and at a loss to explain such weakness... An attack of catarrh?

Aglaya Dmitrevna will not leave her bed at the usual hour, but will say to her husband:

'I'll stay in bed today, my dear. I don't feel able to get about somehow. You might send along Tanyusha.'

And she will never get up any more, nor sit in the dining room before the samovar. When Edward Lvovitch comes on Sundays the bedroom door will be left ajar, so that she, too, may listen to the music.

Two years, fled so fast; lost in so far as the grandmother was concerned, but turned to good account by the grandchild. Raising the jug above her bare shoulder, Tanyusha noticed its healthy roundness and flashed a swift glance at the window: 'Can the swallows see?' Then, wiping herself with a new, fluffy towel, she braced herself, stretched and started at a sensation of strength and desire as yet unknown to her. And the dispassionate mirror that studied each little detail of the growing girl's appearance made a note in its mirror's memory:

'On such and such a date a woman was born.'

White already at the temples, Nicolai, the dvornik, went out before dawn into the street, with his scraper. He crossed himself, looked up at the sky, then turned his attention in a businesslike way to the road. He yawned and swept conscientiously along by the wall, removing every speck of dust and every flake of the crumbling plaster.

All were still asleep in the house. Only he and the swallows were at work. But the greengrocer's cart was already jolting along on its way to the Arbatskaya marketplace.

– XVIII –

UNCLE BORYA

During the years of peace everyone had found his own pigeonhole, had put up his number to enable others to find him, and had gone on growing steadily within its walls. Every talent had been exhibited and weighed. A handful of elites had severed themselves from the masses; and these enjoyed quite special honours.

The poet was pointed out by the finger of the muse; the scholar by the acknowledgment of the unlettered; the artiste by the murmurings of the crowd. The architect stood a full head taller than the builder, while the house decorator was no bigger than a pygmy beside the painter. Two apples grew upon one tree, but the sun reddened the one while the grub gnawed the other. The Lord commanded His stewards to lay out human goods on the counter of life, displaying them with the best on top, the worst below. For the one the glory of the sun; the dimness of the guttering candle for the other.

But life had been turned topsy-turvy by the war, and everything had changed. Who needed Edward Lvovitch's Cosmos any longer? Who needed the bird specialist's old mind? The whole of creation was reeling, and the birds had been scattered by the din of firearms. Turn aside the bullet's flight by an effort of profound philosophic thought! Let pure poetry dispel poison gases! Cast-iron and copper thirst for nameless flesh; this is not the moment to weigh the brain. Glory to him who is needed today, and only for today, by the new god – the god of War, the only god.

And it was then that Uncle Borya, the son of the professor of ornithology, came to be an all-important man; Uncle Borya, who could not tell the difference between Chopin and Scriabin; Uncle Borya, the tolerated nonentity, the undistinguished mechanical engineer, who had not hitched his wagon to a star! Aha! now Uncle Borya came into his own.

He would get up at daybreak and be at the works when the second whistle blew. Where he had formerly stamped buttons he now made field telephones. Instead of ploughshares he now smelted steel of quite a different order. On the Kama, above Perm, he laid a special road to the hyperphosphate factory; not, however, in the interests of agriculture – that could wait – but as a sacrifice to the suffocating god of men. And instead of reels of cotton he now bored the barrels of machine-guns.

Uncle Borya's activities were numerous; he was everywhere, all over Russia, in every country – everywhere prominent and greatly in demand. The only man who was still more necessary was the big, thick-headed, hairy-chested, bull-necked general of the Prussian troops, and just one or two experienced spies who had long since been trained to their jobs; the doctor, too, for that matter – the daring young surgeon who hacked off legs to the knee. That, however, only for the sake of our consciences; for it does not do to live entirely without conscience. Like the general, Uncle Borya was needed for the main business of killing.

Uncle Borya never killed a soul. Indeed, Uncle Borya – Boris Ivanovitch, to give him his name in full – did his job in a quiet, unassuming manner: supervising the works of a large factory, appearing in the morning, leaving at nightfall and looking in on holidays as well. Nevertheless, he had risen to greater heights than those who listened to Edward Lvovitch's improvisations with the lights turned low. He had risen to greater heights than all of them taken together, for now what did it matter whether a straight line was really the shortest way or not?

People whom no one had known or been prepared to acknowledge a short while ago, now suddenly sprang to the fore; not those who were mere cannon fodder, for these were even now only dealt with in figures, but those several rungs higher up, simple enough people, quite ordinary and accessible, yet for all that the only real, active workers. The time was ripe for them, and everyone realized that they were the people who counted.

Uncle Borya, who had reached an age that commands respect, now wore a 'French' and grew younger. Uncle Borya shaved off his beard, leaving, however, his grizzling moustache.

Tanyusha would say to him: 'You've grown so good-looking that I fear for Lenotchka's heart!'

Uncle Borya's wife frowned, but he was pleased. He was even gay. He no longer shunned all general conversation, retiring into the background, but would wait for his turn and put in his word. Everyone realized that not only Uncle Borya had an opinion of his own, but that he knew things as well. Formerly, they had simply not been able to think of what to talk about with Uncle Borya; after all, they could not be expected to discuss steam boilers. So they had tried to think of something in the nature of steam boilers – something not above the heads of all the rest and equally uninteresting to them all.

Uncle Borya came to be needed by very many people and for a great number of things. It was he who settled Myortvago, who had just got married, in the Zemgor.[1] Myortvago was now called a 'zemhussar'[2]; his uniform, however, reminded one of an army uniform.

Uncle Borya was seen in the company of big guns in the commercial world. It may be that these people were trying to get round him and make use of the prominent engineer; possibly it was just a matter of supplies or something of the sort. But no doubt could ever have entered anyone's head as to the good faith of Uncle Borya – that particular Uncle Borya, Tanyusha's uncle and the ornithologist's son. Other Uncle Boryas engaged in national service served their own ends at the same time. It was a time when personal interests often coincided with those of the Government and country at large, a thing that happens less frequently in peacetime, though it does happen then, too.

On Sundays, when Edward Lvovitch played, Uncle Borya, beardless now and wearing his 'French', would sit in the light near Aglaya Dmitrevna's lamp, listening with pleasure to Scriabin, whom he took for Chopin.

On one occasion when Edward Lvovitch came to the end of one of his improvisations, the one where the life of sounds ebbs away of itself and one can actually hear its ebbing, Uncle Borya was the first to exclaim: 'Marvellous! You are in form today, Edward Lvovitch! Very pleasant to listen. But all the same I must be going. The works are waiting for me. We have Sunday and night shifts going these days. Steaming away for all we're worth!'

He said goodbye, and left. And nobody said anything else to Edward Lvovitch, nor did he play again that night. A little desultory conversation followed, and the party broke up early.

When she went to bed, Tanyusha thought about Edward Lvovitch, and for the first time it occurred to her to wonder: 'Has Edward

---

[1] Abbreviation for Union of Towns and Country.
[2] Ironic name for Zemgor officials. Exempt from conscription, these wore handsome, military-looking uniform; whence the suffix 'hussar'.

Lvovitch ever been in love? He has never married.' And then: 'How unhappy he is!'

On top of her big pillow, Tanyusha had another little one with a lace border. On it she laid her head, a little on one side so that her ear sank into the light down, and fell asleep.

– XIX –

THE SCRATCH

The friend of Tanyusha's childhood and the ornithologist's great favourite, Vassya Boltanovsky, had just finished his studies at the university. After going up for his last examination he ran home, washed and looked at himself in the glass.

During the period of his examination he had grown thinner; on the other hand, his eyes were merrier. He was still what he had always been – a whirlwind... Moustache, not so bad; beard, a poor affair. The jacket of his suit – the only one he possessed besides his university uniform – was nothing to boast of either. As for the examinations – devil take them! They were all over anyhow, and a jolly good thing too!

And now there was absolutely nothing to do. Suddenly, somehow, there was nothing left to do. Vassya was staying on at the university, which meant there was a good deal of work still before him. But in the meanwhile there was nothing whatever to do. How queer! It mightn't, perhaps, be a bad idea to go and order some visiting cards. Or what about shaving his beard off? He put his hand over his beard up to the lips. The effect wasn't too bad. A grubby sort of feeling lasted on after the exams – a sort of inky-booky dustiness. Should he be manicured? Well, but that was just silly, of course; as for the beard, well...

While he lathered Vassya's countenance, the hairdresser remarked judiciously: 'You are quite right. With your type of face there's no need to have a beard. You have a well-defined chin with a cleft in it, so that there's no object in covering it up. In a way, it adds to your appearance... Head up a little, just a little more... There are rumours of victories from the front.'

Vassya lunched in the Troitskaya dining rooms at the end of the Tverskoy Boulevard. He knew everyone who lunched there – the little hunchbacked man with the cockade, the Armenian girl who studied at the Conservatoire, the unhappily married couple, who would begin to quarrel in whispers during the second course, and the university reader with his fancy tie; and, of course, Anna Akimovna, who sat at the window on the left and managed to get through ten slices of bread in the course of her lunch.

When he had finished his borsh,[1] Vassya asked for some sucking-pig – 'preferably a bit of the side.' He was given a piece in jelly with some horseradish in sour cream. Vassya drank off the contents of a little jug of bread kvass. He also ate some kissel with milk – all of which was holiday fare. When he wiped his mouth with his napkin (his own, the ring was marked) he remembered that his beard had been shaved off. How pleasant – so smooth! And such a fresh feeling behind the ears – the hairdresser had cut his hair, too.

Vassya went striding along the boulevard on his way to Sivtzev Vrazhek, swinging a thick cane and looking with undisguised gladness at the people he passed. For, today, Vassya was a real man at last, quite definitely grown up. He pitied the students he met: what a lot they had still to go through!

At a bend of the boulevard he met a pleasant-looking young girl who bestowed on him a glance. Vassya returned it, and hurried on to Sivtzev Vrazhek, the sooner to see the professor – and Tanyusha. The professor, by the way, would not be at home, since he was still at the university, busy examining.

Dear little house; and how old you are! Vassya had never noticed that before. But today, having shaved off his beard, he noticed it at once. The professor's little house stood upright, yet slightly awry. The gate was visibly out of the perpendicular. And a lot of the plaster had come off the walls.

Tanyusha's window above was open. Vassya stepped back to the middle of the road and sang in a falsetto voice:

'Vi rosa, vi ro-o-o-sa...'

Tanyusha glanced out of the window.

'Come in, Vassya; I'll open the door. Well – passed?'

'Everything. A free citizen.'

'But where's the beard? What did you do that for?'

Vassya went up to the porch wondering: 'What does she mean by "what for?"' But as soon as the door was opened he immediately real-

---

[1] A favourite Russian soup, whose principal ingredient is beetroot.

ized that he had been desperately in love with Tanyusha ever since his childhood, and that it was absolutely final, which wasn't in the least surprising, as there had never been anyone better or sweeter or lovelier than she in all the world – never was and never would be. If that had somehow never entered his head before, there remained not the slightest doubt about it now... He must fall on his knees and creep upstairs behind her, or do something of the sort – to express himself in some way or other! She was so severe – white blouse with a little collar – and here he was dying of love!

When Tanyusha held out her hand and said: 'D'you know, Vassya, that suits you much better, ever so much better!' Vassya was full to the brim of emotion, and sat down on the staircase, announcing that he would not budge an inch, and that unless Tanyusha stroked his head he would die on the spot.

She did not stroke his head, nor did he die; and both went up to Tanyusha's room, where things became somewhat less strained. The glass looked at Vassya without his wretched little beard and thought: 'Oho! Why, he's really in love!'

'How's grandmother?'

'Better today, but far from well on the whole.'

'The professor's not home yet?'

'Grandfather is examining. But you simply must wait till he returns. He has been asking after you. What are you doing this evening?'

What a question! Vassya had nothing whatever to do in the evening, nor during the whole of the summer.

'I'm not doing anything.'

'Then you'll stay here, won't you? Do stay, I'm free today.' The cat came into the room. Seizing it by the scruff of its neck, Vassya raised it to his face, whereupon the cat scratched his newly shaven chin. Vassya dropped the cat and wiped the spot with his handkerchief.

'Curse the beast!... Tanyusha, I love you, just like a dog.'

And he coloured, thinking – not without reason – that he had said something foolish. Why hadn't he simply said 'I love you!' without adding on a dog?

Ever truthful, he corrected himself: 'Tanya, what I added about the dog was quite unnecessary. Leaving the dog out of it altogether, simply, I'm head over heels in love with you.'

That sounded more absurd still. Though of course if she had wanted to understand she would have. But she said quite calmly:

'You'd better rub it with a little eau-de-cologne. Show me. Yes, she's scratched you quite deeply. Well, it's your own fault...'

If you hadn't shaved off your beard, Vassya Boltanovsky, the scratch wouldn't have been noticeable. What a moment to choose! And it hurt. Vassya's passion began to cool.

They sat down side-by-side on the couch and talked about the summer holidays. It looked as if Tanyusha and her people would have to stay on in town, on account of grandmother's illness. Then they remembered mutual acquaintances who were at the front. Ehrberg had met his death long ago; he had been the first of their friends to be killed. There were others, too. And many of their old friends were now at the front. It was rare that letters came from Stolnikov, though they did occasionally get news from him. A good fellow – Stolnikov! Lenotchka was a Sister of Mercy, though in Moscow and not at the front. She wasn't going into the country in the summer either. Lenotchka talked a lot about the wounded, and was in love with several doctors. The white uniform with the red cross suited her to perfection.

'Do you know, Vassya, I couldn't. I could, of course, only – how shall I put it? ...I don't feel suited somehow.'

Tanyusha was grave today; she, too, was tired after her examinations. They went downstairs to the dining room. The professor came home hungry; he embraced Vassya and congratulated him. While he lunched, Tanyusha played for her grandmother, who was lying in bed – playing her favourite piece at her request. The old lady was sinking without any actual illness, but in a way that made it clear to everyone that her end was near. The life forces in her were ebbing away, and she was slowly and quietly passing on. As far as such a thing was possible the others even got used to the idea. During the months of her illness the professor's back had become markedly bent, but he grew fitter and gained in strength.

That evening a friend of Tanyusha's, one of the pupils of the Conservatoire, came to see her, and Vassya told them their fortunes.

'An eight of clubs on the heart; you'll soon get a love letter.'

The girl was pleased: she was expecting a letter.

Afterwards he saw Tanyusha's friend home. And when he was alone once more he could not be sure with whom he was really in love – Tanyusha or her friend? However, he made up his mind: with Tanyusha! Though it was rather queer, for he had known her from her childhood and they had been just like brother and sister. But having come to this decision, he again regretted that he had, for some reason or other, stuck on that dog... 'Just embarrassment!'

He went back home to the students' quarters. A pile of books and an unwashed cup stood on his table. In the dregs of the tea were several flies and yellow cigarette ash. Tomorrow he would have to send his linen to the wash. And really he ought to go away somewhere for the summer. He decided to look up his relations on the morrow; it had to be done.

And all of a sudden – just like his love for Tanyusha that day – life rose up before him. Adolescence was over, and a new and difficult road was opening out before him. Maybe it was true that it would be a good thing to have a companion on life's way. But who? Tanyusha? The friend of his childhood? It was with genuine tenderness that he thought of her now. And as he thought of her he admitted to himself with astonishment that he did not know Tanyusha in the least. He had known her before; but now he did not.

It came as a shock. How had it come about? And another thing: he was still a boy, whereas Tanyusha was a woman. That was what he, behind his books, had overlooked!

In his confusion, he raised his hand to pull at his beard, but there was nothing there but a smooth chin and on it – a scratch.

It was impossible not to be in love with Tanyusha; but to love her in a special way, like in novels, also was impossible for him, Vassya Boltanovsky. Well, but what was to be done about it? It was quite uncomfortable even and somehow not quite right.

It was all very sad. So he took a book and read on till his eyes would keep open no longer.

Vassya Boltanovsky possessed a happy capacity: he could sleep like a dormouse, and would wake up as fresh as early morn. That was why he loved life and did not know it.

– XX –

BEHIND THE BLINDS

On a chair by the door sat the cat that had scratched the postgraduate student's shaven chin the day before. Well, then, he shouldn't have grabbed her by the scruff of her neck! The cat was washing herself and feeling bored. She had met with a great failure the night before: the old rat – the famous old rat of the basement – had escaped from her claws.

He had got away, fairly mauled. She had already got him in her claws... and how ever could it have happened? Not that there was any taste in the old rat; that wasn't the point. But how could it have happened? The hunter's amour propre was wounded in the cat. She was bored on such occasions, and her eyes, which usually blazed in the dark with a green glow, would grow dull.

Settling herself comfortably, though without bending her forelegs – so as to be in readiness for war – the cat began to drowse, leaving only her ears to keep watch. Another couple of hours still remained before dawn.

The old rat was still trembling from the terror he had experienced. Crouching into the narrowest crevice of the floor, he was engaged in licking his wounds. It was not the wounds themselves that were dangerous; it was essential that the young rats should not see them. For they would follow his movements, dog his footsteps and worry him to death at the first sign of weakness. That was the great danger. They would not spare his grey hairs and grizzled back. What an ill-starred night that had proved!

Above Aglaya Dmitrevna's bed stooped a long, lean figure in grey. Stretching out its hand, it dug its sharp nails into the nipple of the wasted breast beneath the coverlet. The old lady gave a cry and groaned with pain.

Death stood at the bedside and listened to the old lady's moan, then withdrew to a corner. It had been keeping watch for over a month at the bedside of Tanyusha's grandmother, shielding her from all the attractions of life and preparing her for admission into the void. When the night nurse fell asleep, Death would hand the old lady her drink, cover her up with the blanket and wink at her fondly. And, not recognizing Death, the old lady would say to it in her weak little voice: 'Thank you, dear one; thank you so much!'

And when the old lady went to sleep Death would yield to an impulse to play impish tricks: fling off the blanket, pinch the old lady in her side and stop up her mouth with the palm of its bony hand to impede her breathing. And it would laugh quietly, chuckling and displaying its blackened teeth.

At daybreak Death would hide away, skulking in the folds of the blanket, in the chest of drawers or in the window chinks. If the blanket had been drawn back sharply, or a drawer pulled out, nothing would have been discovered but some dust or a dead fly. For Death was invisible by day.

Its teeth bared and its tail twitching, the old rat stood surrounded by the young ones, which were watching him out of their beady black eyes and listening to his squeals. Whenever he stirred, the semicircle of young ones retreated at once, for they feared the old rat; there was strength in him still. But their eyes never once left him, and they watched him licking his coat where a red mark showed with an oozing drop of blood.

The cat, too, heard the old rat's squeals, and her ears quivered slightly. But all was quiet; all were asleep in the house. The rats were alarmed and would not come out that night.

The old lady reached out towards the acid drink. The bony hand aided her, and for a second the two dry knuckles met – the old lady's and her death's. A cold shiver ran up her arm.

'Oh, my death!' moaned Aglaya Dmitrevna.

'Here I am. Lie still, I'm here,' said the lean one in grey. And to comfort the old lady: 'There isn't anything there at all, so there's nothing to be afraid of! You have had your day. You had a good time when you were young; you danced and wore pretty dresses and the sun smiled upon you. Can you say that you had a bad time? And your old man? Can you say that you weren't happy with him? And your children? Didn't they bring you joy?'

'You took away my son, Tanyusha's father, rather early,' complained Aglaya Dmitrevna.

'I took your son because I needed him. But I left you old people your granddaughter for your solace and joy.'

'And how is she to live without us? And my old husband cannot live forever either.'

'Oh, the old man will go on living; he's hale enough. And she, too, is growing up. She's an intelligent girl and won't come to grief.'

'And how am I to get on without him in the next world? And how is he to stay on in this one without me? We have been through so much together.'

At this point Death laughed, convulsed with merriment, though without malice.

'So that's what you're thinking about! Don't worry – just lie still in your grave and rest. They will get on without you all right. What joy does one get from people who are old and ill? What are you but a burden? All that's nonsense!'

The cuckoo could be heard from the study calling four times. In all probability it was light beyond the window, but heavy blinds shut out the dawn.

'Oh, my death!' moaned Aglaya Dmitrevna.

'The little pillow must be set straight,' said the night nurse; 'everything is tossed out of place.'

She smoothed the pillows and sat down again to doze in the easy chair by the bed.

The light filtered down into the basement, and the young rats dispersed by devious ways. The old wounded rat dozed, too. The cat was engaged in catching a big drowsy fly on the window, now squeezing, now letting go, so that the fly went on creeping. It was summertime; quite light already.

Just before daybreak Tanyusha had a dream, her third; and again Stolnikov was laughing, looking cheerful and pleased.

'On leave? For long?'

Stolnikov answers joyfully: 'For always now!'

'What d'you mean – for always? Why?'

Stolnikov holds out his hand, long and flat, like a board. On his palm is written in red: 'Leave of an indefinite length of time.'

And suddenly Tanyusha is frightened. Why indefinite? Hadn't he written quite recently that they wouldn't be seeing each other for some time because he had refused to be sent to Moscow? – 'It is not possible to leave the front at present; not that I want to either, as it is hardly the moment.'

Stolnikov wipes his hand on a handkerchief; and now his hand is quite small, and the red has come off on the handkerchief. Tanyusha wakens. What a curious dream!

Six o'clock only! Tanyusha flung out her arms and went to sleep again. A shaft of light through a chink in the blind threw a bright ribbon of light across the sheet, and rose in a little pillar on the wall above the bed. On Tanyusha's right shoulder, below the collarbone, was a small mole. And gently, evenly, the sheet rose and fell with her breathing.

– XXI –

THE FIFTH CARD[1]

Stolnikov felt with his foot for the step that had been hollowed out of the ground, and went down into the officers' common dugout, protected by a bombproof shelter. It was stuffy inside and the air was thick with smoke. On the bench nearest the entrance the doctor was playing chess with a young ensign; and there was a group of officers at the table, continuing the game that had been begun after lunch. Stolnikov went up to the table and slipped in among the players.[1]

'You've got to pass twice, Sasha. You mean to play?'

'Yes. I know.'

When his turn came he felt in his pocket for his paper money and said:

'All that's left. How much here?'

'A hundred and thirty for you and the card.'

'Hand over.'

The players' eyes, as though at a command, shifted from the banker's cards to Stolnikov's.

'Well, give me one,' he said.

'Nothing for you, and nothing for us. Two points.'

'Three,' said Stolnikov, and stretched his hand for the stake.

The cards were passed on to the next player.

The war stopped short. Everything vanished save the surface of the table, the money passing from hand to hand and the thumb-marked packs of cards. It was as though Stolnikov had never been a student, nor danced at Tanyusha's party, nor changed from a fresh little officer to a war-bitten captain with the Cross of St. George; as though he had not been to the opera the day before and was not returning to Moscow. The whole world was cut off from the players by a curtain of smoke. He, too, lit a cigarette.

'Your bank now, Sasha.'

'Well, here you are. I'm putting down the whole of my winnings. To begin with... a nine. I'm going on. Three for you; for me... again a nine. Three-hundred-and-sixty roubles in the bank. Half for

---

[1] The game played is a variation of baccarat.

you, and a hundred for you. What's left for you, Ignatov? I ought to get another nine... Your turn... there, take it.'

Stolnikov handed over the 'gadget' – an adapted cigarette-box – with the cards.

There were ten of them playing, so that now he would have to wait some time. All eyes turned to the hand of his neighbour on the left and all ears listened:

'Rotten luck – curse it! Six? No, we've only got seven. I'm taking up half. Whatever are you risking all your fortune for? There, not once the third card! I didn't even get a second... Must break the luck.'

They did so, railing at the run of bad luck, tried passing two banks and placed notes in various pockets 'in case the worst came to the worst.' Then the fourth card came, and growing noble and generous, and altogether a finer being, the lucky player consented to give credit to some of the other players; after which his money dribbled away at three big stakes, and he nervously fingered the note he had put aside in case the worst came to the worst.

The ensign at the end of the table passed twice. He was no longer even called upon to play.

'Gone broke?'

'Clean broke.'

'That happens, my lad. The luck's cycle.'

'I never have any other.'

Nevertheless, he did not go away; he watched, as if luck might fall from the skies upon the head of a non-player; or thinking perhaps that somebody might get rich and offer a loan of his own accord – for he didn't want to ask.

Stolnikov was having a run of good luck.

'This is the second day I'm in luck: yesterday in action, today in cards.'

At the words 'in action' all wakened for an instant to reality, but only for an instant. No other life should exist beyond the one they were living.

A soldier entered, saying:

'There's a droning, your honour.'

'A German? All right, I'm coming. Curse it! Just before my turn for the bank!'

'Give him hell, Ossipov!'

The artilleryman went out, and nobody followed him with his eyes.

As he crossed the threshold there came from without the old familiar noise of a distant engine in the sky. A few minutes later the guns were rumbling.

'Ossipov's going at it for all he's worth. What are the Germans flying at night for?'

A crash – the German airman's answer. But Ossipov had already got his finger on the enemy in the sky, and one could hear the rapping of the machine-guns.

Another crash; nearer this time. All raised their heads.

'Curse him! Hand over the cards... Seven. Better sell the bank, or they'll break it after the seven... Very well, then, give me a card.'

A tremendous crash quite close to the dugout. The candle was overturned, but did not go out. The officers leaped from their seats, gathering up the money. Some earth fell through the beams that supported the ceiling.

'Curse it; he nearly gave us one on the head. We must go out and have a look.'

'Remember the bank's mine,' said Stolnikov, raising his voice. 'My turn isn't yet over.'

The officers streamed out into the open. A searchlight illumined the sky almost above their very heads, but the streak of light was already slanting. The anti-aircraft guns were rumbling and the machine-guns rapping away unceasingly.

'Don't stand about in groups, gentlemen,' said a senior officer; 'you shouldn't do that.'

'He's already gone, sir.'

'He may return and open fire.'

The shell-hole was just beside them. Fortunately, there were no victims. The German had merely scared them.

Stolnikov remembered that he had no cigarettes left, and went along to his own dugout. When he reached it he paused. The sky was marvellously clear. The searchlight was piercing into the depths, calling back the enemy, no larger now than a faintly luminous speck on the dark background. Then there came yet another crash – the giant of the skies had placed his first cast-iron foot upon the earth. Somewhere in the neighbourhood there dropped the empty shell-case of the answering discharge.

'Why doesn't it put the wind up me, I wonder?' thought Stolnikov. 'And yet it might quite easily kill me! In action, yes – one does get scared, but there's never any time to think then. But as for these toys from the skies...'

Then he recollected that the bank was his. 'I've taken four cards. I'll leave everything in. If only I could take the fifth. That would make a jolly good stake.'

And he saw himself uncovering a nine. Involuntarily he smiled.

When the German's last gift struck the ground the officers instinctively rushed to the bombproof shelter. They stood about at the doors listening to the roar of the engine diminishing in the distance and to the dying down of the machine-guns; then, when everything was quiet again, they returned to the table. The German had apparently located the position of the stores fairly accurately, though he had succeeded only in scaring the raw recruits.

'Ossipov will come back. How is he ever to bring down such a bird as that?'

'It was flying too high.'

'Let's sit down, shall we? Whose bank?'

'Stolnikov's. He took four cards.'

'But where is he? Are we going to wait for him?'

'We ought to wait.'

'He went to fetch some cigarettes,' someone said. 'He'll be back in a moment.'

An orderly came running into the dugout – for the doctor.

'Captain Stolnikov has been wounded, your honour.'

And lowering his hand from the peak of his cap, he added in an undertone to the first man to leave the dugout: 'His legs have been shot clean away, your honour! A German bomb it was that did it...'

– XXII –

THE MOMENT

Dark night encompassed the little house, pressing close against its ancient walls and penetrating everywhere – into the basement, under the roof, into the big drawing room where the cat kept watch by the door. It crept in semi-darkness about the old lady's bedroom, where only a night-light was burning. And only Tanyusha's bright, open window scared and chased it away.

So still it was that one could hear the stillness.

Wrapped in a plaid, her feet up on the armchair, Tanyusha saw not a line of the book she was holding. Her face seemed a little drawn, and her eyes were staring straight before her, as though fixed upon a film screen. Pictures of the past and others that were not yet of the past quietly followed each other on that screen, where a hand traced the invisible characters of thought and faces looked out at her and faded away.

Vassya Boltanovsky flashed by with his scratch healed; Edward Lvovitch turned over the pages of music; then came Lenotchka, with a red cross on her snowy overall, her surprised brows arching beneath her nurse's veil. And the front – a black line, uniforms, bayonets, inaudible reports. The hand on the screen wrote on: it was a long time since there had been a letter from Stolnikov... And Tanyusha herself was on the screen, passing by gravely, like a stranger.

Then hazy again... She was tired.

She closed her eyes and opened them again. Things had drawn nearer, back once more to their former places. When minutes and hours of silence have passed something new is born: maybe the rumbling of a drozhky, maybe the squeal or only the rustling of a rat, or possibly a gate may slam in the side-street – and the dead moment is past.

Vassya, with his clean-shaven chin, is on the screen again, breaking up a matchbox and saying:

'Considering that you will get married in any case, Tanyusha, it would be very interesting to know if you would marry me – since you'll marry in any case, devil take it!'

The fragments of the matchbox fall on the floor, and Vassya picks them up one by one, in order not to raise his head at once.

'No, honestly, Tanyusha. It's quite absurdly interesting.'

Gravely Tanyusha answers:

'No.'

Then, after further thought:

'In my opinion – no.'

'Quite,' says Vassya. 'Clear as daylight. One for me, dash it all! And why? I'm most aw-fully interested to hear.'

'Because... I mean... but why you, Vassya? We're just friends – and now marriage all of a sudden.'

Vassya gives a laugh, rather forced.

'And so you're set on having a stranger? That's good!'

Vassya searches for something else to break. There is nothing, however, besides the fragments of the matchbox.

Tanyusha tries to explain:

'In my opinion one marries when someone turns up, or when it dawns on one quite clearly that one cannot part with that particular person and that one could spend the whole of life together.'

Vassya makes an effort to be cynical:

'Oh, come – all one's life! People come together and separate again.'

'I know; but that's only if they have made a mistake.'

Vassya sombrely breaks up a small penholder:

'All that's neither here nor there, whether they've made a mistake or haven't... And anyhow, dash it all! I, personally, am not likely to marry. I value my liberty far too much.'

Tanyusha realizes quite clearly that Vassya is hurt, though she really cannot make out why he should be. He is the best friend she has, a person who can be relied on and trusted.

Vassya fades away from the screen, and the shade of the person about to appear slips by in the haze, as if loath to reveal himself more clearly. And how infinitely disturbing it would be if some genuine image were to appear, with eyes and nose – moustache, perhaps – and be a complete stranger to her.

Suddenly, Tanyusha closed her eyes. Her heart sank within her. A cold shiver coursed through her body; her chest felt oppressed and her lips quivered and parted. A minute thus. Then the blood flowed back to her cheeks, and she cooled them with a hand that still shook.

Could that chilly feeling have been due to the window being open? What a strange, mysterious sensation – mysterious to body and soul alike!

The screen was now covered up. The interval. Tanyusha attempted to return to her book.

'The extract quoted is fairly eloquent...'

'What extract? Quoted from what?'

Tanyusha turned back to find the inverted commas. She had not the faintest recollection whose words they were or what the author's object had been in quoting them.

The nurse's step on the stairs.

'Will you go in to your grandmother, Miss Tanyusha?'

– XXIII –

DEATH

A tremendous event in the basement: the old rat had not returned. However weak he had been, he had continued to force his way by night into the storeroom through the opening gnawed out by a generation of mice that had now completely vanished from the basement.

In the storeroom stood several trunks, a mail-cart and piled-up bundles of old magazines and newspapers, nothing edible whatever. But next door, across a passage, was the kitchen; and to creep beneath its door was not so very difficult. Into the other rooms, especially that big one, the rat did not venture, remembering how he had once fallen into the cat's paws.

The old rat of the basement did not come back. But the keen ears of the young ones had heard his squeals that night.

When Dunyasha carried out the rat's mangled body to the dustheap the following morning, the dvornik said:

'Well done, puss. That's something like! He must be a hundred if he's a day.'

In years the rat had not reached the youth of a human being; but in age he had outlived his time.

Nobody appeared at coffee that morning. The professor sat in the armchair beside Aglaya Dmitrevna's bed. Twice the nurse came in to smooth the bedclothes. Tanyusha contemplated with wide, wondering eyes the wrinkles on the waxen face of her grandmother that death was already smoothing out. The old lady's hands were folded on her breast and her fingers were slender and tapering.

The nurse did not know whether to put in the set of false teeth or not, and could not make up her mind to ask. But the chin had dropped too far without them. The set lay in the glass of water, and seemed the only living thing that remained of the old lady.

A tear rolled down the professor's beard, clung to a curl, swayed and hid away in the depths. A second coursed down the same path, but without being held up. When her grandfather gave a sob, Tanyusha turned her eyes on him, flushed, and drooped down suddenly upon his shoulder. At that moment Tanyusha was just a tiny infant whose little face seeks the warmth of the breast: this new world was so awe-inspiring; never had she attended lectures on history, nor had her mind till now ever learned to swim in the salt solution of tears. At that moment, too, the scholarly ornithologist was a little pygmy, warding off a savage rat with his feet – wrongfully hurt, and seeking the protection of his girl grandchild, no bigger than he, but undoubtedly brave. And half the world before him seemed taken up by the gigantic bed of the old lady who was no longer with them, who had broken with them so wisely and abruptly. At that moment the sun went out and fell to pieces in one soul; the little bridge that spanned eternities collapsed, and in the body all that is deathless began a new and active process.

Beside Aglaya Dmitrevna's bed were left two little children: one quite old, the other quite young. Everything had been taken from the one that was old, while before the young one there remained the whole of life. On the window-sill of the next room the cat was washing herself and idly watching a fly performing its toilet with its feet before flying away.

The only event that had any reality was the one that had taken place in the bedroom of the professor's house in Sivtzev Vrazhek. In the rest of the world everything was as it should be; though there, too, lives were being cut short, creatures born and mountains crumbling. But all that was happening in the general and inaudible harmony of things. Here, however, in the laboratory of grief, the tear that was dim mixed with one that was clear.

Here was reality, and here only.

Grandmother had died beloved.

– XXIV –

NIGHT

Above the old widowed 'bird-professor's' house the night bird spread two wings that shut out both the moonlight and the brilliance of the stars; two wings, to shield him from the world and honour his great grief.

In the easy-chair long use had made so comfortable, out of the glare of the lamplight and haloed by his grey hair – still, so still, around, from thought there to the world's end – sat an old, old man, a thousand years older than the one of yesterday, when Tanyusha's grandmother, Aglaya Dmitrevna, still clung to life with feeble breath.

But in the drawing room, where the grand piano's shining feet were watching the candles burning at the coffin side, evenly and audibly, the nun's voice ran on in a quiet stream, pouring forth its murmuring trickle of solemn words, so superfluous to the silent listener under the dark brocade. And the chin of the dead woman was drawn up firmly into position.

Wholly given up to memories, wholly in the past, the professor looked deep into himself and, in his thoughts, wrote page after page of minute writing, pausing from time to time to read through what he had written and to tie the notebooks together with strong, coarse thread, then going on and on, without being able to bring his life-story to its conclusion – to another meeting. He did not believe in a reunion in another existence; nor was that necessary. But it would soon come in a state of non-existence. Years, days, hours were numbered; and hours, days and years were going by. Earth to earth; ashes to ashes; dust to dust.

The book-lined walls and the shelves of works – all that was dear to him, all that was the fruit of his life – would be left behind when 'she' should call. And he saw her as a young girl once more, a laughing dimple in her cheek, calling to him across the rye:

'Go round, it mustn't be trampled! I'll wait.'

And they had gone along by the edge of the strip... But where and when had that been? And what had made him remember? It must surely have been the sunshine.

They had gone along – and met. But this time she had not waited; she had gone on ahead. And now again, with an old man's halting gait, he was going round the golden rye.

Tanyusha, in dressing gown and bedroom slippers, entered the room. There was no sleeping that night. The night bird shielded grandfather and child from the outer world. Grief sleeps not in this little world.

'We shall have to go on living without granny now, Tanyusha. And we're used to living with her. It's not going to be easy.'

Tanyusha sat at his feet on a footstool, her head on his knees. She had not pinned up her soft plaits, but had left them loose about her shoulders.

'What was it about granny that made her so lovable? Wasn't it that she was so good to both of us? Poor granny.'

And they sat on a long time; they had already wept that day till they could weep no more.

'Can't you get to sleep, Tanyusha?'

'I want to sit up with you a little, grandfather. You are not sleeping either. If you would just lie down, if only on the divan, I'd go on sitting near you. Why don't you lie down?'

'I will; I have been sitting on like this, I don't know why: perhaps it was better so.'

And again they fell silent, a long, long silence – and the same unutterable thoughts in both their minds. Whenever the murmuring of the nun's trickle of words reached them through the wall they beheld the candles and the coffin, then went on waiting for fatigue to come. How good to both of them grandmother had been – grandmother, now lying in there beneath the dark brocade, with the flickering of the candle-flames around her.

One enters the world by a narrow gate, all timorous and tearful that one should have to leave the restful chaos of sounds and the simplicity and comfort of the incomprehensible; one enters the world stumbling against the stones of desire, and goes on in a crowd, straight on, like a lunatic, to the other narrow door. There, before the exit, everyone would like to explain that it was a mistake – that his way lay ever upward, and not towards the ghastly mincing-machine, and that he has not yet had time to look around. But at the gate – a grin, and the turnstile's click.

That is all.

No sleep; but, on the other hand, no clearness of shapes and images. Between sleeping and waking, the old man hears from that last door a young girl's voice:

'I'll wait for you here.'

If only he could go straight after her! But the rye must not be trampled. Everything is bathed in sunshine. And the old man hurries on along the narrow path to where she waits, her slender hands outstretched...

His eyes opened and met Tanyusha's great, bright questioning eyes:

'Grandfather, do lie down and rest!'

– XXV –

A PAIR OF BOOTS

Nicolai, the dvornik, sat in his porter's room gazing pensively and attentively at the boots that lay before him on a bench.

A strange, almost inconceivable thing had happened. The boots had been constructed, not simply made, a long time ago by a great architect-bootmaker, Romman Petrov, a drunkard past all belief, but a past-master the like of whom had not been seen since the day when Romman fell downstairs one winter's night, fracturing his skull, freezing to death and rendering up his drunken soul to its appointed place. Nicolai had known him personally, and had judged him sternly for being perpetually drunk; but at the same time he had marvelled at his talent. And now here were those boots of Romman's making quite worn out.

It was not that this had happened entirely unexpectedly. No; signs of impending old age had been noticeable before, and more than once. Twice Nicolai had had them soled, and three times heeled. On both boots there were patches over the spot where there is supposed to be a corn on the crooked little toe; another patch where there had been a cut from a hatchet (Nicolai had almost chopped off half of a toe, but the tough leather had saved it). There was yet another patch over a place that had worn thin with age. And it had been Romman who had done the soling and heeling. The last time he had fixed on to Nicolai's new heel such a strong protector that the heel's wear was assured for many years ahead. Into each sole he had driven ten smithy's nails with thick heads, and he had fitted the sides with cast-iron bands. The boots became extremely heavy and noisy as a result, but from that time on Nicolai forgot to think about their wearing out.

And how that had happened was a mystery; only, one day when the thaw came, and it became necessary to exchange felt boots for leather ones, Nicolai got them out of a chest beside the stove where they had been put away in the autumn, carefully smeared all over with vegetable-oil so that the leather should not crack. He got them out and noticed that the soles had become detached from both boots, one entirely, the other partially. He noticed, too, that there was nothing but rot between the tooth-like nails and that there was a hole right through. Nicolai bent the sole and the hole widened without creaking. And it was then that he noticed that the uppers had gone, too, to such an extent that with the prod of a finger came a lump that would not flatten out again.

He took them to Romman's successor, the bootmaker who had inherited his workshop, but not his talent. As soon as the latter saw them and held them up to the light, he said at once that they weren't worth mending any more – the leather wouldn't stand it. Nicolai could see that for himself and had cherished no particular hope.

'So that's the end of them, is it?'

'Yes; no good giving them another thought. Time to think of getting a new pair.'

Nicolai returned with the boots, placed them on the bench and, without actually grieving over them, grew very thoughtful.

He thought about boots and about the impermanence of the things of this world in general. If such a pair had worn out, what then could be everlasting? If you looked at them from a distance they seemed to be the same old pair as before, and they looked as if they could be drawn over the foot with the same slick movement as before. But they couldn't. Those weren't boots now – just perished stuff, no good for patching, let alone dvornik's work. But it looked as if the horseshoe protector hadn't quite gone and the nails were all right, though they too were rusty on the inside.

What dumbfounded Nicolai more than anything else was the sudden way in which the hopelessness of their condition had evinced itself. When the bootmaker had put the last patch on he had neither shaken his head nor foretold the perishing of the leather, but had just pointed with his finger: from here to here he would put a patch, sew it on and give a finish to the edges. It was quite a usual repair – not a fight with ruin. If it had been a fight the loss would have been a simpler matter. But, as it was, utter ruin had come about quite suddenly.

If you looked you could see that the inside had gone. And the nails were rusty and the leather perished. Pretty far gone, too. But the point was, the work put in wasn't just ordinary work, but Romman's – famous work. They didn't make boots like that nowadays.

While he set the wick right in the lamp he went on thinking, not so much about the necessity of having a new pair made as of the frailty of the things of this world: it looked as if nothing could ruin them, and everything on the outside was all right; and yet a day had

A PAIR OF BOOTS

come when the wind blew and the rain soaked them, and there was nothing but perished stuff inside; and there were your boots. Everything was like that, too. A house goes on standing, and can fall at any moment. And it's the same thing even with people.

One of the dvorniks of the neighbourhood, an elderly man, past mobilization age, looked him up that evening. Nicolai told him about the boots and they looked at them together and fingered round the insides.

'Nothing to be done. You need a pair of new ones, so fork out. You can't get goods like that made nowadays, not even in factories.'

'That'll be all right. It's not the money I'm upset about, it's the work. It was famous work.'

They smoked together. And all at once the atmosphere in the dvornik's room became smoky, musty and heavy.

'And another thing,' said Fyodor, 'everything's unsettled now. There's the war for one thing, and all sorts of things getting messed up. The sentry was telling me today the things that are going on. He says we may be taken any day. And none of us, he says, will turn up at the post no more; we'll sit at home and drink tea, he says.'

'I've heard.'

'And no one can tell what's happening in Peter,[1] he says. Maybe they'll depose the Tsar. But how's things to go on without the Tsar, I don't know.'

'How can they remove the Tsar?' said Nicolai, and again gazed at the boots. 'It wasn't us as put him there.'

'Who knows! things are like that nowadays. And it's all because of the war – it's all the war.'

As he went out of the dvornik's room, Fyodor once more ran his fingers round the inside of the worse boot and shook his head.

'Done for.'

'I can see that for myself,' muttered Nicolai.

When his neighbour was gone he threw the boots into the chest, and gloomily listened to them striking against the wood. A good thing that the felt boots had leather sewn on. Taking his shovel from the passage, he went out to his evening work.

---

[1] Popular diminutive for St. Petersburg.

– XXVI –

'FIRE'

It was shortly after nine when Vassya Boltanovsky rang at the street entrance of the house in Sivtzev Vrazhek. The door was opened by Dunyasha, with her skirts tucked up.

'Miss Tanyusha and the master are in the dining room. Don't kick over the pail, sir. I'm scrubbing the floors.'

Tanyusha came out to meet him.

'What brings you so early, Vassya? Coffee? Well, then, tell us all you can.'

'A lot has happened... Good-morning, professor... Congratulations – the Revolution has come!'

The professor raised his head from his book.

'What have you been able to find out, Vassya? Haven't the papers come out today either?'

Vassya told them all he knew. The papers hadn't come out because the editors were still bargaining with Mrozovsky – even the *Ruskiya Vedemosti*, which was simply scandalous! In St. Petersburg there was actually a revolution on; the power was in the hands of the Duma, which had constituted itself the temporary Government; and it was even said that the Tsar had abdicated.

'The Revolution has come out top, professor. The news is accurate. There's no doubt about it this time.'

'Well, we'll see. It's not so simple as all that, Vassya.'

And the professor buried himself in his book again.

Tanyusha willingly consented to stroll round Moscow. There was no staying at home those days. In spite of the hour, which was early for Moscow, there were many people in the streets – not out on business either.

Tanyusha and Vassya went along the boulevards to the Tverskaya, and along the Tverskaya to the town duma. A crowd stood in knots in the square, without, however, blocking up the way; and there turned out to be quite a number of officers, too, in the crowd. Something was going on in the town duma. It appeared that there was nothing to prevent them from entering.

People who obviously did not belong to the place, and were not officials of the duma, were seated before a table in the rectangular hall. A pass was required of those who entered; but, as there were no passes, people were allowed to filter in after just a verbal statement. Vassya said that he was a 'representative of the Press,' and stated curtly, with regard to Tanyusha, that she was his secretary. It was clear that the assembly of faces was a somewhat fortuitous one. Nevertheless, to the question: 'What is this meeting?' came the answer: 'The Soviet of the Workers' Delegates.'

The conference was not a particularly lively one. A certain bewilderment imposed a restraint on the speeches. One soldier from the side spoke out more boldly than the rest; and he, too, was addressed as 'delegate.' The soldier shouted angrily:

'What's there to talk about? It's not talking that's needed, but doing. Come on to the barracks, that's all. Our fellows will join in all right. What else are you waiting for? You fellows behind the lines have got into the way of doing a lot of talking and all to no purpose.'

The people in the duma went out in a small crowd. But at the very entrance the crowd grew. Climbing up a little above the rest, someone or other made a speech; but the words carried badly. The usual timidity of the people made itself felt; there was only the presence of a few soldiers and officers with empty sleeves to their uniforms to spur them on and encourage them. A small group, however, moved in the direction of the Theatre Square, and the crowd went on after it. At first the people glanced about them, on the lookout for the appearance of the mounted police; but there was not a policeman in sight. The crowd grew steadily, and from the Lubyanka Square several thousand people went along the Lubyanka and Sretenka. In several groups, voices dragged out the *Marseillaise* and *You Fell a Victim* – but the singing was discordant; the Revolution had no anthem of its own. They reached the Suharevka, but at the sight of the Spasky barracks the crowd wavered again. Many said that there would be firing from the barracks.

Vassya and Tanyusha went with the foremost. It was both alarming and stirring.

'You aren't afraid, Tanya?'

'I don't know. Are they going to shoot?'

'I don't know. I think not. You see, they know in there that the Revolution has triumphed in St. Petersburg.'

'Why don't they come out – the soldiers, I mean?'

'Well, probably they can't make up their minds to. But they will now, when they see the people.'

The barrack gates were locked, but the small side gates had been left open. The indecision of the crowd was manifest; it was possible, of course, that an order had been given that it was not to be excited. The sentry was consulted. To the surprise of those in front the sentry let them in, and part of the crowd, about two hundred people in all, trooped into the barrack-yard. The rest remained prudently outside.

Only a few of the barrack windows were open. Soldiers in tunics, with excited, curious faces, could be seen at the windows. They were locked in.

'Come out, comrades! There's a revolution on in St. Petersburg. The Tsar's been dethroned!'

'Come out, come out!'

The people waved leaflets, tried to throw them up to the windows, and asked that officers should be sent out to them with whom they could parley. And while they smiled up at the soldiers, in a confident, friendly way, they did not know themselves to whom they were appealing – new friends or foes. Apprehensively, distrust flitted in and out of the windows.

The barracks was silent.

The people crowded up to the very doors. Then, suddenly, the doors were flung open and the crowd sprang back at the sight of an officer in field uniform and a whole platoon of soldiers on the staircase. The soldiers' faces were white, and the officer stood as though made of stone, without replying to questions or uttering a word.

It was strange, very odd. The noisy crowd was allowed to shout in the barrack-yard – and shout terrible new words, mutinous and provocative. But the soldiers did not come out. From some of the windows they called down:

'We're locked in. We can't come out.'

From others sceptical exclamations reached the crowd:

'All right, jaw away! Just you wait till the machine-guns sweep you away! That'll be a revolution for you!'

As though in reply, the platoon of soldiers, one after another, rifles levelled, ran out swiftly from a side door and lined up before the crowd. The young officer was in command. His chin could be seen quivering. The soldiers, mere boys, were white-faced and bewildered.

Almost at the same moment came the command:

'Fire!'

And the volley.

Tanyusha and Vassya were standing in front, right before the muzzles of the rifles. Catching each other by the hand, both leaped back involuntarily. The flanks of the crowd dispersed and ran to the gates, while those who were in the middle drew back, to press against the walls.

'Fire! Fire!'

Two more volleys.

With his shaken nerves aquiver, and endeavouring to screen Tanyusha, Vassya muttered, in a voice that was very nearly tearful:

'Tanyusha, Tanyusha, they're firing at us – at people on their own side! It cannot be, Tanyusha.'

There was nowhere to run: either they would be killed or else a miracle must happen.

When the firing came to an end Vassya looked about him. No groaning, no wounded, no dead... There was a moment of deathly stillness, broken only by cries that came from the gates where the crowd was scattering. Then, suddenly, the shrill pipe of one of the urchins who everywhere and always run in front of a crowd:

'They're firing blank cartridges, blank cartridges!'

And, darting to the front, the urchin began to make faces at the soldiers:

'You're firing blank cartridges, you are!'

Several workmen ran up to the soldiers, caught at their rifles, broke up their line, and shouted at them, trying to persuade them about something. Somehow or other, in obedience to the officer's call, the soldiers struggled free from the crowd and disappeared into the hall.

Again the din began and the shouting up at the windows; and again the crowd in the street came surging towards the gates:

'Come out, comrades; come out to us!'

Tanyusha stood wedged against the barrack wall, trembling. Tears stood in her eyes. Vassya held her by the hand.

'Tanyusha dear, what has happened! How awful! And how very queer! How could they fire today!... Blank cartridges, I know, but still, how could they fire at the people! Tanyusha!'

Trembling still, she tugged him by the sleeve:

'Vassya, let's get away from here. I'm cold.'

Keeping close to the wall they quickly slipped out of the barrack-yard, skirted the noisy crowd and, in silence, arm in arm, got back to the Sretenka, and into the first cab they came across.

'Sivtzev Vrazhek.'

Tanyusha took out her handkerchief, wiped her eyes and, smiling, shot a guilty glance at Vassya:

'Don't be angry, Vassya.'

'But am I?'

'No; I was very upset, that's all. It's the first time I – '

'I, too, got rather a shock.'

'D'you know, Vassya, it seemed so sad, so sad. I wasn't frightened, not even when they fired. But the soldiers looked so unhappy, Vassya, that I felt sorry for the whole world. Not brutes at all, they weren't – just pitiful human beings. And it's so shameful.'

'Not their fault, Tanyusha.'

'I'm not blaming them... But how awful, Vassya, when there's a crowd and when people with rifles... I thought that a revolution was something heroic. But here all are afraid and cannot understand...'

Then, after a pause, she added:

'D'you know, Vassya, I don't like your revolution.'

– XXVII –

THE 'MIRACLE'

Its feet are rounded into wheels; steam and oil in its veins; fire in its heart. All these three years it has worked for blood, and blood only, though it is spick-and-span itself, having been cared for, and its brass and number polished till they shine. Today it has brought the living remains of one who in the world of yesterday was Stolnikov, the young officer who failed to guess the fifth card.

The ardour with which society Sisters of Mercy meet the wounded at the Moscow stations is no longer what it was; there is now something almost official about it. For it is a theatrical affair no longer, merely a matter of daily experience. They go up and chat mainly with the officers, though they did not go up to Stolnikov. The dreadful body, which was now no more than a trunk, was looked after by his orderly, Grigory; and Grigory it was who helped to lay him on a stretcher.

The senior medical officer said to the junior:

'A miracle that this... is alive. And he'll pull through, see if he doesn't!'

The medical officer wanted to say 'this man,' but did not get to the end: the Trunk was not a man. The Trunk was nothing but the trunk of a man.

When they arrived, Grigory had wanted to pin the Cross of St. George on Stolnikov's breast. But the latter had shaken his head, and Grigory had put the cross back into its case and the case into his breast pocket.

There were no relatives; and acquaintances did not come to meet him. They did not know. Stolnikov had let no one know. And he was weak, even though he was a miracle. He had lain for six months in the hospital of a little town, the risk of moving him being too great. Now, however, he would recover.

He was taken to hospital, and there the doctors wondered at the 'miracle'. Not one of them could say a word of comfort to the armless and legless officer. The young doctors came up to him to make sure that a blue scar had formed over the bones of the knee and that what was left of the right upper arm could move. They went on massaging without knowing exactly why. And Stolnikov would watch their faces, their moustaches, their skilful hands; and when they went away his eyes would follow them: there went people on feet as he, too, had done – left-right... left-right.

Being a 'miracle,' he was given a room to himself, and Grigory, who was discharged from the service on account of his age, never left his side.

Two of his old university friends came to see him. He was grateful to both, but asked them not to come again, as he didn't want to see people for the time being. They understood. It had indeed been painful for them, too: what was there to talk about with him? About the bright or the dark side of life? About the future? Flowers were brought from Tanyusha. He said:

'Thank her from me. When things are easier I'll let her know. I shall soon be discharged from this place, as there's nothing more they can do for me. Then I'll settle down somewhere or other... with Grigory. Come and see me then.'

He lay there another three months. He was 'fit,' and actually put on weight. The doctors said: 'A miracle. Just look at him. There's nature for you!'

And Stolnikov left the hospital. Grigory took two rooms for them both in the students' quarter, in a side-street leading off from the Bronnaya, and was as tender with him as a nurse.

The tie that bound them? – the helplessness of the one and the homelessness of the other. Both the simple-minded soldier and the limbless officer had got to know something out of the ordinary run of experience. They used to have long talks together in the evenings; though it was Stolnikov who did most of the talking and Grigory who listened.

Grigory would strike a match in the dark, place a cigarette between the Trunk's lips, and put a saucer for the ash beneath his head. He did not smoke himself. Or else Stolnikov would read aloud, Grigory listening reverently to the incomprehensible book and turning over the pages at a sign from him. Little by little Stolnikov learned to do that himself, by means of a pencil to which a rubber was attached – his 'magic wand' – which he held between his teeth. He read aloud to Grigory nearly the whole of Shakespeare, and Grigory listened with grave astonishment... Curious imagery, incomprehensible conversation. He understood it all in his own way.

Like a baby, the Trunk learned to live. His brain was ever working at contrivances. The idea came to him to place a sloping ladder above the head of the bed in order that he might raise himself up by the muscles of his neck; his body being otherwise over-weighed by the stumps of his legs – though there was really no reason why he should raise himself up. He was able with his lips to take a cigarette from a shelf on the wall; holding it between his teeth, together with the magic wand, he could press the button of a cigarette lighter fixed to the shelf and smoke. It took him over a week to learn how to do it; on one occasion he was all but burnt alive in his bed, after which he finally mastered it.

Stolnikov's means were slender, but sufficient for such an existence. He bought himself a bathchair, and thought out a means of propelling it which was not beyond his powers. It was in that bathchair that Grigory took him out for walks along the Tverskoy Boulevard and the Patriarsky Ponds. He also set up a typewriter and learned to write, holding in his mouth a little bent rod with a rubber end and turning the paper up by means of a lever fixed to the bathchair by the left shoulder. It annoyed him that Grigory should have to adjust the paper for him, so he had long sheets stuck together and wrote with narrow spacing. A collection of strange-looking objects they had themselves devised, and which had been made either by Grigory or the carpenter, according to instructions, were set out over the whole of his table. Without a word Grigory would slip over his head a hoop with a spoon and fork adapted to his use; and the Trunk learned how to use these complicated instruments by the movement of the skin of his forehead. Water and tea he drank through a straw. Often, seeing his weary helplessness, Grigory would say:

'If you'll let me, sir, I'll feed you. Why do you worry yourself for nothing?'

'Just a moment. And it's not for nothing. I'm alive, which means I've got to learn to live. See?'

Their speech on practical matters was of the briefest.

The Trunk had no artificial limbs. The doctors had admitted them to be of no use.

'If you like... for the look of the thing. But apart from that... They can still be got from abroad – but only for the right arm, there's some sort of hope for that one.'

But for the look of the thing he could put on his 'French' and have the sleeves stuffed.

He wanted to put it on the day he was expecting Tanyusha's first visit. But he changed his mind and stayed in bed to receive her for the first time.

And Tanyusha, who knew the full extent of Stolnikov's misfortune, was taken by surprise:

'How well he looks, even though he does lie motionless.'

The old ornithologist came with Tanyusha to visit the young man. They did not remain long. Before going, she promised to come again when he should ask for her.

Home again, and full of the memory of her visit, Tanyusha cried and cried – and it was seldom that she wept. Stolnikov was nothing to her – just a casual and fairly recent acquaintance. But of all the people she knew he was undoubtedly the most unfortunate; nor could she conceive of anyone as wretched.

As she stood half undressed by the mirror, before going to bed, Tanyusha caught sight of her beautiful arms bent slightly back to tress her hair into one thick plait. There was life and youth and strength in those arms. And, suddenly, imagining the blue scars over the sawn-off bone, she started and recoiled. Falling face downward on to the pillows she sobbed aloud from pity, terrible pity, for the man to whom such pity might never be told. It was worse than seeing a dead body... A human being crushed by life and stirring still beneath it...

'He hates me, of course; he must hate everyone.'

– XXVIII –

BACK FROM THE FRONT

Morning, noon and night, shadows of soldiers in ragged old army kit, carrying with them the dirt of the trenches and bundles full of unwashed shirts, with kettles clattering against the butt-ends of their rifles, flowed from the stations, past the Smolensky marketplace and along the Arbat in one big stream, that split up farther on into many lesser ones. Like civilians, they went along the pavements in separate groups, without attempting to get into formation. Each man, in the depths of his being, bore back the war from the front, although his thoughts were of the war no longer, but of his village.

There were no faces. There was nothing but uniforms and resounding boots. The faces had disappeared behind the unshaven cheeks and into the hollows round the eyes, vanished into insomnia, into the deserter's conscience and the dull obstinacy that refused to look around. And thus they trudged on, neither looking round, nor knowing the way, nor speaking, careful only never to lose sight of the back of the man in front.

They went on in a herd, following the signposts, till they got lost in the side streets. Then the man in front would ask the way of an apprehensive passer-by, while the rest dragged dully after him.

And then again they would go surging into the station halls, throng the waiting rooms and platforms, prepared to wait, as they had waited in the trenches, until a signal should hurl them in an attack upon the train – long-distance train or short, or only to the summer resorts round Moscow: it mattered little where it went as long as it took them nearer home. Others, who no longer cared, were sucked into the city, where they spread alarm and the foul trench lice.

There were some who had their rifles with them and others who had left them behind, or sold the cumbersome burden, keeping only the bayonet to dangle in its sheath at the belt, in the hope that it might come in useful in their work on the land. And meeting on their way some trim little cadet, marching along in well-polished boots, they would stare at him in surprise, not troubling their dulled and wearied wits.

In the Arbat one of the soldiers turned down an alley on the right, without bidding anyone farewell. First he straightened his reversed rifle behind his back, with the bayonet attached, then set straight his forage cap as well, and quickened his step. It was evident that he knew the way. Farther on, along Sivtzev Vrazhek, he strode alertly, though his unshaven, grimy face bore signs of great weariness. With his free hand he pushed to open the gate. It turned out to be bolted, and behind it a dog began to bark… There had been no dog before… He knocked loudly with his fist, then caught sight of the bell, and rang.

It was with a look that hovered between confusion and simulated boldness that he met the stern gaze of Nicolai, the dvornik.

'What do you want?' asked the dvornik severely.

'My respects, Comrade Nicolai. You don't say you don't recognize me?'

'Dunyasha's brother?' The dvornik peered at him suspiciously. It was already dusk.

'The same – Private Kolchagin, a grey hero on leave, back to billet himself on you again.'

They shook hands. But Nicolai's look was one of disapproval.

'How's it you've stopped fighting?'

'Don't go on forever.'

'Run away, eh?'

'Right! And I didn't ask no authorities neither. Whatever the war was, we've gone and put a stop to it.'

'O-oh! Back to the village?'

'Back to the village and no mistake, when I've rested. I've been mucking about a whole month on the journey.'

'O-oh!'

The sight of him both gladdened and frightened Dunyasha – the journey had made her brother look so dreadful, poor dear!

'You'll tramp about all over my kitchen. And what've you dragged along your rifle for? Is it a Government one?'

'Nobody can tell what is and what isn't nowadays. I ought to have a bath, Dunka, and no mistake.'

'The bath water has been heated today, just as if we were expecting you. Got underclothes?'

'That'll be all right. I'll wash them myself, if I can only get a bath. If I don't get it I'll be passing on insects to you.'

Like all good old-fashioned homes, the little house had a bath-house of its own. It was not till late on in the evening that Private Kolchagin came out of it, after having bathed, washed his things (he had taken his bundle in with him), and dried them. He turned up to drink tea, with a red, shiny face, decidedly more cheerful than before, and wearing a new tunic of an officer's cut.

'This tunic is a jolly fine one. I got hold of it just before I left. I've steamed all the insects to death. That's a real bathhouse you've got, and no mistake. I could have stayed in it for ages. Of course, the masters don't live the way we do.'

Dunyasha told him about her mistress's death.

'Well, she was old. And we at the front died young, we did, killed off by the enemy and sickness; and all for the good of capitalism.'

'Whatever's that?'

'How am I to know? We've had enough of all that lying!'

Yet he asked his sister not to gossip about his arrival, and was evasive in his replies to her questions.

'What was there to stop on for? There wasn't no war on.'

He stretched himself out on a bench for the night and immediately dropped off to sleep.

While Dunyasha was clearing the table her sleeve caught on the tap of the samovar. A tiny stream of water dripped on to the floor, ran away in several directions in search of chinks in the boards, trickled down into them, and disappeared. The cat raised her head and remained a long time staring at the water flowing from the tap; at length she wetted her paw in the advancing pool, gave it a shake of distaste, and stalked off.

Dunyasha had gone to her room. When she came back the samovar was empty, and Private Kolchagin, deserter, was snoring loudly.

– XXIX –

AT THE MEMORIAL

'A walk, sir, today, if only it keeps fine.'

Before pushing the bathchair out of the blind alley Grigory threw a short cape over Stolnikov's shoulders.

'No need, Grigory; it's warm.'

'It's on account of those shoulder-straps, sir. You never know.'

Officers' shoulder straps were torn off those days. Was it possible that a disabled man should be insulted? But the masses were ignorant, and Grigory was uneasy.

'No need, Grigory.'

The bathchair came out on to the boulevard. Opposite the beginning of Bogoslavsky Street a crowd stood round a thin, spectacled gentleman with a sharp beard, who was arguing with a soldier. The soldier was expounding on trench lice, while the gentleman was talking about France and England. The people round them were listening attentively.

Glances were cast at Stolnikov's bathchair and many eyes followed it on its way. Then the people turned away to listen again, craning their necks forward in an effort to reach beyond the people in front of them and putting more faith in the men's expressions than their words.

One of the listeners remarked in an undertone:

'What a lot of those disabled men about!'

A nurse came up to the Trunk, pushing a perambulator. The blue eyes of a baby girl gazed out beneath the white hood, and when the perambulator and bathchair were side-by-side two glances met – an adult's and a child's. But the adult did not smile.

The nearer they got to the Pushkin Memorial the more groups they met round people who were arguing about the land, about the constituent assemblies, about various parties, but mostly about the front. Fragments of sentences reached them.

'...and the people that took cover behind the lines...'

'...and why have I got to shed...'

'...How am I to know what sort of fellow you are? Anyone can put on an army uniform...'

'...Educated people are needed, too, to instruct the others. Only...'

AT THE MEMORIAL

As usual, the biggest crowd of all had gathered before the memorial. A bandaged officer on crutches was speaking. His cap was being passed round, and all were giving unquestioningly on behalf of the disabled men. On one side, in front of a seat, stood a little table, at which a man sat, slipping paper money into a collection-box. People were coming up and giving, sometimes not knowing themselves for what or whom it was collected.

The crowd parted before Stolnikov's bathchair, so that Grigory was able to take his master almost up to the memorial itself. The speaker, who was already hoarse, pointed out Stolnikov to the crowd, and, mopping his brow, cried:

'What did men like that – there, look – shed their blood for? Was it to hand over Russia to the Germans now? No, citizens, we can't allow that!'

It was evident, from the way in which the trousers bulged, that the speaker's leg was bandaged. There was a red, recent scar on his cheekbone, and whenever he opened his mouth the skin of the scar stretched and looked shiny. When the officer finished, a civilian in spectacles took his place, and the people drew close, with interest. A moment later confused murmurs rose from the crowd, for the civilian was speaking against the war. Somebody shouted:

'You ought to be ashamed of yourself! Here's an officer who has lost both arms and legs.'

The civilian cried:

'That's precisely why we have had enough.'

But they would not let him be. Two sailors and a soldier yelled at the crowd:

'Free speech, comrades; it's quite impossible if you go on like this!'

Stolnikov turned his head, dug his teeth into one of his shoulder straps, tore it off, and said to Grigory, who had bent down to him:

'Take them off. The other one too, both of them, and throw them at him.'

'At whom, your honour?'

'At the black fellow who's talking. Throw them straight at his head!'

Grigory obeyed, and the shoulder straps struck the speaker on the chest. A roar rose from the crowd; the man in black vanished, and with him the two sailors and the soldier.

Stolnikov's bathchair was immediately surrounded. There came shouts of 'Well done!' and a lady squeaked something incomprehensible, urging everyone to go and give it to the Germans. A Sister of Mercy with frizzy hair came and stood beside Grigory and put her hand on the bar of the bathchair. By means of signs – her voice could not be heard – she invited the men to take off their hats to the disabled officer. Those in front did so; those at the back pressed forward.

Somebody called out:
'Silence, citizens; he's going to speak!'
And the crowd was silent.

The circle widened. Stolnikov's eyes travelled over the crowd; then, breaking in upon the hush, he spoke out, clearly and to the point:

'I have nothing to say to you. You are slaves, all of you! And that fellow in black, who talked against the war, may be a scoundrel, but he's right all the same. Devil take your war! Grigory, get me out of this!'

The first row broke up. The Sister of Mercy let go the bathchair. The back rows had not heard well, but called out: 'Quite right!' 'That's true!' 'Thank you, your honour.' A bearded gentleman explained to his wife: 'Clean demented – a cripple. Embittered, of course.'

And only one soldier, whose tunic collar was open, panted out in his enthusiasm:

'Bloody well got it in the neck! Now they too know how their legs were hacked off. Ho! Jolly fine!'

He took out a handful of sunflower seeds from his pocket and set to. From behind his left ear a cigarette stuck out.

The cheery soldier's name was Audrey Kolchagin.

XXX –

THE DVORNIK

It was October, yet no snow had fallen. There were frosts at night, but during the day it thawed. Before daybreak the dvornik, armed with shovel and broom, worn to one side, would push open the gate of the professor's little yard and spend a long time sweeping the pavement clean, casting unfriendly glances as he went in at the neglected pavement and road before the neighbours' houses, and thinking how lazy people had become with all that new freedom. It was light out of doors and the street not yet swept.

One day the greengrocer stopped for a moment to have a chat with his old acquaintance and fellow-countryman. They rolled themselves cigarettes and smoked. The horse sidled up to the house.

'How's the old gentleman – all right?'

'He's all right. He took it very hard, of course; but he's got used to it. It's easier for him, having his granddaughter. It would have been pretty bad without her.'

The greengrocer knew the professor quite well – had known him, in fact, for twenty years. It was he who had found him the dvornik who lived in his village.

'There's a lot of talk going on in the marketplace,' said the greengrocer, looking away. 'Mostly the soldiers what have just come. Nothing'll make them give up their rifles. The people ask them: "Well, and who d'you want to go and shoot at?" "Anyone," they says; "at the gents." "Well, and then what?" "And then," they says, "we'll finish the war for good and begin to take away the land." "But you've finished doing your bit in the war, deserters!" "Deserters," they says, "and what about it? We've got freedom now! Was I feeding the lice for nothing?"'

'The people are ignorant,' said the dvornik.

'I should think they are. But they're strong. Just look at all the men that are coming from the stations. And they keep going all the time, night and day. You go to the front, and you'll find there's none of them left there. And they've got to go on living somehow before they get back to the villages. Well, and so they're having their heads muddled.'

'Who's muddling them?'

'Their speakers. There's a meeting in every square. To do for the bourgeoisie and to get all the power in their own hands. And the fellows listen and take it all in.'

The horse again sidled up to the window. The greengrocer pulled at the reins.

'I don't think that it's all going to end peacefully. If it had been in the old days, well… But nowadays there's nobody to restore order. And they've got rifles, too.'

'It's nothing to do with us,' said the dvornik.

The greengrocer remained silent. They finished their cigarettes and said goodbye to each other. Then the cart started off again for the Arbatskaya marketplace.

A wintry sun was just about to peep forth, but was covered up by a milky stretch of cloud. Several gates in Sivtsev Vrazhek swung to with a bang, and there came a smell of smoke. Carrying a cardboard case under his arm, and thrusting his hands with a shiver into the sleeves of his army tunic, a man, whose appearance suggested that he was engaged in some kind of clerical work, went past, clicking his heels. The dvornik gazed after him a long time, wondering in his deliberate way who would come out top – the gentry or that mutinous soldier gang. Then, as he passed through the gates, he had a good look at them also; they were in need of repair, but would go on standing for years. And he said to himself:

'I ought to tell the master it wouldn't be a bad thing to have a dog, in case we get thieves. We get a lot of people loitering round these days with no homes to go to, and the street is badly guarded. Instead of keeping watch the watchman goes off to sleep, or else he's drunk. And there's no police. What with one thing and another, it's a rowdy time just now – not normal.'

He retired to his dvornik's quarters in a brown study, his face austere and stern.

The stove burnt up. Then he stamped up the dark staircase in his imperishable hobnailed boots for tea, which he was in the habit of having in Dunyasha's kitchen.

He was a solitary figure, morose, elderly, slow thinking, but thorough. As he entered the kitchen he made a wide sign of the cross, muttered a gruff good-morning, and sat down to his tea in silence, stroking his moustache so that it should not get in the way. While he ate he collected the crumbs in his palm, and when there was enough of them tipped them into his mouth.

'As soon as the master is up, Dunya, give us a call. I want to talk to him about a dog.'

'What d'you want a dog for? There'll be it to feed, too!'

'I want a dog to guard the house. What with everything that's going on these days.'

'But the gates are locked.'

'The gates! That used to be enough, but nowadays they get over gates. A lot of people are about, and they're over before you know where you are. But a dog will bark; it would be a warning anyway. You give us a call as soon as he's up.'

'All right, I'll give you a call.'

He finished his second cup of tea, turned over the cup and wiped his moustache with a checked handkerchief.

'D'you want any wood brought?'

'Yes, enough for two stoves. We're not heating the dining room today, it's warm enough as it is.'

He stumped down the back stairs again, the protectors of his new boots ringing.

'No snow yet! and it's quite time for it.'

A village scene flashed through his dvornik's mind: fields, forests, plains, all buried in deep snow – a clean snow, not beaten down by sledges, nor mixed with earth or dung. Snow was a friend, not something smudgy and stained.

It flashed through his mind – and the soul of the dvornik of the little old house grew urbane once more.

– XXXI –

ENVY

'Why doesn't he come, Grigory?'

'He'll come all right, sir. It's early still.'

'And how will he manage to get here? Will he be led?'

'He'll find the way himself. He lives two doors away. He's even been to the little shop all by himself.'

Lieutenant Kashtanov, who had been blinded in the war, did not come until it was close on nine. Hearing footsteps and voice, Grigory went out and led the blind man up to the Trunk's table.

'Well, where are you, Sasha, old friend?'

'Here. How are you? There, you're giving me your hand again,' Stolnikov added. 'No good, you know: I've got nothing to hold out.'

'All right. We're both of us fine specimens. There's not much to choose between us, is there?' and reaching out in the direction of the voice, the blind man patted him on the shoulder.

At first they were silent. They smoked. Grigory gave them tea. Stolnikov was worked up and kept his eyes fixed on his friend. Before him was a human being who was just as wretched, perhaps, as he was himself – if that were possible! – a human being who could not see the world, with its colours and its seductive contours. He himself could see the world, but could not embrace it; Kashtanov could embrace the world, but without being able to see what and whom he was embracing. At that moment, Stolnikov saw the world as a woman.

To begin with they talked not of themselves but of the events of the day, and of mutual friends in the battery. But when Grigory left them to go to his room the conversation turned almost at once to their misfortunes; and hurriedly, half in whispers, embarrassed and yet interrupting one another, they vied in the telling of their terrible tale of suffering; told each other all that they had thought out in their hours of solitude during the long useless days of the one and the eternal night of the other.

Clutching at his temples and waving his hands about wildly, the blind man, Kashtanov, poured forth in whispers:

'You say – arms and legs. But what good are they to me? Where am I to go? And what am I to do with these hands? You know, Sasha, there's nothing but utter darkness; and sounds from out of the darkness, voices, noises, music, laughter – all that simply doesn't exist, Sasha. Just dreams, unsubstantial dreams. You can see houses and look out of the window, you are taken along the streets; but I haven't got all that. Just night. You were saying just now that you can feel your legs. Now I can feel the light – as I knew it. There are houses and people and women before my eyes, so that I just long to rush up to them... But they aren't there, Sasha; they just aren't there – lost in the night. When I know that it's dark – evening – I feel better. But when I feel the sunshine on my face, and feel it warming me, then, Sasha, it's really unbearable. The sun caresses me, while I curse it for its weakness. Why can't it drive away this everlasting darkness?'

Interrupting, in just such a whisper as though they had a secret, Stolnikov broke in:

'That's better all the same, Kashtanov. Now, you can't see, and you say there's nothing there. But I can see, and know that there are things – only not for me. You go by yourself to the little shop – you came to me alone – but I have to be wheeled along by Grigory, and fed by him with a spoon. Try to understand... Am I a human being? You at least are equal to others during the night. I – never. You can embrace a woman.'

'But she's not there, Sasha! I have no eyes to see what she's like!'

'I know you can't see her, but you can embrace her all the same. Now, I can see, and am able to love – maybe I do love, Kashtanov, and have loved her a long time. But I can't touch her, or even take her hand. I'm repulsive to her, Kashtanov. Why, I'm not a human being, but a stump, a trunk – a mistake! I can't even pass water by myself –

curse it, curse it! And when I howl I haven't got anything to wipe away my tears with, I've just got to shake my head. They run down into my nose – curse them, curse, curse!'

He sobbed, and shook his head. Then Kashtanov rose, took out his handkerchief, groped for Stolnikov's face and wiped his eyes:

'Steady on, Sasha.'

They were silent; but not for long. At their first words their heated discussion broke out again; and, choking, Kashtanov went on in a loud whisper:

'I know it's all as you say, Sasha. Only, I tell you, Sasha, I would willingly give not only my arms and legs, but all of myself to see with my eyes – just for one moment. You say you love someone; but d'you know how I loved? And she's alive, and came to see me once, and I heard her voice... Oh, I know every little intonation of it! She had eyes, Sasha... What am I talking about? – had – well, yes, used to have for me, though no longer now... Such blue, blue wonderful eyes. Well, and now they aren't there any more – for me. You said – embrace. But I must embrace with my eyes; I want to see her smile, otherwise every word would seem a lie. I'd rather have no one at all. And have I got to embrace the sunshine, too? And there's the sea and distances and forests in the world, and beauty and pictures – but where, Sasha? The devil has made away with it all. Try to understand me! I don't want arms or legs, they're no good to me. But I could just dig my nails into these eyelids and tear them off!'

'You, Kashtanov, can cure yourself. I've read somewhere that there is a way – on the temples, some nerves or other of the eye are stimulated.'

'Don't lie to me! Why do you say that? Can't you see that both my eyeballs have been taken out? I've only the sockets left!' 'Who knows? Something or other may be invented.'

'Invented! More likely that artificial limbs will be invented for you!'

'Yes, but then am I to stroke breasts with pieces of iron!'

And whatever they talked of they invariably harked back to the same thing – the woman whom the one could not see and the other could not touch. They were young, the blind man and the maimed. And they talked on till anger and envy surged up quivering in their souls: blind bitter against maimed and maimed envious of blind. And they envied each other the woman who had no existence, who spurned them – the amazingly beautiful woman with the blue eyes, with the delicate skin.

Grigory entered, noticed their haggard faces and heard their bitter words.

'The neighbours are asleep, your honour,' he said, thinking to calm them. 'They'll make a fuss again. It's late, your honour.'

He led Kashtanov home, and on his return put to bed the helpless and exhausted Stolnikov – the pitiful remains of him who had been a handsome and gallant officer, a good comrade and a fair dancing partner.

Three years had passed since he had danced light-heartedly at Tanyusha's birthday-party on the day that heralded her eighteenth spring.

– XXXII –

OCTOBER

October snow should have been flying those days like little white butterflies and moths, piling the roads, layer upon layer. Children should have been snowballing, all damp above their collars and their fingers red; and the fur of their little winter coats should have had an odour of spices when their mothers hung them up close to the stove. And from eyes to lips should have leaped the laughter of delight such as the first downy snow imparts when it is still so clean, so delicious to the taste, so busy and caressing.

But there was no snow yet. And they were leaden bumblebees that flew over Moscow in those days   over the roofs and in and out of the windows. For people were hurling terrible balls at each other, whose bursting shook the iron plating on the little house in Sivtzev Vrazhek.

The leaden snow began in the Tverskoy Boulevard. After a morning's work in the university laboratory Vassya went along to the Troitskaya dining rooms, whose windows looked out over the boulevard. He went in at the usual hour, and sat down near the window where he always sat, placing the table-napkin with the ring he had marked on the table beside his plate. Life had been running for so long on its tiny, time-worn wheels along the rails of routine. And though the price of jellied gammon had taken a big leap up, pancakes with jam and huckleberry kissel – lilac-hued islands in lakes of milk – could still be ordered on Sundays.

After soup with little dumplings came some pickled pork with mashed potatoes. Then, just as he was wiping up the remains of the sauce with a little bit of bread, the firing began at the other end of the boulevard, opposite the house of the Governor of Moscow. From the windows figures could be seen in the distance, running down between the trees of the boulevard – just passers-by, or people thirsting after a new order, or defenders of the old? The courses in the dining rooms followed each other rapidly. Vassya drank up his biscuit kvass and went out into the boulevard. The leaden bumblebees were already flying from their nests, without aim or reason, over the boulevard. And it was not long before the first of them to arrive crashed through the windowpanes of the famous students' dining rooms.

There was no snow in the thoroughfare of the boulevard, and darkness fell rapidly. The reports of unseen firearms were already thundering in various parts of the city. Someone was firing at someone else – brother at brother, of course. After the rifles came the machine-guns, and after these the guns. That evening and all the night through and for five consecutive days the inhabitants of Moscow crouched in their rooms, listening to the firing of the heavy guns and to the rapping of the machine-guns. The leaden Terror swept over the roofs, seeking the foe, and flew in at the windows, pockmarking the outer walls of the houses.

During the first night it grew light near the Nikitsky Gates: a house was burned down, blocking up the entrance to the boulevard; and the Troitskaya dining rooms, where Vassya had eaten pickled pork and mashed potatoes that day, were reduced to ashes. His table-napkin, that was not entirely consumed by the flames, went on smouldering, and the ring he had marked cracked as it charred.

When that house was burnt down another caught fire, this time a huge one on the boulevard; and, instead of an inhabited house, the pale dawn saw a blackened coliseum which there was no one yet to gape and wonder at.

Out of the houses that were in flames or under fire rushed well-to-do and needy; and all were mown down by the machine-guns. Every shot brought victory nearer; every shot lessened the number of foes. From a little boarding-house in the same building as the dining rooms had been ten old women crept out with bundles and rushed wildly about. Some fled, protecting themselves with their shawls against the leaden rain; some died of fright; others were riddled with bullets, or were burnt alive – and victory drew nearer. A handful of young soldiers in the corner house were firing at a handful of young cadets in the house opposite. Some were killed, and others succeeded in sidling along the walls and hiding – and the long-awaited reign of equality and brotherhood drew nearer by another fraction.

His arms outspread, his rifle tossed aside, a soldier lay in the road, dead, his teeth grinning up at the sky; and so it was he never came to know for whose truth he had died nor which side would count him among its fallen heroes.

Taking cover beneath an archway was a pale-faced little urchin in a fur cap, coughing and spitting blood. A moment before he had been firing away gaily, feverishly – little matter at whom or where; firing at cadets and at every slinking shadow, both at brother and grandmother, missing mostly, his bullets pelting at the plaster of the houses. And now he himself had a bullet in his lungs, and was among the living no longer. Farewell, poor foolish little fellow! And freedom came yet another step nearer.

Behind strong walls, in a room where the windows did not look out on the street, civilians who were incapable of setting or loading a machine-gun held council, deliberated, managed affairs and issued orders. But power was not theirs, nor did they count. For it was chance that settled what should be, chance and the blithe careless bullet, for which the men who had left the front no longer had any use. There was, too, the Kremlin, the Arsenal and the Alexandrovskoie training school; and the general muddle, and the few people who are always in the right, and are successful only when they go on without plan or thought. But what was truly alarming was that, beneath the aerial arch of shrapnel and bullets, thought whirled and wandered and grew confused – thought that had but yesterday crept forth from the brain was now arguing, wavering, despairing and getting entangled in the threads of guesswork and unfamiliar ideas.

Victory was to come to those accustomed neither to thinking, nor weighing, nor valuing, and who had nothing to lose. And they did conquer, too. After some deliberation the people in civilian clothes proclaimed: 'We have conquered'; and driving away the real conquerors, filled the places of highest authority in the dead city.

All this was perfectly right and just; their enemies among the civilians would have acted in just the same way in their stead.

Vassya Boltanovsky lived in the students' quarter in the Bronnaya.

At night he could see from his window the fiery reflection in the sky, and slept no better than anyone else. At times it struck him as strange and unnatural that he, who was young, no coward and full of life and vigour, should be sitting at home siding with no one. And a moment later he would say to himself: 'Yes, but there are no sides; it's just the play of the elements, a fire caused by a match that has been dropped by chance. Go out into the street without a weapon? What for? Get hold of some firearm or other and shoot? At whom? Which of the two truths shall I fight against? Not two truths either, but many. Nature has one truth and Man another, in complete opposition to Nature's. And there are others too, quite different. Everyone fights for his own truth; such is the struggle for existence. And then some fellow goes and dies for others – going right against his own interests! Self-interest has its own right; self-sacrifice also.' And he wondered to whose side he – Vassya, research student and Tanyusha's friend – belonged. Certainly not to the side of any of those aiming at power; no – his idea of right was that it should be possible to go on working hard and that Tanyusha should be happy. There was far more sincerity in that!

Towards morning, Vassya fell asleep. But he awoke early, roused by reports quite near the house. It was merely a casual, random firing; possibly with intent to carry on a persecution, possibly just out of mere mischief. Who could want to shoot at the peaceful students' quarter!

Work that day was out of the question; or should he attempt to get to the laboratory by keeping to the side streets?

About nine o'clock Vassya went out and managed somehow to get as far as the Nikitsky Gates; but there the firing forced him to beat a retreat. Then he went along in the direction of the Sadovaya and crossed the great Nikitinskaya. Not a soul in the Povarskaya. Curiosity drew Vassya on to St. Boris' and St. Glyeb's; and he thought he might be able to get as far as Arbatskaya Square. But he had hardly reached the corner of Boriso-glyebsky Street before a shell set the air vibrating and burst, knocking off a part of the church's dome. Vassya gasped, and muttered: 'What in heaven's name are they doing now?' And, quickening his step, he turned down a side-street. He had not, as a matter of fact, been able to make out what had happened; but he was deeply shaken. It was quiet in the Dogs' Square. Now there was only the last stage left to attempt – the bit from the Arbat to the university.

When he reached the corner of the Arbat, Vassya stopped and looked with curiosity to the left, whence came the sound of intermittent reports. Chance it?

It needed the deeply ingrained mentality of the civilian and the profound ignorance of the research student to enable him to go on standing there quite calmly, without even noticing the bullets whizzing past. Nobody stopped him; and it did not enter his head that he was being shot at from the whole length of the street. His elbow pressing his books to his side – a student habit-he crossed the Arbat leisurely, unaware that he was being watched with fear and amazement from behind the drawn curtains of the houses. Not a yard away from him, a bullet flattened itself out against the cobbles. No – going along the Arbat was really rather unnerving, and it was very doubtful whether he would be able to cross the square; the Alcxandrovskoie training school was quite near, and there was sure to be fighting going on there. And then it was such a natural customary thing to turn down by St. Nicholas' and come out into the peaceful haven of Sivtsev Vrazhek, where they wouldn't yet have finished coffee in the old professor's house; or even if they had, Dunyasha would be sure to heat up some for him. It was all up with the day's work.

The morning was obviously wasted. But he could make the most of it in another way. There was something to talk about with the professor, who would of course be at home, and impressions to share with Tanyusha, although his impressions were scant enough, being nothing but a sort of haze – sheer rubbish.

He rang, and hearing steps on the stairs smiled a little smile of pleasure.

– XXXIII –

BETWEEN TWO WINDOWS

Those days the rust that was slowly eating away the ironwork of the roofing, and the worm gnawing the beam, and the rats that were making new passages for their impudent nightly invasions, and the damp and the mould and the myriads of tiny creatures that, in the name of procreation and the right to existence, were shaking the foundations of the house in Sivtsev Vrazhek – all these were aided by the vibrations over Moscow, those vibrations of the air caused by a multitude of grape-shot and coward-mocking shells.

The windowpanes shook, displacing the dried-up putty; a little nail broke; flakes of old paint came tumbling down; a brick lost a speck; the soot that clung to the chimney right up to the very top fell back into the stove in greasy flecks. And it was all quite imperceptible, save to the infinitesimal builders and destroyers that were working away without rest or respite.

The tiny new wrinkle on the aged face was not visible to the human eye. High up above the roofs, splitting the air, came a shell that had been fired at random from the Sparrows' Hill by someone who was, obviously, no shot. And the professor's peaceful little house cowered to earth, blinked, held its breath, then straightened itself out – with yet another little wrinkle. But no one could have seen or heard. Only a slight rustling behind the wallpaper – a cockroach perhaps, from the kitchen.

The professor said: 'You must not go home, Vassya. We shall not let you go. Besides, our minds will be more at ease with you here. Tomorrow the firing will be over, then you will be able to return.'

'I'm not afraid, professor.'

'There's no reason why a young fellow like you should be. All the same, there's no object in taking needless risks. It's the worst part of all down at the Nikitsky Gates. And think, you will be doing us a kindness. It will be jollier with you, both for Tanyusha and for me.'

Lenotchka telephoned from the Clear Ponds, where she lived:

'It's simply awful here. They are firing at the Post Office. They say that the Telephone Central has been besieged.'

After repeating the number, the telephone girl asked:

'From what part of the town are you ringing up? What's happening your way?'

'From Sivtzev Vrazhek. It's quite quiet here. And where you are?'

'Awful! We don't know what's going to happen next.' And she put Tanyusha through.

But in many parts of the city the telephone could no longer be used.

'Would you like to come upstairs to my room, Vassya? Grandfather will go and work.'

Grandfather had not abandoned his time-honoured routine. He would work till late on in the night, surrounded by atlases and tables, examining the plumage of the turtle-dove against chalky paper, and making corrections in classifications that were now out of date. He cut with a bone paper-knife the pages of an English journal that had somehow managed to reach him, pulled down his glasses from his brow, ran his nose along the lines, and made pencil marks in the margins. It was all so important – migration, song, little grey-spotted eggs, hooked beak, bright flecks on the wings. It was all so very, very important; it was eternal, and for Eternity.

A bullet – quite a tipsy, stray bullet – came flying over from the Arbat or the Smolensky marketplace, striking the roof with a scarce audible tick.

'I'll go along now, but you young ones can sit up. Granny's room will be got ready for you, Vassya, or the sitting room, if you would prefer it. Tanya will tell the maid.'

'Yes, I'll tell her, grandfather. You go now. We shall sit up in my room just a little longer.'

'All the same don't sit near the windows. You never know... Better sit by the wall between the windows.'

'All right, grandfather.'

They bade him good-night and went upstairs to Tanyusha's room, where both talk and silence were pleasant.

'How is all this going to end, Vassya?'

'Well, they won't be able to take the Kremlin. And there's the Arsenal there.'

'And supposing they do?'

They talked on, discussing the rumours. Tanyusha said to herself:

'Curious! Vassya's no coward, but it's just as if it were all the same to him – as if he were an onlooker. Anyone else in his stead would...'

But who? She ran over the names of her acquaintances, those in the army and those who were not, the living and the dead. Would Ehrberg have fought? Possibly. As for Stolnikov, if he... Of course! Poor man, what a time he was going through... Yet she would have been incapable of realizing to the full what the Trunk was actually going through those days; pain had as yet not touched her soul deeply enough for that.

Vassya smoked, and when Tanyusha opened the ventilator for a moment the rapping of shots in the neighbourhood came to their ears: *tuk-tuk-tuk-tuk-tu*k. That sounded like a machine-gun.

They fell silent and listened, sitting near each other on the divan, Tanyusha thinking about the Revolution and Vassya thinking:

'I know I love her, and that she's only sweet and friendly to me, but in spite of that I love her terribly. What's going to happen about it, I wonder?'

With the thought still in his mind he raised his eyes to Tanyusha and gazed at her intently.

'What is it, Vassya?'

'No – nothing.'

Tanyusha rose and closed the casement.

'Brrr – how cold it is today!'

'Yes; no snow yet either. And it's already nearly the end of October.'

It was nearly the end of October, but only the beginning of the long, great, agonizing October.

Snow began to fall only after those bumblebees of lead ceased flying towards the end of the fifth day of the disturbances. It came at last, needed by all, on the morning of the sixth day, falling in sparse, fluttering snowflakes, whitening the railed-in roofs, covering up the bodies left lying in the streets, freezing and powdering the blood in road and yard.

The disturbances in Moscow died down suddenly. The inhabitants peeped out apprehensively, drawn forth by curiosity and want; for supplies of food, paraffin and wood had run short. One had to go on living somehow, after all. So, muffling their footsteps, they stole sideways along to the half-opened doors of the shops, asking of acquaintances on the way:

'Who's come out top?'

'They say they – the Bolsheviks.'

'What will happen next?'

'What will happen? They can't hold out long. The troops will come and restore order. Firing like this all over Moscow – unheard-of! What have things come to!'

'Is our baker open?'

'Yes, though you may have to go round to the back.'

Glancing about, wide-eyed with curiosity, pressing even closer to the walls, then darting doubled-up along the street, people went upon their business, ready at any moment to hide behind posts, in doorways and in alleys.

And if there was anything to delight the eye it was just the clean, untrodden snow, crisping the air and powdering all Moscow, with its population spent and terror-stricken by the last five days.

– XXXIV –

THE BULLET

It never occurred to Edward Lvovitch that he might buy a new blanket which would reach up to his chin and at the same time tuck in under his feet.

Though he had never got used to the discomfort of having a blanket that was too short for him, he dealt with the discomfort with a measure of rather doubtful efficiency: covering up his feet with his old check-lined coat. It was not that he was stingy; it was simply that no other remedy had ever entered his head. He had never experienced poverty. He lived in a quiet way, and was able to spend a lot on music and books about music; moreover, he still sent money to an aunt in Riga, whom he had not seen for twenty years. It had become a habit and a tradition with him, for he had begun sending when his mother was still alive.

Since his blanket covered up his feet in such an inadequate way, he was obliged to sleep on his side with his legs drawn up. One of his ears listened to the beating of his pulse against the pillow, and the other to the machine-gun in the street going *tuk-tuk-tuk-tuk-tuk*. The object of the firing was a mystery to him, being something totally outside his experience; but the rhythm – that belonged to his world. Little by little the blanket crept off his feet and the cold made his sleep restless. Then he stirred in his sleep, the bristles of his unshaven cheek rasping against the linen pillow-case.

The rhythm of his pulse and the rhythm of the machine-gun did not coincide; yet it was imperative that they should be made to, and systematically arranged on manuscript paper. And then began a most harrowing confusion.

The big-headed little black notes with tails went dashing about all over the place, a number of them settling upon little knolls, on roofs, and blackening the horizon on telegraph posts and in little alleys. The rest went crawling over the blanket, hooking on to the lines of manuscript paper, plucking at them as if they were strings, getting into the wrong key and darting from major to minor. Edward Lvovitch tried decoying them gently and bringing down upon them the lid of legato, but the black tadpoles lashed their tails, broke away and scattered again, some over the little knolls, others over the folds of the blanket.

Edward Lvovitch quite realized that it was impossible to reconcile those that were on the horizon with the rest on the blanket. There could be no question of any sort of melody. Very well, then, let there be dissonances; a musical concept could be built up out of them, too, though it was essential, of course, to have a meaning – one single idea upon which all the laws of harmony should depend. And for all reply he heard nothing but the continuous crackling of the machine-gun and the pitiful ticking against the pillow. It looked as if it were impossible to get them to sound simultaneously. But which of them was it that caused the difficulty? The ones on the knolls were extraordinarily dispassionate and stolid. There was something dead about them, like the crosses of a cemetery against the sky. The usual disposition, Little heads all turned one way, nearly all of them crochets and quavers. Quite different were those that surrounded the pillows, with their ceaseless, irregular ticking. There was an effervescent sort of confusion here in sharp contrast to the prosaic stolidity of the others. Edward Lvovitch made an attempt to catch one of the lively ones by the tail, but missed it, his hand making a wild dive into space. Then he raised himself on tiptoe, barefooted on a mound of snow, and began to conduct a choir of tadpole notes: you never know, they might respond.

To his astonishment the choir turned out to be a magnificent one. Rising off the ground with the utmost ease, his arms flapping sinuously, he flew from horizon to horizon along the huge and endless ranks of notes, becoming more and more convinced that the jarring discords came only from quite near, and that from the remote heights there came the sounds of a wondrous choir, a mighty harmony and perfect music. Then he wanted to draw into his choir the instruments which were farthest away, scarce visible on the horizon; but before he had time to come down from his dizzy heights there came a ring, and he lost his balance.

He awoke, but could not make out what sound it was that had wakened him. He pulled the blanket over his feet and lay listening. Could it have been the front-door bell? But all was quiet. Yes; but there had been a ring all the same, or rather a sound like the breaking of glass. His thoughts turned to his dream: an amazing dream. And what was most curious about it was that it had turned out to be possible to harmonize and merge into one another rhythms that were apparently so different. That was profoundly significant. They should be approached from afar, from above. The idea of a new composition seemed to start up in his mind: conceivable and comprehensible – yes; but could it be given shape?

There was a chilly draught in the room. He arranged the coat over his feet and curled up tight. His chin rasped against the pillow. Then he tried not to move, in order to get warm. There was a chilly draught and the air seemed to be getting fresher. The notes all vanished and the little knolls too, but the rapping of the machine-gun went on more distinctly than before and at more frequent intervals. His ear, however, had got used to it, and he dropped off to sleep.

When it began to grow light, the dawn revealed a little hole high up in both windowpanes, and rays streaming out round each little hole. When it was a little lighter still another little hole was revealed in the wallpaper of the wall opposite the window, and the paper all round the hole was bulging out over the crumbling plaster.

No one had taken aim at the window. October bullets flew everywhere without much thought of their destination. One of them – quite the most useful, although inoffensive – had flown into the composer's room, momentarily shattering his musical dream.

– XXXV –

KOLCHAGIN'S CAREER

On the sixth day Andrey Kolchagin, with several days' growth on his cheek, burst into the kitchen of the little house in Sivtzev Vrazhek, red and merry-looking, though starting nervously from time to time. With him he carried his rifle and a bag stuffed full of a variety of things – a sausage, a round of cheese, a big slab of butter to which some newspaper stuck fast, and some odds and ends which he did not show Dunyasha, though he presented her with an alarm clock, a little bottle of eau-de-cologne that had already been opened, and a silk blouse with lace and narrow sleeves.

'Whatever's this? Where did you get it from?'

'Found it. The case in the yard has been broken.'

'Whatever's the good of it to me? It won't go on me! It's ladies as wear that sort of thing.'

'The ladies' day is over. The gents' too. We've got the upper hand now.'

'Where've you been? You've not been firing, have you?'

'I should jolly well think I have! I was in the thick of it. Took the Telephone Central.'

'Who took it?'

'Who? We took it – the Bolsheviks.'

'You don't tell me you're with that lot?'

'I'm on the people's side against the cadets and the bourgeoisie. It's the end of them now; we've come out top.'

'I can't make out what they're shooting for. It seems just a muddle to me.'

'There's nothing for you to understand. You just take the blouse and the scent. We can get as much as we like of that sort of thing now.'

'What doesn't belong to us?'

'What doesn't belong to us! Get on! You're a silly fool, Dunyasha – just a country girl, that's what you are.'

All the same it would be better, he said, not to show the masters; it wasn't no business of theirs. And 'the masters' was the expression he used. There were no other words as yet, and he was not sure whether the people who lived in the little house, whose kitchen had always offered him its friendly shelter, belonged to the bourgeoisie or not.

He did not remain long, however – did not stay the night, nor even have a bath, though it just happened that the water had been heated. With him he took his bag, empty, after locking up its contents in his little trunk.

He strode along the streets with a firm step, a lock of hair straying in the Cossack fashion from beneath his forage cap, although he happened to be in an infantry regiment. The gaze of those who passed him was apprehensive and unfriendly; he, on the other hand, looked at no one. He was going along feeling himself to be no ordinary mortal, no common private, but someone important, something in the nature of a hero, like he had felt those days in the village before being sent to the front.

He made straight for the gates of the Sovdep,[1] where a number of soldiers had already drifted together, all of them holding their rifles reversed. Here he exchanged a few words with some of the men,

---

[1] Sovdep = Soviet (Council) of Workers' and Soldiers' Delegates.

smoked a cigarette, and inquired by which entrance he should go in with his slip of paper. He came across a few of the men who had taken the Telephone Central with him, but none of them had slips. Then he elbowed his way on, stood in a queue and succeeded in getting in. His attitude, far from being that of a simpleton, was the fearless one of an old campaigner, and the words he spoke were to the point.

The man who was taking down particulars and stamping the papers at a table in the smoky, musty room Andrew Kolchagin entered was a weedy, darkish individual in a lounge suit. There was, however, nothing diffident about him. He was shouting at the soldiers. He entered Kolchagin's name on a slip of paper without even looking at him, thumped down the seal, and said:

'There you are, comrade. Now get along there.'

'But where've I got to go?'

'It's all written down. You've got to be at Khamovniky. Whose turn next?'

There was nothing for it but to walk out. Kolchagin tucked the stamped slip into his cuff.

There was complete chaos in the large building the Bolsheviks had occupied in the Khamovniky. There was no means of finding out who was at the head of affairs, or who was in command, or who was under orders. The soldiers were sitting about in armchairs, on tables and on window-sills, spitting and dropping cigarette ash all over the parquet floor. Whoever shouted at the others was obeyed.

Kolchagin went round the building looking for someone to whom he might deliver his new document. He failed to find anyone. There were several others searching like himself, so he took their papers, verified them and said casually: 'All right, you're in order. Just wait a bit.' After which he began to ask all the newcomers for their slips. And all of a sudden he began to feel quite like a person in authority. He had no power: power had to be acquired, so he set about acquiring it. And everyone realized that this was as it should be. He was now addressed with a certain amount of respect, like a superior.

Then some civilian or other arrived in a ramshackle car and came bursting into the outer room, calling out: 'Good-day, comrades! Everything will be along in a moment.' But no one answered him. He wandered about rather helplessly, transferring his portfolio from one table to another, seeking for an inkpot, and clearly at a loss what to do next. It was then that Andrey Kolchagin, in his forage cap, came calmly forward, a cigarette between his teeth:

'The papers have been verified, comrade. Everything's in order. We'll see about a guard soon, because, if we don't, we'll be having all sorts of people who have no business to be here in and out all the time. And I'll have the door locked, so that nobody can get in without special permission.'

The new arrival was greatly relieved, but he was not given a chance of looking important or playing the chief. Authority was already visibly imprinted on Andrey Kolchagin's face.

Everybody was hungry. Kolchagin picked out five men and sent them 'to see what they could find'. He gave them a slip of paper. He himself wrote badly, but a less illiterate man was discovered, whom Andrey ordered to be something in the nature of a clerk. It was he himself, however, who signed, 'Commander-in-Chief, Comrade Kolchagin.'

These five men got into one of the shops in the Arbat, which necessity forced them to open. There was nobody there, however, to whom they could deliver the receipt, there being no proprietor on the spot. They brought away with them a large round of cheese, all the sausages they could find, a quantity of butter, and various tins and boxes – ail of which was brought in sacks to Kolchagin, who ordered the things to be locked away in his room. Afterwards he himself handed the things out to be divided among the men. And into his own bag – for a rainy day – he stuffed as much as would go in.

Some of the men went away; others stayed on. They slept in the building itself, on the floor, without undressing. A sofa was given to Kolchagin. And that was only to be expected: for was he not one of the chiefs, which meant he worked harder than all the rest? Before turning in, Andrey saw to it that there was a guard, and appointed the men who were to go on duty throughout the night.

The following morning more organizers arrived. They bustled about, talked about typewriters, put up notices on the doors, arranged the tables, went away and came back again. Kolchagin went following them about like their shadows, helping them to move the tables and jotting things down on his own slip of paper. On their departure, he sat down at a desk in the outer room, shouting and looking keenly at all who entered. People came and went, but Kolchagin stayed on.

Days passed in this way. Pens began to scratch in the rooms. At first it was only soldiers who thronged the outer office; then the civil population appeared, scared and hesitating. Things were brought to the place and people who had been arrested; and from it flew orders in the name of the Khamovniky Sovdep. But nothing could take place without the knowledge and sanction of Andrey Kolchagin, now addressed as 'Commandant.' No one had appointed or elected Kolchagin, no one had confirmed him in the post he had assumed. It was simply that he was the right man; he was indispensable and inevitable. And when someone who had come for information gave up hope, after going round all the rooms, he was invariably told he had better go and ask the Commandant. And the man would knock diffidently at the door of the 'Commandant's Office', where Comrade Kolchagin, now renowned in the entire district, sat at a table before a glass of tea with sugar and a roll – clothed in authority, businesslike, shrewd, and a stranger to doubt. Some he would direct to wherever it was they had to go, others he would deal with himself, issuing slips of paper signed with his name and stamped with his own 'Commandant's' seal.

– XXXVI –

THE TRUNK'S NIGHTS

They were terrible indeed, those nights the Trunk lived through. Often during the nightmare of his nights, when he was lying between sleeping and waking, the last revolt of the crippled and mutilated seemed to start up, dreamlike before him.

In little low carriages, with a wooden support in each hand, the disabled of the war went whirling at the pace of a tortoise on to a new war. And he, the most perfect specimen of all – he, the miracle of surgery – went flying on ahead of them – a miracle, too – after the officer in command. Behind him came men twisted crooked as a ram's horn, the faceless, the poisoned, the blind, the deaf, the dumb, the sleepy – whole regiments of mutilated winners of the Cross of St. George.

A new and unheard-of revolution – and the last: all that are still well and whole must be deformed, all reduced to one level! Teeth must gnaw off hands that are whole; feet that can walk must be run over and crushed; eyes that can see pricked; easy breathing poisoned; minds unsettled by thunder. One mould for all!

And women! Give us women that are trunks too, just like us. If they have arms and legs and eyes that can see and lie, they will despise and repulse us. Let them be trunks too. We will leave them only their breasts. We will creep and embrace without arms or legs. And let just such children as we are be born unto us.

Everything must be created anew. Let the clothing of man be a sack; he will work with his teeth. Let the blind and the mad be the only ones to have a right to limbs; let them lead and carry the others. What does it matter? Weren't they blind men and madmen who led us before? If the deaf and dumb wish it, let all the others have their tongues pulled out and their eardrums pricked with a needle! Both young and old; girls too.

Let there be silence in the world for the men responsible for military marches and anthems, and for the beating of drums and the roar of guns. Nightmare – nightmare – great piles of hacked-off legs in the city squares. Round the blaze, in a swift merry-go-round, fly the little carriages of the legless – the revolt of the legless, the holiday of the mutilated – while the insane cast into the fire books that are now useless, and pianos and chairs and pictures and footwear – especially footwear – gloves too, and wedding rings – all the odds and ends that are needed only by the whole, who are no longer and never will be more. So now you understand!

The highest type of beauty shall be the scar and the stump. Whoever is most scarred, most cut about, shall be considered the most beautiful. The blazing pile for him who dares think otherwise. Arms and legs shall be blotted out from icons and pictures; the faces in them shall be made hideous, so that no trace of their former beauty may live, not even in the memory. The ancient statues shall be overthrown and broken, and only the marble torsos left, together with the busts with broken noses. Copies of the Vatican torso of Hercules – the ideal of post-war beauty, the only statue that is worthy – shall be set up in all the big squares.

The world shall be ruled by a blue, shiny stump. And if the world collapses, well, then, let it!

These nightmares of thought and dreams wrung long groans of misery from the Trunk. Bracing the muscles of his back, he would attempt to turn on to his side. He was able to do this suddenly, by a sharp movement, pressing his head against the pillow, his strong neck aiding him. Occasionally, however, miscalculating his movement, he would fall on his face, and cry like a child in his wretchedness. In

THE TRUNK'S NIGHTS

order to get back to a more comfortable position he would have to sway for a long time, brace his neck again and toss about in the hollow of his soft mattress. When he got his breath back he would close his eyes; and then, in the light half-waking slumber of his nights of torment, the nightmare would begin all over again.

Think about something else? But what? Remember the past, when he could walk the world over on those legs, embrace or push away with those arms, when everything was within his powers – playing and fighting, marching and waltzing, every kind of movement and work? When he could… could scratch his shoulder without having to perform those tiring and difficult movements of the head in order to reach the spot, if only with his chin? It seemed to him that never had anyone's shoulder itched as his was itching; and filling him with an icy horror the thought flashed through him: 'And supposing my back or side should suddenly begin to itch, which they never have yet!' Call Grigory? Poor Grigory! What wouldn't he, the Trunk, give to be 'poor' like that, with arms and legs, even though it did mean being an elderly and almost illiterate soldier? He would willingly be anyone, doing any kind of dirty work. A convict? Yes, even a convict. A spy even! Any life rather than his own.

He remembered his invariably morbid and useless arguments with his neighbour, Kashtanov, who had lost his sight in the war. And now he found a thousand new arguments and reasons that went to prove the blind man's life was infinitely more bearable than his, that it was at any rate a life, a real life, full of possibilities. At night, now for instance, in the dark, Kashtanov was on an equality with everyone else. He was lying comfortably in bed, and he could get up and pour out a glass of water for himself, drink it, have a good stretch, and go to sleep again. He was not bound to sleep alone, and he could caress without seeing. And that lucky beggar dared to grumble, dared to make comparisons!

Pressing the nape of his neck against the pillow, the Trunk raised his back slightly, bent his body and slowly lowered himself again; his muscles tense, emitting through his teeth a long, stifled roar, as of a wolf.

A bed creaked in the neighbouring room, and Grigory's feet pattered along the floor.

'Something you can't manage that's making you groan? Is there anything you'd like?'

He gave Stolnikov a drink of water, took out the bed-pan and stayed a long time, tending the cripple as if he were a child, setting the blankets in order, tucking him in, giving him a cigarette and placing a saucer for the ash – all by the glimmer of the night-light. Then he sat down near him on the bed, covering up a yawn with his hand.

'Well, Grigory, do you mean to go on looking after me like this forever?'

'You aren't thinking I'm going to leave you, are you! I'm all right. I only want to cheer you up a bit, that's all. It's not worthwhile thinking about it, your honour. The less one thinks the better one sleeps.'

'Do you really believe in God, Grigory? Or do you only say that, when you are really only trying to believe in him?'

'I believe in God; of course I believe in God.'

'Is your God a kind God?'

'What's He got to be kind for? He's stern.'

'But why has He crippled me, your God?'

'How can you, your honour! It's not the Lord, it's people. It's their doing.'

'But He let them.'

'That means He's got His own ways and it's not for us to know them. You've got to get resigned, your honour, since it's your fate.'

'Well, all right, Grigory. I'll be resigned. Now go back to bed.'

Grigory yawned, and made the sign of the cross over his lips:

'If there's anything you need, just give me a call; don't you tire yourself out for nothing.'

'Thank you, Grigory. You can leave me now.'

He lay thinking about Grigory and his stern God who had ways of His own, and about the people who believed in God and were able to reconcile themselves to whatever misfortune befell them. And, strange – he did not envy them. They were the only ones he did not envy. In himself he could find no such faith, nor did he seek self-deception.

But as he thought about them he grew calmer, and did indeed grow reconciled, letting sleep's gentle fingers brush against his eyes. And in his dreams he saw himself as he had been – in no hurry to make the most of his health; saw his arms and legs – whole; his youth. He saw a woman, too, and joked with her.

The Trunk was not yet thirty. At that age man still has the whole of life before him. But the Trunk was not a man...

- XXXVII -

THE LITTLE CITY OF MONKEYS

A ditch had been dug in a circle, and its outer wall cut perpendicular. The result was a little island from which there was no exit.

In the middle of the island was a tall, dry tree with bare branches, which was admirably suited for the monkeys' gymnastics.

Beneath the tree were little houses, with windows and attics and roofs, just like the houses of human beings. There were excellent swings, a reservoir with running water, and, above it, a ring attached by a cord to a crossbeam. Everything was destined for pleasure.

The huge family of grey, long-tailed apes had a very good time there. They multiplied, and their numbers soon filled the little city.

The superintendent of the Zoological Gardens had been right in supposing that the little city would prove popular with the public. People threw nuts and bread and potatoes at the apes, watched their tricks with delight, and laughed at their lovemaking and family quarrels.

The superintendent then decided to transfer a tawny species to the city. Another little house was added, with a stronger roof. The new citizens were slightly larger than the others, their muscles stronger and their habits more mischievous.

At first all went well. There was some fighting, of course; but then no social life of any stability can exist without it. Afterwards, however, relations became restricted to contests of strength, and a racial persecution began.

One of the tawny apes was a perfect monster. Strong, agile, cruel, and a leader, he became a real scourge to the grey tribe. He never let an opportunity go by of bumping into them, grabbing them by the scruff of their necks and tugging at their legs.

At first he was somewhat afraid of interfering with a certain mother ape in front of whom her lively offspring – a skinny, naked, little creature – was romping. But in the end he crept up stealthily and seized the tender infant with his sharp white fangs and escaped from the infuriated mother by dashing up the tree.

The tawny apes were delighted with the joke; it made them feel conscious of their own strength. It was then that for the first time there entered the monkey souls of the grey ones a sense of fatality, a sense of the impending and inevitable destruction of their patriarchal tribe.

The terror of the greys spread in the little city. And soon their worst fears were justified.

The tawny brute was bored. It was always the same thing. There wasn't even any serious opposition. After he had driven one timid victim to the very end of a twig, and had forced it to take an unsuccessful flying leap down (the grey one had broken its hind arm), none of the greys would venture up the tree. Grabbing their food was no fun either, and he grew tired of it; nor was there any point in it, he had plenty of his own. What he needed was something out of the ordinary.

In his boredom the tawny ape would go on strategical rounds, and after taking a good look at a cluster of tiny trembling monkeys would leap straight into their very midst, and seize all he could by the scruffs of their necks, after which he would sit, a little way off, scratching his side, mocking at the cowards, his lip lifted over his fangs in a sneer. And the greys would herd together again farther off, riveting their close-set eyes on him, their teeth a-chatter. Whenever he jumped, all of them – as though in obedience to a command – turned to look in his direction, keeping a vigilant watch upon his movements, and prepared to dart back as soon as necessary. Whenever he was a good distance away, or was asleep at home, they ventured to lick their wounds, nibble carrots, look for fleas, and hastily, timorously, make love. Even though it had become unbearable, life had to go on. But it was a life of the doomed.

One day, when the tawny monster was feeling bored from having nothing to do, one of the greys risked having a little fun: he leaped on to the ring over the reservoir and began to swing. The tawny brute noticed him, quietly slipped into the grey one by the tail and pulled him sharply down into the water.

The grey ape swam to the edge, but his foe was already there; he swam to the other edge, but was unable to get out here either. He had scarcely time to catch at the edge before the powerful hand of the tawny brute struck him a blow on the crown of his head which sent him back again into the water.

Here at last was a new and interesting amusement. The grey victim's strength ebbed away, and he sank below the surface, sending up bubbles. When its wet head appeared at the edge for the last time, the tawny fellow, who had by this time lost nearly all interest in the game, just flicked him back into the reservoir and held him down for a while. Only bubbles rose that time.

Their teeth bared, their tails between their legs, the trembling apes sat watching the prank from afar.

The tawny fellow waited a little, then jauntily arching its back went round the reservoir once more, and stalked off. Some distance away he sat down, bared his fangs, shook his wet hand, and happening to discover a monkey-nut, settled down to shell it. The fun had come to an end, and boredom had returned.

On the whole, however, the experience had been to his liking, and the reservoir began to claim more and more of his attention. He now took to driving the victims to it himself. Whenever he succeeded in seizing an unwary grey ape with his powerful fangs he would drag him along to the reservoir, fending off the convulsive hands with his fangs, and, reaching it, would quickly push him in. Never in any hurry to drown his victim, he would give him time to get his breath back, retreating craftily from the edge and returning just in time to duck the feeble swimmer's head again, playing in the intervals, amusing himself, leaping on the ring, swinging, and returning again just in time. When he had drowned his victim he felt bored again, and would shake the big, dry boughs with his powerful, muscular arms.

The grey colony decreased in numbers. Dread turned to despair. Other tawny apes followed their leader's example and took to falling unexpectedly upon the trembling, bewildered monkeys, that were by this time almost furless and painfully attenuated. They would go into their houses and drive them out, make off with their food, bite their hands and tear out tufts of their fur. The grey colony gradually dwindled away; the tawny thrived and multiplied.

It was not until the water was drained away, in order that the reservoir might be cleaned, that the superintendent of the gardens noticed the disappearance of the grey apes; and then it was already too late. The keepers were severely reprimanded; and the few grey apes that remained were removed from their free little city to a cage that had been specially prepared for them. There they were given plenty of food. On their cage a little board was hung up with their Latin name, and the wife of one of the keepers was allowed to put a table with monkey-nuts beside it. This brought her in a small but regular income, especially on Sundays; and for the gardens it was an economy on the monkeys' food.

It was impossible to tell by looking at the fattened apes whether they had any recollection of their free little city, their lost home. They would stare out at the public with their little close-set eyes, receive alms and bare their teeth in a grin, and, all unmindful of onlookers, would do in the presence of everyone all that creatures made in man's image are meant to.

– XXXVIII –

THE DISABLED

Ever since early morning Stolnikov's rooms had been invaded by khaki uniforms with empty sleeves, thumping wooden legs, and excited faces with ghastly scars. The Trunk had suddenly become their acknowledged leader, in spite of the fact that they had something in the nature of an organization of their own – 'The League of the Disabled' – and that the first of their claims – 'The war must go on till we win' – found no response in him. The second claim was for help for the men whom the Great War had disabled; but Stolnikov thought very little about that. The only thing that stirred him was the thought of the public appearance of limbless and mutilated men. They had been forgotten; now people would be obliged to give them their say. And the louder, the bitterer, the more biting and insistent it sounded, the better.

It was settled that he, as the most perfect example of the disabled, should be carried in front in an armchair set high upon a stretcher; that the procession should stop before the building of the Soviet and that speeches should be made there.

About two o'clock the men gathered together in groups in the Tverskaya. They sat about on benches, walked up and down in front of the Pushkin Memorial, and wandered about the square. When Stolnikov was brough,t they all gravitated to him. The badge was the same for all: the red badge of 'The League of the Disabled.' The crowd that had collected numbered about three hundred men. Three of the strongest bore the stretcher with the armchair; the fourth was Grigory. Men on crutches and those who had lost their arms walked

THE DISABLED

beside it. Several blind men were led by the arm. Kashtanov among them. Many bandages gleamed white in the crowd.

On the pavement hobbled a horrible-looking little soldier who had no face; only his eyes, without brows or lashes, made dark spots in the shiny skin, pierced by his nostril holes. On one side hung a straggly tuft of a beard.

When the procession halted, five people came out on to the balcony of the Soviet. One of them, a stout, fair, bearded man with an air of self-assurance, who looked like a merchant with intellectual interests, bent his corpulent body over the balustrade and waved a hand. The other four leaned on the balustrade and gazed down at the crowd of deformed men without evincing any particular curiosity. It was a sight that was not new to them.

A ragged chorus of cries rose from the crowd of the disabled. The words 'Till we win!' and 'Shame!' and 'We demand!' could be distinguished. Many of the men waved leaflets. But it was evident that the demonstration had been badly organized, and that the people who had assembled there had come to no agreement with regard to the things they should demand.

Again the fair man waved a hand. Then he began to speak. His voice was hoarse, obviously strained by continuous speeches. It was the sixth time that day that he had had to speak from the balcony – to the sixth crowd of soldiers. His speech had been learned by rote and was the same for all, the only difference being the manner in which he addressed the various crowds. This time he was addressing them as 'Comrades, you who have been disabled in the Imperialist butchery.' The words went striking the Skobelev Memorial, from which the bronze figures had just been removed, and flying on, were lost beneath the low arches of the guardhouse.

The passers-by scarcely paused on their way; they were long since used to demonstration outside the Soviet and were familiar with the words from the balcony. It was only the Trunk's armchair, high up above the crowd, that arrested their attention.

Swaying with every clumsy movement of his bearers, Stolnikov stared hard at the healthy two-armed, two-legged speaker. Tied like that to an armchair, he was more than ever conscious of his helplessness and his inability to make a gesture just when gesture was so indispensable.

In the middle of the speech the crowd began to interrupt the speaker; towards the end of it the roar of voices drowned his words completely. Those who were standing in the neighbourhood of the Trunk's chair turned up their sleeves, waved their crutches and yelled themselves hoarse. The blind, too, uttered incomprehensible cries. The faceless soldier came forward and roared. He was dumb.

The speaker shouted his last words, pointed his hand first to the horizon, then upward, wiped his lips with a handkerchief and made for the door, the others following him.

Something had to be done; but exactly what, no one quite knew. The representatives, who had brought with them the demands drawn up on a sheet of paper, returned to the crowd; the paper had been taken from them, but they themselves had not been admitted into the Soviet. Young soldiers with rifles were standing at the entrance, and others on the pavement were forcing lingering passers-by to move on. Like a whirlwind, a youth in uniform burst out of the entrance. His uniform was cleaner than the others, his belt drawn tighter; clearly an officer in command. He ran down the pavement and, without actually going up to the head of the procession, called out:

'Move along, comrades! Scatter. Enough of that! You mustn't block up the square.'

He went back and led out a small detachment, which occupied the whole of the pavement in front of the building.

The disabled shifted from leg to leg but did not move on, though some of the stronger men on the edge of the crowd fell back. Those who were acting as standard-bearers moved to one side of the street.

Just then, above the hum of the crowd, wild and strident rose a scarce human cry, that broke off shrilly:

'Scoundrels! S-scoun–drels!'

The bearers staggered. With his free hand, Grigory quickly caught the Trunk's body as it fell out of the chair, breaking through the slender board that held him in. Several men rushed up to help. The officer of the guard ran up to them, followed by two of his men:

'Take him away! Carry him off before something worse happens. You heard the order, comrades. Scatter at once!'

The Trunk had lost consciousness. Handing his end of the stretcher to another man, Grigory tied the arms of the chair with the same cord as before, then wound it round the Trunk's chest and the back of the chair. Pushing forward the youth with the bandaged cheek, who was holding the stretcher in front of him, he commanded, in a muffled undertone:

'Get on! No good dawdling here.'

The crowd fell silent and advanced rapidly. Only a section of it, however, followed Stolnikov. The bulk, outstripping the furled banner, scattered towards the opposite side of the Tverskaya.

'I hope nothing will happen,' said the disabled man who was striding along beside Grigory. 'They won't notice that he's lost his arms and legs. And the worst of it is that he's an officer.'

'What can they take away from him?' replied Grigory, gruffly. 'There's nothing left to take.'

And he forced the bearers to quicken their pace, his stern eyes and frown compelling the crowd of curious onlookers they met to get out of the way of their strange procession.

The Trunk came to himself and looked round for Grigory; then his head dropped back again, and he did not open his eyes till he was brought home. Spasms crossed his face at every clumsy movement of the bearers; but beyond that there was no sign of life.

– XXXIX –

THE CIRCLE CLOSES IN

Dunyasha had lit the stove in the sitting room, where the grand piano now stood, filling up half the room. The big drawing room and the dining room had been locked up. Tanyusha had moved into her grandmother's room, next to grandfather's bedroom. The second floor was not heated, for it was not easy to get firewood those days. The last time it had been Nicolai and Dunyasha who had gone together to fetch it, and the greengrocer had let them have his horse and cart. They had brought back some excellent dry birchwood; but from where – that was Nicolai's secret; no object in gossiping. On the way back some people had tried to stop them, but Nicolai had stood firm:

'I'm carting it home. You go taking away other people's wood and not a working man's. You can't put the wind up me, brother! I'm a Sovdep myself.'

Nothing happened, they were allowed to go on.

Edward Lvovitch was playing Chopin, and playing calmly, without starting. Tanyusha, now mistress of the house, was pouring out the tea. The ornithologist was not on the divan but in a deep armchair. Poplavsky was there, too, worn to a shadow; life was far from easy for him. Then of course there was Vassya Boltanovsky, a daily guest – in fact not a guest at all, but one of the family. Among the new acquaintances was a reader in philosophy, Alexey Dmitrievitch Astafiev, whom Tanyusha had got to know through Vassya; and the old professor, who was slightly acquainted with him at the university, thought quite highly of him. Only men were present; not even Lenotchka was there. She had married a doctor just before the Revolution.

The tea was real tea, from an old store, and the bread was white bread, made from flour which had been brought from Dunyasha's village. The sugar was ration sugar; it was still occasionally doled out.

The professor was thinking that there was no lamp in the corner casting its light upon granny's grey head, her little cap and her needlework. Then his eyes turned to Tanyusha, and he noticed that Tanyusha, who was in granny's place at the samovar, was already quite grown-up. She looked sure of herself, responsible and thoughtful – too thoughtful really; it was permissible to be more light-headed at her age, although of course not at such times – there were no carefree people nowadays. And there was Vassya looking at her, his eyes never leaving her face. Nice boy, Vassya, though it was hardly likely that Tanyusha would single him out; a thoroughly good lad, but not Tanyusha's sort. She needed quite a different type of person.

'It's warm in here,' Poplavsky was saying, 'and cosy too – cosier even than it used to be. It's simply freezing at home. I've shut myself up in one room, and there are stalactites hanging from the dining room ceiling. And the pipes have burst.'

Edward Lvovitch rubbed his hands, thinking that it was cold in his rooms too. True, there was the little stove, but it was very difficult to manage even when the wood was chopped up very small and the sticks placed carefully side-by-side. He thought that, but said nothing. It was not the sort of thing he was used to talking about. He had his grand piano, and that was the main thing after all; some people had had theirs taken away. Shrinking into himself, he rubbed his hands.

'And where do you live, Alexey Dmitritch?' Tanyusha asked Astafiev.

'I live in the Vladimiro-Dolgorukovskaya. The house has been handed over to the working classes and there's not a single bourgeois except myself. At present I'm being left alone, but I shall probably be turned out too. It's very noisy, but quite interesting.'

Vassya gave a laugh.

'What's interesting? – when everything you've got has been taken away.'

'That's not such a calamity. Besides, not everything has been taken, my books have been left.'

'Without any shelves?'

'It's true there are not many shelves left. But it was I who burned them. It has been so cold.'

'They'll take the books too.'

'Possibly. It won't upset me very much.'

'But how will you be able to work?'

Astafiev smiled, and hesitated before replying:

'Work? ...Of course it will be impossible to go on working as before; why, it's not possible even now. But – is it really necessary?'

Tanyusha looked at him, and he went on:

'Philosophy has become such an obvious luxury – like all learning in general. For oneself – yes, but for others – I don't know what can we teach others, when life itself teaches so much better than any philosopher.'

Tanyusha wondered whether he was being ironical or was just playing with paradoxes. His words had the effect of making Poplavsky depressed. And the old ornithologist was troubled and up in arms.

'Well, but what is one to do then – sweep the streets? Wisdom that has been acquired throughout the ages cannot suddenly, in a day, cease to be of any value.'

'Well now, professor, there's your own special province, for instance, a natural science – well, one that cannot go wrong in a sense, if you see what I mean. But philosophy, on the other hand, is not even a science, although it does call itself the science of sciences. It's the luxury or weariness of life that breeds it. It's cake. And it's also a grin. And an escape too. Life at the present moment is such that if you escape from it for a moment it will escape from you for days. If one wants to survive one has got to cling on to it – life, I mean – scramble up and push the others off the step, like on trams.'

'That, too, is a philosophy,' said the professor – 'a depressing one, of course.'

'Oh no. Why depressing? We have simply got nearer to nature. Existence has lost its refinements and grown simpler, and manners and customs have got to keep pace.'

'Yes, but life has not lost its refinements,' put in Poplavsky.

'On the contrary, it is becoming more and more refined. People feel more deeply at present. Material existence goes on in its own way, but spiritual life –'

'Is becoming more complex, you think? Personally, I don't think so. The man in the street is something of a philosopher from sheer lassitude, and the philosopher becomes the man in the street. Cynics, both of them. Manners gain nothing from that. And the point is, all that's no longer necessary, as it used to be. Nowadays it's far more important to keep one's muscles in training. As for books, what's the use of them? Except, possibly, popular science books, and talcs too, perhaps, by way of recreation.'

And Astafiev smiled in such a way that his words could be taken either seriously or as a joke.

Edward Lvovitch's short-sighted eyes ranged from one to another; then, his thick voice unusually assured, he said:

'Would you care to hear something crassicar?'

While he was playing, Astafiev watched Tanyusha, who was trying to wash the cups without clinking the spoons against them. He wondered what she was really like, for, despite those still childish features, she was a grown-up woman.

Tanyusha was twenty years old, well proportioned and beautiful. Her face was severe – almost cold – though very Russian. But her smile was spontaneous, wholehearted, sunny; and when it vanished from her face colour remained in her cheeks, and her eyes were playful and gentle. Then the Diana in her would return once more. In the evening, her grey eyes seemed dark and blue. Her hair was drawn back smoothly from a lofty forehead. She belonged to the type of unfashionable women who are incapable of making an awkward movement and who do not have to think what to do with their hands, or how to hold the head. It was in the presence of other people, in society, that she was like that. Alone, she was entirely different; then her eyes would dilate, a little line would appear on her forehead, and she became a frail and frightened little girl, wondering where she ought to go and at whose door she should knock, a little girl with nobody in the wide world to direct her and advise her. She would look out of the window and see a grey sky, take a book and find no answer in its pages; she would sigh, and her blouse would seem too close-fitting; and her heavy hair dragged back her head. All the objects in the room were long since familiar; and they would stare at her dispassionately, too logically, somehow. Then she would go to grandfather and press against his rough cheek. And grandfather would stroke her head and think: 'What's going to become of my Tanyusha?'

Edward Lvovitch played with quite unusual assurance that day; and while he played he felt certain that people had lost their heads and that the truth was known only to him, Edward Lvovitch. Only he was in possession of the unquestionable truth. And nothing could take away what was unquestionable. Music, the world of sounds, the power of sound, composition – these were the things that were unquestionable. His finger was striking one of the keys, and the key was responding exactly as he wished and expected.

Snow was falling beyond the window. Neither horses nor pedestrians were to be seen in the street.

At the Khamovniky, in a large building with lighted windows, people in tunics, leather jackets and army uniform were bustling about, leaving the building in groups, getting into cars and dashing about far faster than was necessary. While Edward Lvovitch played, the clumsy fingers of a soldier traced the letters of the composer's surname and brought down the seal. For a grand piano is a thing which can be taken away with even greater ease than life itself these days. Added to which, a piano was greatly needed for a workmen's club.

Entering the composer's name on a blank form, the same soldier went on this time with far greater ease and assurance, almost showily – to sign his own name, with a red flourish below: 'Andrey Kolchagin.'

And he set his seal to the form.

– XL –

A THING

The entrance door slammed with a bang, but the sound of voices still rose from the stairs, while at every jolt some bass string of the grand piano rumbled with surprise.

The room looked out on to the yard, so that Edward Lvovitch did not see his piano loaded on the cart.

One of the men who had come to take it away returned, however, knocked, and entered to repeat a few words of consolation:

'Don't you worry yourself overmuch about it, citizen. If they decide that you have a special right to music you'll get it back; if not your own, at any rate some other one. But we can't do nothing against orders, and the workmen's clubs are in real need of musical pianofortes, so it's clear as daylight we can't let everybody keep them. You can see that yourself, can't you? But there's no use worrying yourself for nothing; nobody will interfere with you and everything's being done for the good of the country. You as an education chap ought even to be glad. But of course you can always send in a complaint if you like.' And he departed.

Although Edward Lvovitch ate, drank and slept like everyone else, he differed from everyone else in that he somehow scarcely noticed what he ate and drank; and he went to bed only because it was impossible to play at night – everyone else slept. Added to which, everyone else had interests he understood very little about – family interests, business, political. Each, from the score of his own life, performed an opus which was well-nigh incomprehensible to the composer, and that seemed somehow to sin against all the rules of counterpoint. It was quite likely that all that was quite necessary; but, at all events, one could quite well do without it if one had that universal and all-embracing thing called music. Experience proved it. Edward Lvovitch was over fifty; he had no ties of any sort, family or others, and if in his youth there had been something of the kind it had all been long ago transmuted into sounds and fitted into the five lines of manuscript paper. Nor did he notice, of course, how from a human being, ordinary as a chromatic scale – albeit a human being with a perfect ear – he changed to a citizen.

When the man who had called Edward Lvovitch 'citizen' went away, there remained little dusty spots where the piano legs had stood, and three bright little ribbons running from the spots to the door. A quantity of music, especially manuscripts in a big old music-case, now lay on the shelves – useless all of a sudden.

There remained in the room yet another long-kept thing that not a soul needed – Edward Lvovitch himself. The thing went on standing in the middle of the room, fingering the few hairs on its temples, then seated itself on a chair by the wall. The round music-stool with raised seat stood in the middle of the room, unoccupied; it would have been strange somehow to sit on it. And it was difficult to decide which way to face – though what did it matter now that his piano was gone?

For half-an-hour the thing sat on, fully conscious of the importance of what had just happened, but very vague as to the details, and especially at a loss to know what it should do next. There was even a moment when the thing smiled and said to itself:

'It simply cannot be! It's probably something connected with their life and nothing to do with me. It's absolutely inconceivable that for some reason or other someone should come and take away – well, what amounts to – no, not what amounts to, but what actually is – my soul. Just take it and carry it off on a cart? Besides, without an instrument it's impossible not only to work out a symphony, but even to sketch in the simplest little song. And, well – how can one live without it? If that goes, then what is left?'

It was so absurd, so like a practical joke, so utterly impossible, that the thing sitting on the chair against the wall attempted to smile. Then, for a moment, it closed its eyes. And all at once the three bright little ribbons on the floor disappeared and the legs stood on the dusty spots and everything came back. Opening its eyes, the thing beheld once more the spots and the lines to the door.

Then, from a far corner of his memory, from an old manuscript-book, where all he had jotted down had turned yellow and faint, there suddenly peeped out in a half-forgotten tune the realization that there had been a similar event before. Details came back to him: an object like a case had been borne out, and it, too, had left an empty space. The case had been smaller and lighter, and narrow. The case had been a coffin. And in it had lain Edward Lvovitch's mother, who had been his companion right up till the time he had begun to grow elderly.

But there was a difference. What could it be?

In the first place, that time Edward Lvovitch had gone out of the room behind the case and had followed it along the streets to the grave. The case had been lowered into the earth. And then – then Edward Lvovitch had gone home again to his flat – he had had a flat of his own in those days, and no one had disputed his right to it – and his flat had seemed empty. And then something soothing had occurred, something comfor... Well, yes. He had sat down and begun to play. And he had gone on playing till dusk. And as he played he forgot his loss. And every time he felt an emptiness creeping into his life he had hastened to fill it with the sounds of his piano.

And now? But here his thoughts grew painfully confused. Edward Lvovitch, the reasonable being, disappeared, and in the chair appeared a faded, old and useless thing.

The little stove had gone out and his feet began to feel cold. At first he thought of lighting the stove again, then realized that there was no object in doing that now. So he put on his little fawn overcoat and his felt boots and went out, stepping carefully so as not to tread on the little ribbons that rubbed along the floor.

Then it was as if a dim little light in his memory shone forth, bidding him to go after – after that case in which the whole contents of his life had been laid – go after it, because then he would be able to complain. But where should he go after it? By which streets? In which direction?

They had carried it beyond the Dorogomilovskaya Gate that time. Then along the road and through the gates. There, in a far corner on the left, was a little railed-in grave, and near the grave a seat.

Edward Lvovitch was very tired, but he found the grave easily – he knew it so well. Even the graves around were familiar. And it was so good to meet again, to be once more among such simple, quiet, pleasant – yes, they really were like friends. Fifteen years, or maybe sixteen even, had gone by since then. How cosy that grave looked – his mother's – yet so simple. And he sat down on the seat.

His mother had died when she was very old. And he was almost an old man now himself. His hair was thin and grey. When it had been thicker and not yet grey there had been times – again some little tune from an old manuscript-book came stealing back into his memory – times when there had been things to complain about to her. There had been his first unsuccessful efforts, the indifference of the public, the misunderstanding of the critics – various things which had hurt him then, not trifles either – though, of course, not like that unprecedented thing. And if he were now – if for instance he were to complain to his mother now too – he had been so intolerantly wronged this time – she would be sure to understand; the rest of the world might not, but his mother – his old friend! She would understand!

Taking his hat off, most unlike a citizen, though very like an unwanted, long-kept thing in. his shabby little overcoat and his wretched felt boots patched with leather at the heels, the grey-haired little man, whom not a soul needed, slipped off the seat on to his knees, in the snow and, burning his bald patch against the ironwork of the railings, began to cry, sobbing like a child. In cemeteries one is supposed to weep for others, but he cried for himself, because he had been wronged, because they had taken away the plaything of his life – such a poor little thing, so like a child, though in reality already a little old man. And like a little child he forgot all his words save the one short little word 'Mummy' which he repeated over and over again. There were no other words. He wiped his nose on his sleeve and his copious tears bored little holes in the snow and froze to a clear icicle on a spiral of the railing. Through the mist of tears he looked at the little holes and at the icicle and set his sobs to music, putting in the signature, and bars, with a minim and a crotchet rest in each.

When his tears came to an end he rose from his knees, looked round, smiled a little disconcerted smile, bowed politely to the grave and took a few aimless steps round, as one does in an entrance hall before the guests go, then made his way to the gate, stumbling in the snowdrifts of the unswept cemetery.

Stumping along the streets in his felt boots, making way for the people he met and trying to protect his face from the cold in his wretched fur collar, he slowly went back home.

At home his room and his unheated stove awaited him. It was dark in the room, and neither the dusty spots nor the lines on the floor could be seen. The thing pushed open the door with care, went in, groped about in the dark for the chair by the wall, and sat down.

– XLI –

THE LITTLE BRONZE SPHERE

Tanyusha came to see Stolnikov again. This time he received her seated in his bathchair and wearing his 'French' with its useless sleeves. The chair was drawn up to the table where all his 'inventions' were set out, with a little bronze sphere in the midst of them on a sheet of dark-green paper.

When she entered, Tanyusha experienced the same discomfort as before, a discomfort which had made her shrink from the prospect of a second visit. Even to enter the room seemed somehow strange.

She couldn't shake hands. Ought she to bow, she wondered? And of course she must look friendly and cheerful as if nothing had happened. She must compose her features, which was hardest of all. And she blushed before she had even crossed the threshold.

Tanyusha realized that she must not ask after his health or say 'How are you?' but must begin to talk about something or somebody and tell him things that would interest him. But it was so difficult. And she was greatly relieved when Stolnikov began to talk himself:

'It's nice, so nice, to see you, Tanyusha. I'm calling you Tanyusha like in the old days, though you are quite grown up now. But then I have turned into an old man, as it were, though Grigory calls me a little baby. And how are your studies getting on, Tanyusha?'

She began telling him, but noticed that he was scarcely listening. She saw that he was absorbed in thoughts of his own.

'Is there anything you need?' she asked. 'Can I do anything to help you?'

'Please. I should like to smoke. If you can do it without minding, will you take a cigarette and put it right between my lips? There, thank you. As for the ashtray, Grigory is in the habit of putting it just in front of me.'

'What's that little ball you've got?'

'That little sphere?... Yes, that's a wonderful little ball.'

And, suddenly, his expression altered and he whispered hurriedly:

'That sphere, Tanyusha, can change and upset everything, everything... You don't believe in miracles? I personally find it possible to believe in this particular one, and don't they say that I myself am a miracle, a miracle of surgery and endurance? And now I'm looking at that sphere. And it's going to move, Tanyusha. I'll make it move, make it move by looking at it.'

She did not understand, but the Trunk was not looking at her.

'There must be such a power, you see, and power develops and grows. It begins in a small way – by acting on a sphere and making it roll; but if that happens, well then, you see, everything will be possible in the future. Gymnastics of the will is all that's required. If I can force it to move then I don't need arms or legs any more. I shall be stronger than most people – than anyone, in fact – without them, don't you see?'

Swaying gently, the muscles of his face tense, he riveted his eyes on the sphere as though pushing it mentally. The cigarette fell into the ashtray that Tanyusha had placed as he had bidden her. And just as intently, her eyes wide, Tanyusha sat staring at him, full of pity and pain, thinking in a frightened way:

'What's to be done? Heavens, what's to be done! He's gone out of his mind.'

Closing his eyes for a moment, Stolnikov seemed suddenly to grow calm again. He smiled his former smile, as of old, and looking straight at Tanyusha, said:

'No, Tanyusha, don't think that. I'm not mad. This is something quite different. This is the only way out for me, my only salvation. My life, you know, isn't easy. But if I've got to go on living, I must make life bearable; and life at present is not bearable. Living like this is intolerable. One can believe or not, as one likes. And then my little sphere isn't such folly either. People who have lost their arms manage all right with their legs, and people without legs get about with the help of their arms, the deaf hear by means of ear trumpets, the blind train themselves to see by means of some sort of instrument. All these things are miracles, no less than the miracle I'm waiting for. Why, I too, have managed to do a great deal. I can take soup out of a spoon and can smoke by myself, when I'm lying in bed. There are infinite possibilities. Writing with one's mouth is quite a simple matter. But I want to succeed in doing something infinitely greater. There is the world of the spirit we know so little about, but it's real enough, not just guesswork. Mines can be blown up from a distance without any train. Voices from America can be heard in Europe; they say it will be possible for aeroplanes to fly without a pilot. All these things are miracles of course. Technical knowledge. But in the world of the mind there ought to be more miracles still. Fakirs aren't all of them charlatans. And it's not that sort of miracle I'm after. I have no wish to move mountains, only one light little sphere. Man is the source of boundless energy. It has only to be trained and directed. No, Tanyusha, I'm not mad.'

'But I didn't for a moment think –'

'Yes, you did. I know it. I feel more keenly now than others do, well – whole people, I mean. But that's not the point. The point is – ' But now – just will. Look at me, Tanyusha.'

She raised her eyes and met that altered look again, grown suddenly intent, remote and otherworldly. Again there glowed in the depths of the Trunk's large dark eyes a spark that seemed to her like insanity.

'Don't be afraid, just look. Now look at the sphere, go on looking steadily, more steadily, still... now... now...'

Tanyusha's heart sank. Then an incomprehensible thing took place, a thing whose very simplicity and unexpectedness made it appear strange: the little bronze sphere moved, then rolled in Tanyusha's direction till it reached the edge of the table and fell with a thud at her feet. Tanyusha gave a cry. Very shaken, she leaped up and ran to the door. Then, with a rush of remembrance, she looked round, and saw the Trunk's head fallen back and his eyes half-open, white-looking. Grigory entered the room.

'What's the matter, miss? Isn't he feeling well?'

Seeing the Trunk's condition, Grigory shook his head.

'It takes him that way sometimes. He's been playing with that there ball of his again. Oh, miss, what an unhappy man he is! He goes on like that day and night. You go now, miss. I'll manage by myself. It'll pass all right. He'll come to himself, but he mustn't be disturbed. And it would be better for you too not to be here then.'

Tanyusha went out, scarcely able to stand on her trembling legs. What had just happened was so very strange, so horrible. A trick of the imagination? Or had he jolted the table? How pale he had been! And his eyes – how insane! It was the most dreadful thing that she had ever seen in her life.

The frosty air of the streets restored her strength. Avoiding the Bronnaya, she hurried on in the direction of the Conservatoire. Had she met any of her acquaintances on the way, she would not have recognized them.

– XLII –

THE VISIT

They came to Stolnikov at daybreak and roused Grigory by thumping at the door:

'Who are you, citizen?'

Although he knew quite well what they had come for, Grigory answered sullenly:

'And you yourselves? What d'you want?'

There were four of them with rifles, and a fifth – the man who was questioning – wearing a leather jacket and an ostentatious red bow. He waved a nagan[1] before Grigory's nose:

'That's what we are. Where's that officer, Stolnikov, as lives here?'

'What d'you want him for? He's sleeping. What's the good of disturbing him?'

'And what are you – his batman, eh?'

'That's right.'

'Then we'll take you too. In case you don't know it, there aren't no batmen no more. Come on, right about turn!'

And they all trooped into Stolnikov's room.

Grigory's face clouded over, though he had been through too much in his life to be in the least alarmed.

The Trunk, who was lying under a blanket, turned his head towards the men as they entered. He had been wakened by their knocking and had understood. He looked at them in silence, frowning, and his eyes were hard and mocking.

'You the officer, Stolnikov? Well, then, get up; and don't you mind us, there aren't no women about.'

'Better first ask if he can get up,' said Grigory, speaking with surly distinctness. 'You don't know yourselves where you go. You don't tell me you're supposed to go about bothering disabled men?'

The man in the black leather jacket answered sharply:

'Don't you talk too much, comrade batman. We'll take you too, and that without orders to, either. Lift up your master. We've got a warrant with us. Hand over your papers, citizen, and no nonsense about it.'

'Give him the papers, Grigory,' Stolnikov said quietly.

'You disabled?' asked the man in black.

Stolnikov did not reply, but looked mockingly into his eyes.

'When I ask you something, you've got to answer! It's no use your lounging in bed, neither. We've got instructions to fetch you. They'll make out what's the matter with you there. It's not our business.'

The soldiers were looking on with curiosity. Both the face and the voice of the officer lying there were unusual. And they saw that their commander was ill at ease, in spite of his efforts to maintain his attitude.

'He's got no arms or legs,' Grigory said to him in an undertone as he handed over the papers. 'You can't do nothing to him.'

---

[1] A revolver of Russian make.

'Not my business!' barked the platoon commander. 'I've got my orders to fetch him, so no arguing about it. He can walk, can't he?'

'But I've already told you he's got no arms or legs.'

'I don't care if he's got no head! My order's clear, so there's nothing to go on talking about. You'd better look sharp, or you may be taken too.'

'They can't take me; I'm looking after him.'

'Nurse, eh? Call yourself a soldier!'

'Didn't ask you to tell me what I am.'

'Don't you be cheeky, comrade, or we'll find a way of dealing with you all right. Well, now, up with your master.'

His eyes flashing, Stolnikov cried:

'Have you fought at the front, you swine! Or do you only fight against officers?'

The man in black flared up:

'Take him, you boys, just as he is! No need to look at him.'

Not one of the men moved.

Then the man in black went up to Stolnikov's bed, his nagan in his hand, and shouted: 'Get up!'

He met a mocking look. Stolnikov did not stir.

In a frenzy the man in black seized the blanket by the edge and pulled it away. Through the opening of the nightshirt could be seen the glassy shoulder scar; the other sleeve was tucked behind the back and the whole bottom of the shirt behind the hips. Without a quiver of the muscles of his face the Trunk riveted his eyes on the man in black.

'What are you doing, brothers?' cried Grigory. 'How can you!'

One of the men brought the butt-end of his rifle down with a thud.

'Eh, leave him alone,' he grumbled. 'Let him stay where he is. He's not in danger.'

Another backed him up:

'What's the good of him? Can't you see he's an absolute cripple?'

Grigory went up to the bed, shouldered away the man in black and covered up the officer with the blanket. The Trunk lay with his eyes closed, his left cheek twitching and his teeth clenched.

Not knowing what to do next, the man in black turned to Grigory:

'Well now, you put your things together, comrade, and get ready. Hurry up, there, get a move on. What's that typewriter you've got? Take it, boys; they are required for the office. We'll draw up an official report and go. You, citizen, have got to stay at home under arrest till an inquiry is made. It's not my doing. I've got my orders. You hurry up, batman. They'll teach you to hide away officers!'

'I'm not going,' said Grigory firmly. 'Drag me along by force, if you haven't got no conscience.'

The man in black raised his nagan and pointed it at Grigory:

'Ever seen this? Another word!'

But his hand was jerked aside by another. Going red to the roots of his hair, one of the young soldiers growled out:

'Leave him alone! Don't pester, I tell you. Take the typewriter if it's wanted, but leave him here. We haven't got to the right place. One's been hacked about in the war, and the other's looking after him. We aren't monsters. Let's get along.'

The man in black lost all his aggressiveness and put back the revolver:

'Not your business, comrades. I'm the only one that's responsible here and you've just got to carry out orders.'

'All right, but don't you order about too much, neither. Take the typewriter, I tell you, that's quite enough.'

Another took his part:

'That's right; this is a special case, comrade. There's things one's got to understand.'

Completely pacified by now, the man in black thrust his revolver into the holster and turned to the door:

'One of you take the typewriter.'

'All right.'

The four turned their heads towards Stolnikov, looking to one side; then one after another, raising their hands in a salute, they rapped out the military 'Fare you well!'

The young soldier lingered behind, went up to the typewriter and went red again:

'Devil take it! What's the good of it? It may as well stay here.'

And to Grigory:

'Don't you worry, comrade. We're human, too.'

Then to the Trunk, facing him squarely:

'Fare you well, your honour!'

And he stumped out noisily.

– XLIII –

THE CONCERT

Dunyasha was wearing felt boots, and a warm shawl over her blouse; Tanyusha her old overshoes and a grey fur cap. Moscow was in the grip of the last frosts. If only they could hold out till spring – it would be easier then.

On the doors of the Sovdep were posted up numerous notices that had been tapped out on damaged Remingtons. There were no ribbons, and carbon paper was used.

The seals were huge and the signatures reddish, with the mixture of inks. The Commandant received twice daily. Commandant? What sort of functions could his be? The signature 'Kolchagin' had been scrawled very large, and the flourish executed by a pen that was rusty.

'Whom d'you want to see?'

They were admitted, but were obliged to wait. Fortunately Kolchagin came out himself, saw them and said:

'Just a moment, if you please.'

And very sternly he shouted at somebody else:

'It's no good coming back here, citizen. Once a thing's said, there's no going back on it.'

Even Dunyasha was overawed. Tanyusha looked at him with interest: here was a man who had lived in their kitchen, and that very same man was now at the head of affairs. Upon him depended the fate of Edward Lvovitch, and, doubtless, that of many others as well.

In his own private 'office' Andrey Kolchagin was a very different person. He shook hands with embarrassment, and was obviously nervous:

'Please excuse me for keeping you waiting. It's me you've got something to ask about? Well, to think we should meet here, Tatyana Mihailovna! But, of course, times have changed. We're bringing about a new order, you see. Sit down, won't you, and have some tea? Dunya, you sit down too. I haven't seen you for ages. I'll just go and order some tea.'

'Oh no, please don't; we have come on business and there are other people waiting.'

'That doesn't matter; they can go on waiting. They've mostly come about nothing, though of course one's got to settle their business.'

Dunyasha's brother did not know what attitude to assume; he was fidgety, yet very anxious not to lose his air of importance. Tanyusha was wondering what to call him, for she had been in the habit of calling him Andrey. Dunyasha came to her aid:

'Andryusha, it's about the piano that's been taken away from Edward Lvovitch, Miss Tanyusha's teacher.'

Tanyusha explained. But although he had signed the order himself, he could not think to whom they were referring.

'Can't it be returned to him? He's a composer and a master at the Conservatoire. He can't get on without a piano. What's he to do?'

Then Andrey remembered:

'The chap with a squint that used to play at your house all the time?'

'Yes, yes; that's the one.'

'And who was it took it away?'

He made inquiries, and found out that the piano had been taken for a workmen's club. However, it had not been yet sent on, nor had the club been opened. So he called someone over the telephone, mainly to show them how businesslike he was, and after bawling into the mouthpiece and scowling, left the room:

'I'm going to find out about it and give the order at once.'

He was obviously glad of the opportunity of doing something quickly, in an authoritative way. He disappeared, did what was to be done, and after a quarter of an hour returned:

'It can be restored to him. Of course it's quite a different matter with a musician. It was taken away from him by error.'

To make things doubly sure, Dunyasha alluded to past favours:

'You do your best for Tatyana Mihailovna, Andryusha. She sent you your shirts to the front, she did.'

'Of course I will. What d'you think! I'll drive to the depot with you myself. It's a special case – an error. Can't see to everything. Times have changed, of course, but we've got nothing against the population: we know how to distinguish between them. Don't you worry, Tatyana Mihailovna. If there's any misunderstanding at home, if they come to your house, or want to requisition things, don't you worry about it, just you come straight to me.'

He went out again, wrote something down on a slip of paper and set his seal to it. It was the order.

'Now, if you please, we'll drive to the depot. I'll come along myself to make sure.'

They went out. A car was waiting for them at the gates – a noisy, rusty affair that had lost all its paint. Kolchagin spoke to the chauffeur sharply, with a stern air of importance:

'To the depot, comrade, where the things were stored the other day.'

At the depot, the warehouse of a large business premises that had been closed down, were quantities of furniture, carpets, pictures with broken frames, writing desks, pianos, mirrors – everything scratched and chipped during the hasty removals. There were two grand pianos, and Tanyusha had no difficulty in recognizing the one she knew so well. But, heavens, what a state it was in! Dusty, grimy, its lid all scratched. She rejoiced over it as if it had been a dear friend.

'This one, Audrey, this one! But how are we going to get it away?'

Kolchagin was determined to be magnanimous and authoritative to the end:

'I'll order it to be fetched.'

'For certain? When?'

'I'll order a van. Don't you worry yourself. If it doesn't come today, it'll come tomorrow. Just leave the address.'

Tanyusha stroked the polished surface of the piano and raised the lid just a little: it wasn't locked. Had it by any chance been damaged on the way? She sat down on a case and ran both hands over the keys. Dear Edward Lvovitch. How glad he would be!

At the sound of the piano a couple of soldiers and a man in civilian clothes peered into the warehouse.

Kolchagin stood looking self-satisfied and important, his holster at his belt:

'Perhaps you'd play something?"

Tanyusha looked round in surprise:

'Here?'

'Why not? We'd like to hear you. Of course we're not much of an audience.'

Tanyusha was overjoyed. Play to them? Why, she was ready to do anything if they would only return the piano. It was cold for the hands... She glanced round and saw that more curious faces had collected at the door of the warehouse. Play to them? Oh, she would play.

Dunyasha found a stool, which she dusted and placed before the piano. Tanyusha breathed on her hands to warm them, smiled happily – how queer to play here! – and began to play the first thing that came into her head.

THE CONCERT

The keys were like little black and white blocks of ice, and the pinpoints of frost pricked her fingers. But the sounds were warm and echoed her joy. She played for her master, and for him alone, for Edward Lvovitch, whom no one found interesting, for the elderly child who had been so hurt. It was the first time that she was able to show her gratitude for the joy of music, for the years of close and severe supervision on her way to success, for everything. She was ready to go on playing as long as ever Dunyasha's brother and those people at the door wanted her to. What did it matter whether it was in a cold warehouse or in a brilliantly lit drawing room, to people who understood or to soldiers? And how strange it was, and how wonderful!

She played with effort, for the keys were slippery with rime. And she felt her toes turn to ice in the old overshoes on the pedals. But she went on playing all the same.

When she came to an end she did not know whether or not to play something else. Her fingers were icy and no breathing upon them would restore any warmth. She turned round with a guilty smile and saw them all looking at her in silence – looking at her with funny, kindly, wondering eyes. There was already a crowd at the doors; those in front had come forward. And they were silent – waiting. It seemed she had to go on playing to them... Her chilblains brought tears to her eyes... Well, if she must –

Kolchagin's voice broke in:

'Thank you very much, Comrade Tatyana Mihailovna! Of course, this isn't the right place.'

'Thank you ever so much,' joined in some of the others. 'Now that's real music.'

Dunyasha came to her aid:

'Your hands are just about frozen. My, isn't it freezing in here! My feet are numb with cold even with felt boots on.'

A man in a leather jacket came up to her:

'You really must come and play at our club, comrade. Will you? We are opening a club and there will be a piano. You really must come. We'll do all we can to thank you, you may be sure – rations and so on, everything that's usually done.'

'Yes, yes, I'll play,' Tanyusha replied, in bewilderment. 'As often as you like. Anything to have the piano returned.'

At that, Kolchagin affirmed authoritatively once more:

'As I've said, either today or tomorrow – depends on the van. The order's ready. Once I've said I'll do it, and there's no need to worry about it any more.'

They left the warehouse. all three of them together. At the gates, everybody said goodbye to Tanyusha and thanked her again for playing.

'How nice they all are,' she thought. 'I believe I played badly. But how nice they were! They listened wonderfully well. And altogether how nice everything is. If only they return it, if only they return it!'

The Commandant's car rattled rapidly along over the snow and drove up to the little house in Sivtzev Vrazhek. Tanyusha and Dunyasha got out.

'Well then, you just see to it, Andryusha.'

'It'll be returned, once I've said so'; and then in military fashion to Tanyusha: 'Fare you well, Tatyana Mihailovna! If anything happens, you just come straight to me.'

With an air of importance, Andrey raised his hand in a friendly salute to the dvornik who had come out:

'Comrade Nicolai!'

And to the chauffeur:

'Back to the Sovdep.'

The dvornik followed the car with his eyes, shook his head and muttered under his breath:

'That's the new leaders! Dunka's brother, a deserter. Ho!'

– XLIV –

THE FIRST KISS

'Nobody been, Dunyasha?'

'A comrade, who asked to see you.'

'What comrade?'

'A soldier – quite oldish. He asked me to say – 'Grigory of Bronnaya Street.' He asked you to call in.'

Tanyusha had not been to see Stolnikov for a very long time. She would have gone to see him, but she felt that her visits not only gave him no pleasure, but actually upset him somehow. And she had not forgotten – and he, too, would remember, of course – the scene with the little bronze sphere. Poor man, it must be painful for him to see her – a healthy girl with whom he once used to dance. After that strange scene she had been to see him several times, though never alone, usually taking with her Vassya Boltanovsky, who had an amazing faculty for remaining natural and friendly, and even gay. It was easier with him.

This time Tanyusha went alone. Could anything have happened to him that Grigory had come to ask for her?

It appeared, however, that it was Stolnikov himself who had sent Grigory to ask her to come.

Although he seemed a little embarrassed, he was quite simple and natural with her this time.

'I have been missing you so much that I made up my mind to disturb you. I'm always alone.'

'Why, of course, Alexander Ignatievitch! I should have come myself, only I wasn't quite sure that you wanted to see – '

Stolnikov's eyes were laughing:

'It's always nice to see you, Tanyusha, only I don't always feel up to receiving visitors. But today I'm all right, I can breathe freely.'

All the same, she did not know what to talk about.

'Shall I bring you some books? I looked out some in a hurry and brought them along with me, only I don't know if they are the kind you like.'

He thanked her and said:

'You needn't set out to entertain me, Tanyusha. I just wanted to look at you. You are growing up to be such a beautiful, sweet person. Only of course, times are so hard just now.'

She told him about her various household cares, how Edward Lvovitch's piano had been requisitioned, how the poor man had nearly gone off his head, and how she had been to the Sovdep with Dunyasha, whose brother was Commandant there. She tried not to lose the thread of her story, aware all the time of Stolnikov's eyes – so simple and gentle today – immovably fixed on her face. And she was actually carried away by her tale.

From time to time Grigory would look in, and his eyes, too, rested on her in a kindly way. He had long ago come to approve of her: did she not come to see the cripple and make things easier for him? A real lady, and a nice one.

During a pause, Stolnikov said:

'I wrote you a long letter, Tanyusha. I didn't send it, because it's not worthwhile now. I mostly talked about myself in that letter. I've got to tell somebody, and whom can I tell? It would have been simpler for you, and you would have understood me better.'

Tanyusha was silent.

'In that letter I tried to set down what I feel. The world is quite a special sort of place for me now, not what it is for other people. It's as if I didn't belong to it somehow. Sometimes I feel dreadfully bitter, and at other times resigned. It would be quite impossible to go on living otherwise – quite impossible. So I wrote to you. About myself – out of weakness, of course – and you, too. As though blessing you on your way through life. You don't mind, do you, Tanyusha?'

'Why, no, of course not.'

'Well, then, only don't let it embarrass you, I'll tell you... I love you very much. In a nice way, you know. Why, even an insect – I mean – how shall I put it? – even such a – well, not quite a human being like me longs to have something to feel in his heart and caress. And I have your name to caress, Tanyusha. You must forgive me. I thought of it as a way of keeping a hold on life.'

Both were silent. Then he went on:

'Well, there's old memories. I don't shun memories. One can sometimes go on living on fragments of the past...'

What an unusual Stolnikov today! And how can he speak so simply? How very strange!

'Well, to go on. You know, Tanyusha – what a sweet name you have – you know, it's possible that the world of humans, with all its happenings and all its personal joys and sorrows, is overestimated, and that it all leads to very little in reality. Well, take sleep, for instance. Sleep is happiness and given to all alike. Or the blissful moment of perfect freedom – death.'

'Don't, Alexander Ignatievitch.'

'Oh, I'm not being melancholy, Tanyusha. That's by way of being philosophical. Don't think I want to weep over my fate – wretched as it is. I'm thinking of something quite different just now. Only it's not easy to put into words.'

He searched for the right words; then, after some little time, suddenly turned his big eyes on Tanyusha and, with boyish confusion, said in a tone he forced to be light:

'Well... and I made up my mind to ask you to help me – unpleasant help – in my thinking, or, rather, to help me in my life – in so far as I do live, of course. Will you?'

THE FIRST KISS

'Tell me. I would do anything, only I don't know– '

'Tanyusha, it's this... On the whole, it's not so very complicated, only a trifle odd. It's this. You will be going home in a moment; it's quite time too. Only, before you go, you will kiss me.

And, trembling all over, he added:

'There's your sacrifice. For all mine, for all I've been through...'

Tanyusha's heart froze. An intolerable dread, worse than on that occasion with the little bronze sphere, overcame her. But it lasted only a moment. The Trunk was sitting with eyes closed, his head thrown back.

She rose, went up to him and, with horror and infinite pity mingled, put her arm around his head, stooped and approached her lips to his. He opened his eyes – enormous eyes at such close quarters. Then, trembling in her agitation, she put her cold lips to his hot, dry ones and kissed him, while he held his breath.

Not by the slightest movement did he respond; he remained sunk in a torpor, his face otherworldly.

Tanyusha took a step back, then went to the door. So faint that it was scarcely audible, she murmured:

'Goodbye.'

He neither stirred, nor opened his eyes, nor replied. Tanyusha went out.

It was Tanyusha's first kiss. Her first kiss had been given to a man who could not be called a man, nor even a human being.

– XLV –

'IRA'

Grigory had left the house early that morning, to stand in a queue for groats. The Trunk was sitting at the table in his bath-chair. In the middle of the table, as usual, lay the little bronze sphere. From the open window came the rattling of wheels and the shrill voice of a woman:

'I've been standing ever since before daylight, and then, just as I went up, they closed. All sold out, they said; no more till tomorrow.'

Another voice answered:

'My goodness, whatever is happening!' Stolnikov's room was on the second floor. When Grigory took him for walks, he would first take down the bath-chair, then carry the Trunk downstairs in his arms, like a baby.

It was spring. But the only carefree creatures – and even they in appearance only – were the swallows and sparrows.

The little bronze sphere lay motionless. And, fixed on it, motionless too, were the Trunk's steel-grey eyes.

The little bronze sphere was a small, insignificant object. But around it had grown circles, and the first circle had caught in the Trunk's existence – his joyless, scarce human existence. And beyond it there were other circles, even larger and larger, with Moscow in the first of them, Russia in the second, in the third the Earth, and beyond that illimitable space. The Trunk's existence, in Eternity, was utterly insignificant, as indiscernible and non-existent as a point in mathematics; and yet it was the centre – brilliant, blinding. From it emanated rays that illumined the whole world with the light of terrible thought and significance.

The Trunk snapped the threads of vision and threw back his head. Instead of the sky he beheld a dirty ceiling, with a yellow streak above the window. There was a starless void in his soul: impossible to feed the soul with lies. And he had no hands with which to dash away the moisture that was dimming his eyes. Why, in the name of heaven, should he have to endure it? On what thoughts can the remains of a man go on living? What could give him the strength to go on? And what was the object?

Clenching his teeth, he bellowed:

'Kill me, Grigory! Slave, kill your master!'

Grigory was standing in a queue for groats and six lumps of sugar.

The Trunk leaned the stump of one of his legs against the lever he had himself devised and the chair rolled back a few inches. That was all that was in his power to do. The little bronze sphere receded into the distance and grew dim. The circle closed in to the limits of the Trunk's own useless life. In the streets a woman was exclaiming:

'Look at what they've done! How are we to go on living without bread?'

A coarse voice answered:

'All right, you won't peg out, and if you do the loss won't be great.'

The Trunk leaned against the lever again and rolled the chair to the window. His chest was on a level with the window-sill. The windows of the houses opposite were open; on one of the window-sills stained pillows and blankets, that had evidently not been washed for

'IRA'

some considerable time, were heaped up. The many-storeyed houses hid from him all but a tiny strip of the sky. A little cloud was floating over it, and the heights were blue and wondrous. It was spring – useful to someone, kind to someone. Like a sharp blade, a swallow cut across the sky and disappeared into its nest.

Then, resting the stump of his arm on the window-sill, he strained all his muscles and lifted himself out of the seat. He was like a little child trying to scramble up on to a chair. There was more room beyond the window. Resting his chin on the cold ledge, he raised his inert body by the powerful muscles of his neck, and remained thus, motionless. If the chair were to roll away he would fall on the floor. But the chair was standing firmly by.

Then, aided by the movement of his jaw, he managed to reach the framework of the windowpane and dig his teeth into it. Get his chest on to the window-sill – that was all he wanted. Its edge was cutting into his chest and hurting him, but he bore the pain; and, with a final effort, he got the whole of his body on to the ledge. The chair rolled away, impelled by his movements, and the plaid with which Grigory was in the habit of wrapping round the stumps of his legs fell on to the floor.

He was now lying on the window-sill, lightly clad in a long shirt – harassed and spent by extreme effort. He lay on his face, his head turned to the street. Now he could see more of the sky. What was that, on the ground?

Resting his weight on his chin, he worked his way to the edge of the window and hung his head down. Below was an unswept stone pavement, and there, just under the window, lay an empty packet of 'Ira' cigarettes. He smoked those cigarettes himself; that packet might quite well be one of his own.

The window-sill was cold to the touch. A passer-by came down the street, glanced up, saw the head looking down and passed on. The street was now empty.

The Trunk crept still nearer the edge, and again stared down at the 'Ira' packet. Then, raising his head, he saw the cloud disappearing behind one of the roofs. The sky was now cloudless. Somewhere, in meadow or village, it must be good to be alive. But only for those who have something to live for, and something by which to live; for those for whom it is worthwhile to cling on to life and go on struggling for the future. There was no bitterness or anger in his heart towards them or anyone. Nor was there any love. There was just nothing at all.

Above him the fathomless sky; below, on the dirty stones of the pavement, an empty packet.

At the window opposite, where the pillows lay heaped up, appeared the figure of a woman. Seeing the Trunk, she gave a cry and called to the back of the room:

'Nastasia, Nastasia!'

The Trunk made a sharp movement, freed his chest, arched up his neck and threw down his head. His body tilted, remained motionless and slowly sank back on the window-sill. Then, with a childish moan, he again repeated the movement, with all his might. The monstrous clod that was his body swayed, remained suspended again – no longer this time than the space of a second – and began to overbalance. Then the packet marked 'Ira' drew suddenly nearer, leapt up, and grew bigger and bigger – huge...

– XLVI –

WITH CARE

Staid and grave, in his patched uniform and grey puttees, Grigory slowly went down Great Nikitinskaya Street, looking in through the dirty panes of the empty, boarded-up shops. He remembered having somewhere seen what he wanted when he had passed that way before – somewhere, it seemed to him, to one side of the church.

He was not mistaken. There in the window, resting on legs, stood a massive coffin, ornate and expensive-looking, but covered with dust. He might, perhaps, be able to find something simpler.

A lock hung on the door, and across the door was a board with seals. Grigory went into the yard to make inquiries.

The woman he stopped at the gate to ask could not at first make out what it was he wanted; finally, however, she answered in a frightened voice:

'I don't know, comrade. I don't know nothing. The undertaker's has been shut and boarded up. He didn't use to live here. You'd better ask at the House Committee if you need one.'

At the House Committee he was informed that the shop had been requisitioned, and that the former proprietor had gone without leaving any address – had quite likely run away.

Grigory frowned.

'What's one got to do nowadays when one's got to bury someone?'

'You have to go to the Sovdep, or to one of their police stations. Nowadays they give out coffins. There's so many dying that there's not enough to go round. You'll have to stand in a queue. Or else, if you happen to know a carpenter, you can go to him. Only it's impossible to get the right sort of boards now. It's no better for the dead than for the living, these days. Is it your wife that's gone and died?'

Grigory went out without replying.

He did not go to the Sovdep, however, for a neighbour had told him that the coffins were only given out just to take the dead to the cemetery. There they had to be emptied and afterwards returned. And not everybody managed to get one, either: you had to wait. So it was better to knock one together yourself, as best you could. They were burying so many people without coffins at all.

Grigory made a detour to go to the Arbatskaya, where it was rumoured that there were tapers to be had in a little ecclesiastical shop. He was served with apprehension. When it came to paying he turned away to take the money out of his big leather purse, for under the valueless money of the present day lay a gold ten-rouble piece, sewn up in a little piece of stuff, and with it five silver roubles.

When he came home he placed the tapers by the dead man, crossed himself and went out again on business. He had noticed a little shop in the neighbourhood where there was a light to be seen in the evenings. He called in there to inquire if they hadn't by any chance an empty case he could have. At first he was told that every bit of wood had been burned, but afterwards he succeeded in negotiating an exchange. For five pounds of flour he got a case which had held crockery – quite a good solid case with iron clamps – on which, printed in large letters, were the words: 'THIS SIDE UP. WITH CARE.'

The rest of the day Grigory spent in the shed near the house, sawing, planing and fixing on legs to the case, which grew shallower, but remained square, as before. The words 'THIS SIDE UP' disappeared, and only 'WITH CARE' was left.

Heavy-hearted, and grieving that there should be no coffin as became a Christian, Grigory carried the case into the room, set it down on the table and lined it with a blanket and a snowy sheet, placing in it a pillow for the poor broken head.

He saw to everything himself. The blind man, Kashtanov, who was sitting on a chair in a corner, listening and straining to follow Grigory's movements, could do nothing to help him. Not one of the neighbours looked in. They had heard of the tragedy, but had all of them troubles enough of their own.

A policeman came, took down particulars, and said: 'A doctor will be sent to certify death.' But no doctor was sent that day.

Grigory was just as unsuccessful with the priest. The old priest of St. John Bogoslov's refused to hold the burial service for a man who had committed suicide. Grigory was advised to have a service held in the cemetery itself. The following morning he went to the Dorogomilov cemetery, where he was obliged to spend a long time bargaining. Nothing was charged for the burial ground, but he was asked an unheard-of sum for the actual digging of the grave. And as his last flour had gone on the coffin, there was nothing for it but to promise some silver in addition to the requisite paper money.

A hearse was out of the question; even a simple cart was not to be thought of. In those days the poor were taken to be buried in quite unpretentious ways – on little sledges in winter and handbarrows in summer. The body was carried if there were enough people.

The Trunk had no friends except the blind man. Grigory was his family, his nurse, his only friend. It was for him and him alone to follow the dead man to his last resting-place.

A barrow was sent him by the dvornik, with injunctions to return it by six o'clock without fail, as it was used for bringing the bread ration that had to be distributed among the inmates of the house.

Kashtanov could not see how Grigory placed the white cross for heroism over the sheet on the officer's breast. But he heard when he began to hammer; and, rising, he crossed himself till the last nail was driven in. Then he went up and felt the case, his cheek twitching, and went stumbling to the door. He could not follow his unhappy friend; nor would tears come to his blind eyes.

At three o'clock, after tying the square case in a spare sheet, Grigory carried it down into the yard without difficulty, placed it on the barrow and set out for the Dorogomilov cemetery. Despite the legs he had fixed on, no one could have recognized a coffin.

The people he passed did not cross themselves. On the grim case lay Grigory's cap; and on one side – standing out black against the white wood of the case – the words: 'WITH CARE.'

– XLVII –

AXIOS

Yet another death to her list of sorrows, a death most merciful and just – a death of release.

Crouching quite small on a corner of the divan, Tanyusha turned her eyes inward and saw, on the shelves of her soul, the little black-bound volumes that were the annals of lives she had known.

Here, in a cold-looking binding, was a slender volume with Ehrberg's name on the back. She knew very little about him, and thought of him seldom. His had been the beginning of an intelligent life, traced out for a long way ahead; a life of both arithmetical and geometrical figures; a prudent life; then suddenly – a mistake in the calculation. He had been the first of Tanyusha's near acquaintances to go – so young, yet ever since his boyhood seeming so grown-up. Such a severe, logical introduction... And yet, the very first chapters were torn.

Then there was the little old dumpy volume, fragrant with lavender, the volume that had so many times been lovingly looked through, and that bore the sacred name of grandmother. The first page had been written in such a familiar, ancient writing. Dear, tired grandmother, who had fallen asleep beloved, after a full, busy life of love and peaceful blessing. The marriage taper, with the moiré ribbon wound about it yellow with age, had burned on till the end.

Books of death. And now here was another death, and a black book no one had read. Who could venture to turn over the pages of torturing thought, of passionate search for self-deception, of stifled outbursts of envy of the living, of morbid conflict between reason and a belief in miracles, and of physical longing to have done with life? A terrible book! A book written by a great martyr, to whose lifeless lips she had in horror and pity given her first kiss.

And as she sat there, crouched in a corner of the divan, she was suddenly swept by the very same feelings, as deep and intense as before. Terrible! How terrible life was!

And how easy spring had been. What sunshine at seventeen, and in what orderly ranks problems had risen and been solved. How mighty knowledge had been, what harmony in music... Where had it all vanished to, what had happened?

Why had it happened that her life was, as it were, preceded by death, the deaths of people she knew? Crosses at the beginning of life's journey and funeral chants before the hymns of gladness... And what lay on ahead?

Ask grandfather? But grandfather was old; what would he answer? It wouldn't be right to worry him with questions like that. Vassya? Vassya was such a dear, thoughtful, faithful friend. He might find something, perhaps... No, but it wouldn't be what she wanted. He would be upset; he would try to amuse her and divert her attention, and that was not at all what she required. He would tell her something funny, or, if he could find nothing to say, would ruffle his hair over his temples and sit in a corner, breaking up matchboxes. No, Vassya couldn't. He didn't know himself. Why hadn't he been all day? It was nice and restful all the same to be with him.

She went through in her mind the names of acquaintances who had remained in close contact with them, and thought of Astafiev. If he were prepared to answer – but how should she ask? Did one ever ask about such things? And what exactly was it she wanted to ask? She had more faith in Astafiev than in the others. He was the most unusual of all the people who came to the house those days and the one they knew least about. It would be nice to see him oftener and get to know what sort of person he really was, and something of his life. She would ask Vassya, who saw him quite frequently.

It was a spring day and twilight had fallen. The window was open. Tanyusha rose to look out into the street. Quiet; scarcely a passer-by. She sat down at the piano and put her fingers to the keys. But, tired of thinking, her fair head sank on to her hands. She remained a long time motionless.

When she rose, the tears in her eyes – chance tears, a young girl's tears that had come she knew not why – had dried. It was because of them, perhaps, that her lassitude had passed. Maybe she had needed them.

She drew herself up to her full height, set straight the scarf she had thrown about her shoulders and was suddenly overtaken by a sensation of lightness quite new to her.

It was cool in the room and night was falling. What could it be? Could everything have been pervaded by death and the loss of people she had known? And, if so, why that sensation of lightness and that desire to do something, to know a lot, meet people, and look for one among them who would know more and answer better than the rest?

She was amazed to find how good it was to be alive, amazed at the ease with which this sensation of living overcame both thought of death and death itself. Go somewhere, do something – at once. See somebody. And just occasionally, if only just occasionally, laugh without thinking of tragic things, without setting black against white and wondering which would triumph. Those little black volumes on the shelf – yes, but the white pages had not been begun. She ought to make haste and begin.

And she said to herself:

'I'm twenty already.'

And then:

'Is there such a thing as complete happiness in the world? Where ought one to look for it, I wonder? And what is happiness, really? Where's the key to it? And where can I find a big wide door in the world which the walls of the old house can never make narrower?'

She put her arms behind her head, braced herself and uttered aloud:

'I want to live! Live!'

She did not see the reflection of the tall figure, straight and youthful, with arms thrown back, in the dark gleaming mirror, nor did she hear the confused rumbling of the piano strings answering her; nor knew that evening stood on guard, listening to the great significance and simplicity of her words, and that in their agitation those silent witnesses of her growth, sedulous keepers of her soul's secrets – the walls of the little house that had known her as a child and heard her first lisping words-were listening, holding their breath.

Then the walls whispered to the strings, and the strings passed it on to the spring air, and the evening sky sent forth its first star as messenger of their verdict:

'*Axios*! She is worthy!'

– XLVIII –

THE PILGRIMAGE

Steadily, with even step, lifting his boots out of the mud, the old soldier, Grigory, was walking to Kiev with a bundle and tin kettle on his back and a single purpose in his mind.

He was going to Kiev because he had no one and nothing left in the world – neither friend, nor son, nor plot of land. Only his enduring faith in a stern God remained – a God who had left Moscow to go to other Russian towns and maybe farther still.

He had been told he would never get there. But those who had nothing to lose or to keep were free to roam the wide world over.

Pilgrims and paupers in search of truth and alms, indigent friars and wandering cripples were all tramping from one end of Russia to the other, and not one of them missed going to Kiev.

Grigory was strong in body and soul, neither blind nor destitute, nor yet bereft of reason; he would get there, the old soldier.

When the mud grew stickier he took off his boots, tied them together by the straps, and threw them over his shoulder; then went on squashing into the mud with his bare feet. He would get there all right; from village to village.

And the villagers quietly waited, knowing what to expect. Perhaps it had not been worthwhile after all to fell so many trees. The newly hewn-down trunks were lying useless, and the wood was rotting. There were jugsful of that useless paper money at home. What could be bought with it? Townsfolk came for grain, dragging with them calico, bright-coloured stuff, some of them silk as well, and blouses trimmed with lace; all sorts of odds and ends, some useful and some quite useless – all in exchange for a handful of grain. But the grain had taken to hiding deeper and farther afield, as though afraid lest the peasant should lose his own share of it, lest all his collection of goods should doom him to hunger. The womenfolk were pleased with their new finery, and had taken to wearing thin stockings with clox and low-necked blouses. But a good farmer should take thought of the future.

Cringing, afraid, summoning to their aid all their cunning, the villages waited. Those townsfolk weren't to be trusted; they didn't deal openly, and they were envious. One could only pray they wouldn't bring along an armed force after them.

Grigory followed the high road, sparing himself as much as he could and choosing the shortest route whenever he knew the country. He neither bartered, nor bought, nor begged. But he was sober-looking, his beard had grown long, and his eyes were honest and stern; so that whenever, crossing himself, he entered a hut the peasants, whether well-off or needy, were always ready to give him a bit of bread and a night's shelter. Nor would they accept any money, observing, in the case of people like Grigory, the old tradition of hospitality. To their questions, Grigory, who was a silent man by nature, would answer briefly but with thought and wisdom.

Going the same way, walking, riding, straggling uncertainly, hobbling and bent, with doubt and fear in their hearts, were many others – emigrants dropping into eternity – fleeing from Moscow to the south, from the new order to the good old times they hoped to find elsewhere. But though they were all going the same way, Grigory walked alone. It was not fear that drove the old soldier on, but his isolation and the austerity of his uncompromising thoughts.

On his strong shoulders Grigory bore his ancient faith and his sense of right and wrong from the land of sin to the saints of Kiev, or maybe farther still, to wherever his steadfast faith and the straight road might lead. He was no refugee, no traitor to his country, no coward, but a man who had shaken off the dust of lies and of dishonesty grown bold.

On the frontiers he would come across fires and wild confusion, and there were frontiers without number: here today, tomorrow a hundred versts away; now behind, now in front; coming and going, and sweeping houses and cattle away like a hurricane. Impossible to make out what was happening. Ragged heroes – White today, Red tomorrow – grave upon grave. What were they fighting each other for? Grigory found it all quite incomprehensible.

With a crackling of machine-guns, the wave of hatred and death, or just mischief and lawlessness, went rolling on. And all in the name of freedom; and all were fighting for freedom, Grigory reflected. And what did that freedom amount to? They were both afraid and spreading fear; they couldn't leave each other alone in their terror. Put them all at one table before one bowl of cabbage soup and they would all be alike, in thought and desire and appearance. Why were some on one side and others on another? How did they themselves distinguish between each other? And did they? The same grass grew on their graves, the same sun shone for them, the same rains drenched them. It was past all understanding... But what Grigory could not understand was sin and riot.

The shaggy eyebrows beetled grizzling over Grigory's eyes. The knapsack on his back was a good strong one. No one interfered with him.

Now and again he would leave the main road and go past ploughland and fields of winter crops. And, as he went, the rye grew tall and ears appeared. Fields stretched away from horizon to horizon, from clear distances to hazy. And all that vast expanse was Russia, baptized in toil and in vain mockery at human effort, caressed by the harrow and trampled by the boot of the soldier sent to fight against his will, sought out and rejected.

When the mud dried, Grigory got a pair of bast shoes in order to spare both feet and boots. The light bast shoes sent the dust flying up around him, and the staff left little short-lived rings in it that vanished at the first breath of wind... That way passed a man, and not a trace of him – any more than of all those who had passed that way before – remained.

Grigory walked from dawn till noon, when he would leave the road to rest. There on the grass, beneath a shady tree, he would listen to the outpourings of the lark, driving into the blue the little nail of its song, while his ear caught the rustling of the young cool grass, muttering to the ants and tickling his hand.

Thus, stubbornly, leisurely, step by step, Grigory bore away with him the Russia of the past to the places of sacred rest; not with war cries and curses, not in loads or trucks, not guarded by bayonets, like others to whom fate held out no hope of return, but along the ancient road of pilgrims and wanderers – those bearers of a simple human truth and seekers after the eternal.

Whether the old soldier ever reached Kiev, whether he found there what he sought, or turned up north to the hermitages of Perm or crossed the seas to Bari or Jerusalem, whether he carried on his truth or cast it from him on the way, together with fasting and his worn-out knapsack – that no one knows.

PART II

– XLIX –

SPRING

Slowly, lingeringly, came the long-awaited spring, flowing in dirty streams along the Moscow streets, spreading contagious diseases and the stench of unswept yards. Not even the professor's little house, from whose roof the snow had not been cleared away in time, had remained entirely intact.

In other houses, water and filth from pipes that had burst in the winter came dripping through the ceilings and oozing through the walls, whilst in the flooded basements the last yellow blocks of ice were melting.

However, now one could remove those little stoves, take off those soaking felt boots, and even open the front doors, which had been nailed up that winter in fear and to keep out the cold.

It was Nature herself who saw to the spring-cleaning of the city. But human beings helped too, when it was obvious to them that life, however hungry and absurd, must still go on.

In the yard of the big house in the Dolgorukovskaya, where nearly all the flats were tenanted by workmen's families, the clearing and cleaning was carried on under the orders of the House Committee. There were plenty of spades, very few wheelbarrows and only one cart – without a horse. The snow and refuse was taken out into the street and got rid of at the first opportunity by emptying it into the running water of the gutter. It was Denissov, the chairman of the House Committee and former assistant in the now boarded-up grocer's shop in the same building, who conducted the proceedings himself.

The inmates of the house worked listlessly, under the threat of a search, if not of an arrest. It was the women who worked hardest. Among the men, the strongest and ablest was the tenant Astafiev, the last member of the intelligentsia and bourgeoisie to stay on in the house. Denissov went up to him:

'Getting used to it, Comrade Astafiev? It's heavy, unpleasant work, isn't it?'

'I have no intention of getting used to it, but if it's got to be done, well, I do it. It would have been better to have carted it all away with the snow during the winter.'

'Couldn't manage it in the winter. Of course, the work isn't to your liking, you being an educated man. All the same it's got to be done, Comrade Astafiev. It was us that sweated for you before. Now it's your turn too. Times have changed.'

A smile curled Astafiev's lips:

'My work is no worse than anyone else's. There's nothing so dreadful about it. Only I don't seem to recollect your ever having worked for me. I thought you spent most of your time behind the counter.'

'It's not a matter of former occupation, but of who's accepted, the revolution.'

Astafiev lifted a big spade, emptied it into the wheelbarrow, and brought it down upon the contents with a vigorous clap:

'Everyone has accepted it in the way that suits him best,' he replied. 'You in your way, I in mine. We're quits there.'

Denissov walked away and Astafiev said to himself;

'He'll probably try to turn me out all the same. And he will, of course, in the end. Well, I'll find somewhere or other to go to. Not such a misfortune as all that.'

He wheeled out a barrowful into the streets and dumped it on to the kerb, for the gutter was so full, without that extra load of his, that the water would no longer sweep anything along. It wouldn't? Well, then, it needn't. And he returned with his empty wheelbarrow, his boots squelching in the dirty liquid.

On the way back he met one of the women, obviously weak and delicate, pushing a wheelbarrow. He had an impulse to go and help her, but changed his mind.

'What does it matter! Let her go on pushing it.'

He took out his pipe. He smoked shag, there being no other tobacco. He maintained that it was a pure tobacco, and pleasant to the palate when once one was used to it. And he had got used to it, with the same case he had got used to Havana cigars abroad.

Astafiev had been given a very considerable part of the yard to clean. But he got through his work quickly: there was no point in quarrelling with the chairman of the House Committee. When he had finished he put away the wheelbarrow and spade in the shed and went home, wiping his feet on a newspaper that was lying about on the stairs.

Astafiev had had a flat there once. Now two rooms of it were left, the third being occupied by a timid, cowed workman who lived by himself. The workman would return home in the evenings and go straight to bed, so that Astafiev saw very little of him.

The second room, his library, had been coveted also; but for the time being he was able to keep it. Because he belonged to the teaching profession 'he had been given an official document certifying his right to it. The room was cold and uninhabitable in winter, but in summer he meant to receive visitors and work in it, if there was anyone to receive and anything to work at.

When he came in he changed his clothes, filled a new pipe and settled down to read.

A whiff of spring air entered the room, together with a smell of dung and dirt. And he discovered that he was not in the mood to read. Wouldn't it be better to do something? Plenty of things that needed doing: there were those frayed trousers to mend, the handkerchiefs to wash with clay soap, and the lamp to see to – that lamp of his made out of a little bottle, in case the electricity was cut off again. It was Saturday today. Tomorrow he was going to see the ornithologist in Sivtsev Vrazhek. What sort of a girl was that granddaughter of his? Not like the rest, not easy to fathom. But she seemed rather charming.

There came a knock at the door. Astafiev wondered vaguely who it could be. A humble, yet strong-looking, muscular man entered the room, wearing a threadbare jacket and a pair of brown boots, very down at the heels. There was no sign of a shirt under the waistcoat.

'Excuse my troubling you, Alexey Dmitritch. I don't exactly know how to ask you – '

'Ask straight out.'

'Yes, of course, straight out. Only these days one needs everything oneself. But I thought there might be some old book I could read, not too difficult.'

'I have a great number of books. Help yourself. Only I don't know which you would care for. What is it you want to read about?'

'I don't know how to explain. Something about how to order one's life. I feel a bit in the dark about it.'

'But don't you have to be at work today, Zavalishin?'

'We're having the day off. There's no raw material at the works, so we've come to a stop. We're being paid, so I don't mind.'

'You can have a book, only what has any book to give you? Do you imagine it will teach you to live? Or explain how? Just sit down, Zavalishin. We'll have a talk. Books won't help you in the slightest. But are you really in such a bad way?'

'It's not that so much as that I'd like to understand.'

'What is it you do not understand?'

Zavalishin grew confused, fidgeted and hunted for words:

'Well, when I look around, I don't know, but nothing seems real somehow.'

He managed, however, to explain, if somewhat lamely. Before it had been all the same to him; live and wait; everything would work out of itself. But today everybody was saying one had got to set about living in a new way. And the new ways were no good. A lot of shouting, but no sense in it that he could see. Yet, all the same, there must be something in it.

'You're in too great a hurry, Zavalishin. You must wait.'

'I can wait all right; we used to wait before, too. But I'd like to know what I'm waiting for.'

Astafiev thought: 'That's their working man. Scum, of the same stamp as our intelligentsia. That shop assistant, Denissov, is infinitely better, even though he is a cad: he's one of the builders anyhow...'

And he said:

'I quite understand your position, Zavalishin. You're up against it because you feel a want of stability about things. Life used to be pretty rotten before, but it was stable anyhow. Today everything's gone to the dogs and the new order hasn't yet materialized, and it's sickening going on in the old 'hope deferred' way. But you've got no real strength, Zavalishin.'

'I haven't got much strength, of course. And it's true that I've got tired of things. But what I want most of all is to understand.'

'What the devil have you got to worry about? You're on your own, you've got health, and you're being paid – up to the present, at any rate. Don't you care a damn? D'you drink?'

'I can drink all right when there's something to drink. But I don't ever have a real good drink, so's not to be drunk at my work.'

'You must drink more, Zavalishin. Perhaps I may be able to get hold of something this evening. If so, we'll drink together. It's impossible to think things out when one's sober.'

'You're laughing at me, Alexey Dmitritch!'

'Not in the least. I'll tell you straight out – you're not fitted for life.

What sort of a builder of life d'you call yourself? You have no real faith, no audacity, no nerve, you can't steal; well, they'll just pick your bones clean and chuck you out. And you've got all sorts of notions in your head into the bargain. It's far better to get drunk. When a man is drunk he is wise as well.'

'But drinking is the last resort! What sort of help is that, Alexey Dmitritch? ...I came to you for help, you being an educated man.'

'You ought to go back to the village. Haven't you got one?'

'No, I'm town-bred. Where should I go?'

'That's unfortunate. Well, listen, Zavalishin. I don't know what sort of a man you are, whether you take offence easily or not – though that's your business, I don't care. Do you want me to tell you what I really think? Well, here am I, an educated man, who has read so many books... Well, you wouldn't even be able to read, much less understand, the titles of them. Only the trouble is they don't give you anything – for the understanding of life, I mean. It would make no difference if they hadn't been written. I'm as tired of things as you are sometimes. I'm not a builder either: I'm no good, even though I do happen to be stronger than you. It's all quite simple'. Do you want to get on? If you do, you must be a scoundrel and leave off whining. The times are evil, and you won't gain anything by being honourable. But if you'd rather not then it's better, I tell you, to soak in spirits and deaden your mind with drink. It works excellently, in making one die off sooner. What sort of a fighter are you? Nobody is afraid of you, which means nobody respects you. You're a timid man, and timid men go under these days. Some Denissov or other – you know that brute and swindler of a chairman – will squash you flat with one nail one of these days, just because you look stronger than he. He'll never go under. But all that's your lookout, of course.'

They were silent. Presently Zavalishin rose.

'Well, thank you most humbly for that advice, too, Alexey Dmitritch. Of course, it isn't interesting for you to talk to a simple man like me.'

'Oh, nonsense, Zavalishin! I'm a simple man myself – simpler maybe than you are. Well, look in this evening. We'll drink together, at any rate.'

And he turned to him with a good-natured smile.

'You mustn't be offended with me, you know. I talk like that because life isn't exactly a bed of roses for me either.'

'I understand, Alexey Dmitritch. I didn't think anything.'

When his lodger had gone out, Astafiev said to himself:

'Maybe I did wrong to speak to him like that. Perhaps I was mistaken in him. He's timid all right, but there's no doubt about his being scum, and that was an evil little spark that flashed in his eye. I have offended him. Well, it's a good thing he's capable of getting angry. Something may come of him in that case... Interesting!'

A smile curled his lips.

'Came for help, for books! So that I and my books would be to blame for all his woes, so that he might have someone to hate and a reason for hating.'

That evening Astafiev strode briskly home to the Dolgorukovskaya, carrying under his coat a bottle of spirits and some odds and ends of food of very poor quality to eat with it. Would he come, he wondered?

Zavalishin did come, knocking this time less uncertainly.

'Are you busy, Alexey Dmitritch?'

'We'll get busy together in a moment.'

Before night, Zavalishin was drunk and Astafiev worked up and brimful of curiosity. He was examining his client as though through a microscope, thinking with astonishment: 'Oho, he's not so simple as I thought! Something may come of him after all. A great scoundrel, perhaps. His fists are fine ones, and that's the main thing.'

The workman's bleary little eyes roved over the empty plates.

'We'll say I'm boozed,' he spluttered. 'All the same, I can understand what's what all right. Thank you for the learning, and I don't want to go under, I don't. And maybe I've got my own... which... various plans. Thank you very much for the invitation and for not turning up your nose – an educated man.'

Astafiev frowned:

'All right, enough of that. Get along to bed – you sot!'

Startled, Zavalishin looked askance at him:

'What d'you mean?'

'Go to bed, I tell you! You bore me. If you wake up a scoundrel, so much the better for you. But you'll remain scum whatever happens.'

And, taking him by the collar, he gave him a vigorous push to the door.

– L –

BOOKS

Lingering over the illustrations, the old ornithologist spent a long time looking through one of his books. Before putting it into his portfolio, crammed already full of volumes, he examined the half-binding and stuck down, with moistened finger, an edge of the coloured paper of the cover. The book was a valuable one and in good condition.

Suddenly, however, he remembered that his name was written in it. He drew it out hurriedly and, sitting down at the table, carefully scratched it out with a penknife from the author's inscription:

'To my greatly revered Master... from the Author.'

He put on his hat, which was now very old indeed, and his coat, that hung in the room itself, adjusted his portfolio as comfortably as he could under his arm and went out, locking the door with a little key of American make.

Strangers now lived in the dining room of the little house. Dunyasha had a room upstairs, next to Tanyusha's old room, which Andrey Kolchagin now occupied, but used very little, since most of his nights were spent at the Sovdep, where he had a divan to sleep on in his 'office'.

Occasionally Dunyasha would help Tanya with the housework – just a friendly, helping hand. She was a maid no longer, but a lodger.

The professor was still fairly hale. On his way to Leontievsky Street he did not have to sit down more than three times, and he rested only because the heavy portfolio seemed to pull his arms out of their sockets. During his brief rests on the seats he counted the number of times he had already been to the little bookshop in Leontievsky Street, and calculated how many more times he would be able to go before his store of books came to an end.

One day there happened to be no money left in the house. Bread, nasty ration bread, was given out free, but Dunyasha, who at that time still looked upon herself as a maid, announced that there were neither potatoes, nor groats, nor provisions of any kind left, and that there was nothing whatever for her to cook.

Tanyusha imagined that her grandfather was not without means, and was very embarrassed by the discovery that he had none. She borrowed a small sum from Vassya Boltanovsky.

That evening she spent a long time discussing various household problems with Vassya, and the following morning disappeared. Towards midday she returned, and excitedly, without the least trace of embarrassment, announced that an offer had been made to her to play at concerts given at the workmen's clubs:

'Extremely interesting, grandfather. And I shall be given provisions for playing.'

Poplavsky looked in that day and told them what amazing old books it had been his good fortune to see in the Writers' Bookshop in Leontievsky Street. Books it had been impossible to buy before now suddenly appeared on the market:

'I found a complete first edition of Lavoisier's works. Extremely rare for Moscow. And I saw a curious little book on mathematics, with ecclesiastical print, dated 1682, the first, I should think, ever published in Russia. The title was curious too: *A Convenient Method of Calculation whereby any Man may conveniently discover the Number of Any Kind of Things when Buying or Selling*. There are also logarithmic tables there that go back to the time of Peter the Great.'

'Well, did you buy anything?'

'I? No, professor; quite the contrary. I was selling my own books. They pay well, and one can sell there on commission too.'

Out of sight, on the lowest shelf of the big bookcase, lay a quantity of presentation copies of the professor's scientific works. As he left the house to take his morning stroll he picked out a copy of each.

At the bookshop in Leontievsky Street he was welcomed with respect, for behind the counters were young university readers and demonstrators with whom he was acquainted. They took his books, paid for them, and told him that they were very glad of books like that, since there was a great demand for them for the new universities and the public libraries in the provinces. They asked him, too, if he would bring some more. And no one was at all surprised to see a famous scholar – an old man – bringing his books for sale himself.

More out of curiosity than anything else, the old ornithologist, who was a great book-lover, rummaged among the miscellaneous collection of books in the shops, and was filled with delight by the discovery of a copy of a most rare edition: *The Description of a Hen with the Profile of a Human Being*; with three illustrations. He turned over the pages lovingly, joyfully, and in a way old people have, chuckled and gurgled over the description of the figures: 'The portrayal of the hen in profile is fairly faithful, and represents an old woman just as she really is. The second figure gives the head full face, revealing in it a real satyr. The third represents it yawning, and shows the tongue as well.'

He turned the book over and over in his hands, and finally inquired the price. In those days rare old books had no value: 'We are selling the editions of the time of Peter the Great and Catherine cheaper nowadays than symbolist poetry which has only just been published. And we don't buy them ourselves. That volume got in here by chance with some library we bought. Now what do you say to this: we will let you have that little book if you will promise to bring along your books on commission?'

'Yes, but this is such an exceedingly rare edition, even though it is not so very old.'

'So much the better. It will be in good keeping in your hands, professor.'

The old ornithologist went home in the best of spirits. That evening, Vassya read the book aloud while they were having tea, and the professor rejoiced like a child over every word of it. The following morning he filled his portfolio with 'useless' books and took them to the shop where his acquaintances had been so very kind to him:

'I have a little money, Tanyusha, so there's no need to worry.'

But roubles had long since risen to hundreds, and millions were not far off now. The presentation copies did not last out long. Looking over his shelves, the ornithologist discovered new commercial values in them. There were the duplicates, to begin with; then the popular editions he did not require for his scientific work, though of importance in so far as his collection was concerned; then atlases and tables, which were not absolutely indispensable; and lastly, books he had been, given-books with autographs. The professor's shelves were emptying – but then Tanyusha was so pale and did get so very tired after those concerts of hers at the workmen's clubs. He imagined she knew nothing of his frequent visits to the bookshop, and was glad to think that he, who was an old man and of no use to anyone, was not a burden to his dear grandchild, and was even able to do something to help her. He did not know that Tanyusha's children's books that used to stand in her small bookcase had long since been sold at the very same shop, and not badly either, as the price of children's books was always high.

On the other hand, her grandfather was never once given rissoles of horseflesh for his dinner; and Tanyusha would add real sugar to his glass of tea, quietly dropping into her own cup a little tablet of saccharin.

'Sugar is probably very dear now, isn't it, Tanyusha?'

'I don't know, grandfather; you see it's given to me.'

– LI –

STRANGERS

Tanyusha was not at home. She was playing in the workmen's quarters, in a club called after Lenin.

On the table in her room an old photographic album lay open. In the little window of the album were the portraits of grandfather and grandmother when they were both of them quite young – grandfather in a frock-coat very small at the waist, and grandmother laced tight in a corset, her hands on her crinoline. Grandfather's spectacles shone, so that instead of one of his eyes there was just a white spot. The photograph was very faded indeed.

Further to the right was a photograph of Tanyusha's mother in a fashionable gown of the nineties.

No one was in the room. Over the album, Time bowed his grey head, whispering as he pored over the photograph:

'The same, she was just the same – the eyes, the hair, the mouth, the same grave expression. She, too, wanted to live just like Tanyusha, and she, too, did not know what life would be like.'

Time turned over the pages.

Two students: the elder, with a little beard, in the uniform of a technologist, was Uncle Borya; the other, a handsome university student, with a tiny moustache and a lofty forehead, was Tanyusha's father.

Through the cardboard of the album, from one little window to another, a young girl and a student looked at each other, fell in love and married. And here, too, in the album, was a very small child with a big head, baby eyes, surprised-looking brows and fluffy hair, dressed in a garment that rose inelegantly at the back, as if propping up the nape of the neck. That was the first photograph of Tanyusha herself.

Everyone had a father and mother – older, if not quite old. But Tanyusha had no old parents. At their age in the photograph they might have been her contemporaries and friends. Both had died quite young, before being able to advise her how to live in order to be happy. When she was still a little child their place had been taken by grandfather and grandmother. Her mother had had time to pass on to her no more than her grey eyes and golden hair, and her grave, thoughtful look. The eyes were questioning eyes. But who could reply to them? And what was there to reply?

As for her father, he was a stranger to Tanyusha, yet at the same time very near and dear. She did not remember him at all. He had died young, when she was not two years old. It seemed strange to her that she should be the daughter of a student who had not reached full manhood. That her mother should have been a mere girl was somehow understandable. Of her mother she had the vaguest recollection, as though all she could remember were nothing but what she had been told about her, as though from an obligation of knowing one's own mother: an intuitive feeling rather than an actual remembrance.

Her mother was Tanyusha herself, living in the past. She, too, had been called Tatyana. Whenever Tanyusha looked through the old album she would linger over her father's photograph, to gaze with interest at his face, thinking at times that she too, perhaps, might meet just such a person as her mother had met; there were such preordained encounters, though it was difficult to imagine the man she was destined to meet as different from her father. She was even just the least bit in love with her father in that photograph, and she would look out for him whenever she opened the album.

Time went on turning over the pages, locks of his hair drooping over the album. The little girl, Tanyusha, grew and shot up, and here she was again in a white school pinafore. History whose dates were not yet forgotten had begun from that moment. The fifth form: recent history still. The old album was taking on a fresher appearance, and its record would doubtless have been brought up to date had it not been suddenly cut short. The pages were all full.

On the last page was a quite new photograph of a man, the sort of photograph about which one says: 'That's someone I know. A very nice fellow, I can't remember his name.' For some reason or other it had been put into the last little window, and there it had stayed – the first link with the outer world. If it were to be taken out of its frame (for the album was a family one, after all) the little window would remain unoccupied. So, without justification, the stranger remained in the family.

Time smiled.

'But weren't her grandmother and grandfather complete strangers to each other once, and her father and mother too? And isn't the man whom sooner or later Tanyusha will meet a complete stranger to her also?'

Time sprinkled a little dust over the pages, added a little touch of yellow to the photograph of Tanyusha's mother, gave a little rub to the corners of the leather binding, and left the album lying open at the same page as before.

Tanyusha was not at home. She was playing Bach in one of the clubs on a very poor piano, badly out of tune.

Before her item, Comrade Braudey had spoken from the platform on international relations, and the following item on the programme – humorous sketches and a raree-show – was to be given by the popular club entertainer, Comrade Smehatchev, which was the pseudonym chosen by Alexey Dmitrievitch Astafiev, reader in philosophy at the University of Moscow.

Astafiev was standing in the slips, listening to Tanyusha's playing. He had on a battered top-hat; his cheeks were smeared with flour, his nose just slightly coloured. His mere appearance was calculated to provoke mirth. As a rule he was encored.

Tanyusha had a pseudonym too. She was called by the maiden name of the mother (the sweet young girl in the album) and figured on the club posters as Comrade Tatyana Goryaeva, pianist.

Watching her nimble white fingers, Astafiev said to himself:

'How serious she looks – just as if she were playing at a real concert. And they're just cracking sunflower-seeds! Now, I merely play the fool for those rations they give us and forget my bitterness; but she comes here for the same salted herrings and plays to them with all her soul. So that's what she's like, is it?'

– LII –

TWILIGHT

Vassya ran in to see them that day as usual, but left early, before dark. He was firmly resolved to go to the government of Tula to get food, and was taking great pains over the preparations for his journey, going about collecting such 'goods' as could be bartered.

He had brought with him a very modest but fresh little bunch of wild flowers:

'They are for you, Tanyusha. Guess where I picked them.'

'Have you been out of town?'

'No.'

'Well, I don't know – somewhere in the garden?'

'You'll never guess. Here's a buttercup and here are harebells. And, look, this is an ear of wheat. I picked the whole lot in the streets of Moscow. And the grass I picked under your fence. In some places the whole road is overgrown.'

The ornithologist carefully examined every flower and felt the grass:

'Do you know, Vassya, that bunch is worth pressing. It's a bit of history. You really must keep it. It ought to go in a museum.'

'I'll pick another bunch, professor. One can even make little garlands of them on the outskirts. Some of the roads are entirely covered up. But this I picked in the heart of the city, without going beyond the garden circle. This one is for Tanyusha – from her trusty knight.'

He watched her hands while she was putting the flowers in water, and the professor's eyes lingered with a caressing look on his face. Vassya caught the look:

'Why are you looking at me, professor?'

'Merely looking. Just come here for a moment.'

When Vassya came up to him, the professor, without rising, put his arms about the boy:

'Well, bend down to an old man so that I can kiss you. You were right, Vassya, when you said you were a trusty knight. I loved your father and I love you too.'

When Vassya was gone, and Tanyusha had settled down with a book in her favourite place on the corner of the divan, the ornithologist gazed a long time at his beloved grandchild:

'Tanyusha...'
'Yes, grandfather?'
'Doesn't our knight, Vassya, suit you?'
'How do you mean – doesn't suit me – grandfather?'
'Well, I mean as a husband. He doesn't, I see. A pity. A pity for him and for you too. He's very fond of you. Do you know?'

Tanyusha laid down her book:

'I know, grandfather. I get on very well indeed with him. Vassya has sterling qualities and we are the best of friends. But as to what you were saying – about marrying him, I mean – well, of course I wouldn't marry him, grandfather.'

'I see.'

'But, grandfather, do you mean you want me to get married?'

The old man was silent for a moment.

'Well, but in any case you will marry,' he said. 'Better not too young on the whole. Vassya is rather young for you, of course. You must be about the same age.'

'I don't want to get married, grandfather. I like living with you best.'

'Well, well, we'll see about that later on.'

The windows were open and the air fresh. Stillness brooded over Sivtzev Vrazhek. In the deep restful armchair in which Aglaya Dmitrevna had reclined for so many years in the twilight the old ornithologist now nodded, his grey beard spread decoratively over his breast. Tanyusha ceased turning the pages and running her eyes over the lines; she was thinking, listening to the stillness.

It was quiet on the floor above, where the Commandant of the Sovdep, Kolchagin, lived with his sister; it was quiet, too, beyond the wall in the rooms inhabited by strangers; in the basement, also, where a family of rats was thinking out the expedition that lay before it that night.

The whole of the professor's little old house was sleepily recalling the past and guessing at the future. The clock the old man was so fond of – the cuckoo clock on the wall – ticked on.

* * *

It was a long time since the streets of Moscow had been swept. Between the cobbles, timidly at first, then with increasing boldness, peeped a little eye of green. In the gutter and along by the fences the grass grew with greater assurance, and here and there the yellow eyelet of a flower dodged the stinging nettle. If it were not for that violent visionary-man, who was no whit less stubborn, and who, too, meant to remain alive at all costs and raise his puny body on the city stones, grass would have triumphed over stone; would have eaten through and adorned it; would have swept away the living and the whole of human existence into history and painted its pages green with oblivion and legend.

When twilight fell, the restless bustling in the houses died down. The sparrows and swallows were long since asleep in their nests and in the apertures of the attics, the curtain of their bluish lids drawn over their keen-sighted eyes.

The professor's little house had fallen into decay, had grown greyer and older, during that last terrible year. In the daytime it would still make a brave show, but when night fell it grew painfully bowed and grey, and its plaster and beams would groan.

Sad that the old house should go! There had been comfort in it and quiet gladness and content, grown greater with each added year. But it was tired, the old house. Time for it to slip into eternity; it needed rest. Drills and picks will pull up the cobblestones; asphalt will cover the ground, wood-block paving will be laid, and the walls of big new houses with every convenience and comfort erected on the site of the little pillared houses, dead and pulled down – old nests with kindly house-sprites and walls that witnessed to bygone days. Then the grass will retreat to the fields and stay there for many a year, till that page, too, is turned, till the varnish that is fresh today is worn away, and thought runs to seed. Then moisture and rubbish will again return for the obstinate buttercup to every chink in the city of stone. Maybe the grass of oblivion will triumph then, as it triumphed over the Acropolis of old and the Forum of Rome, as it triumphed over many a pile of stone unknown – nor ever destined to be known – to archaeologists, burying even the memory of it forever. Yet maybe for a few brief hours of the ages, man will shout aloud his victory once more.

* * *

'Grandfather! Are you asleep, grandfather?'

The twilight had merged into darkness. The air was fresher. Tanyusha lit the lamp:

'Were you asleep, grandfather?'

'I believe I dozed a little.'

'Shall we have tea?'

With the help of both his hands the professor raised himself out of the armchair:

'Well, do you know, Tanyusha, I shouldn't be sorry to have a cup of tea.'

– LIII –

THE WHITE FROCK

The clocks had been put on three hours and Moscow woke very early.

First it woke in Presna, in Blagusha, in Sokolniky, and in all the stations. Then Zamoskvopetchie, Pogozhskaya, Suharevka and the Smolensky marketplace bestirred themselves, yawning.

A lorry rumbled along the Tchyornogryaskaya Sadovaya. A policeman standing on duty in the middle of the Pokrovka road whooped at a starved and mangy dog. Down the boulevard from the Sretenka to Trubnaya Square ran two women, chattering excitedly, in a hurry, probably, to take their places in a queue for sunflower-seed oil.

And lastly, all at once, as though at a single command, from all the houses, slamming doors, sneezing in the sunshine, came pouring out the shabby, sleepy, earthen-faced figures of Soviet workers – copyists, heads of departments, chairmen of committees, couriers, experts, workers in the transport section, and skilled workmen. The majority went on foot to their work, not trusting to the trams that bumped along the refuse-littered rails in the Great Nikitinskaya, screeching round the Lubyanskaya Square and trying to squeeze through the chink-like archway of the Red Gates. Trams were very few and far between. Not many were fortunate enough to get on them, and those who did elbowed their way in, scowled at each other angrily and shot sidelong glances at the woman-conductor.

The day began early in the professor's little house too, in Sivtzev Vrazhek, where the swallow that had built a nest beneath the roof, as it had done in the free happy days of Moscow's past, was now rearing its fledglings.

The windows were open. A teaspoon clinked against the ornithologist's favourite big cup.

'Are you going to be at home, grandfather?'

THE WHITE FROCK

'I'll stay in and write till lunchtime. You, Tanyusha, ought to go for a walk today. Just look at the weather!'

'Yes, I'm going to. I have something to do quite a long way away, at the Red Gates. I shall not be home before two o'clock.'

After washing up the cups in the kitchen, and putting them away, Tanyusha, with quite an unusually cool, clean feeling of freshness, slipped on the frock she had ironed the day before – a white frock with wide short sleeves, drawn in at the waist by an elastic band. It would have been nice to have had white shoes to go with it, but extra shoes were a luxury that was not to be thought of those days. Her straw hat had been remodelled, cleaned with lemon powder and trimmed with a bit of coloured ribbon from an old store.

The familiar white girl in the glass smiled back at Tanyusha. With both her hands she tucked her hair beneath her hat and, growing serious, drew nearer to the glass to look at herself, face to face. Then, turning sideways, she set her dress right, took leave of herself and disappeared into the depths of the mirror.

Bruised, poverty-stricken, littered with refuse and dirt, Moscow was nonetheless wonderful that summer morning; still a dear city and a fair one, with its irregular beauty and Russian charm. Its streets, crooked and cobbled, its alleys and squares, for all the present desolation and repression, need and dread, were bathed in sunshine, which was mellowing the walls, dancing on roofs and domes, and edging the violet shadows with fringes of gold. The Moscow River was still swirling under the Stone Bridge, and, just as before, the Yausa veiled the impurity of its waters behind the iridescence of a rainbow.

In the Arbat all the shop windows were boarded up and thick with dust. There were no goods displayed and few signboards, and those that still remained had lost all meaning. Huddled at crossings and street corners, small boys were selling cigarettes, ready at any moment to take to their heels.

It had occurred to one woman to place a little pail of wild flowers – bunches of white and yellow flowers, forget-me-nots and heartsease – in the Arbatskaya. Tanyusha paused, gazed at them, inquired the price and went on. And yet how nice it would have been to carry a little bunch of flowers on such a glorious morning and sniff at them, or pin them at her throat or at her waist.

The trees in the boulevard were bursting into leaf. The straight alley was like life, luring her on with its dancing sunbeams, startling her with its shadows, looking, far on ahead, like a straight, narrow road. It was so pleasant, so easy, to be walking under the trees, even though there did happen to be a shorter way. Here, on the boulevard, it was as though nothing whatever had happened. True, the houses were greyer, grimier, uncared-for. But here, between the trees, it was just as pleasant as it used to be, if not pleasanter still. Was it that the trees had not been clipped and the foliage was thicker?

Sitting on one of the seats were two youths in army tunics and puttees, but with caps that belonged to no uniform. They shouted an indecent word after Tanyusha and giggled joyfully. But, deep in thought, she did not even hear them. Over her brows, left exposed by the brim of her hat, sunbeams were flashing, dazzling yet gentle. She seemed to be treading on air.

She followed the boulevards as far as the Strastny Monastery, cut diagonally across Sovietskaya Square, where the erection of a temporary obelisk on the site of the Skobelev Memorial had just been begun, and reached the Kuznetsky Bridge. She was not tired; but there was a climb before her now.

The street that had once been such an imposing and brilliant street of shops had lost its old air of gay pretentiousness. In the windows of the arcade, odds and ends had been left behind, forgotten. There were a large number of temporary signboards of various new establishments with clumsy-sounding names; and the type of people she met seemed out of keeping with the style of the rich Moscow street. The nearer she got to the Lubyanka the greater the number of people in army and government uniforms, in new 'Frenches' with uncomfortable, badly cut collars, in army breeches of an exaggerated cut, some even in leather jackets, notwithstanding the summer weather. Many of them carried portfolios. Few passed the girl in the white dress without a look in her direction; some plainly tried to look their best, throwing out their chests and striding past with martial gait, peering under her hat. But Tanyusha did not resent it today: it was so sunny and bright. Let them look if they liked.

What would she not have forgiven on that day of brilliant sunshine; to what would she not have replied with a smile! But why was she alone today? Among all the people she passed – dressed with taste or flaunting their poverty, walking head erect or with a crushed and abject look, good-looking or ugly, strolling or hurrying – there was not one who cared, not one whose thoughts were not of himself just then, but of her, Tanyusha, a little tired already and intoxicated by the sunshine... If only there had been just one!

Why did one have to live in such times? Oh, why? Would it go on for long? How different it had all been before!

As she crossed the street she looked around. There it was, the Kuznetsky Bridge Street, where she so often had gone on foot to buy music. There it was, different, yet unchanged; the same outlines, the same capriciousness and assurance about the bend in the street, the same church at the corner. No, Moscow could not be changed!

In the Myasnitskaya she met Uncle Borya, just before the entrance to his office, his department of 'Industrial Research.' He was glad to see her. He gave her hand a vigorous shake and asked after the health of her grandfather – his father, whom he could so rarely come to see on account of his busy life, that allowed him no time for anything besides his work and procuring stores.

'How nice you look,' he commented. 'A white dress – quite a lady.'

He accompanied her to the corner. There, in a hurry to get back, he stopped:

'Well, I must leave you, otherwise I may not be in time for the distribution. Meat is being given out today. No joke, I can tell you. Well, goodbye, my little niece.'

And she went on, alone again.

Before the General Post Office she paused. Why not turn down on the right to the Clear Ponds? She could go on home by the side-streets; it wasn't such a long way round.

As soon as she came into the alley she felt as fresh as before. It was quiet here and the clear notes of birds could be heard.

She reached the pond. The banks were trampled, the fence had been pulled down and taken away for firewood, and in the water, near the banks, eggshells were floating, and bits of newspaper and rotted straw-matting. But the trees and bushes were gazing down at themselves in the water just as before, and the cool air was the same, and so were the tiny ripples. No boats, though; they must have been hidden away or burned during the winter. And, then, who thought of going rowing these days?

Tanyusha remembered how she had been in the habit of going to see a school friend in the neighbourhood, with whom she used to go to the Clear Ponds to skate from early afternoon till evening, when, about seven o'clock, she would return to Sivtzev Vrazhek, breathing freely, pleasantly tired, cheeks rosy with cold – home to Granny's wing, home to be petted by grandfather and to sweet rusks with her tea. All that, of course, could never come back.

She retraced her steps and saw a man in a soldier's uniform, with frightened eyes, small and close-set.

'Won't you buy some bacon, citizen – real bacon from Kiev? I'd let you have it cheap; do buy, citizen.'

And he was already drawing out a dirty bundle from his tunic when Tanyusha answered:

'No, I'm afraid not.'

The sun momentarily disappeared behind a cloud and the pond darkened. Tanyusha turned away.

Could it be that the boats and the skates and the light-heartedness of old – could it be that these things would never return?

She came to the end of the boulevard, walking not between the trees but on one of the side-pavements, crossed the road and hurried down the shady side of Kharitonievsky Street, full of cares in her white dress, full of cares and alone – on that lovely summer's day.

But when she came out into the Sadovaya, and saw a house with a little green fence and the Red Gates and, far away down the street, the Suharevka Tower, she stopped again involuntarily, as she had done at the Kuznetsky Bridge, and said to herself:

'All the same, how lovely, how very lovely, Moscow is! Dear Moscow! And how like it used to be – unchangeable. It's the people who change, but it is always the same; saddened a little, perhaps, but just as absurd and straggly as it used to be, and just as dear and beautiful and homely.'

– LIV –

A DECLARATION OF LOVE

The lorry could not take all the performers home to their very doors, and Tanyusha and Astafiev were put down in Strastnaya Square.

They were carrying bundles, which contained the provisions they had earned: a little sugar, five pounds of flour, a pound of groats, a little jam, and a couple of herrings, each. The club in that locality was rich, and paid them liberally. In Astafiev's bundle were also his battered top-hat, a large paper collar and a gaudy tie, all of which belonged to his buffoon's outfit. He had washed off the flour and paint as best he could at the back of the stage.

'Well, you go along the Malaya Dmitrovka, and I take the side-streets.'

'No, we'll go together,' said Astafiev. 'I'm going to see you home.'

'But there's no need, Alexey Dmitritch. I'm not afraid.'

'But I'm afraid for you, especially with such a bundle. It's after midnight, too.'

Tanyusha knew that it was no small sacrifice on the part of a tired man who had performed, as she had herself, in two clubs that day. But it was rather frightening to go by oneself at night, and in any case Astafiev would not hear of it. Poor man, he would have a long way to go back to the Dolgorukovskaya!

She was grateful to him: he was a true comrade. But she did not allow him to carry her bundle. She wanted to carry home herself all the treasures she had earned. And it was not a burden, it was a joy. And, best of all, there was some sugar for grandfather.

The jolting of the lorry had made conversation impossible, and it was in silence that they started to walk home. Tanyusha was the first to break it.

'Don't you find it difficult to perform in such parts, Alexey Dmitritch?' she asked.

'What? Play the buffoon? No; anything else would be more difficult – speeches, for instance, on international relations. I could never bring myself to make them. To do that sort of thing one must either be an idiot or a knave.'

'It seems curious, all the same, that you should have taken to acting. What made you do it, Alexey Dmitritch? What gave you the idea?'

Astafiev gave a quiet laugh:

'But what else was there to do? Give lectures on philosophy? I did do that as long as it was possible – until I was turned out of the university, in fact. And the idea of acting occurred to me simply enough. I used to recite short stories in public at various charity entertainments – as an amateur, naturally. And I used to give impromptu raree-shows to various student societies, which turned out quite well. So when it came to changing my profession, I remembered those performances. Acting is quite a profitable business. One gets flour and herrings for it, anyhow. So that's how I came to be Comrade Smehatchev, with a whitened mug. I'm a success, as you see.'

'But you find it hard, don't you?'

'You find it hard and so do I, and so do all the rest of us. Only, you suffer in all earnestness for your music, while I at any rate do get things off my chest by making fun of all those people – the guffawing asses.'

'But why make fun of them, the workmen, Alexey Dmitritch? I don't like that in you!'

'You're warm-hearted and I'm not – very. I'm not fond of people in the mass; I can only really get to like someone I know and respect, and think highly of, too; someone in whom there is that which really makes him dear to me. But the mob – no. So here am I, lecturer and philosopher, powdering my face with flour, colouring my nose and playing the fool before the conquering mob, that pays me for it in herrings and fermented jam. And the trashier and more pointless the stories I tell them, the worse the taste of my witticisms, the better pleased they are and the louder they laugh. I often get a lot of comfort out of that.'

He paused, then went on again, without exasperation:

'All the same, you do know me just a little, Tatyana Mihailovna, so you will be able to understand that I don't find it easy to think out and declaim all that rubbish. And the sillier it sounds, the more I rejoice. Possibly there is something of the joy of revenge in it – revenge on them, the lords and masters of our age, and on my own useless science, my unnecessary knowledge and vain intellect.'

'Why vain?'

'Because it gets in my way, in the way of my new career – not my own, but Comrade Smehatchev's. The philosopher Astafiev is always trying to put real satire into Comrade Smehatchev's mouth, true wit and some sort of artistic meaning. He, Astafiev, is ashamed of Smehatchev, but that's quite unnecessary, and only goes to prove that Astafiev himself, philosopher and lecturer though he is, has not yet raised himself to the philosophic heights, is not yet free from the coquetry of scholarship, is not a Hercules nor yet a Stoic. It would seem that that is very difficult. To live like Diogenes did, in a tub, is easy enough. But to get rid of an empty affectation is quite a different matter. The phrase 'Stand aside, you keep the sunshine off me' – the phrase centuries have been repeating – is nothing in reality but a cheap affectation. A genuine Stoic ought to have said, quite simply, 'Go to the devil!' – or, better still, yawn without saying a word, go to sleep or scratch his back. What unlucky chance dragged in Alexander the Great, when it was quite dull enough without him, and when it obviously didn't require his presence to make the crowd of idiots gape at the tub and its inmate. But, instead of that, Diogenes let out an historic phrase, to his own and everyone else's satisfaction. It's just that sort of cheap philosophy that appeals so much to the man in the street.'

'Don't, Alexey Dmitritch!'

'But why? Isn't it true?'

'It may be true, but if so, then it's very unlovely, that truth of yours. It doesn't warm the heart. And it doesn't make things any easier for you. As for me, I find it distinctly unpleasant.'

Astafiev was silent. Under a lamp-post at one of the street corners, Tanyusha turned to look into his eyes. Astafiev's face was drawn and grey, and his eyes sad.

'You're not offended with me?'

He searched for an answer. He wasn't offended – that wasn't the right word. But he was sorry for himself. Just a 'No' would not have been an adequate reply.

'You are right in a sense, Tatyana Mihailovna, and I'm subtilizing and getting involved. That too is an unconscious affectation.'

When they were near the house, Tanyusha said to him:

'Do you know, I used to be afraid of you. You are so clever and original, so out of the ordinary. But I'm less afraid of you now; in fact, I'm not afraid of you at all.' He was listening attentively. 'And that's because I have come to understand a great many things since I have been earning my own living and seeing a lot of quite new people. The thought somehow came to me that we are all just frightened children – you and I and grandfather and the workmen and Comrade Braudey, all of us. We all talk and think about strange, trifling things, such as herrings and the revolution and international relations. But those aren't the really important things. I don't know what is. I just know that those aren't. What do you find important, Alexey Dmitritch?'

'I'll tell you in a moment... For me it's necessary and important to see you sometimes, Tatyana Mihailovna, and talk to you just as we are talking now; and that you should worst me in our conversation. And what do you find important?'

'I? I can't help feeling that for me the most important thing would be to be sometimes near a simple, healthy-minded person, preferably not a philosopher, nor a raree-showman either.'

'Isn't that rather unkind, Tatyana Mihailovna?'

'No, I'm not unkind; you said so yourself. But I do want air. I don't want to have anything to do with the gloomy prison that's drawing you all so irresistibly, and where you'd like to shut me up too.'

'Who would – '

But Tanyusha interrupted him:

'I'm twenty, Alexey Dmitritch, and do you imagine I enjoy hearing those everlastingly gloomy grievances and bitter words? And all the time about oneself, which makes it worse – all around oneself and for oneself. And everybody is the same, even the best. Grandfather, it's true, thinks about me, but that's the same as thinking about himself. And you, Alexey Dmitritch, do you ever think of anybody beside yourself?'

Astafiev's sleepy face was suddenly lit up by his intelligent smile:

'Extraordinary how an excess of words can denaturalize the idea with which one starts out. You stemmed my flow of words with an excellent remark, and have forced me to abandon my position. And then you yourself were carried away by the coquetry of thoughts and words, and I am saved again; at any rate no longer feel embarrassed. Sheer idiocy, our intellectual tongue. What is it you really want to say? What were you asking me about just now? Whether there existed someone else for me besides my own self? I can answer quite simply: Yes, you exist. If you hadn't, I shouldn't be seeing you home and so afraid for your safety. So, you see, you weren't quite right.'

'I'm grateful to you, Alexey Dmitritch.'

'Not at all.'

Then, pronouncing his words very clearly, as he always did when he was finding speech difficult or when he did not feel sure of his own words, Astafiev went on:

'All that's neither here nor there – sheer nonsense. Words. But it's hardly nonsense that I – that you seem to be beginning to exist too much for me. Yes, that's precisely what you were thinking about just now: the beginning of some sort of declaration. It can't be followed up tonight – for one thing because we have reached your house, and secondly, because your 'words are still faintly rankling. It's probably my masculine amour-propre that has been wounded. Well, goodbye. My kind regards to the professor.'

He shook hands with her, waited till her ring at the gate had been answered by a banging of the dvornik's door, and, turning away abruptly, strode down Sivtsev Vrazhek.

Tanyusha stood leaning her forehead against the cold gatepost.

'Are declarations of love ever as cold as that? And why am I feeling so utterly unmoved?'

– LV –

IN THE THICKET

At seven o'clock the trusty knight was already at the front door of the house in Sivtsev Vrazhek.

Tanyusha looked out of the window.

'I'm ready, Vassya,' she called down to him eagerly. 'Do you want to come in? Have you had your breakfast?'

'Yes, thanks; and there's no time to lose now. You'd better come straight out, Tanyusha. Don't forget to take a basket with you. I've got a big bag and enough bread for both of us.'

'What's the bag for?'

'What for? Why, for fir-cones, of course! We'll bring some home for the stove. And, in any case, a bag may come in useful.'

What a glorious summer day! A slanting ray of early morning sunshine glided over Tanyusha as she stood framed in the window, white and radiant and friendly. How good it was to be alive – sometimes.

'You're very smart today, Vassya.'

Vassya's smartness mainly consisted of a fairly new pair of sandals on his bare feet and a Russian shirt with a leather belt. He wore no hat, not only for hygienic reasons! – the hair ought to be allowed to breathe freely! – but also because his own was too shabby and greasy to wear; and hats, even if one could afford to buy them, were no longer sold anywhere.

To be smart meant in those days to be wearing clean linen and well-mended clothes, no matter how fantastic the costume. In the absence of all material, buttons and trimming, former dandies ingeniously contrived to make themselves suits out of curtains, and linen from tablecloths; while ladies wore hats made of green and red cloth ripped off card-tables and desks in the Soviet offices. Prosecution had been attempted, but abandoned: the offence was so difficult to prove.

As for well-pressed trousers, they were not only considered to be a prejudice of the bourgeoisie, but actually something in the nature of a defiance of the new ways of thinking.

He, in an embroidered shirt and sandals, and she, in her old white dress drawn in at the waist, spotless and ironed, made a young couple whose smartness would have satisfied the most fastidious taste. The baskets on their arms and the empty cloth bag on Vassya's shoulder did not in any way detract from their appearance: for who would think of going out without a bag! The morning sun was caressing. Both were young and light-hearted. A whole day in the forests lay before them. What was happiness if not that?

Big and small, the houses in Sivtzev Vrazhek smiled after them. Even the professor's little house, darkened with age, took heart that day and beamed in the sunlight. Tanyusha, grave and businesslike as a rule, was ready to laugh at all Vassya's flow of nonsense. And Vassya felt just like a schoolboy. Their legs seemed to run of their own accord; they had to be held back in their haste. What was happiness if not that?

The train consisted exclusively of trucks, and the passengers were mostly dairywomen returning home with empty cans. There were only two morning and two evening trains on the local lines. On the other hand, no special permit was required, as for long-distance trains.

It took the train nearly an hour to crawl ten versts, and it stopped at three stations on the way, for a very long time, and without any apparent cause. Tanyusha and Vassya got out at Nemtchinov Post.

'Well, here we are; the journey's over. Where do we go now, Tanyusha?'

'Let's get to the woods as quickly as possible.'

'There's a small wood quite near. But half-an-hour's walk from here through the fields would bring us to a wonderful forest that stretches right down to the Moscow River. Shall we go there?'

Their legs went on without any urging. They avoided the clump of neglected and half-ruined villas on the way. These villas were now in the hands of the local Sovdep, and it was possible to get hold of one only after a great deal of trouble, cunning and solicitation – and even then only in the name of some organization, which could quite well be imaginary if the application were made through acquaintances. Although there was a wood quite near, a number of the little houses had been pulled down during the previous winter for firewood.

They came out into the fields, all trampled by the roadside. For all

IN THE THICKET

the sparseness of the corn, golden waves rolled over the barley, and the blue eye of the cornflower twinkled in among the ears. A lark was singing in the sky, invisible. Nature was stubborn: living herself and calling upon all else to live.

Tanyusha took off her shoes and went barefoot in between two ruts. From time to time she trod upon green blades of grass, deliciously cool to the soles of her feet, blades that started up between her toes and slid out again caressingly. Vassya undid the collar of his shirt and sang all the way in an uncertainly pitched voice, dreadfully out of tune: he had absolutely no ear. Such singing would have jarred unbearably on Tanyusha's musical sense had it not been for the radiance of the morning. Only at his most despairing tremolos did she stop up her ears and cry to him, laughing:

'Do have pity, Vassya! You'll scare all the birds away!'

'Well, anyhow, the frogs will be pleased when we come back this evening. My singing is just their style.'

They enjoyed themselves like children: ran after each other, adorned themselves with garlands of cornflowers, chewed unripe grains of corn and sweet tips of grass. About ten o'clock they left the fields and, entering a deep ravine, struck at last the road to the forest

At first the forest closed in round them with low trees – young oaks, little birches, hazels; then it encompassed them with the freshness of ancient birches and aspens and firs. The road that wound its ways through the forest was little used, and its ruts curved round the bushes over a network of roots, while in the spaces between the ruts grew mushrooms with little pink and green hats.

They scarcely met a soul, and the people they did meet were on foot. About four versts of forest stretched to the steep banks of the Moscow River. Either the berries had already been picked or else it was not a good spot for them, for they saw very few; but the nuts were already beginning to swell and to harden their milky kernels in carven green hoods.

Towards noon they passed the scattered little villas and houses of the village and reached the river. Vassya got some milk on the way, and they came to a halt on the high riverbank.

Never had the greyish doughy bread – ration barley bread eaten with coarse salt – seemed so nice. Tanyusha marvelled at the research student's housekeeping ability when in his basket stood revealed, not only a bottle for the milk, but two thick glasses as well:

'You take this glass, Tanyusha, it's my drinking glass.'
'And the other?'
'The other's for shaving, to tell you the truth. But I've given it a thorough good wash. I can tell it from the other by the bubble-like bump on the glass – here, d'you see?'
'What a funny, dear person you are, Vassya! Let's touch glasses.'
It was Vassya's turn to give a little cry and turn red when Tanyusha's bundle revealed two big rissoles:
'Well, I'm blessed! This is sheer dissipation – food for the gods!'
'And don't imagine that it's horseflesh, Vassya. It's absolutely the genuine thing, and I fried them myself in real dripping.'
They each ate half a rissole, leaving the other half for supper. And they ate in silence, as though performing a ritual, their thoughts turned for a moment to serious matters.
They finished up with baked potatoes, and all at once the provision basket became distinctly lighter.
'Berries for dessert?'
'If we can find enough. We must pick some for grandfather too.'
'There's a glut of bilberries and whinberries in the other wood.'
They sat on the edge of the steep slope, enjoying the marvellous view over the river banks. Below, on the other side of the river, was a tiny hamlet; and far, far away one could catch a glimpse of Arkhanghelskoe.
'Lovely!'
'Yes, isn't it.'
'Are you satisfied, Tanyusha?'
'I'm happy. And you, Vassya?'
'Means I'm doubly.'
'Why – doubly? And why – means?'
'With my own happiness and yours too.'
Tanyusha looked at Vassya, and her eyes were thoughtful and gentle:
'Dear Vassya, thank you.'
'What for?'
'For everything. For your true and vigilant friendship.'
'Yes, for my friendship – that's true. And thank you, too, Tanyusha, for being alive; for my love for you. It's a nuisance to you, I know, but it just keeps me alive. Lord! but I love you so, Tanyusha, that...'
Vassya sprawled on the grass and thumped at it with his clenched fist.

'It may be silly, but I do need it so badly. Don't you listen to me, Tanyusha? It's the sun's doing; it has turned my head. Lord, what a perfect ass I am today!' and he made a few inarticulate sounds. 'Jolly pleasant feeling all the same.'

They remained sitting there, he with his face in the grass, she looking thoughtfully out across the green expanse. And when Vassya raised his head Tanyusha said quite simply:

'Shall we go back to the wood now?'

'Yes. Now we'll go back to the wood. To the wood... quite so.'

They leapt to their feet.

'Come along. The oldest wood begins two steps away. It's forbidden to fell any of the trees, and there are firs that date from the time of Tsar Alexey Mihailovitch. You'll see for yourself. We're sure to scratch our legs, but it's so wonderful that it's worth it. I've been there many times and know every inch of it.'

The tall grass brushed against their legs. The paths grew scarcer. Bending aside the branches of the tall undergrowth, they penetrated into the ancient forest, and it was like entering a grotto. Although it was noon – the noon of a hot summer's day – they suddenly found themselves in a cool, damp atmosphere.

The treetops interlaced above them in domes without number, and all the earth, in spite of the thick shade, was spread with grass, lush, cool and tender. Through the soft, spongy loam white blades were slowly pushing their way up to the open and turning green in the light.

There was no trace of a path farther on in the forest. The green wall of undergrowth stretched on as far as eye could see, and the ancient trunks stood out like sombre pillars. At one spot lay a rotting pine that had fallen many years before. The scattered bark now formed a pathway through the saplings and bushes, and the top was lost in the distant gloom. The trunk was as thick as the height of a man, and they were obliged to go round it.

'Where are you, Vassya?'

'Here, quite near you. I've got into such a tangle of undergrowth that I don't know how to get out.'

'It's nice here, Vassya. What a wonderful forest! Can you see me?'

'I can just see your dress gleaming, but not your face.'

'I'd like to live here.'

'You'd get bored. You'd long to get back to the civilized world.'

'The civilized world is not a very pleasant place just now.'

'Wait a bit. Things will get better.'

'Do you think so?'

'How can one think otherwise? Look at all our wealth! Just this forest alone; think what it's worth! And up north – oh, I've barked my shins against the knot of a tree '

'What were you saying about the north?'

'I was saying that up north, where I used to live as a kid, the forests are much denser. There are pine forests that go on for thousands of versts. When one thinks of them, people and politics and housing problems and regulations just seem ridiculous.'

'Do you love life, Vassya? Aren't you afraid of living?'

Vassya's shirt appeared through the bushes:

'Well, I'm absolutely stuck now. The basket makes it so difficult to get on, too... But about life, how can one not love life? Of course I love it! The only thing I love more than life is you, Tanyusha.'

'You're beginning again.'

'It's the truth I'm telling you. I'll even go so far as to say this to you – wait a moment, Tanyusha, don't move; I'll help you out afterwards. Just listen to me for once. I swear by this forest that I don't ask anything of you, but that I'd give my life for you, Tanyusha – just wait a moment; hear me out. I swear by this forest that if ever you need my help – well, in anything whatsoever – you must remember that I'm your true friend for always and that I'd do anything for you – even die for you, Tanyusha, and gladly too. There, that was in deadly earnest, and now I won't say another word.'

The twigs ceased rustling and the birds were silent.

'Vassya!'

'What?'

'Where are you?'

'I've got stuck'

'Come here.'

'Can't; there's such a tangle here. And I'm being pricked all over.'

'Well, then, stretch out your hand.'

Again the twigs crackled, and through them appeared Vassya's large hand.

'Oh, Vassya, you have been scratched!'

'That's nothing.'

'Poor dear!... Well, take hold of my hand.'

Tanyusha leaned against a shrub and reached Vassya's fingers:

'Got me?'

'Yes.'

'Only don't pull, or I shall fall. Vassya, dear Vassya, I know and do value it all. It's only myself that I don't know still. It's so nice to be here with you; but at home, in town, there's something that troubles me all the time. My mind is never at rest. There are a lot of things I can't understand, well… in myself. Only, don't judge me, Vassya,'

'But am I likely to?'

'It's so difficult for me, Vassya – so difficult.'

'Well, but I do understand.'

'Vassya dear, you are my only real friend. There; now let go my hand. We've got to get out of this thicket somehow.'

The twigs parted still farther, and Vassya's tousled head stretched forward till his lips met Tanyusha's fingertips:

'We'll get out all right. I said I'd always help you! There ought to be a path not far away from here. I'll see you safely out, Tanyusha, never fear!'

– LVI –

A SECOND CHAT

Astafiev had heated some water on his stove and was in the act of washing away the last traces of flour and paint when his glass reflected the chink of the opening door and, in the chink,, the bloated face of his neighbour, the workman.

'No need to spy on me, Zavalishin. Come in.'

'Busy washing?'

'Washing flour off my face.'

'Got dirty?'

'Seems like it. How are you?'

Zavalishin entered and warmed his hands before the stove.

'Very well, thank you,' he replied distinctly and with assurance. 'I'm making a lot of money.'

'Still at the works?'

'Not me. I'm on a different job now. I followed your advice and clear directions, Comrade Astafiev.'

'I don't seem to remember ever having advised you. Where is it you work?'

'You said I ought to struggle and not stop at dirty work, 'or else you'll go under, Zavalishin,' you said to me; 'they'll do for you.' Well, so now I'm struggling.'

Astafiev looked at his neighbour with curiosity:

'Well, and does it work?'

'Can't complain. I'm getting on. I've even come to you to invite you, Comrade Astafiev, so's to pay you back like, and thank you for inviting me. That's if you don't mind, of course it's not homemade imitation stuff, it's real cognac, from a pre-War brewery. Two bottles of it.'

'Got it through a bit of dirty work, you mean?'

'That's right – through a bit of dirty work – the real human stuff. You wouldn't mind, would you?'

'Curious!'

'Nothing curious that I can see. Have you got two glasses, by any chance? I'll just go and bring along something to eat with it – a joint of meat and a few other things.'

Again Astafiev looked with interest at his neighbour. There was a marked change in him. He was better – indeed quite well-dressed; no trace of his former timidity and abjectness could be detected; and yet his self-confidence did not seem quite genuine. It smacked too much of showing off – bravado.

Zavalishin brought along the cognac, which though not of a particularly good brand was nevertheless real, pre-War cognac. He also untied a parcel and produced a joint, caviare and some dubious, greyish-looking rusks – positive luxuries in those days. They moved the table nearer to the stove.

Zavalishin half-filled both glasses:

'To your health, learned comrade! I'm deeply grateful to you for everything – for your learning, for your advice and for bringing a fool to his senses.'

'But what is it you do, Zavalishin? D'you steal, or have you joined a band of brigands, or what?'

'What d'you take me for? I'm earning my living at a regular job, I am.'

'But where?'

'Ah, that's a secret, that is, Comrade Astafiev. It's a job anyhow, a real job too. It's work that's absolutely got to be done in the interests of the country. But one oughtn't to let things out.' 'Well, then, devil take you, drink!'

They drank in silence, helping themselves to the caviare and to thick chunks of meat. Astafiev was hungry, and being a man of strong physique he needed a good deal of food. The cognac warmed him and restored his vigour. Zavalishin, on the contrary, got tipsy almost at once, but went on greedily drinking. His face became suffused with blood; his small eyes narrowed and looked down dully into his glass.

The damp wood crackled in the stove.

Seated in his armchair, Astafiev forgot all about his visitor. His mind seemed to grow to double its usual size. He thought of Tanyusha, of their last conversation; but mingled with their words were his own platform witticisms and some doggerel with which he had been entertaining the mob. And the sound of music – Tanyusha playing Bach – still lingered on.

The thump of Zavalishin's fist on the table made him start.

'Stop, don't budge or – '

'What's the matter with you? Are you drunk?'

The workman raised his tipsy eyes.

'I don't w-want him to move.'

'Whom?'

'In general, I – don't w-want.' He gave a shrill laugh: 'I'm like that. Don't you w-worry, c-comrade; I can do anything I like.'

'Not everything, Zavalishin. As a matter of fact, you're a weak man, even though you do look so muscular.'

'Me weak? Me, you mean? I can quite easily kill, I can; that's how weak I am.'

'Think, why even a child can kill a man, especially with a revolver. That doesn't require any strength. And beyond that you can't do anything.'

'What can't I do?'

'Create. Do things. Well, make cigarette lighters, for instance.'

'I'm not a locksmith.'

'Well, then, plough a field.'

'Whatever's the good? The peasants do that.'

'But what a lordly proletarian! The peasants till the fields and you eat up the bread. No, Zavalishin, you're not fit for anything; you can't even drink cognac in the right way. You give your mouth a swill with it before swallowing it and get drunk after the very first glass.'

'We swallow it in our own way, Mr. Astafiev. We weren't taught how to do it at the university. We didn't have time to learn to sip. We always gulp it down like this!'

A SECOND CHAT

He filled up his glass and swallowed it at one gulp; then, hiccuping, began to cut a slice of meat with trembling hands.

Astafiev emptied his glass, filled another – keeping up with his neighbour – and returned to his thoughts. He was feeling pleasantly dizzy. Soon, however, he was again roused from his deep reverie by the sound of Zavalishin's mutterings.

Resting his arms on the table, and his drunken head on his hands, Zavalishin was looking at his companion out of red, blinking eyes.

'You could be put in quod for saying such things,' he was mumbling. 'For the cigarette lighters and for the peasant; even have your account closed.'[1]

Astafiev frowned in distaste:

'Tchekist! Go home to bed if you're drunk, Zavalishin. We'll finish the bottle tomorrow.'

'Tomorrow? Tomorrow I've got a free day, a sort of d-day off. There's no urgent raw material tomorrow.'

And again he broke out into a cowardly titter.

'No material tomorrow. What there was came to an end today. I, Zavalishin, finished them off. Click, and it's over.'

And suddenly he brought his fist down again on the table.

'Don't ask questions, I tell you!' he shouted. 'Not your business, it isn't!'

He filled his glass with a shaking hand and drank it off at one gulp. The cognac burned his throat. His eyes dilated. He stretched his hand out for the food, but collapsed as he did so, his forehead striking against the table.

Astafiev rose, took his visitor by the collar and gave him a shake. Then, raising his head, he saw drunken panic writ large on the pale face. Zavalishin's teeth were chattering and his tongue wobbled in an incoherent mumbling. Astafiev raised him by the collar, held him up and dragged him to the door:

'Heavy carcass! Well, get along, you hero!'

He trailed Zavalishin to his room, threw him on the bed, pulled up and straightened out the legs. The drunken man was muttering still, and Astafiev bent down to listen:

'Oh, Ma, oh, Ma, what shall I do, what ever shall I do?'

Astafiev went back to his room, collected the remains of the food,

---

[1] Sent to execution. The expression became current in Bolshevik prisons.

both bottles, empty and half-empty, and carried everything back to Zavalishin's room. When he returned to his own he opened the window and lay down on the bed, picking up from the table the first book that came to hand.

– LVII –

BAGMAN[1]

The heavily laden carriages jolted one against the other and the train came to a stop. The journey, that had formerly taken no more than twenty-four hours, now lasted nearly a week.

The train stopped for hours and days at various little stations and intermediate stops, and the passengers were driven into the woods to gather fuel for the engine. On two occasions, carriages were disconnected. And, groaning and swearing, the grey mob of bagmen had made a dash for new places, stamping along the carriage roofs and squeezing on to the platforms at the ends of the carriages. Among these passengers, hurriedly elbowing his way, fighting for a place and dragging along with the greatest difficulty his portmanteau and bag full of odds and ends, was Vassya Boltanovsky, the research student and the trusty knight of the little house in Sivtzev Vrazhek.

Vassya had long since forgotten when he had last washed. Like all the rest he would slide his hand under his shirt and scratch chest, shoulders and back as far as he could reach, scratch till he bled. He had only been obliged to travel on the roof one night. Usually he managed to occupy a luggage rack inside, from which he would look triumphantly down at the serried bodies below, doped with dirt and sweat and lack of sleep, and their own grumbling and witticisms over their fate. The lucky ones slept on the floor, in the corridors, under the seats. For the unlucky there was nothing for it but to sleep standing; and at every jolt their heads would nod.

---

[1] This term was coined during the Revolution, and applied to the traders who brought supplies of food in bags from the country to the famished towns. This trading was prohibited, since it contributed to the depreciation of the rouble and sent up the price of food. It continued, however, till the N.E.P. (New Economic Policy) came into force.

Towards the end of the journey there was more room in the carriages. Most of the bagmen left the train and scattered in the villages. Vassya travelled on farther than most, thinking he would be able to exchange his goods with great profit in the more distant villages. On the way he made friends with several experienced bagmen, who had undertaken the fantastic journey for groats and grain once or twice before.

When they left the train the bagmen separated into groups, straightened themselves and, adjusting their bags as comfortably as they could, set out in all directions.

Vassya's companions were two experienced, middle-class Moscow women and an 'ex-engineer' – as he called himself – who wore good boots and a khaki uniform, but a reddish brown kepi instead of a forage cap. He was always taken for a soldier and called comrade. Vassya made friends with him on the way, and readily acknowledged his authority and experience. Though dirty, unshaven and sleepy, like everyone else, the engineer had an amazing faculty for keeping a good heart. He would relate his former experiences on 'campaigns,' manage to get boiling water, pacify the people who quarrelled, exchange salt for tobacco, let tired women have his seat for a while, and once, during one of the long stops, actually helped the inexperienced stoker to mend the engine. In the carriage he was looked upon as a sort of steward; and to Vassya, whom he called Professor, he was particularly gentle and kind.

This engineer, Protassov, was about thirty-five. Strong, vigorous, friendly and courteous, he was able to suit his manner of speech and subject of conversation to the people with whom he was speaking. The passengers never failed to say goodbye to him when they left the train; and the inexperienced invariably came under his protection.

He left the station with his little group of wayfarers and set out.

'Well, we've got here, anyhow,' one of the women remarked, 'but the question is – how are we going to get back with our sacks full?'

'We'll see later on,' he replied. 'People are travelling all the time.'

'I know, but not all of them get back.'

'It will be difficult getting past the raids.'[2]

'We'll get through somehow. No point in worrying about it now. We must concentrate on exchanging our goods to the best advantage.'

---

[2] Every measure was taken by the Government to stop the illicit trafficking of the *bagmen*.

'My legs won't go.'

'Never mind. You'll soon get into the swing. And we'll take a rest in the forest.'

'What, in the rain?'

'We'll find a dry spot. Or else we'll take shelter in some hut or other.'

'What a life!'

'All the same, it's better here than in the train.'

It was true; they were finding it restful to be out in the open after being in the stuffy carriages.

Following the sodden, autumnal roads and the footpaths across dank fields, they got as far as a small village, where they were met with suspicion by dogs and men alike. It was plain that no trade could be done with the villagers; one could only hope to get dry and warm and make inquiries.

They gained admittance into one of the huts, where the peasants' attitude became more friendly as soon as it was known that the unexpected visitors had brought some tea with them. The peasants responded by bringing out a pot of milk and a good crust-end of bread – real bread, good and satisfying, not at all like their Moscow rations. For a few pinches of tea, bathwater was heated and a night's lodging promised them. That was a stroke of good fortune, a bath being what they most urgently needed.

For the first time for a week, Vassya was able to undress. He spent a long time destroying the insects, under the supervision of his experienced wayfarer. Then they put on clean linen and had a good night's rest, unbroken by the bugs – harmless insects to which they no longer had any objection.

The following morning, at dawn, they set out once more along the roads and across open country in search of wealthier peasants with larger stores of food.

At the very first village they came to the women of the party remained behind. Vassya was lucky. For the first things he bartered – one of Tanyusha's old dresses and a summer blouse – he received what was worth its weight in gold: a whole half-pood[3] of groats. Protassov highly approved of the bargain. While Vassya was tying up his sack he watched with horror a young peasant woman thrusting her red, work-roughened arms into the sleeves of Tanyusha's blouse, trying it on

---

[3] 1 pood = 36.11 pounds avoirdupois.

above her old greasy one, and setting it straight over her chest with clumsy fists. But he had made a beginning – and a good one, too – for Tanyusha.

The peasants looked at the traders sombrely, but tried, nevertheless, to find out for what they could get the engineer's boots, with which he had no intention of parting. They offered the merest trifle for his scythe and whetstone – it was early yet to think of haymaking. Vassya was interested to know how the engineer had come into possession of a brand-new scythe, and Protassov explained that he had received it at his works, where all sorts of strange and unexpected things were given out in place of rations, the workers taking anything readily enough in the hope of being able to make an exchange.

When they left the first village, Vassya and the engineer decided to keep, as far as possible, to the main road and to stay in the neighbourhood of the railway. The worst part of their journey was the nighttime, for the villagers did not trust the people from the towns, and were unwilling to let them into their huts. But, once admitted, they readily asked all sorts of questions about Moscow, about the Germans and prices, and about what was to be expected next. That the war was over they knew; but they had the vaguest and most fantastic notions as to who was now ruling Russia, and whether it was true that the Tsar had been removed and what it was the Bolsheviks really wanted. Rumours of taxation interested them more than politics, and they were eager to know whether the grain was going to be taken away from the peasants, and whether the landowners were not coming back. Though they listened to the answers with bated breath, it was plain that they had little faith in the townsfolk and put their own interpretation on their words.

On the fifth day, after parting with the blouses, calico, carrot-tea and tobacco leaves, the traders had their bags full. In the last village they stopped at, Vassya sold the professor's hunting-boots for a pood of white flour and a pood of millet, which transaction the engineer did not approve, thinking they had not got sufficient value for the boots. By this time Protassov, too, was loaded with provisions. They decided, therefore, to hire a cart to the nearest station and pay for the transport in money. In this also they were successful.

When they were outside the village the owner of the cart turned round to his fares and took stock of them.

'From the look of you,' he said, addressing himself to Vassya, 'you wouldn't be one of them masters, and you don't look like a comrade, so I'm just going to call you Mister.'

'Well, and whom am I like?' Protassov asked him.

'How am I to know?' the peasant replied unwillingly. 'You aren't from these parts, and to look at you one would say that you was in the army.'

The cart came in particularly useful, since Vassya, who was totally unused to such kinds of adventure, not only felt weak, but had even had a touch of fever the night before.

The drive passed without mishap. What they found most difficult was getting themselves and their sacks on to the train, which as usual was packed. They were obliged to spend the first night at the station. The next day they were lucky again, and managed to settle, first on the buffers, then on a platform at the end of the carriage. At the following stations they were squeezed into the carriage by new crowds of bagmen, who filled all the space near the doors and even swarmed over the roofs. There was no air in the carriage, and they were forced to travel standing; but, once in, they were grateful enough for small mercies.

The train went faster this time, without long stops, and on the third day they neared Moscow, after having successfully got over the first raid, from which they had bought themselves off for practically nothing. Vassya was in a hurry to reach Moscow, for he was feeling every moment weaker. The windows had been opened to let in a breath of fresh air, and Vassya had felt very cold. Towards nightfall he was no longer cold, but hot. The engineer looked at him and shook his head doubtfully:

'What's up with you, I wonder. I only hope you haven't caught a poisonous semashka!'[4]

'No, it's nothing. Only the sooner we get back the better.'

Outside Moscow they were stopped by another raiding detachment. The roofs were cleared by the firing of blank shots. The passengers were driven out of the front carriages, and many had their bags taken from them. But, evidently satisfied with those nearest at hand, the raiders seemed content to let the others go scot-free. The bagmen defended their property by fair means and foul; they clung on to the bags, swore at the raiders, wheedled and bribed them, tried to keep in a serried mass, in order to block up the passage into the

---

[4] The popular substitute for 'louse'; derived from Semashko, the name of a Russian Minister of Health. The reference is, of course, to typhus.

compartments, and stowed away their stores under seats, skirts and coats. But Vassya and his companion were fortunate again. Their carriage was the last one, and the raiders had neither strength left nor time to search it thoroughly. After a halt of over two hours the train at length moved on. The chief danger was over; there was no longer any risk of their being deprived of the goods which they had got with such pains.

'As soon as you get home,' Protassov advised Vassya, 'you must wash and get rid of the semashki. Then drink as much scalding tea as ever you can and go to bed. It would be as well to call in a doctor if you happen to know one.'

He was right. Vassya was really ill. After the nervous strain of the raid he felt an overwhelming weakness. He sat on his bag, like a bag himself. There was such a throbbing in his temples that at times the very thumping of the train was drowned by it. And his bitten, itching body was covered with cold sweat.

'Everything seems blurred, as though swimming before my eyes.'

'I'm not surprised,' replied the engineer, with a look of pity. 'I'm afraid it's something serious, my lad. It's a good thing that we shall soon be in Moscow. We'll drag along the bags somehow or other; we may even be able to get a cheap cab.'

Rattling over the points, groaning at the bends, slowly, as though intentionally prolonging the journey, the heavily laden train crept painfully, sullenly into the Moscow station.

Vassya straightened his back and tried to hold erect his burning head, thinking the while:

'It seems I'm in for it. Well, anyhow, I've brought back a lot of things. It will be a bit easier now for Tanyusha and the professor.'

And then, with a wan smile:

'I shall see her soon – Tanyusha.'

– LVIII –

'STIFFEYS'

The chairman of the House Committee, Denissov, had given out a notice to all the tenants: those among them who had no documents to prove that they were employed by the Soviet were to appear at the police station with spades at three o'clock on the following morning:

'You are to go and do public work.'

It appeared that nearly all the tenants had documents; and the workmen were exempt. Denissov let off two of the others on his own authority; one on account of illness (the man was dying of typhus) and the other on account of extreme old age. Only seven people had no certificate: three women and four men, among whom was the university reader, Astafiev:

'I work in workmen's clubs. You know very well that I act.'

But Denissov was plainly glad that Astafiev had lacked foresight: 'Since you've got no document you'll have to go, Comrade Astafiev.'

'But I don't get home before night.'

'That's nothing to do with me. If you don't go I shall be obliged to report it, and you'll be taken by force, and not brought back either. It will only make things worse for you. The bourgeois are getting a rough time of it nowadays, Comrade Astafiev. Please be there at three o'clock without fail. Here's your slip from the House Committee. You'll get it signed and bring it back to me. We'll let you have a spade. I'm very sorry, Comrade Astafiev, but everyone would be trying to get out of the job if we weren't firm about it.'

Astafiev knew that he could evade it if he wished: Denissov was not above taking a bribe. But, thinking it over, he decided to let the matter alone: 'I ought to have this experience as well. And one must admit that in principle it's fair.'

At three o'clock, the gates of the police station were still closed. At half-past a fairly big crowd had gathered before them – a strange collection of resigned-looking men and women, the majority of them without spades. Who these men and women were it was not easy to tell; but, though badly dressed, most of them looked as if they belonged to the bourgeoisie and to the intelligentsia. Two elderly men were wearing officers' coats, though these were worn-out, shapeless and dirty, with ordinary buttons. The majority of the people in the crowd were elderly.

The gates were unlocked at four o'clock and the people let in to have their House Committee slips collected and their names taken down. The officials grumbled that so few spades had been brought, and ordered a dozen or so to be given out. Four troopers were detailed to conduct the crowd of sixty.

Along the dismal streets, unlighted and unswept, the crowd advanced, keeping at first good order; then, towards the end, plodding on in straggling groups. It was impossible to get away. The cards to certify that they had presented themselves would not be given out before they reached their destination. To their questions about the nature of the work they were going to do, the sleepy troopers answered roughly that they didn't know themselves; their orders were to take them to a spot not far distant from the road, two versts away, and hand them over to another escort.

'Last night it was to clean the rails and sleepers of the Nikolaevsky railway; but tonight it's to a different place.'

One of the women, a lively bustling creature of the lower-middle class, judging from her speech, was eager to tell everyone that it was not the first time she was going to do work of that kind, and that it was of her own free will, since she had offered to go in the place of an acquaintance for almost nothing. In her opinion they were being led, not to mend and clear railway lines, but to bury 'stiffeys'. It was dirty but not heavy work, she told them. And the amount of bread one got for it was regal – sometimes a whole pound; and it was good bread too, of the kind given out to the soldiers.

What 'stiffeys' were Astafiev did not know.

The men and women were placed in a row on some wasteland and told to dig a great pit. Those who had no spades had to wait and take turns with the others.

What 'stiffeys' were Astafiev found out, or rather guessed himself: it was the dead that went by that gentle name. When questioned, the troopers replied that they would have to bury people who had died of typhus and other illnesses, and that the bodies would be brought not only from various hospitals but from the stations as well.

The spring soil was damp, and the work went rapidly, even though the people were unused to it. The pit was dug shallow, but as wide as possible. Among them were a few who acted as foremen, teaching and shouting directions to the others, not unwilling to display their experience and authority.

About six o'clock the first lorry arrived, crawled snorting across the pathless strip of land, and came right up to the pit. By this time the crowd had finished digging one pit and had started on another near it. In the dim light of the rainy dawn four workmen in overalls threw into the pit a dreadful load – 'stiffeys' clothed in a few rags, some actually stark naked.

Astafiev, who was standing near the lorry, felt the air growing every moment more difficult to breathe; it even seemed to him that the drizzle was no longer fresh and clean.

Two more lorries arrived later on, and Astafiev counted forty bodies in all. After each batch the crowd was ordered to throw in earth and to economize space. But the first pit was already full, and they were obliged to pile the earth above it in a barrow. The experienced exchanged opinions: 'Heavy rains would probably wash away the earth.'

The gravediggers looked on gloomily, frowning and turning away. The women stood it better than the men, and more whispering went on among them. Only the bustling little woman seemed as though used to the sight, and evinced neither horror nor disgust. Indeed, it was with a curiously lively interest that she went up to each lorry as it arrived, peering into it and getting in the workmen's way.

'Again from the hospitals or from the stations,' she explained to the others. 'And all undressed, every single one of them! The boots have all been removed, too; not a pair left, in spite of their having died of typhus.'

The last lorry remained stuck in the damp, trampled earth, some distance away from the pit. The two accompanying troopers, in helmets with red stars, edged with black piping, asked for volunteers to unload it, promising an extra pound of bread each:

'If no one offers, we shall have to pick ourselves.'

Astafiev glanced at the crowd and, seeing reluctant, gloomy faces, was the first to come forward. The little woman was already bustling round the lorry. Two others, the men in the refashioned officers' tunics, were called out by the troopers:

'You needn't mind; there aren't any contagious bodies here. They're all of them quite clean.'

These last 'stiffys' were ghastlier than all the rest. Though without boots they were almost all of them dressed; and their clothes were caked all over with blood. Astafiev and his companions were ordered to pull them out by the legs and look sharp about it:

'Nothing to stop and look at! A dead man's a dead man, and that's all there is to it.'

Clenching his teeth, and trying not to see the faces, Astafiev touched the nearest corpse. Through the dirty linen he could not help feeling the slippery cold of death against his hands. He summoned all his masculine willpower to his aid, but his lips would not assume his customary smile of scepticism. He could not rid himself of the idea that the horrible corpse had been a man, and a well man, no longer, perhaps, than an hour ago. It seemed to him that he must know the man – that it was impossible that he should not know him, that here was a night-stricken victim of the Terror – an acquaintance, possibly a university friend or some officer he knew.

As though in reply, one of the troopers said to the other:

'Mostly bandits.'

Suddenly Astafiev noticed that the bustling little woman, who was working with him, was hurriedly fumbling round the torn collar of the corpse she was supporting by the shoulders. Feigning that she was unable to hold up the body, she lowered it on to the ground for a moment; and in her closed fist gleamed a gold cross and chain. Then, in the same bustling way as before, she seized the body by the shoulders, muttered something to herself, and looking anxiously into Astafiev's eyes smiled at him as if he were an accomplice.

'It was you yourself that offered, so now get on with it,' one of the troopers shouted at her, adding in a lower tone: 'What a woman! It's all the same to her; she might be shoving bread into the oven! Her favourite occupation, it looks like.'

Astafiev worked on like an automaton, without thought or sense of time, no longer feeling either horror or disgust. And as he dragged the corpse nearest to him off the lorry, he mechanically counted: 'One, two, three, four, five, six...' There were twenty corpses in all; and those underneath, crushed and soaked in the blood of their own as well as that of other bodies, were the ghastliest of all.

Astafiev strode from the pit to the lorry with firm step, head erect and looking straight before him. The troopers watched with curiosity the tall, clean-shaven man with the pale, stony face, who was better dressed than all the rest and wore a leather belt. Fortunately for his bustling helper, he drew their attention away from her thievish, fumbling hands.

The order was given to fill in the pit. Astafiev went to fetch his spade, but the moment he touched it he felt that his wrists and the edge of his sleeves were sticky, and saw that they were a brown-red. Dropping his spade, he went to one side and, squatting on his heels, wiped his hands on the ground and the young blades of grass with the same dull indifference.

The world was there around him; but it was empty, dead and meaningless.

Astafiev wiped his hands dry on his handkerchief, then threw it away, and, going past the lorrymen and the troopers, headed straight for the road. The soldiers fell silent and made way when he passed. The one nearest him ventured a 'Where're you off?' but did not repeat the question. The other said: 'Leave him alone. In any case they'll all be let oil in a moment.'

Astafiev came out on to the road and went on without looking back in the direction of the town. When he had gone about half a verst he felt tired, and sat down by the roadside against the wall of an abandoned cottage.

The lorry with the two soldiers snorted past him, and a little later on, with tired but hurrying footsteps, the bourgeois workers passed him, singly and in groups, no longer under escort. Many were munching as they went the bread that had been given out to them.

The bustling little woman was not among them. Astafiev saw her in the distance, lagging a long way behind. She was walking quite alone, her spade over her shoulder.

'I've left my spade behind,' Astafiev said to himself.

He got up and started back. When he was on a level with the woman she took fright and made as if to avoid him. But Astafiev went straight up to her, seized her with a strong hand by the collar of her half-masculine coat, and said:

'Hand over all you've got. Give up those crosses.'

The woman ducked and struggled to get free. In the eyes that tried to smile there was a mortal terror.

'What am I to give up?' she squealed in whispers. 'I haven't got anything.'

'Give them up,' Astafiev insisted. 'I'll kill you if you don't!'

The woman's shaking hands fumbled in her pockets and drew out a ring and four crosses, two of them on broken gold chains.

Without uttering a word, Astafiev searched her pockets himself, flicked out a handkerchief and found two more crosses. Tossing the ring back, and paying no heed to her hissed expostulations, he strode on to the place where they had worked. The spot was now deserted. Above the trampled earth rose long clay mounds, and along it gleamed the marks of tyres.

'My spade's not here. It must have been taken,' he grumbled.

Going right up to the second of the filled-in pits, he threw all the crosses upon it. Then, after a moment's thought, he climbed onto the heap and dug them deep into the soil with his heel, and sprinkled some fresh earth above them.

Being no believer, he made the sign of the cross neither over himself nor over the grave; took no farewell. Turning abruptly, he took the same road back and walked to Moscow.

– LIX –

I KNOW

The old ornithologist missed Vassya exceedingly. The latter had been gone over a week and was not yet back from his journey in quest of provisions:

'It's high time he were back, Tanyusha.'

'You love Vassya more than you do me, grandfather.'

'Well – hardly, though I really am very fond of the boy. Vassya is a good lad. He is so generous and warm-hearted.'

Poplavsky entered, wearing a thick knitted jersey under his old black frock-coat, and a pair of sodden galoshes, which he left outside the door.

'I should leave trails,' he said. 'My galoshes let water through; I must get some rubber solution. Do you suppose, professor, that anyone is likely to make off with my galoshes if I leave them behind the door? There are your lodgers.'

Poplavsky, who had talked of nothing but physics and chemistry formerly, was now left unmoved even by the name of Einstein, of whose book rumours had just reached Moscow. In the Writers' Bookshop, where the ornithologist used to call in on business, the shop which was temporarily Moscow's centre of culture, there was much talk behind the counters of the theory of relativity; and, as a curiosity, the mathematical formula of the end of the world had actually been fastened with drawing-pins to a desk. Poplavsky knew, of course, that the theory of light-bearing ether was exploded; but the young professor's thoughts were very far from all such matters. His thoughts – and there were many like him – were concentrated on treacle, saccharin and the insufficiency of fats; and on yet one other thing – the horror of the Terror which had just begun:

'Have you heard? Again forty people shot yesterday!'

I KNOW

In his distress the ornithologist shook his head and sought to turn the conversation away from the subject of death into different channels. The little house in Svitzev Vrazhek was warding off the world; it wanted to go on living the same peaceful life as before.

At eight o'clock, punctual as usual, Edward Lvovitch arrived. The composer had grown much thinner and had aged of late. The crooked pince-nez that were always slipping off his nose were ornamented with a bit of plain fine string instead of the worn black cord.

When there came another knock at the door (the bell was out of order, like everywhere else) Tanyusha started up more hurriedly than usual, ran to open the door, and returned rather livelier than before, followed by Astafiev.

Recently, Astafiev had taken to calling in frequently. He would stay a long time, sometimes longer than the professor himself – who was in the habit of going to his room early and reading in bed.

Tanyusha got ready the samovar with Astafiev's help. The professor's spoon clinked against his big cup. The old man liked to see his little flame of learning attract intelligent people round him with whom it was pleasant and cosy to sit and talk:

'Science must be carefully preserved. Generations go by, but the light of science remains. Science is our pride.'

Poplavsky was drinking his tea and munching black rusks in silence. He was hungry. It was Astafiev who kept up the conversation:

'What have we got to be proud of, professor? Our logic? Do you know, I sometimes think that science, especially natural science, has led us astray from the path of true thinking – concrete thinking in images. Primitive man thought pre-logically. Things for him were all linked together. That is why his world was so full of mystery and beauty. But we have thought out a *loi de participation*, and the world has lost its hues and fairy-tale quality. The loss, of course, is ours.'

Force of habit prompted Astafiev to stir his sugarless tea; and when Tanyusha passed him the sugar basin he said:

'No, thank you; I have some of my own.'

He took a little box from his waistcoat-pocket and dropped a tablet of saccharin into his tea.

'Why won't you take some? You know we really have got enough.'

But Astafiev obstinately pushed the sugar basin away from him:

'Don't let us break the good old-established rules of housekeeping, Tatyana Mihailovna.'

'One should be able to bring logical thinking into harmony with thinking in images,' the professor said.

'No, that can't be done, professor. There's no possible synthesis. Take, for instance, the case of Edward Lvovitch. Living as he does in a world of musical images, in a world of beauty, how could it be possible for him to accept the logic of the present day? Why, it would mean giving up art entirely!'

Edward Lvovitch fidgeted on his chair and murmured:

'I must confess that I don't quite forrow you. Music has its own raws, its own rogic one might even say; but it's not at arr the same rogic you are talking about. I find it very difficurt to exprain.'

The ornithologist nodded at him approvingly.

'I don't quite understand you either, Alexey Dmitritch,' he said. 'I can follow your reasoning, but it's you yourself I cannot anyhow make out. It's as if you found it easier than anyone else to accept and justify the present-day mode of existence. Here you are disavowing science and prepared to think like a savage, pre-logically. True, it all comes from your mind and not from your heart. But you know it's precisely this contemporary life of ours that rejects culture and logic, for there is certainly nothing logical about it.'

'On the contrary, professor. It's precisely this contemporary life of ours that is a purely mental structure, real mathematics, a scientific puzzle. Logic and technical knowledge are the new gods we have adopted in place of the old ones we have discarded. And if they are not capable of helping us in any way that is not their fault, and that does not in any way detract from their holiness.'

Tanyusha listened to Astafiev, and other words he had uttered in that very room came back to her mind. Astafiev was made up of contradictions. Why was he saying all that? Just for the sake of being paradoxical? And would he be saying something quite different on the morrow? Why did he do it? And yet he was sincere. Or was it just put on? Why was he like that... Because he was depressed?

She gave up thinking of the meaning of what Astafiev was saying, and listened only to the words. Scanning them, obviously speaking not because he wanted to, but for the sake of keeping up the conversation, he went on:

'The people I find most odious are airmen and chauffeurs – gas meters, electricity meters. They simply do not take into account that the noise of the propeller and the violent and unjustifiable din of the engine jar on one. They burst in upon one's life unbidden, and look upon themselves not only as messengers of truth but as the highest type of beings.'

'They are the men of the future.'

'Yes, they have that dreadful stigma. On the whole I prefer football players, to mention just one of many negative types of people. They at least are absolute idiots and ready to admit it. In airmen, on the other hand, and in some engineers one is conscious of intellect, even though that intellect does happen to be warped.'

Tanyusha's eyes travelled to her grandfather. The old man was listening to Astafiev with displeasure, putting no faith in his words and trying to repress a feeling of hostility. The cheap levity was out of place in a serious discussion.

'Why is he like that?' Tanyusha wondered sadly.

Edward Lvovitch did not play that evening, and left early. The ornithologist took Poplavsky into his own room to ask him his advice about certain books he wanted to sell. Astafiev was left with Tanyusha:

'Why do you talk like that, Alexey Dmitritch? You don't believe yourself all the things you say.'

'That's because I believe neither myself nor other people. It's really hardly worth talking at all. Although you exaggerate. I am right to a certain extent.' After a moment's silence he went on: 'Yes, stupid of me. I believe I offended the professor with my schoolboy tricks. I am so utterly weary of thinking and talking. I don't know myself what it is I want.'

'I thought you stronger.'

'I used to be. But not now.'

'Why is that?'

'Probably something has gone wrong with my calculations. I have an idea it's partly your fault.'

'Mine? Why mine?'

Astafiev, who was sitting in an armchair, stretched out his hand and laid it on the divan, near her. Glancing at the large hand, she involuntarily and scarce perceptibly edged away.

'You understand why, Tatyana Mihailovna. You ought to, at any rate. I don't conceal my feelings; I don't even attempt to, even though they may seem strange in me. But the worst of it is, I do not command the right words; I don't know how they are uttered… Doesn't it seem to you, by any chance, that I have fallen in love with you?'

That was not the first time he had declared his love. The first time had been on that occasion by the gate. And this was just as cold.

'It doesn't,' she answered slowly. 'You probably find me attractive and you want to imagine that you are in love. But what you feel bears no resemblance to love.'

Astafiev smiled unpleasantly:

'And what do you know of love, Tanya?'

No one ever called her Tanya, and she disliked that diminutive. Why did he do it?

She raised her eyes and looked him full in the face:

'I? I know!'

She said it quite simply. And Astafiev felt that it was true: she did know. She knew far more than he who had seen and loved and known so much in life.

'I do know,' Tanyusha repeated. 'And so I am able to reassure you. You don't really love me. You probably don't love anyone. You cannot love. It's not in you.'

'And you, Tanya?'

'I'm different. I can and want to. Only there's no one to love. I might perhaps have loved you. I could have – before. But being with you is so cold, so dreadfully cold. Before, it occasionally seemed nice. But only for a few minutes at a time. Because, you know, you aren't always like that.'

'That's pretty much what I gathered,' said Astafiev.

He slowly withdrew his hand from the divan. His world shrank and grew dismal. He remained silent, miserably unhappy.

Simply and gravely, as though to herself, Tanyusha went on:

'At one time I thought I did love you. I looked up to you. Now I don't think I do love you. And once you stop to think about it, it's not love, is it? Now if without wondering about it at all...' Astafiev was silent. She heard steps outside the door: grandfather and Poplavsky would enter in a moment. And raising her voice, she said: 'On what day is our concert in the Basmany district, Alexey Dmitritch? On Wednesday or Thursday?'

'On Thursday,' Astafiev answered in a firm voice.

When the ornithologist entered, Astafiev rose and took leave. As Tanyusha undressed to go to bed that evening she thought of many things: of grandfather's supply of sugar which was running short, of her free day on Wednesday, and of how poorly Edward Lvovitch was looking. Then she thought about Vassya, who was due back from the country. She thought, too, about Astafiev. He was right. Logic kills beauty and mystery. Then looking into the glass and seeing herself in white, her arms bare, her fair hair down in a plait and her eyes tired, loving no one except grandfather, she fell upon her bed and buried her face in the pillow so that dear grandfather should not hear if she should for some reason or other, suddenly burst into tears.

– LX –

THE MAN IN THE YELLOW GAITERS

Coming up on a level with Astafiev, the man in the yellow gaiters shot a glance at his face, paused for a second, then strode on faster and turned down the first side-street.

Something about his eyes and gait struck Astafiev as familiar, though such faces and such an assortment of clothes, half army, half civilian, were common enough in those days.

When he reached home Astafiev busied himself with his housework. There was the stove to clean, the little flat stove with the corrugated iron bottom which gave out such a good heat and which was so economical of fuel; then the iron funnel which let the smoke out into the street through a hole in one of the upper panes of his window needed examining, and old condensed milk tins had to be hung up under the joints[1] in the funnel; and there was the winter in general to prepare for. Up to the present there was no firewood to be had, but some would undoubtedly turn up from somewhere or other. If the worst came to the worst he could always fall back on his neighbour, Zavalishin. A scoundrel of course and a tchekist – but still...

There came a knock at the front door. With sooty fingers Astafiev took off the door-chain and the hook, and turned the key. This complicated system was due to Zavalishin's caution. The man had grown quite a coward of late. Was it that he was nervous for his stores of food and his bottles?

'Comrade Astafiev?'

---

[1] To catch the sooty drops that dripped from the horizontal part of the funnel.

'The same,' replied Astafiev.

On the threshold before him stood the man in the yellow gaiters.

'May I have a word with you... just for a moment?'

'Of course; but... might I ask... but you are... who are you?'

'Let's go in first, Alexey Dmitritch,' said his visitor in an undertone.

'Well, how are you? Which way? In here?'

'In here, in here.'

After showing his visitor in, but allowing himself not even time to shake hands, Astafiev went out into the passage and up to Zavalishin's door. He listened for a moment, gave a little knock, and receiving no answer pushed the door slightly open. Zavalishin was not at home. Astafiev nodded:

'Well, that's a bit of luck, anyhow! All the same – you never know.'

His visitor, who had not taken off his things, was still standing, patiently waiting:

'Are you sure you know who I am?'

'I recognized you, of course, though you are an amazingly good actor. You can speak freely here; we are alone in the flat and the door is on the chain. What are those curious gaiters you are wearing? You know they do hit the eye dreadfully.'

'That's why I put them on – so that people shall look at my gaiters and not at my face. The more conspicuous one is, the less.'

'And that's how you wander through the streets of Moscow? Almost without any make-up? You'll get caught... my dear friend.'

Even though he was alone with him, Astafiev could not bring himself to call his visitor by name.

'Of course I'll get caught – sooner or later. Better later. Listen, Alexey Dmitritch, you're an outspoken man, tell me straight out: can you give me a night's shelter?'

'Very urgent?'

'Very.'

'Well, then, I can. I ask because my flat is not a particularly suitable place. I'm the only bourgeois left in the whole building, and there's a man living in the flat who is something in the nature of a tchekist, though principally a drunkard. Still, he's seldom at home – not even every night. Does that suit you?'

'Not in the least; but if you'll let me, I'll stay, as I have no alternative. Your tchekist had better not see me.'

'I won't let him in. He doesn't seem an inquisitive sort, and, as I say, he's a confirmed drunkard. He is my disciple in dirty work. He goes as far as to affirm that it was I who was responsible for his first step in that direction.'

'Is there any likelihood of a search? There are general perquisitions going on everywhere nowadays. Whole houses are searched.'

'Hardly likely. We have workmen's families living in the building; though of course everything is possible.'

'Of course. Well, then, I may stay?'

'Yes. Take off your things. The food I have isn't up to much, but we'll have something to eat all the same.'

'Yes; that, too, is urgent.'

They put out what food they had in silence. The man in the yellow gaiters had a bit of bacon and Astafiev some groats. Their supper was a highly successful one.

'When your tchekist comes home we had better not talk at all. I'll turn in, I'm dreadfully sleepy.'

'There's no need to keep silent. I do have people in occasionally. By the way, did you happen to meet anyone in the yard?'

'One fellow with a curled-up moustache and the expression of a shop assistant.'

'With a curled-up moustache? That must be Denissov, our chairman. That's unfortunate. But not a calamity, for how is he to know who you are?'

'Well, we'll hope for the best. I say, Astafiev, I'm most grateful to you. You're a sportsman, and that's really why I came to you. Didn't you recognize me in the street?'

'I didn't pay any attention. I saw, of course, that you had outstripped me.'

'I didn't want to come in at the same time as you. I walked down the street three times, waiting for you to turn up.'

'Why?'

'On the off-chance.'

'And are you in luck on the whole?'

'Not for the moment. I'm in a pretty bad way. But I think I shall be successful in a couple of days.'

Astafiev smiled:

'When you say 'successful', that means thunder and lightning all over Moscow, if not all over Russia. Well, that's your affair; I'm not inquisitive.'

They chatted for half-an-hour over their meal, recalling their meetings in Russia and abroad, and mutual friends at the time of the first revolution,[2] most of whom were in exile or dead.

'In burying yourself in science, Astafiev, have you broken entirely with the past?'

'Yes; one cannot remain a fighter when one no longer believes in anything.'

The eyes of the man in the yellow gaiters seemed to sink deeper under his brows.

'Well, but few of us have real faith,' he said slowly, 'and they, mostly, are the fools and the simpletons. That's not the point, Astafiev. One must have something to live and die for. One cannot just go on dragging out a meaningless existence, with nothing but the illusion of words to comfort one. If one has to go under, one may as well... But, I say, I do so want to go to sleep. Where are you going to put me? I shall not undress anyhow.'

At dawn Astafiev, who was asleep in an armchair, against which he had placed two more chairs – he had given his bed to his visitor – was wakened by the tread of feet resounding on the asphalt of the yard. He rose, went up to the window and saw that the flat opposite was lit up brightly. Down below he could discern vague forms of soldiers with rifles tramping about. It might be a search. Against one of the windows there appeared for an instant a shadow in a forage-cap, then another, belted. Yes – there was no doubt about it: it was a search.

'It really does look as if his luck is against him,' thought Astafiev, and smiled, though not without a tremor, his usual smile. 'We shall both have to answer for it. Well, but perhaps it's just a search in that particular flat.'

Figures continued to appear against the bright patch of the window and disappear again. Astafiev watched it for some time; then, after a smoke, tried to force himself to remain in his armchair. But the window drew him irresistibly. Half-an-hour later the windows of the flat above lit up, and Astafiev felt himself going cold:

'Then it really is a search. That, then, is the end.'

It was impossible to leave the flat without crossing the little yard. Besides, as far as he could make out without opening the window, sentinels were standing at all the main entrances, not only to the flats but to the dvornik's quarters as well.

---

[2] The abortive attempt of 1905.

'Wake him? Or let him sleep on?'

There seemed somehow no point in wakening him. What would be the good of both of them being nervous? In any case it was impossible to leave the flat. Perhaps the search wouldn't get as far as them.

Quietly he pushed the armchair up to the window and watched the fourth, the top, floor lighting up, his eyes immovably fixed on the windows.

'There are no tenants on the bottom floor,' he recollected, 'that's why it's dark there. They probably went in, and finding nothing to search, left again at once. Now they'll go to another entrance. I wonder which?'

The search in the top flat was a drawn-out affair. It was already light, and the shadows in the yard became flesh and blood in khaki. The soldiers were sitting about on the steps of the entrances and even on the asphalt, clearly worn out with fatigue.

'They're searching a very long time. Means they're not after people, but stores. The usual general perquisition. But of course they'll take along the man who's not down in the books, together with the tenant who gave him shelter. I wonder if he's got any papers? But of course, once caught, it will take them no time to find out who he is. A dainty morsel for the Tcheka!'

There were heavy footfalls in the yard, and a group of men in leather jackets emerged from the entrance. There was one terrible moment, and Astafiev's heart beat loudly. Then, after hanging about in the yard for a while, the group moved in the direction of another doorway, the one opposite Astafiev's window.

A fresh delay; the last, this time. Windows lit up on two storeys at once; then on the third floor, and almost simultaneously on the fourth as well. The searchers had evidently divided up into two parties, and the work was going on more rapidly. The soldiers in the yard were dozing as they sat, with their rifles across their knees.

Astafiev no longer counted the minutes and half-hours. His nervous tension was succeeded by a mortal weariness.

'In any case, there's nothing for it but to wait.'

He smoked with closed eyes, raising his eyelids only at the noise of steps in the yard or when loud snatches of the soldiers' conversation reached him. The morning light was already merging into the patches of the lighted windows. There were rosy tints in the sky. Astafiev's cigarette came to an end and he fell into a light slumber.

Three hours at least had passed since the first alarm. Besides – what did it matter?

Then again, the stamping of feet in the yard made him start up and go to the window. From behind the curtains he could see the same group of people standing in the middle of the little yard. The soldiers who had been drowsing before had joined it. Although it was impossible to make out what they were talking about, Astafiev gathered that they were holding a council. At length the group moved in the direction of his entrance, while a certain number of soldiers detached themselves from it and walked away with gestures of discontent.

Then, on a sudden, heavy footsteps were clattering on the stairs.

'About time to wake him!'

He entered the second room, littered with books, in which his visitor was sleeping:

'I say, get up!'

He tried pulling at his shoulder, but his visitor was sleeping soundly. For all reply he uttered a few inarticulate sounds.

'After all – why?' Astafiev said to himself. 'In any case, there's no escape from here. I'll wake him when they begin to knock. Meanwhile, they're only on the bottom floor, and we're on the third.'

He was perfectly calm now. But it was a tragic calm. He was the philosopher again. He glanced down at the pale, puffy face of the sleeping man in the yellow gaiters, and his twisted smile hovered over his lips. Then, turning away, he saw in the dim light the reflection of his own face in the glass. He set his hair in order, lit another cigarette and went out into the hall.

He had not long to wait. Again there came the clatter of heels and the loud talk of men coming up the stairs.

When the knock came, Astafiev did not even start. He took a long pull at his cigarette, but did not stir from his place by the door. Behind it there was a hum of voices, and he had no difficulty in distinguishing the words:

'One can't go on like this, comrade! The men are dead-beat and it's already light.'

'All right. This is the last, then we'll go.'

Again a knock, and another voice:

'They're sleeping like logs! There's no waking them!'

'They'll start breaking in the door in a moment,' thought Astafiev. 'I ought to wake him.'

Behind the door several voices broke out louder than before: 'Enough, comrade! We must put it off to another time. Going on like this... Two nights running. How can you? We, too, are human beings.'

Throwing away his cigarette, Astafiev put his ear to the door. The men were getting more vociferous in their murmurings. Finally a sharp, shrill voice exclaimed in exasperation:

'Well, all right then. Right about turn! Couldn't even stick it to the end of one block! You might be a lot of women, the way you've crumpled up. There won't be anything to do here tomorrow. Everything will be in order.'

'We're not made of iron! You try working like us,' came a reply.

But already the heavy heels were jingling downstairs. Then, just as Astafiev was moving away, he was almost deafened by another thump of a fist on the door:

'Hey, here's a goodbye to you! Sleeping like that, you blasted bourgeois!'

Taking out another cigarette with shaking fingers from the packet, Astafiev listened to the last footsteps dying away on the staircase. Slowly he turned, and as he did so came face-to-face with the man in the yellow gaiters:

'An unpleasant surprise, it appears, Alexey Dmitritch?'

Astafiev blew a ring of smoke:

'On the contrary, a real pleasure. Have you had a good sleep?'

'Excellent! You, too, seem to be quite a good actor.'

'Such is my present profession. I'm inclined to think they have gone away for good now.'

'Let's hope so,' the man in the yellow gaiters replied in the same tone. 'By the way, I forgot to warn you yesterday that I shouldn't give myself up alive. There's no point in it.'

'I quite understand,' said Astafiev. 'And I can see that for myself. But for the moment you can put back that toy of yours.'

He laughed, and his laughter was both heartfelt and gay:

'Well, you really are in luck's way! Now what do you say to a cup of carrot-coffee? No good leaving the place yet. Can you light a primus?'

– LXI –

THE TRUSTY KNIGHT

When Tanyusha opened the door she beheld a stranger carrying two large sacks strapped over his shoulder. The man was wearing a semi-army uniform and pince-nez, and looked the type of intellectual who is living the simple life.

'Well,' he said, 'I don't think there can be any doubt about it. You are Tatyana Mihailovna, aren't you?'

'I am.'

'Here are some provisions: flour, groats and so on. This is the first lot. The rest I'll bring along presently. It's too heavy all at once. I was told to deliver it into your own hands.'

'But who sent it?'

'I was told to say, "from your trusty knight."'

Tanyusha was overjoyed; then anxious:

'From Vassya? But where is Vassya? Hasn't he arrived?'

'He's arrived all right. We arrived together, but not as we should have liked. He's ill; and, in my opinion, seriously ill. He caught something or other on the way.'

Dear Vassya was ill – her best friend and trusty knight!

Tanyusha asked his fellow-wayfarer in. Ridding himself of the sacks, the visitor introduced himself as Protassov, Pyotr Pavlovitch, adding:

'I used to be an engineer, but now I spend most of my time bartering.'

He told her how Vassya had borne up till the last moment, collapsing finally on their arrival at the Moscow terminus, where he was not only unable to carry the sacks as far as the cab, but scarcely even able to drag himself along; how he, Protassov, had taken him home, made him undress and wash as best he could, and had taken away his clothes to steam and clean them:

'I have a first-rate stove in my flat and a boiler. I have some firewood too. Everything has been adapted to present needs. My style of living is quite unproletarian.'

'Where is Vassya now?'

'At home. He asked me to bring along the sacks. I have inspected them, of course, to see that they are free from any sort of dirt.'

'You think it's typhus?'

'I'm afraid so, to tell you the truth. He ought to be seen by a doctor. I'm depending on you, Tatyana Mihailovna – that is, if you're not afraid of contagion. One doesn't catch it from the air of course, but all the same...'

The engineer looked at Tanyusha with a confident smile: a girl like that wasn't likely to be afraid!

'Why, of course, I'll go at once! I know a doctor quite near, in the Arbat. I'll take him to Vassya. It's the doctor who has always looked after grandfather.'

'Splendid! You'll be as quick as you can, won't you? I'll be getting along home.'

Tanyusha made Vassya's fellow-wayfarer promise to be sure to call in soon – tomorrow evening – and thanked him for bringing the sacks.

'I'll bring along what's left tomorrow.'

'You must be very tired after the journey.'

'Not very. I'm as strong as a horse and used to it. I never get worn-out.'

They talked like old acquaintances. Protassov was about thirty-five. He badly needed a shave and was somewhat shabby, although he had evidently found time to change his clothes. There was a good deal of manliness and kindliness in his face. He talked to Tanyusha as to a junior, but with a certain masculine courtesy:

'I recognized you as soon as I saw you.'

'How?'

'He said to me: 'Go there and knock, and it will probably be Tanyusha herself – Tatyana Mihailovna – who will come to the door."

'In that case it wasn't so difficult to recognize me.'

'No; but he added: 'She's a wonderful girl; quite out of the ordinary.' So you see that was how I was able to recognize you at once.'

Tanyusha was embarrassed:

'Oh, but Vassya... he's such a funny person!'

Nevertheless, pronounced so simply, so freely, with a smile so open, these words from a stranger were pleasant to hear: 'You must have made friends with him on the way.'

'Yes. He's a charming kid, a real dear. A great idealist, which is a good thing.'

'Vassya's such a good comrade. You, too, are probably an excellent comrade. It was you who helped him on the way.'

'It wasn't difficult for me,' the engineer said simply. 'I'm as strong as a horse and used to anything.'

They parted company in the Arbat, outside the house in which the doctor lived. Tanyusha enjoined him to come the next day without fail, directly after dinner.

'Grandfather will be so pleased to see you. He's very fond of Vassya and has been lonely without him. You will tell him about your journey.'

When Tanyusha was alone once more she said to herself:

'What a nice man! Extraordinarily nice! Such a gentle smile, and so tactful and cheery – just as if nothing had happened. And how good he's been to Vassya.'

The engineer strode along home, rubbing his shoulders, that were sore and stiff after the weight of the heavy sacks, and thinking his own masculine, practical thoughts. But a smile hovered about his lips.

* * *

Vassya Boltanovsky was lying in bed.

The outlines of his room, every inch of which he knew so well, were now all blurred: the corners had lost their sharpness and were filled with a quivering mist; the window was throbbing, and scorching his eyes with its excessive light; and the engraving that hung on the wall facing his bed was swimming in space.

His pillow was peculiarly uncomfortable and restless; his head could not settle comfortably upon it. It felt like a stone against the nape of his neck, lay all awry, suddenly stood up on end and tickled him with one corner, crept over his head, impeding his breathing, got under his shoulder and raised his entire body up high. The blanket was too hot, yet did not warm his feet; and though he felt choked by the heat and stuffiness, his feet groped for the end of the blanket to wrap themselves up tighter. There was, in the room, a din reminiscent of the thumping of train wheels, and every beat reverberated in his temples and in his left side. He wanted to drink, but the water bottle, which Protassov had placed on the bed-table, rolled far out of reach and taunted him from afar, darting away from his outstretched hand.

Even when Vassya closed his eyes, his chest would soar up to the ceiling and sink down again, rocking gently as upon waves, dazing him. This prevented him from going to sleep; this, and faces, unfamiliar faces, that thronged round the seat on which he was trying to settle himself with his sacks, although the seat was far too narrow and too short for him. It was curious that the train was continually jolting over points, even though he distinctly remembered having already got to the Moscow station and having had time to undress. Now he was trying in vain to make his way through the crowd of bagmen, searching for the sack with the groats, which was exceptionally valuable, as it was in exchange for that sackful that he had parted with the professor's boots. The ornithologist was angry and stamping his foot; Vassya had never seen him do that. It appeared that the boots were on Vassya's own feet and were making them dreadfully cold. It was impossible to take them off, nor was there time; there might not be a single free place in the carriage, and then Protassov would go off alone.

'It's a good thing I asked him to see that Tanyusha gets the bags,' he thought, 'otherwise I'd have to wait till somebody turned up and telephoned. If it is typhus, I believe I shall have to have my head shaved.'

These words suddenly reached Vassya's ears, and the truth dawned on him:

'I'm raving. It was I myself speaking just now. That means I must be jolly ill.'

Opening his eyes, Vassya noticed that the window had grown darker. There was the same din in the room as before, though it might be from a car in the street. Raising himself with an effort, he reached for the water-bottle and drank from it greedily, his teeth chattering against the rim.

The water gave him a sharp sensation of cold, just as though ice had been laid on his chest and stomach. His feet, on the other hand, felt warmer and his head was clearer. The bottom of the bottle knocked violently against the wooden bed-table and Vassya's head fell back on the pillow.

'Yes, I'm ill, really ill. I need someone to see to me.'

Someone could only be Tanyusha. Neighbours, landlady, acquaintances – none of them could help. And they would all be nervous.

The cold made Vassya feverishly draw the blanket closer round him. Again there was that knocking in his temples, and his head was aching agonizingly. And again the hard, turbulent pillow began its restless dance.

Vassya found it very pleasant when a cold hand touched his forehead and an unknown masculine voice pronounced:

'Of course – a high temperature. There can be no doubt about it.

He ought to go into hospital. Only there is nowhere for him to go these days. The hospitals are all full.'

The words did not penetrate into Vassya's consciousness; but another familiar voice, that could be nobody's but Tanyusha's, soothed him at once and filled him with joy:

'Well, what's to be done, doctor? Can't he be left here at home?'

'He'll have to be, of course. But who is going to look after him?'

'I could.'

Of course it was her voice. Vassya lay very still, just as though he had been caressed. And all at once those sensations from the hard pillow left him; his body felt warmer and the ache in his head passed away. But he had no wish to open his eyes; he wanted the dream to go on.

'Well, but how are you going to do it? He needs a trained nurse. Typhus is no joke.'

'I'd look after him by day and we will find a night nurse somehow.'

'The nurse I could find. Only what about paying her?... You could pay her in provisions, with flour. I've got someone in my mind – an experienced nurse who has worked in a hospital and whose husband was a doctor. Only he's got to be cleansed. And the whole room has got to be cleaned. He's just back from a journey, did you say?'

'Only arrived this morning.'

'Quite. He needs a great deal of care. Do you mean to stay on here for the moment?'

'Yes. Tell me, doctor, what ought to be done.'

'What ought to be done... Well, I shall have to get what there is to get myself. The chemists have nothing nowadays, and they don't let private people have anything either. You'll have to stay two or three hours with him alone.'

'I'll stay as long as necessary.'

Vassya heard the sound of voices, and knew that the talk was about him and that it was Tanyusha speaking. He knew, too, that he was ill and happy. More he did not need to hear or understand.

'Are you in pain, Vassya?'

He opened his eyes for a moment, saw the dear familiar form, smiled, and sunk once more into the rest and non-existence he had so longed for. The trusty knight was happy. Vassya slept. If it had not been for the flushed, hot face, he might have been taken for a healthy, happy person, peacefully sleeping.

Thus passed a minute or an hour or eternity – till the hard, turbulent pillow broke in again upon his sleep. But now there was a strong hand curbing and calming its violence. And a voice was murmuring: 'Vassya! My poor knight; poor, poor Vassya!'

– LXII –

CONVERSATIONS

The socialist revolutionary was searched for high and low. There was no doubt about the old fighter being in Moscow. It was generally known that he not only frequented acquaintances, but actually went so far as to give a full report about events in the south at a meeting of a group of socialists. And at that meeting the old terrorist was wearing yellow gaiters.

An individual with an Armenian type of face, in a round lamb's-wool cap and a bright waistcoat under his unbuttoned coat, was quietly talking to a dark girl beside the parapet of the Moscow River.

'I know all that, of course; that's why I've turned Armenian. They are real prattlers, those people. And do you know where my gaiters are? Sold them in the Smolensky marketplace myself. I badly needed money – and gaiters are valuable goods.'

When they parted, the Armenian gave the girl's little hand a squeeze:

'Well, dear – farewell. Or perhaps – goodbye. Miracles do happen. Come, let's kiss. Now go, and don't look back.'

She was moving away when he called her back:

'One moment, dear friend. You remember the address, don't you, in case anything goes wrong or turns out differently? You'll leave the note there.'

'Yes; I haven't forgotten anything.'

'You don't believe in God? Nor do I. But all the same I'll pray for you in my own way – for you and our success!'

When she disappeared behind the bend the Armenian tugged his cap over his head, buttoned up his coat and started off in the direction of the district that lay beyond the Moscow River.

* * *

Like lightning the rumour of the attempt on the great man's life[1] spread over Moscow; like lightning flashed out dread and hope. All were certain that the man in the yellow gaiters had had a hand in it, and all were equally sure that many people who had not the slightest connection with the plot would have to answer for it.

Stories were told of how soldiers, who had taken aim at the breast of a thin little Jewish girl in an outhouse, fired an uncertain volley; how one of them had had a fit of hysteria, and how a former workman who worked at the Lubyanka Tcheka – a confirmed drunkard and qualmless executioner – shot the wounded girl dead, with his Colt.

There were many such rumours – fantastic, alarming, true and absurd; and, cowering and shrinking, Moscow awaited the morrow with terror.

It had not long to wait.

* * *

The greengrocer, the crony of Nicolai the ex-dvornik,[2] was getting on in the world. To bring a whole cartful of vegetables, as he had done before, from the kitchen gardens round Moscow straight to the Arbatskaya marketplace was, of course, out of the question. Business had now to be done on the quiet, and a sharp lookout kept; though, as a matter of fact, carrots, cabbages and turnips weren't things that could be requisitioned and dumped into a basement and sold, or rationed out little by little in the name of the country. It all needed special handling and no delays. That was why the kitchen-garden business was flourishing on the outskirts. Only it was difficult to keep guard over the stuff; people were so bold these days.

The greengrocer gave Nicolai a full account of all this in the dvornik's room of the little house in Sivtzev Vrazhek.

Nicolai assented:

'Regular thieves, the people are nowadays! Now take a dog – even a dog knows what it may do and what it mustn't. But human beings go nosing round, ready to make off with anything as soon as your back's turned. They'll even pinch things under your very nose.'

They then turned to politics and abused the shag:

---

[1] Dora Kaplan's assassination attempt on Lenin's life.
[2] The dvornik system had been abolished.

'It might be sawdust.'
'Well, that's what it is.'
'No real taste in it, there isn't.'
Their pipes had made the air thick and heavy in the dvornik's room, and had lent the place an air of cosiness.

The greengrocer, Fyodor Ignatyitch, who was well versed in all sorts of matters, expounded the events of the day: 'They say they've again been shooting I don't know how many people. Probably some were shot because they deserved it – thieves, brigands, raiders. But lots of folks were shot for nothing at all, just to scare the others.'

'Nobody ought to be killed,' Nicolai said severely. 'Judge if there's something to judge, let some off and send some to penal servitude to get better – but don't kill.'

'Well, that's what I say – if it's what they've deserved. But in this case they took a lot of people, kept them for ages and then did for them as a warning to others. One of them, for instance, was an old chap. What was that for? And another one was a lad. There wasn't no reason for it. The same for all. And a boy, you know, can grow into a man what's better than all the rest.'

'To kill a youngster is worse than anything else. One can't forgive a man for that.'

'That's what I say. Now one lady I used to supply with cabbage had her kid taken and done for; the lad wasn't seventeen. But they'd made out their lists and took him. And it seems he wasn't guilty of nothing at all.'

'Just like beasts!' Nicolai said sternly.

'Beasts what do no good neither.'

'What good comes of killing? He who lives by the sword shall die by the sword.'

'They can't even organize anything. Now say I want something: is there anywhere where it can be got, I ask you? And there didn't used to be no shortage of goods in Moscow!'

'They've grabbed the lot.'

'That's what I say. Stealing isn't so difficult, but you try coming by goods honestly! You've got to know what you're about. Just look at the men at the head of things! There's your soldier chap, Dunyasha's brother, Andryusha, the deserter.'

'Andryusha's gone.'

'Got the sack?'

'No; just did a bunk. They came and asked for him. He got caught out over something or other; been putting things into his own pocket, you bet. He was well off, far better off than the masters. The old gentleman hasn't got nothing at all, and his granddaughter eats salted herrings. But Andryusha and Dunyasha always had sweets with their tea. They used to invite me too, sometimes. "We've got as much as ever we like of this sort of thing," he used to say, "and meat too, every day."'

'So he's made off, has he?'

'That's right; didn't even tell Dunyasha. Probably gone back to his own people in the village. Or perhaps he's got copped – we don't know. All we know is that the Commandant has disappeared; and he was at the head of things, you know.'

'I know. Some of them do get caught. Means he didn't give satisfaction in something or other.'

Nicolai told the greengrocer about his plans. It wasn't much he needed, but you couldn't keep alive on just a quarter of a pound of bread a day. The young lady, Tatyana Mihailovna, gave away her salted herrings, saying she'd got plenty. But where was she to get plenty from? Dunyasha helped too. But now that Andrey had run away she had nothing to eat either. She had asked the young lady to take her back as a maid. But how could they feed her, and what was the good of having a maid when they had only two rooms? So now she too wanted to go back to the village. Andrey used to give her money, so she had a little put by; but then money had grown so cheap. It might perhaps be enough for the journey. Of course she didn't come from far, only from the Tula government. But he had a long way to go. And of course they didn't take people for nothing.

'That is a problem!'

Whereupon they agreed that it was indeed a problem, and that there was no way out that they could think of. The greengrocer rose to go home, and Nicolai accompanied him out of the dvornik's room to have a little breath of fresh air:

'The frosts will be here soon; you see if they aren't.'

'They'll come all right. They don't have to wait. Can't stop them with any regulations.'

They took leave of one another at the gate. Giving the pavement a sweep with his battered broom, Nicolai looked up at the sky, set right the broom by striking the end a couple of times against the paving-stones, and went in, pondering:

'These are bad times, but those were bad times too. They used to hang and flog before, and no good came of it. There's not much to choose between them.'

And although he loved the warmth and the smell of tobacco, he opened the door of his dvornik's room for a while:

'If one was to go to bed with the smoke of this present-day shag about, the fumes would go to one's head, and no doubt about it. Whatever do they make it from! Regular swindling I call it!'

– LXIII –

SISTER ALYONUSHKA

A doctor and a Sister of Mercy were standing at Vassya's bedside. The doctor, Kuporrossov, was an elderly man, with a brusque manner and a warm heart. He was the only doctor the ornithologist would have anything to do with.

'That's a doctor one can trust,' the professor would say. 'He realizes that medicine isn't a science like any other. A kind word is what helps a patient most. He's a good fellow, Kuporrossov. By the way, how on earth did he get such a name?[1] Yes, he's a level-headed fellow, who can really be relied on.'

Kuporrossov had always attended Aglaya Dmitrevna and the professor; Tanyusha, too, from the time when she had had scarlet fever. He never appeared in Sivtzev Vrazhek unless called in; besides, he was kept very busy by his practice, which was for the most part among people of limited means.

It was the doctor himself who had brought the Sister of Mercy to Vassya's bedside. Elena Ivanovna was very young, but already a widow. Her husband, a doctor, had died of typhus. Dr. Kuporrossov had been very fond of his young colleague, and after his death had taken his widow under his protection. He had found her work and trained her in the difficult art of nursing, treating her like a daughter, and calling her affectionately 'Alyonushka'. He could be very exacting and severe, however, where the nursing of a serious case was concerned.

'It's a matter of life and death here, Alyonushka. The utmost care

---

[1] Kuporrossov is the Russian for vitriol.

SISTER ALYONUSHKA

must be taken of him. Above all, fresh air and cleanliness; drugs won't help. The lad is young, so we've got to pull him through.'

Alyonushka – Elena Ivanovna – was a short, plump little woman, bursting with health and vigour, with a little uptilted nose and great blue eyes, not in the least beautiful, but exceedingly pretty. She had been called 'Puff' at school, and the other children had been in the habit of pinching her during lessons. She had always squealed, for what she dreaded above all was being tickled.

But it was when Alyonushka laughed that she was the most amusing. The laughter was uncontrollable, beginning in a clear, bell-like way, and breaking off towards the end on a strange bass snort, something like the grunting of a little pig. It never failed to delight her friends; but the moment she emitted the grunt, Alyonushka would be overcome with confusion and grow serious.

This little foible had been a source of utter misery to her, but she had been quite unable to cure herself of it.

Later on, however, when her fiancé a young doctor, confessed to having been bowled over by that very laugh of hers, she decided that it was not such a misfortune after all. After their marriage her husband, in bursts of tenderness, used to call her his darling little grunter.

There was every likelihood of Alyonushka being happy with the doctor; but their married life had been all too brief – no longer than six months. He had been sent to a typhus hospital at the front, and very soon afterwards Alyonushka had received a letter from him, in which he complained of not being well. That letter was his last.

It was a long time before the infectious laugh was heard again. Instead of remaining in her married woman's station, Alyonushka chose to become Dr. Kuporrossov's daughter and pupil. And he it was who trained her to become a nurse.

'I'm off to see another case now, Alyonushka. I'll be home at seven. If anything goes wrong let me know at once. It would be better to send someone than to come yourself. Let him drink as much as he wants to, and change the vinegar compress as soon as it gets hot. The rest as usual. You know all that has to be done by now.'

'Yes, doctor.'

'Well, that's all right then. I'm trusting to your nursing. Don't let anyone in, except that young girl and his friend, the one who has already been. They're very nice people. They'll give you a hand, and, if necessary, relieve you.'

'All right, doctor. Who is she?'

'The young girl? She's the granddaughter of a certain professor, an old patient of mine. She's called Tanyusha. I've forgotten her other name. She's an admirable girl – plays well, I believe, or something.'

'Isn't she beautiful?'

'Eh? Beautiful?... I suppose so. I don't know.'

Dr. Kuporrossov was not a connoisseur of feminine beauty. It was possible that Alyonushka was a beauty, but, on the other hand, she might be a fright. It was for others to judge of such matters.

When Dr. Kuporrossov was gone, Alyonushka took stock of her surroundings, drew up the hard armchair closer to the bed, regretted the absence of cushions and took out of the basket she had brought a little yellow-backed volume, Knut Hamsun's *Victoria*. She had read the novel before, and had liked it so much that she had decided to read it again; besides, there was nothing else to read. When she had settled herself as comfortably as she could in the armchair, in such a way that she would be able to remain sitting thus for some considerable length of time, she turned to look with curiosity at the face of her sleeping patient.

Vassya was sleeping restlessly, his head continually tossing over the pillow. Alyonushka had to straighten his pillow and change the vinegar compress on his forehead. It was a long time since he had been shaved, and shadows lay on his hot, flushed face. But the cleft in his chin was visible, and that at once predisposed her in his favour:

'Poor thing, what a nice face he's got!'

Tanyusha and the engineer had done their best to make Vassya's room tidy. On the bed-table was spread one of his handkerchiefs, with the initial 'B' embroidered in one of the corners.

A lock of his hair, which was always in the way, lay matted and damp over the compress. Alyonushka drew it aside on to the pillow:

'He'll have to have his head shaved.'

Then she began Knut Hamsun's tender love story. Alyonushka understood love in exactly the same way as Knut Hamsun. Love is a restless thing; and the novel in no way suffered from her having to wrench herself away from it from time to time in order to rearrange the cloth on Vassya's forehead, or bring the slightly acid drink to his parched lips, or smile kindly at the patient, who was neither aware of her smiles nor able to appreciate them. For Vassya was rarely conscious.

An alarm clock stood on the bed-table and the hours drew out. The night would be a sleepless one; all Alyonushka could hope for was to drowse a little in her armchair. In the morning she would be relieved by that beautiful girl, the professor's granddaughter, or by the man who had come and gone away with her. Were they by any chance engaged? Or was she perhaps engaged to the patient?

And again Knut Hamsun went on telling of love. How marvellously he wrote about it!

When it grew dark she lit the reading-lamp, shaded it from her patient's eyes, took out of her basket a bit of ration bread, a little pot containing something edible, some salt wrapped up in paper, and an apple. She ate at Vassya's writing-table, resting Knut Hamsun against the inkstand and going on reading through her meal. When she finished she wiped her fingers on the paper, collected the crumbs, put the little pot with the remainder back into the basket, decided to eat the big, rosy-cheeked apple later on, while she was reading, and, before settling herself in the armchair, went up to the looking-glass to set straight her veil.

When Alyonushka looked at herself in the glass she would bend her head slightly, so that her little nose should not appear too tilted.

Half asleep, Vassya murmured:

'What's to be done? Whatever is to be done? Is it leaving at once?'

Then shouted:

'You might at least wait! How am I to manage like this!'

Alyonushka went up to him and changed the cloth on his forehead, wringing it out in her plump little hands. Just then Vassya opened his eyes and asked in astonishment:

'Who are you?'

'Lie still.'

'No, but who are you?'

'I'm a Sister of Mercy. Well, how do you feel? Any better?' Vassya closed his eyes for a moment, then said quite audibly: 'I do so want a drink.'

Alyonushka took the glass and helped him to drink; and Vassya again looked at her attentively, with bloodshot eyes.

'What is your name?' he asked.

'Elena Ivanovna. You shouldn't talk; the best thing for you is to try to go quietly off to sleep.'

Vassya smiled wanly and said:

'I'll try.'

SISTER ALYONUSHKA

He did go to sleep, and Alyonushka thought:
'What a nice smile he's got! Poor thing, what a wretched time he's having!'

Alarmed by her lodger's illness, the landlady came and knocked at the door. Alyonushka went out and came to a friendly understanding with her at once, calmed her fears about the infectiousness of typhus, and assured her that there was no danger as long as everything was kept very clean. They talked about necessary arrangements and came to an agreement about them. The landlady offered to boil water if it were needed. Vassya had been with her a long time and was her favourite lodger. Before she left, Alyonushka, too, had been given her meed of praise:

'How young you are, and your cheeks are just like milk and roses! Anyone would recover in your care. Why, you're just a girl. You don't mean to say you're married?'

'I'm a widow.'

That melted the landlady completely.

'If ever you have to go away for a bit I'll stay with him,' she volunteered. 'But how are you going to sleep?'

'Oh, that's all right. I'm used to sleeping in armchairs.'

Whereupon the landlady brought her a cushion to sit on, and a big soft pillow to make sleep in the armchair more comfortable.

'Thank goodness, it's warm in here. You won't freeze. I've got a supply of wood and keep my stove going all day, just the other side of the wall. That's why it's warm in this room, too. Everyone envies me, as a matter of fact.'

Late that evening, Dr. Kuporrossov called in for a moment. He felt Vassya's pulse, told Alyonushka to keep a temperature chart, approved of everything and kissed Alyonushka on the brow:

'Well, I must be off. And you, dearest, have a little snooze in the armchair anyhow. Well, then, see you tomorrow. I'll be round in the morning, soon after nine.'

Knut Hamsun went on with his story, and it was curious how vividly Alyonushka visualized the love and torments of his hero.

– LXIV –

THE FIFTH TRUTH

As many as five truths have been recorded in Moscow from the time of the Boyard Kutchka[1] down to our day.

The first truth was that of the rack – 'the long and short of it', as it was called. The home of this truth was the Secret Service chamber of Zhitny Dvor, by the Kaluzhsky Gates. Here, at the inquiry, the executioner extorted it by torture, with rope and horizontal beam, inflicting strappado on the naked body; while at the table, the recorder scribbled line upon line with his quill pen.

The second truth was that of 'the ins and outs of it'. Hands were clamped in a hoop, fingers in pincers, and sharp splinters of wood were driven in beneath the nails. When the first method failed the other was tried.

The third truth flourished near the churches of Peter and Paul, in a chamber in Preobrazhenskaya, where it was in the hands of the all-powerful Prince Fyodor Yuritch Romodanovsky, 'a man with a peculiar character, with the appearance of a monster and the ways of an evil tyrant; a man utterly incapable of wishing anyone well'. His justice made 'the devils scratch their necks'.

A fourth truth was almost established at the Kadashy church, beyond the Moscow River, where there lived in the fifties an eminent merchant, Shestov, the mayor who defended the interests of the poor people of Moscow. But so unreal a truth could not hold out for any length of time.

After that the people lost count of the truths of Moscow: popular sayings no longer tell of each individual one – neither of Butyrsky nor of Tagansky,[2] nor of Gnezdikovsky.[3] Grown wiser, the nation has reduced all these truths to one single one: that truth 'once stood, but has gone into the wood', 'and you are right and I am right and truth is everywhere and nowhere'.

The fifth truth was born in our days in the Lubyanka.[4]

* * *

[1] The Middle Ages. [2] Moscow prisons, notorious for cruelty. [3] The headquarters of the Secret Service. [4] The Central Tcheka. [5]

THE FIFTH TRUTH

After the truth had been extracted from him, the wretch, who was no longer of any use, was 'shortened by a quarter and a half.'[5] Many places in Moscow that still live in the nation's memory were chosen for this purpose. Along the Red Square, from the Nikolskaya to the Spasky Gates, there sprung up, later on, a whole row of little churches on 'bones and blood, and one by a pit'.[6] Ivan the Terrible 'truncated folk in the Square of the Blessed Virgin', before St. John's, later called the Great. 'And the heads were thrown into the yard of Boyard Mstislavsky', to give the devils bowls to play with.

There were other such places at different times: at the Serpyhovsky Gates, on the other side of the Moscow River, near the Bog, by St. Barbara the Martyr's, at the corner of the Myasnitskaya and Furmanny Street – wherever convenient, and in winter even on the ice of the Moscow River.

There were many, very many, such places in Moscow, where 'goats had their horns set straight', where 'the tongue was sewn lower than the sole of the foot', where people were 'weighed up on a bone steelyard', 'heads washed,' 'buckles cleaned', 'sides tinned', people 'taken out for a walk in the green lane', 'brushed over with a dry besom', 'had the gag put in firmly' and 'tortured in three goes'.[7] The Russian language is most rich and musical and beautiful. Rich it is and will become yet richer.

At the time of the fifth – the Lubyanka – truth one began to 'turn out people into the street with their things', 'liquidate', 'put to the wall' and 'settle their accounts'. And new places were discovered in Moscow – the Petrovsky Park, the cellar of the Lubyanka, the 'Takov' Company, the garage in the Varsonofievsky, and various other places.

* * *

Businessmen had formerly had their headquarters in the Lubyanka, and eight and ten per cent, interests had prevailed. Between eight and ten there is an enormous difference: eight is good, but nothing unusual, ten is relative wealth. But all that belonged to the past. The new people, who did not look ahead, knew perfectly well that life was theirs only for today, that even a hundred per cent, was a mere trifle,

---

[5] Beheaded. [6] Pit into which the bodies of the executed were thrown.
[7] Old popular names for various methods of execution.

THE FIFTH TRUTH

and that there was either the whole world before them or a shameful death on the morrow.

The new people put aside faith – or so they thought. They certainly did think so. But they had a faith of their own for all that – a naive faith in the destructive power of the Browning, the Colt and the nagan,[8] in the power of rapid action. How were they to know that grass grows according to its own inviolable laws, that man's mind does not bow with his neck, and that a bullet can pierce neither faith nor unbelief?

A huge yard; old buildings; on the entrance doors notices with the orders of the day posted up. Here reigns supreme the power of might and direct action. Meek people come in fear and trembling, stutter their entreaties and go away weeping, transparently guileful. For might in here is securely buttoned up in army tunics and leather jackets.

On the left from the entrance there is a turning leading to a narrow doorway, and farther on to what used to be a goods depot and what is now a 'pit' – a light basement where but a short while ago there was a smell of books and the fresh fustiness of samples, now the famous Ship of Death. The floor is laid with Dutch tiles.

There is a gallery at the entrance where two young soldiers stand, Red Army soldiers, who have been transferred to the detachment of the Special Department[10] – mere boys, with hairless lip and empty mind, infected with army discipline and fear of punishment. The gallery runs round the sides of the 'pit,' and a spiral staircase leads down to the seventy men who are lying stretched out on boards on the floor and on the big polished table below.

One of the condemned has scrawled over the walls in pencil:

> My life has been so short
> And ruined is my youth
> To the wall all innocent I go
> Farewell to you my spring!

A grave has been drawn: a high mound, with a death's-head rather merry-looking, like a face; and below the skull two bones; and below

---

[8] See note on p133. [9] The basement where prisoners were kept before being shot. [10] Of the Central Tcheka.

THE FIFTH TRUTH

the cross-bones a name. The young bandit evidently wanted to part with life gracefully and leave a memory like that recorded in those slender little volumes that were on sale near the Ilyinsky Gates:

'The notorious bandit and robber, the renowned raider, Ivan Kazarinov, nicknamed Vanka the Flame.'

Hard by, in the 'Ship's' common cell, are the small fry counter-revolutionaries, socialist-revolutionaries, Menshiviks, spectacled men with scanty little beards and decayed teeth, cowards without temerity or fire – mere human scum.

In the gallery appears the fisherman, with leather belt drawn tight, the commissary of death, Ivanov; and with him, heavy and horrible, the executioner, a short, thick-set individual with restless eyes, always a little tipsy. This is Zavalishin, whose duty it is to accompany the young robber's soul to the next world.

On some boards strewn with naphthalene, a book in his hand, lies a man with a trim grey beard – a former Minister of the Tsar. Brought hither from St. Petersburg, he is hardened already to prison life. Next to him lies an argumentative Menshivik, busily writing out statements, waiting his chance to ask every examining magistrate a question that will nonplus him. Sitting near him is a speculator who has been selling shoe leather and been caught. And not far off, swinging his legs, sits poor Styopa, one of the bandits who has so far escaped recognition.

But Commissar Ivanov happens to belong to the same notorious gang, and knows him at once for a mate:

'Hullo, Styopa! Where are you off to?'

'To the Moghilevsky[11] government, it looks like.'

The boy is pale, and his eighteen summers and cocaine-tainted life weigh heavily upon him.

Soon he is to be taken to a special cell. Farewell, Styopa, poor lad – poor wild mother's darling!

Zavalishin gazes down into the pit with drunken eyes. Paid by the job, with extra rations, the executioner is a trusty servant. His beard is unkempt, and his bloodshot eyes swollen and bleary from drinking rectified spirits. At nightfall he drinks, and is ready to treat them all; few, however, are willing to be in his company. Zavalishin is a terrible figure to them: for is he not a pitiless executioner, capable, if ordered, of dispatching his own mother for a bottle of pre-War spirits?

---

[11] Pun on the word for grave – 'moghila'.

THE FIFTH TRUTH

Down the road, down Furkassovky Street, is the headquarters of all strife, the Special Department of the Central Tcheka. Order reigns here; all are reduced to abject submission; no poetry, no futile stir and bustle. Here, issuing orders that are heard by no one, looms omnipotent over all the wise and oppressive genius of strife and retribution – the tall, stern comrade of the old school who had tasted to the full the horror of Tsarist penal servitude. He was the penniless idealist, accessible to no one, the avenger of the people, who had taken upon himself the whole responsibility for the blood that was being shed – and whose name posterity will forget.

New victims, foes of the nation and revolution, are taken from the motorcar and led straight from the square through the gates. An inquiry takes place in the investigation office. Then the prisoner is led to the same cell – with boards for seats, whence he is transferred to the large one – with bugs. Then on to Avanessov's notorious office; after which he is taken straight through the yard to an ancient building which has been converted into a prison of the Tsarist type. On into the dread silence of the Special Department, whence long zigzag passages, cold and empty, lead to the office of the examining magistrate. This is the home of the fifth Moscow truth. – the Lubyanka Truth.

– LXV –

COMRADE BRICKMANN

A small, scanty-haired individual with a smashed chest was writing out a report in a tiny, clear handwriting, his elbows set wide apart and his left eye close to the paper.

The telephone bell buzzed on the table.

'Yes, yes, it's I. ...When was he arrested?... All right, comrade. Only send along the case papers as soon as possible, because I know nothing whatever about it... Well, all right. I'll have him up myself... That will be all right.'

The man's voice was as thin as a woman's, and had little shrill notes in it.

After finishing his report he went through the case papers, carefully turning over the pages with hands that were thin and like a child's, with tapering fingers. Then he opened a packet of papers that had been taken during the search and muttered to himself, frowning:

'A lot of rubbish as usual – they can't make out anything.'

He rang, signed an order and handed it to the soldier of the Special Department who entered:

'Take this to the Commandant's office, comrade, and see that the man is brought to me at once.'

He got up, walked up and down the room, coughed in a corner, peered out into the passage and asked whether he might have some hot tea. A brisk, self-assured woman with curly hair under her kerchief brought him some. It was weak and tepid.

'Do you know if there's going to be a distribution today, Comrade Brickmann?'

'I do not.'

'They say that cranberries are going to be given out, but it might be sweaters.'

'I don't know.'

'Oh, but then who does?!'

The soldier reported that the prisoner was at the door.

The examining magistrate coughed, sat down at his table, placed before him his finished report, took up his pen and assumed the air of a man busy writing.

The door-handle rattled, and behind the door the soldier said:

'On your left, to the table.'

It was Astafiev who entered; tall, in a somewhat creased suit, unshaven, calm.

The examining magistrate raised his eyes, and with no more than a glance at the man who had entered motioned him to a chair beside the table:

'Sit down. You are Citizen Astafiev?'

I am.

He continued for a couple of minutes to look over his report, reading it only with his eyes, while his mind was busy thinking out questions. Putting the report away, and drawing up Astafiev's case papers, he asked:

'You are a professor?'

'A reader.'

'Well, yes, same thing. In philosophy?'

'Yes.'

'And why have you been arrested?'

Astafiev smiled:

'That is for you to know.'

'I do know. But what do you think about it?'

'I think that I just happen to be arrested for no particular reason at all.'

'So you believe we arrest for no reason?'

Astafiev burst out laughing; he was genuinely amused:

'I believe that does happen – nineteen times out of twenty, at any rate.'

'You are quite wrong in thinking so. Mistakes may occur, of course, but they are rectified. We are obliged to be careful, as the Soviet rule is surrounded by enemies. It is better that a dozen innocent people should sit in prison than to let one single enemy slip through our hands. Don't you agree with me?'

'No, I do not. I think, on the contrary, that it is better to let the guilty slip through your hands than to deprive a dozen innocent people of freedom.'

'That's where we differ. The proletariat has not acquired power in order to risk losing it because of some sentimental prejudice of the intelligentsia. As long as the Soviet Government is surrounded by enemies...'

And in a small, grating voice, without any pause at the commas, the examining magistrate poured forth a long stream of words that Astafiev had so often read in the leading articles of the *Izvestia* and *Pravda*, and that had so jarred on him with their mixture of truth and falsehood, of common sense and the fantastic. While he was absent-mindedly listening to them he was painfully conscious of an overwhelming tediousness, and longed only for the magistrate to finish. At the same time he remembered having seen the man and heard him speak somewhere before. He wondered where it could have been.

Breaking off suddenly in the middle of his popular dissertation, the examining magistrate asked him in the same tone:

'A man in yellow gaiters came to see you last week. What is his name?'

Astafiev answered with indifference:

'It is quite possible that someone or other called in to see me in yellow gaiters; I don't remember.'

'Did he stay long?'

Astafiev frowned:

'But haven't I just told you that I don't remember any such person?'

'Who came to your flat last week? Give me the names of everyone who was there.'

'What exactly is it you are accusing me of?'

'This is not a trial and I am not bound to answer you. When everything is brought to light you will discover for yourself. Meanwhile, kindly answer my questions.'

The big, healthy, handsome man looked down at the small, puny form of the examining magistrate:

'Drop all this questioning. How am I to answer you when I don't even know what I am accused of? If I were to give you a name you would have the man arrested. What do you take me for?'

'For an enemy of the Soviet Government, by the look of things.'

'Do, by all means.'

'But do you realize, Citizen Astafiev, what that may mean?'

'I can guess, though that cannot influence me. But do tell me – where could I have seen you before? I seem to know your face.'

The examining magistrate started nervously, and a shrill note came into his voice:

'That has nothing to do with the case. Will you answer my questions or not?'

'Wasn't it abroad that I met you? Was it in Berlin, by any chance? Aren't you an emigrant? I seem to remember... at some emigrant meeting or other... I have it! Isn't your name Brickmann? But you were a Menshivik,[1] I believe, in those days, weren't you?'

Comrade Brickmann fidgeted on his chair and rang the bell.

'Will you kindly answer my question?'

Smiling broadly, Astafiev went on, somewhat ironically:

'I seem to remember that you opposed Lenin at that meeting in Berlin. Tut-tut!'

'Take the prisoner back!' Brickmann shrilled to the soldier who had entered.

'The slip, if you please.'

While Brickmann signed the slip, Astafiev went on talking to him in a benevolent way:

'You shouldn't get excited, Comrade Brickmann; it's bad for you.

---

[1] A member of the moderate section of the Social Democrats.

Just look how thin you are. Take my example. What does it all matter? It's certainly not worth bothering about.'

'I do not need any advice, Citizen Astafiev. As for you, you will have to remain in prison for some time, if nothing worse happens to you. You may go.'

When Astafiev had been led away, Brickmann took the inquiry form attached to the case papers and wrote in his fine clear handwriting, setting his elbows wide apart, his sunken chest almost touching the table. When he had finished he rose, walked up and down the room, coughed again in a corner, felt his pulse, glanced at the door, and went up to the tarnished glass that hung in a frame near the window.

The glass dimly reflected his emaciated face, with its fair little beard, the large eyes over the puffy sacs, and the projecting ears.

He had never been able to breathe freely since his student days, when his chest had been smashed by the butt-ends of rifles in various prisons for the transported. There was no joy in his life; and the only way of prolonging it – useless as the life of a consumptive is – was by a steadfast faith in the revolution, in the future happiness of humanity, in the golden age which must inevitably follow the period of dogged and pitiless struggle against the foes of the working classes.

True, he was not a workman himself; how could he be – with his bashed-in chest? Notwithstanding, he, Brickmann, was destined to become one of the heroes and defenders of the new order, which, born in Russia, was later on to embrace the whole world. With his poor health he should have a strong will, an iron will – invincible; herein lay the whole justification of his life.

He again went up to the glass, threw his head back a little and tried to hold himself erect. And again the glass reflected the puny body with the arresting eyes, bloodshot and feverish. The pockets of his 'French' stuck out, but his chest had not been able to stretch the khaki.

Comrade Brickmann did not smoke: smoking brought on a racking cough. He liked fresh air, but he was afraid of opening the window, because cold air, too, made him cough. In his pocket he carried a little phial, into which he would spit, a little phial which shut hermetically.

Today he had lost his self-control. That wouldn't do; that mustn't happen again! There wasn't enough evidence against Astafiev, but his tone, his speech, his manner – everything pointed to his being a very real and dangerous foe. His case ought to be gone into further; it ought to be cleared up!

A vision of Astafiev – broad-shouldered, healthy, ironical – suddenly flashed across his mind.

He took up the telephone receiver and, pressing the hook impatiently, began in his thin, high-pitched voice:

'Hullo, hullo...'

– LXVI –

AT HIS BEDSIDE

In the words of the expression recently sanctioned by the Moscow bureaucracy, Alyonushka 'came into contact' with the landlady of the flat where Vassya Boltanovsky was lying ill. As a result of this 'contact' they succeeded in getting some semolina and a little sugar in exchange for the millet Vassya had brought from the country.

'He might be your fiancé, the way you look after him, Elena Ivanovna.'

'Now you've said it! It's only that he needs something light. Just look how thin he's got!'

As she changed her patient's shirt – she had previously warmed the clean one by the landlady's stove – Alyonushka gazed with pity at Vassya's protruding ribs and the hollows above his collarbone. His helplessness touched her and stirred in her tender feelings towards him. Vassya could do nothing for himself; and in moments of consciousness and extreme weakness he would suppress his sense of shame and take advantage of her nurse's aid.

The critical stage of his illness was now over. He had regained full consciousness, but was still extremely weak. Every morning, Dr. Kuporrossov took Alyonushka out into the hall to say to her:

'Take careful note of his temperature, Alyonushka. He needs feeding up; a little at a time, but at frequent intervals. Thirty-five-point-two this morning? That's just as dangerous, don't you see, as a high temperature. If this goes on we'll have him freezing to death. Give him hot kasha[1] and plenty of butter. Milk is good too. As soon as he's a little stronger

---

[1] Thick lemolina gruel.

he may have meat also – rissoles, since veal and chicken aren't to be had these days. See that he doesn't tire himself out sitting up in bed and talking. It's better for him to remain lying down. And don't you do too much talking, either, Alyonushka; don't talk his head off. Dear me, it does make one feel sorry. Such a nice lad!'

Vassya's head had been shaved for the second time, as well as the beard that had grown in the interval. He was now lying clean and white and thin, his hazel eyes open, and the little cleft in his chin. He spoke very quietly and said almost nothing beyond expressing his gratitude:

'Thank you, Elena Ivanovna. Why do you do everything yourself, when Marya Savishna might give you a hand – at any rate, with the dirty work? It makes me feel dreadfully uncomfortable.'

'Nonsense! The room must be got nice and tidy. They'll be here soon.'

That meant, of course, that Tanyusha and Pyotr Pavlovitch were coming.

As soon as the critical stage was over, and Vassya was fully conscious again, he lay very still, inwardly rejoicing at the return of life, and straining as hard as his weakness would allow him to remember the visions that had passed before him during his illness. He wanted to distinguish between what had been delirium and what had been dreams, and to discover in which of his experiences there had been an element of real perception. The only thing that was completely real was the ever-present Sister of Mercy, whom the doctor called Alyonushka in such a nice way.

Alyonushka had flashed before him, both in moments of delirium and moments of consciousness. She had always been there when his lips were parched or the heat was stifling, when his heart stopped beating or pounded too hard, when his head seemed on fire and his eyes looked through misty, mauve circles. When Alyonushka came up to him he felt better at once.

But it happened sometimes that other shadows and visions eclipsed her, and that other voices took the place of hers. Tanyusha's and Protassov's, of course; and always both of them together. Two voices speaking in whispers, sometimes to him, Vassya, and sometimes to each other.

Tanyusha's voice he always longed to hear; but hearing it together with another voice, so far from soothing him, had actually upset him. Sometimes he had felt an impulse to catch it and make it speak to him alone, make it say things he must at all costs hear – awfully important things – or, at any rate, words of comfort and compassion. But the other voice, a masculine voice, even, calm, assured, almost light-hearted, always got in the way. Alyonushka's voice was for him. The other two voices sounded, as it were, for each other, although they might be talking of him and for him. It was difficult to explain; but that was how he felt. And at the sound of those voices he had always stirred uneasily and called out in delirium.

Then another memory swam into his mind. During moments of consciousness – if, indeed, it were not a dream – he had answered questions (Did he want a drink or to have his pillow straightened?) and had seen the person who was speaking quite distinctly, though only to forget again at once. It was as though the person went out of the field of his attention, beyond the confines of the world in which he was engaged in his struggle with death. There had also been longer moments of lucidity – the one, for instance, when he had lengthily contemplated Alyonushka's features while she slept in her armchair, and had wondered at her healthy colour and at the ingenuous and good-natured set of her lips. On another occasion he had examined every line of the doctor's face while it was bent over him one morning, and had smiled when the doctor said: 'Well, your eyes are a bit brighter today, citizen; time to get well again.' He had also seen Tanyusha quite clearly, gazing at him with a frightened expression and with such pity that he had felt inclined to cry. But there had been something strange about the face he loved so well. Then, again, he had once seen, both his friends, Tanyusha and the engineer – though this might only have appeared to him – sitting side-by-side, near his bed and close to each other, not saying a word, but looking at one another with an expression he could not understand.

It had not been his imagination. He had apparently been fast asleep; then he had wakened with a pleasantly clear head and a feeling that his illness was over and that he had reached the stage when one feels reluctant to stir, so as not to dispel the restfulness and clarity. Opening his eyes, he had seen his room in all its detail and, lit by the lamp, two faces gazing at one another in silence, as though frozen in contemplation. It seemed to him, too, that Tanyusha's and Protassov's hands were clasped. This he might not have noticed had Tanyusha not made a sharp movement, as though disengaging her hand when he had tried to turn his head abruptly towards them. Then he had closed his eyes and felt his peace and clarity vanishing, and had again been overcome

AT HIS BEDSIDE

by a torturing semi-consciousness, and a weight on the crown of his head and an ache in his temples. He remembered all that now – but oh so dimly; it might almost never have been.

This was only his second day of full consciousness; but as he was still very weak he had slept all through the first day and had not seen Tanyusha.

'Sister, was Tatyana Mihailovna here yesterday?'

'She was. She always comes about three o'clock, when I go home. She has missed only two or three times all the time you've been ill, and those were days when she couldn't come. Marya Savishna took her place by your bedside.'

'What a lot of trouble I have been giving you. Have I been very ill?'

'Well, that's all over now. But you did have a rather bad time.'

'A long time?'

'Don't you know? It will be three weeks tomorrow.'

'As long as all that! And have you been with me all the time, Elena Ivanovna?'

'All the time.'

'And every night? Then when did you sleep?'

Alyonushka broke into a bell-like laugh:

'I slept at night, and sometimes dropped off a bit during the daytime also.'

'Did you sleep in the armchair?'

'When you were very bad I slept in the armchair, and when you didn't toss about too much I added chairs to it and slept like in a bed. Marya Savishna let me have a blanket and pillows, and made me a real bed; only I was afraid of sleeping too soundly.'

'How on earth can you stand it? You must be dead-tired! And yet you look positively flourishing! It makes one quite envious to look at you.'

'Oh, but I'm so strong that nothing has the least effect on me. Besides, I'm pretty used to it. But you are doing too much talking, you know. The doctor's orders were that you shouldn't.'

'It can't do me any harm with you.'

Nevertheless, Vassya was tired out.

Five minutes later, when there came a gentle knock at the door, and Tanyusha's voice asked in a whisper: 'Well, how is he today?' Vassya did not open his eyes, although he heard Alyonushka's answer: 'Much better.'

'Asleep?' asked Tanyusha.

'He seems to be.'

Neither did Vassya open his eyes when there came a man's light footfall after a second knock, nor when Alyonushka left the room, bidding the visitor a simultaneous greeting and goodbye. It was better to go on lying like that with his eyes shut, for if he opened them he would have to talk; and before being able to talk he had to think, which was difficult and irksome.

Breaking in upon the peace of his weariness came a whisper, and he heard the engineer say:

'I've got to go now. Do you mind staying on by yourself?'

'No, of course not, if you've got to go. But you'll come to see us this evening, won't you?'

'I'll be round as usual. Well, goodbye for the moment, Tanyusha.'

'As usual? And he calls her Tanyusha?'

Vassya opened his eyes and saw her following his old wayfarer with a tenderness in her eyes that he had never seen in them when she had said goodbye to him.

Then he remembered.

How long did Alyonushka say? Oh yes, three weeks tomorrow.

– LXVII –

THE TRAITORS

The people who stood at night in queues, waiting under the faded red-and-white signboards for the doors to open and for the distribution of rank millet to begin, were the last people to be disturbed by the thought that the war was still on and that Russia was in it no longer. They had quite enough worries and troubles of their own, and had forgotten the war long ago. All that remained of it for them was its legacy of graves and widows and ruined families, and an accursed memory that the sufferings of the present were effacing.

The jurist Myortvago, for whom Uncle Borya had found a post in the Zemgor[1] (the zemhussar uniform suited him to perfection) – the jurist Myortvago, whose wife had not been obliged to part with her

[1] See note on p.56.

jewels – was not in particularly bad circumstances. He had, of course, made a great mistake in not leaving in time for Kiev, and farther, as others with greater foresight had done. While preparing for his departure, which was now a far more difficult matter than before, Myortvago would express the opinion that we Russians had proved traitors to the Allies, and that the disgraceful (the word he used at home was 'disgusting') peace of Brest-Litovsk had left a deep stain on the honour of the Russian people.

The traitors, meanwhile, stood in queues in the damp snow, munched bread in which there was as great a proportion of chaff as flour, and dispelled with vinegar the tainted smell of mare's flesh which they made into rissoles and fried in mineral or castor oil.

In the towns and in the grainless villages they went about ragged and parched, with unsmiling faces and no desire to prolong the life they clung to merely from habit and animal instinct. Deep-dyed in treason, they were not, even in thought, with the soldiers[2] who, though going to their death, were at all events well clothed and fed.

Uncle Borya, who had formerly worked in connection with the National Defence, who had gone over to the mutineers when they had taken the law into their own hands, and who was now working as an experienced 'expert' in the Industrial Research Department, would say of himself:

'Well, I'm working in the V.C.N.H.[3] – not with them, of course, but in the Research Department. Nothing political. Our department is entirely self-governing.'

He would enter the office of his chief – a rather bewildered young communist, who stood in awe of learned men and was afraid of betraying his embarrassment in their presence – with all the buttons of his jacket done up, down to the one that dangled by a thread and might easily come off at any moment. On entering he would bow and hold his head on one side, at a loss to know what to do with his hands. His embarrassed chief would ask him to take a seat, and Uncle Borya would sit down on the edge of a chair.

From the point of view of the jurist Myortvago, whose speciality turned out for the time being to be of no use to anyone, Uncle Borya also was a traitor for having accepted a post under the Soviet

---

[2] The reference is, of course, to the soldiers of the other Allied armies.
[3] Higher Council of National Economy.

authorities. True, he did not judge him too harshly; for, as he said, it was not everyone who could remain true to his principles.

Uncle Borya would turn up at the Myasnitskaya with a portfolio containing projects for the standardization of tractors and for adapting these tractors to agricultural purposes. He also carried a strong Swiss bag, in case food rations were distributed. But as the tractors were not yet being given out, and as there was no particular hurry in so far as their standardization was concerned, he would go along to the Malaya Zlatoustinskaya, after looking in at his office, to see if there wasn't by any chance a distribution of some sort in another department. And the self-seeking traitor, Uncle Borya, would arrive home late in the evening, bringing back in his bag a pot of black treacle, a pinch of yeast, half-a-dozen tainted herrings and, just occasionally, a piece of thick rubber – enough for two soles. In the eyes of those who did not happen to be 'experts', Uncle Borya was a lucky fellow. Before going off to sleep under a pile of blankets and winter coats, with a fur cap on his head (the little stove gave out no heat at night), he would say to his wife:

'There's a possibility of my being able to get the rations of the teaching profession.'

'Really?' his plain, dried-up wife would answer eagerly, thrusting out her nose from under the heap of old blankets.

'I'm not certain about it, but there's a hope. They're even discussing giving us the special rations of the Kremlin officials, but that would concern only a very few of us.'

'Aren't you likely to be one? How nice it would be if you were!'

'I don't know. It's not so easy. But I might.'

White flour was given out occasionally to those who were entitled to the Kremlin rations, and real meat regularly.

Even Uncle Borya was like that. What, then, of the soldier who had left the front, taking with him a government bayonet and a trifle or two from among the things that had fallen into the men's hands when they broke into the territorial depots? The soldier knew perfectly well that he had taken things that belonged to the Government, and was not at all sure that he hadn't done wrong. He would remember his theft whenever he poked at an old yoke with the rusty bayonet. But no suspicion of treason, of his heinous treason towards the Allies, ever entered his head; and if anyone had pronounced before him the word that should have branded his soul with shame, his blue Slav eyes would simply have opened wide in a stare of utter incomprehension.

In peasant coats and overcoats, in blouses and jackets torn at the elbows, cold and hungry, robbed both in war and in peace, driven out of their minds and starved by the revolution and the blockade, the great and many-tongued Russian nation – beast and hero, torturer and martyred – turned traitor. It betrayed Europe, whom it did not know, to whom it had taken no oath of allegiance, from whom it got nothing, and to whom it had sacrificed a million lives to no purpose – *pour ses beaux yeux*? Heaven knows why!

For all these reasons, 11th November 1918 passed uneventfully enough in Moscow and the rest of Russia.

All woke early, as there were a number of urgent matters that had to be seen to. All went to bed early, as one could never be sure of the electric light; and paraffin was not only dear but almost unobtainable. The central electricity station burned notarial and tide deeds, rent-rolls, old paper-money and the archives of Tsarist government offices.

Neither Armistice Day nor the days that followed it stood out in any way from the rest of the cold, snowy days of the month. True, there did appear short notices in the papers about the armistice which had been signed on the Western Front, but it was not an event that could be of any interest or have any meaning for the people who stood in queues, thinking of fats and sugar. Lists of names of those who had been shot during the previous week were printed with admirable frankness in the very same newspapers. This was of interest to relations and friends; the rest repeated from hearsay the numbers, which they did not believe to be accurate, and one or two names that seemed familiar. Like hunger, like cold and like typhus, shooting became a common event; it troubled the mind at night only, when fears massed thick over the restlessly sleeping citizens of the freest country in the world.

In the streets of European towns, people read extra editions, sang, danced, and embraced one another. Happily the sounds of exultation did not reach the towns and villages of Russia, nor the ears of those whom Europe had stigmatized as traitors.

Virtue triumphed, vice was punished.

If in the skies beyond the snowy clouds there had assembled at that time an Areopagus of supreme judges, it is doubtful if its verdict would have differed from the verdict of man. Traitor and martyr, the Russian people had no council for the defence either in heaven or upon earth; and absorbed in its own troubles, it appeared before neither the Judgment-Seat of God nor man.

'The verdict was given by default.'

– LXVIII –

HE WHO CAME

How is love born?

That, Tanyusha, nobody knows. Its coming is eagerly awaited – and it appears unexpectedly. It is painted in the popular hues all know so well, and it comes up stealthily, wrapped in an inconspicuous cloak, cheap and grey. But that makes it no less lovely and no less desirable.

Sudden and illogical, love has a way of taking one by surprise. Astafiev had been right when he said: 'Logic kills the fanciful and beautiful;' and Tanyusha also had been right when she said to him: 'Once you stop to think about it, it's not love, is it? Now, if without wondering about it at all...'

Tanyusha did not think, she just knew. Someone had come and knocked, someone who was not in the least unusual, just a simple, ordinary being, who had been a mere stranger a short while ago, and today... oh, would the evening never come and bring him back again!

His hands were rough. That came from work and frequent washing with grey soap. Other people's hands – smooth, warm hands, friendly too, and caressing – she did not want; their touch meant nothing to her, or was actually unpleasant. But to this man, who had so suddenly become a friend, she felt she could give her hand, happily and for always. It was impossible to explain; there wasn't any explanation. It was self-evident.

It was eight o'clock, Tanyusha's eyes followed the lines of the book, but the offended book remained mute; it was not used to such absent-mindedness. Grandfather had sunk deep into his easy-chair, and he, of course, would not be listening as she was, listening keenly. From among all the footfalls in the street he would never catch the one she was waiting for, the one that would be sure to stop at the front door and pause for a moment (why was that?) before making itself known by a knock. Curbing her haste, Tanyusha would lay down her book and go to open the door,

'Who is it, Tanyusha?'

'Pyotr Pavlovitch, grandfather.'

'Ah, how nice! How do you do, how do you do? What news have you got to tell us?'

'None, I'm afraid. How are you, professor?'

'Fair, quite fair. How nice of you to have come; Tanyusha has been longing for your visit.'

'Grandfather – '

'Well, what harm is there in that? It's dull for us without you, Pyotr Pavlovitch.'

The engineer sat down next to Tanyusha, on the divan:

'Well, I really have been longing to get here. I've been round half the town after some stupid bit of information I wanted. Do you know, professor, the mines on the Don are scarcely being worked at all. We're done for, of course, if there's no coal.'

Protassov told them about projects of which Tanyusha had no knowledge, and which did not interest her in the least. Nevertheless, she listened to him with attention and pride. That was what he was like: if he wanted to do anything, nothing could stop him.

'Plans are plans,' said the professor. 'But will you get a chance of carrying them out? I wonder whether all the energy you are expending will not be in vain.'

'It's a difficult business, of course, very difficult. There's such chaos everywhere and not much in the way of funds. Plenty of money for other purposes, but for the things that really count – well, we just have to beg it penny by penny. But what's to be done? We can't let Russia go to the dogs. We've got to adapt ourselves to lots of things – anything – to get life somehow back into its normal channel.'

They drank tea, and Protassov related how he had been sent during the war on a special mission to Spitsbergen, and how he had been ice-bound on the way. He made his story as interesting and graphic as if it had been a holiday voyage. The professor was interested to know whether he had not by any chance seen there a rare species of birds of which there were detailed descriptions but, up to the present, no stuffed specimens. Protassov had not seen the birds, but was not entirely at sea in bird-lore. The professor and he entered upon a conversation that proved interesting to both of them. The old man became quite animated and scattered names in profusion. As the engineer's knowledge was limited, his part in the conversation consisted chiefly of questions. But he did know a good deal, considering, and Tanyusha watched him with pride, frequently turning away to look at her grandfather. She saw that he liked their new visitor, and was pleased.

When, punctual as his cuckoo clock, the professor left them to go to his own room, Tanyusha and Protassov remained together alone.

'I am so grateful to you for enlivening grandfather. It's dull for him when you are not there.'

'What a clear mind he has!' said Protassov, 'and what vast knowledge! We still have many people like him in Russia. It's only real workers that are so scarce. Science is a wonderful thing; there's nothing petty about it. Now politics is built on shifting sands. It's unstable: one thing today and another tomorrow; not a thing of any real importance.'

They talked of her grandfather, of Spitsbergen, and of past episodes in the engineer's life that Tanyusha had not yet heard about. They never mentioned love, nor was there even the remotest allusion to it in their conversations. But Tanyusha was so interested in all that the stranger – now quite suddenly become an intimate – had to say, and Protassov, for his part, was so carried away by his stories, that the minutes and hours flew, by faster than either of them would have wished.

When he said goodbye, Protassov asked her:

'Shall you be at Vassya's about three tomorrow?'

'Of course,' Tanyusha replied.

'Well, then, I'll look in too. He seems to be well on the way to recovery. Only I wonder why he is so depressed. He ought to be cheered up.'

Both of them guessed at the cause of the convalescent's sadness… But Vassya would soon be up, and it would no longer be necessary for them to go to see him.

One day it somehow happened that there was nothing whatever to talk about, so they sat on in silence, both of them wondering how it would be if their hands were to meet, and if they were perhaps to lean towards one another.

There are certain moments which have to be got over, and one had now come. And at this point Protassov suddenly turned and, without any hesitation, took Tanyusha's hands and raised them to his lips. Tanyusha not only did not draw her hands away, but trustfully, with a shy tenderness, inclined her head towards him. And thus they sat on a long time, leaning against each other. The minutes went by and the cuckoo called, but they said not a word.

The following evening they waited to see if such a moment would not come again. It did come; and this time it was simpler still. But though sweet, it was already too little.

Ah, Tanyusha, nobody knows how love is born, although it has always, from time immemorial, come in the same way.

Protassov would go striding home with a swinging step, his pleasant smile still lingering on his lips; while Tanyusha, all alone once more, would go to bed, moving slowly, so as not to spill the brimming cup of her new feeling. And she would remain awake a long time, revolving in her mind all that her heart, which had never loved so well, could still not fully understand. But life seemed to have acquired meaning now, to be desirable and full of expectation.

He who came, came simply, unexpectedly, and at the right moment.

– LXIX –

MOSCOW, 1919

The walls and fences of the Moscow houses were stuck and frozen together. The clever artist, Ivan Pavlov, lost no time in making sketches and engravings on wood of the fast vanishing charm of the wooden cottages. He would sketch today, and in the night would come shadows, some daring, some cowardly; and, keeping a sharp lookout, these shadows would tear away the boards, beginning with the fences.

Shadow after shadow, in caps with earflaps or bound round with scarves, in gloves with torn fingers, they laboured for all they were worth, the boldest among them going so far as to use the hatchet. They would work their way in, pulling down staircases and taking doors off their hinges. Like ants, they bore off all, bit by bit, rafter by rafter, the out-jutting nails scratching both them and the trampled snow as they went. Along the street went a door, keeping close to the fence. On two shoulders, in silence, swam a beam. Bent under their loads, they bore off each what he could – old women, odd scraps of wood; strong men, a beam.

And at dawn, on the spot where there had been an old wooden cottage, nothing remained but a brick chimney over a stove, sticking up out of plaster and snow. Not a trace of the wooden cottage. But over there, above the neighbouring houses of stone, rise wreaths of kindly smoke: people are warming themselves, cooking something or other.

At daybreak, people creep out of the houses, carrying baskets and bags, looking out for the flapping white calico signboards with the faded red letters. Doggedly, they stand in queues, not knowing themselves what for. The doors open late, and the frozen people are let in shivering, in strict order, each with his number written in chalk on his sleeve or in indelible pencil on the palm of his hand. They take whatever they are lucky enough to get, not what they need most, but whatever happens to be there – a bit of grey soap, a pot of plum jam, a little bottle of tea-essence. Those who manage to get something are followed out by the envious glances of those still waiting. Very soon, however, the doors are slammed and the people told that there is nothing left, the official shouting that they may come on the morrow or never at all, for all he cares.

In Granatny Street, adorned with pillars and snow, a little house stands dreaming behind its garden railings. It has no roof. The roof has been taken off long ago. The walls, too, are half down; only the pillars are whole. The pleasant home of some noble family is dying. Its day is over. On the gate there is still the 'dvornik's bell.' The snow in the garden is deep and white and clean.

The bright domes of St. Vassily the Blessed are also covered with snow. Under the painted low vaults inside, a little priest in a calotte runs by; in the chantry, where a service is being held, old women in black are mumbling, wrapped up in shawls; and the deacon is wearing a short winter coat under his cassock of brocade, and felt boots on his old, chilly feet. The censer sends forth cheap incense into the cold air.

Along the snowdrifts of the unswept streets, past the Memorial of the first printer, Fyodorov, upon whose shoulder perches a hungry sparrow, down from Lubyanskaya Square to the Theatre Square speeds a dray drawn by a horse that happens to be still alive. The driver is a strapping youth: 'There's a scarcity of drivers, so get on with the job! Drivers have got nothing to be afraid of. They can go and get firewood themselves and hay for the horses. The only difficulty is oats. Nowadays, drivers can make more than most people, and everybody looks up to them.'

Along by the walls of China-City, from the Vladimirsky to the Ilyinsky Gates, nothing but cigarette lighters and flints. The lighters are made in factories by workmen who are not paid, since there is nothing to pay them with, and no point in paying them. But where the flints come from is a mystery. It is rumoured that a dealer had kept a whole boxful by chance, and that he is now the wealthiest man in Moscow. Nevertheless, a wink will bring forth a bit of fat from under floorboards, not here, but in some archway when no one is looking. On the other hand, there is as much cigarette paper as ever one could want, sold openly by the sheet. This cigarette paper is nothing but copy-pages carefully torn out of commercial letter books. People buy it by the sheet and smoke letters – 'Dear Sir, in reply to your favour of... Believe me, yours faithfully.' It is said that it is possible to live a whole week comfortably and carefree on the proceeds of the sale, sheet by sheet, of one volume of such paper.

Wrapped up warmly, people go up and down the Tverskaya, carrying portfolios and knapsacks on their backs. They work for rations; the ink is frozen and the typewriters have no ribbon, but there is a rumour that honey has been brought from the Ukraine and is going to be given out. How one longs to taste something sweet after that cursed saccharin!

On one of the lateral walls of the Tverskaya Chapel something incomprehensible about opium[1] has been written up. Many other walls and buildings bear inscriptions. Futurists have covered the walls of the Strastny Monastery; and on the walls of the Alexandrovskoie training school there are whole rows of names of the world's great men. Among these are some pygmies too; and many of the great have been passed over and forgotten. People read the inscriptions with astonishment, but have no time to think about them.

What is written up today is faded by tomorrow.

There, encompassed by its crenellated wall, stands the Kremlin. Within the walls are people who are unused to being there; bayonets at the gates, and passes stuck upon them. One may not enter by all the gates, not even with a stamped slip. The Nikolsky and the Troitsky Gates are the only ones through which one is admitted.

Coldly towers Ivan the Great, dead like everything else: the palaces,

---

[1] To discourage worship, the Bolsheviks used to write up, 'Religion is opium to the people.'

the cannon and the bell[2] – all that never comes to life except at Easter matins. But there is no Easter now, nor are there any Matins.

The Arbat, on the other hand, is full of life and bustle, full of people going to the Smolensky marketplace and returning from it. A former 'lady' is carrying a loudly ticking pendulum clock and a pair of white slippers. That means she is selling the last of her possessions; for who could want a pair of white slippers in winter! Back from the marketplace, another former 'lady' is carrying a carpetbag, containing frozen potatoes, perhaps. Potatoes are first put to thaw very gradually in cold water, after which the black parts are cut off and the potatoes cooked in the usual manner. It is not every day that one can get the meat of a horse that has fallen dead. If an inexperienced person were to cook the potatoes the result would be an inky mess. Herrings are best put to smoke in the heat-tube of the samovar. All this needs to be known. One has to adapt oneself to whatever comes along.

People cling on to life tenaciously – chew oats, hide from each other tablets of saccharin and, hunger overcoming distaste, stuff themselves with rank millet. The sugar which soldiers have used as stakes at cards is highly valued and in great demand, for it can be bought somewhat cheaper than ordinary sugar. And, as a matter of fact, if the dirt is skilfully washed off and the sugar dried and cut into bits, it is not so bad; it is sugar anyhow.

By nightfall, the people are worn out with worry and fatigue. They go to sleep without undressing, in caps and felt boots, sleeping for the most part in the kitchens, where the warmth of dinnertime lingers on. Rags are stuffed into the chinks of the doors that lead into the other rooms, where it is bitterly cold. If there happens to be a stove, all sleep round it, forming a star, with their feet towards it. In the houses where there is electric light, the light is left on without any thought of economy, because everything is now free. One man had the idea of going to sleep with an electric bulb in each of his felt boots; it is a little warmer like that anyhow. People are growing wise. Unfortunately, the electric light does not act everywhere, as many lines are burnt out and others closed down; then one is obliged to make a night-lamp out of a bottle and work by its inadequate light. Oil is expensive, and reeking kerosene has to be used instead. An old bootlace makes the best wick. All this needs to be known.

---

[2] The huge bell that fell from the tower and still stands, broken, below.

As soon as the people are asleep the rats come up from the basement, creeping through an infinity of new passages – bold, impudent rats, with long tails and jet-black beads of eyes. They overrun the rooms and kitchens, clatter among bottles and jars, upset frying-pans on the floor, squeal and bite each other, and get up to the very ceiling, from which housewives hang their remains of meat and rancid butter. They no longer go about alone, but in herds, in gangs, boldly, fearlessly; and when they find no provisions they bite what they can see of the sleeping people.

In the summer of 1919 Moscow was conquered by rats. Strong tomcats were hired out to the neighbours, sometimes for as much as a whole pound of flour a night. Others, in their foresight, would deny themselves their last morsel to feed the kitten they were training. It was of the utmost importance to have a cat in the house. It was only a matter of keeping the kitten till it was grown; afterwards it would provide for itself, possibly even for its masters as well.

The first foe was man, the second, rats, and the third the pale, malignant louse, from which there was no escape in marketplaces, dens and stations. And to die just then, besides occasioning a lot of trouble to one's relatives, was hardly less expensive than to go on living.

There was not only misery, however; there were joys as well. Every extra bit of bread was a joy, every unexpected gift of fate. A joy, too, was the help of a friend who had nothing himself but who came nonetheless to sympathize and help saw up a damp log. Morning was a joy when the night had passed well – without loss or alarm. The sun was a joy when there was a prospect of its giving some warmth. Water was a joy when it could be turned on one of the storeys. There was joy whenever there was no real misfortune, or when it happened to others and not to oneself.

Life was hard that year, and man did not love his neighbour. Women ceased bearing, and children of five were looked upon as grown-ups, which, indeed, they were.

Beauty fled that year and in its stead came wisdom. From that time on there have been none wiser than the Russian people.

– LXX –

IN THE CELL

Astafiev was lying on a wooden couch watching a shadow quivering on the ceiling. The shadow was vague, and flickering because the light of the lantern was flickering just outside the window, with its whitewashed panes.

The cell of the Special Department was meant for four, but held six; and there was no space between the couches. Next to Astafiev, sleeping peacefully, lay an ex-general, Ivan Ivanovitch Klarik. His looked like a case of mistaken identity, though it was possible that he might have been taken as a hostage. He was an old man, quiet and in no way remarkable. On Astafiev's other side, with open eyes, like himself, lay an elderly workman from Pressnya, who had been arrested a couple of days before, either for libel or unguarded speech. He had just been brought back to the cell after a night examination, during which the examining magistrate, a brute of a Lett, had threatened him with death – though for what Timoshin had no idea.

Timoshin could not sleep; he felt a gnawing ache in his heart. Never had he had such a feeling before. It was as new to him as his insomnia. And feeling utterly unable to grapple with it by himself, he asked Astafiev in a whisper:

'Aren't you asleep, Alexey Dmitritch?'

'No, I can't get off to sleep.'

'I can't either.'

'Did you have a bad time of it at the examination?'

'I should think I did. And the worst of it is, I can't make out what he wants to see me for. "We'll settle your account,"¹ that's what he says. But what for? Could they, Alexey Dmitritch?'

Astafiev sat up on his couch with his back to the wall, drew up his knees and clasped his hands round them:

'They might do anything. Are you very afraid?'

'Well, it would be funny if one wasn't... Wicked to take human life for nothing... And I've got a family too. Do you think they might?'

'How am I to know? You may be shot or let out tomorrow.'

¹ See note on p.189.

'Well, but I'm a working man, although it's true I've got a cottage in the country.'

'Have you been guilty of anything? What are you accused of?'

'I'm not guilty of anything, Alexey Dmitritch. I swear before God I'm not! He went on at me about my being in with my boss – made out that I'd helped to hide him. But the boss – that's our manufacturer – ran away long ago. I don't even know where to. And he made out that I'd helped him. That's not a bit true; it's the first I've heard of it. So what is there to shoot me for, Alexey Dmitritch?'

'How am I to call you, Timoshin?'

'Me? I'm Alexey too.'

'And your father's name?'

'My father's name was Platon, so I am Alexey Platonytch.'

'Well, then, Alexey Platonytch, don't you be afraid. That examining magistrate of yours is only threatening you. He's evidently trying to get some information or other out of you. He won't have you shot.'

'You don't think so, Alexey Dmitritch? But if that's what they decide, there's no appeal against it. You yourself said they could.'

Astafiev closed his eyes. Surely he wasn't going to lie awake all night?

'And even if I did hide my boss, they'd not go and take a man's life for it, would they?'

'How old are you, Timoshin?'

'How old? I'm fifty-two, getting on for fifty-three.'

'You want to go on living a long time?'

'As long as I've got to live; it doesn't depend on us.'

'Well, however long you live, Alexey Platonytch, you'll not live to see anything new. You wouldn't miss anything.'

'I've got a family in the village. And I'm not old, Alexey Dmitritch; I can go on working perfectly well.'

'And what joy do you get from your work?'

'None, of course; but still there's the pay. Though one can't make anything these days. Just starvation, that's what it is. But one manages somehow.'

'There – you see. What is there to be afraid of, then? If they kill you, well, let them – damn them! What have you got to regret?'

'How can you, Alexey Dmitritch! Take a man what's alive and well and kill him all of a sudden – for nothing at all! What justice is there in that?'

Astafiev yawned. If only it were a good sign, announcing sleep and not simply boredom! Here was a man without any object or joy in his life demanding justice!

'Don't worry yourself, Timoshin; go to sleep. They're just frightening you. You'll soon get back your liberty; then you'll be able to live as long as ever you like.'

Astafiev had been in that cell for over four months and had already been examined by the consumptive magistrate three times. Apparently it was the man in the yellow gaiters who was at the bottom of it all. Queer fellow! What had possessed him to go about in those gaiters? He was no coward, though: he had been hunted up and down Moscow for three whole months and hadn't been caught yet. He had even read reports in various 'societies for the deliverance of Russia'. And the attempt on Lenin's life was his doing, too, of course.

'If it's proved that he spent the night with me, then that's the end. Who got wind of it, I wonder? Who could have given me away? There's my neighbour, of course, Zavalishin. He's a tchekist; still, it's not he, I feel sure. He couldn't have done it. Besides, he wasn't at home that night. No, it's not Zavalishin. There's more likelihood of its being that chairman of ours, Denissov. Well, of all the – '

Astafiev got off his couch and crept up to the window. On the white glass of the inner pane[2] appeared a little shadow. Creeping along the frame, the shadow ran up to the ventilator that opened out into the cell. Astafiev raised his hand and waited in readiness. The moment the mouse thrust out its little muzzle, preparing to enter the cell, he gave it the lightest of raps with his finger between its twitching whiskers, and the mouse tumbled down with a squeal.

Pleased and smiling, Astafiev lay down again on his couch. That was luck; otherwise that little rogue would again have eaten up the bread. Not finding any the night before, it had gone to the box and eaten several chessmen which the general, a great hand at modelling, had made out of crumbs. A queen, a castle and two pawns had had to be modelled again.

The mouse had made a passage between the two frames and lived under the window-sill. At night it would creep into the cell and make itself at home among the prisoners' parcels and on the table; and if it found nothing edible there it would climb up on the couches. One

---

[2] Of the double window.

night it had actually bitten one of the general's toes! Ivan Ivanovitch's blanket was too short and was always slipping off his feet.

Suddenly Atasfiev felt a desperate longing for freedom.

'How idiotic! Why, out there, just beyond the window and the wall, are the streets and people and cabs... Two windows and a few bricks; and a few rude human wills that could be thrust aside with a word, a gesture, a convincing argument. What a farce! Not to fear death, and yet not to struggle to get free, not to break down doors, not to come to grips or be under fire.'

Clenching his fists and grinding his teeth, he thought:

'Oh, to scatter them all like chaff!'

It was good to feel the play of muscles in his arms and back – powerful muscles, which prison life had scarce been able to weaken... Then he was struggling with hands and teeth, running up the stairs, dodging the bullets, knocking down the sentry at the entrance of the yard, running out into the street, hiding behind the corner and, changing his direction, going quietly home, watching from afar all the commotion he had caused among the tchekists, the rush of cars and the futile agitation of the executioners.

No, not home, where he would be found at once, but by a circuitous route, in a maze, through side streets and alleys – to Sivtsev Vrazhek; not to enter, but just to tap at the window, and wait till the casement was opened to give a low call:

'Tanya, don't be afraid. It's I, Astafiev, the comedian Smehatchev. I'm being pursued. Hide me, Tanya!'

And she would say:

'Heavens – you! Why, of course. Quick!'

And as he entered he would take her in his arms for the first time and hold her in a long embrace.

From the neighbouring couch came a whisper:

'You aren't asleep, Alexey Dmitritch? It's rough on you too!'

And after a pause:

'I saw how smartly you gave that mouse a rap on the nose. There's a queer creature – living of its own free will in a prison!'

– LXXI –

AMONG THE INFLUENTIAL

Uncle Borya refused outright. 'No, Tanyusha, I can be of no use in this matter. I do meet him now and again at meetings of a purely technical order in connection with the Defence of the Realm, but our relations are only official and don't go beyond wishing each other good-morning and goodbye. Our department is entirely self-governing, you know. It's purely scientific and has nothing to do with politics. So you see, Tanyusha, there's really nothing I can do.'

'I quite understand that it would be awkward for you personally, Uncle Borya, but all I want is a recommendation, in order to gain admittance to him.'

'That makes no difference, Tanyusha. It's a matter of a political nature, and a very serious one too.'

'But, uncle, Astafiev was arrested by mistake for no reason whatever. He had nothing to do with politics!'

'How am I to know? And you can't know either.'

'I'm sure of it, uncle! If one were to take the necessary steps, he could be set free at once. The thing is to gain admittance to somebody influential.'

'In times like these, Tanyusha, the best thing is to leave things alone. You'll only sully your own reputation, and do him no good. And our family is rather too well known. If, as you say, he's not guilty of anything, he'll be set free in any case.'

'But he is a friend of ours, Uncle Borya, and he has no one else to take any trouble on his behalf.'

'I quite understand, Tanyusha... and what I am saying is in his interests too. Taking steps on his behalf might only make matters worse, by attracting attention. Now perhaps if his relations – '

'He has none.'

'There, you see!'

'What, uncle?'

'That's just what I was saying, that I – well, that it doesn't concern me in any way. And I'm afraid that any recommendation of mine – well, I'm not in their good books. I don't mean that there is anything definite, but all the same they don't trust us experts.'

'Then you don't want to, Uncle Borya?'

'I do, Tanyusha, very much. I should so like to have been able to do it, but I can't do anything – nothing at all. I am very sorry. I should so like to help, but there's really nothing I can do. It's the times that are so dreadful. Oh, Tanyusha, I really don't know if we shall ever see better days again. It's a perfect nightmare!'

Tanyusha was silent. She thought for a moment, then, swiftly raising her head, looked at him keenly.

He shrank a little under her gaze and murmured again:

'Yes, a perfect nightmare, and there doesn't seem to be any way out.'

Then Tanyusha rose, and took up her bag:

'Uncle Borya.'

'Yes, Tanyusha? What is it, my dear?'

'Nothing. Goodbye, Uncle Borya.'

He accompanied her to the door, keeping just behind her. In the porter's lodge, where there were a number of workers, he shook hands with her.

'I do understand you, Tanyusha, really I do,' he whispered, in a voice that strove to be gentle, although he was obviously ill at ease. 'You're a plucky, kind-hearted girl, but all the same I would advise you to wait.'

Tanyusha was silent.

Glancing about him, and in a lower whisper still, he added:

'In any case, you know, I would certainly advise you – that is, if you do gain admittance to him – not to mention me. It's all the same to me personally, of course, but it might make a difference, you know. They look upon us experts as a dangerous element, not to be trusted. It might spoil everything.'

Without a smile, without even turning her head towards him, Tanyusha said out loud:

'You needn't worry, uncle. I'm not going to spoil anything for you.'

And she went out.

In the evening, when the new friend of the little house in Sivtzev Vrazhek came as usual, Tanyusha had a long business talk with him. They went over various names, discussing to whom and through whom she could gain quickest admittance. Protassov's circle of acquaintances was small. Nevertheless, he took it upon himself to pay several business calls on the morrow:

'I don't know whether anything will come of it; one can but try. I'm banking on a friend of mine who has access to him. He's not a bad sort; in fact, he's fairly reliable. We can have an inquiry made through him, anyhow. As for the recommendation – well, I don't know about that.'

The following morning, Protassov went to see the man in question. He had not seen him for some time. Their meeting was friendly.

'Well, and what are you doing nowadays?'

'Oh, bartering.'

'Queer fellow! Do you mean to say you make on it?'

'Enough to live on.'

'But why don't you work along your own lines? There's a dearth of people who are experts at anything.'

Protassov told him what he had come about, and asked him to help him to get information as to the nature of the charge on which Astafiev had been arrested and the fate that awaited him. His friend consented, though somewhat reluctantly:

'All right, I'll ring up one chap I know. Only one has to be careful with him, so don't be surprised.'

And he telephoned.

'Hullo! That you?... Yes, yes... Knew me by my voice? I say, old man, how did it end up last night? Did they stay on long? ...Yes. Do you think anything will come of it?... Well, that would be all right... Yes... So – not before the day after tomorrow. All right, I'll ring you up. Well, so long. I say, just a moment; there's something I wanted to ask you. Ah, yes, could you by any chance let me have some information about a man who has been arrested – I'm being bothered to death by his relations. I'll just look up his name... What? Oh no, nothing serious, just seems to have been taken for no earthly reason, but I'm sick of having his people pestering me. His name...'

It was half-an-hour before the information came through. It was not reassuring:

'There's nothing definite, but they've got very strong suspicions about him. The case is in the hands of Comrade Brickmann, and he likes to drag things out.'

'And if steps are taken on his behalf?' asked Protassov.

'That does help sometimes. Do you know him personally?'

'No, but we have mutual acquaintances. There's a girl trying to get something done for him.'

'Who is she?'

Protassov thought for a moment, then named Tanyusha. He trusted his friend.

'Isn't she related to the professor?'

'She's his granddaughter.'

'Well then, what could be better? The professor is famous and highly respected. Couldn't he see to it himself?'

'He is too old.'

'Well then, Protassov, what is it you want me to do? Give you a recommendation for her?'

'Yes, if you could.'

'All right. Do you answer for her?'

'Why, of course.'

'Oh, I didn't mean anything. You never know. Do you happen to be in love with her? Pretty? Well, and to whom do you want the recommendation? Because, you know, I can only give you one to the chap I've just rung up. I'm on much better terms with him than with any of the others.'

'And who is he?'

His friend mentioned a big gun, great enough for Protassov to have heard of him. It was not the personage Tanyusha wanted to see, but his friend merely laughed when he heard who that was:

'Oh dear, no, it's absolutely no use trying to get to him. No object in it either; and extremely difficult, because he won't admit anyone. He wouldn't even stop to listen. My chap is nearer the less important matters. Only – between you and me – he's not a first-rate fellow; not up to much, to be quite frank. But he is in power at the moment. One's got to be very careful in what one says to him. You'd better warn that girl of yours.'

'Are you on friendly terms with him?'

'Oh, I've known him a long time, from the time when I was still in exile. There's no real friendship between us, but we see each other quite often. You know, I'm not a communist myself. I have nothing to do with politics, I'm only on committees. But you know, Protassov, you are making a great mistake in not working. There's a real dearth of the right sort of people, and you're a first-rate worker.'

'That's probably why my factory gave me the sack.'

'Do you mean to say you were sacked? That must have been pure chance; then remember, too, all the engineers were sacked without distinction. Would you like me to get you a job? Are you working anywhere at the moment?'

Protassov named a firm which had nothing to do with technology or mining, and where it was more a matter of his putting in an appearance than actually working.

'Lord, what a hole! There's nothing for you to do there!'

'That's just it, I don't do anything! I just call in from time to time to get a little packet of yeast or a pot of jam.'

'How futile! Ill get you an engineering job.'

Protassov thought it over for a moment:

'Well, of course, I should like to work. Only I haven't much faith in the work of the present day. And I don't want to work for nothing.'

'The work that is being done just at the moment is pretty poor, I admit. But it will improve little by little.'

'And who is going to do the improving?'

'Who? You'll do your share; you and I and all the rest of us – all the people that count. Just at present it's the fools and the greenhorns that have got the upper hand. That's why things aren't as they should be. But you wait. There'll come a time when everything will settle down and become normal. It can't come all of a sudden, Protassov.'

'I know. But by that time there won't be any plant left whole.'

'We'll get new.'

'There won't be any money for it.'

'We'll get the money too. What a pessimist you are, Protassov! Do you imagine that Russia will go under?'

'It might.'

'No, my dear fellow, there's no fear of that. It's just lassitude that makes us think such things. I have no illusions myself, I know our present rulers well, and there's one thing I can tell you, Protassov Russia won't go under. It's not the country to go under. You don't believe it any more than I do, you only just say so.'

They parted as friends, and Protassov took with him the letter of recommendation Tanyusha needed.

'He's not at all a bad fellow on the whole,' Protassov said to himself. 'Of course Russia won't go under, and naturally one has got to work, so that she shall not. But it wouldn't do for everyone to lie jokingly over the telephone, and be hail-fellow-well-met with all sorts of scoundrels. However, one can't blame him. If he were to behave differently he couldn't get on with his difficult job as smoothly and easily as he does. One has got to work, of course. If only the general atmosphere weren't so oppressive, and there were fewer fools about!'

– LXXII –

THE WOLF PROWLS

Strange how fearless the wolves had grown.

The snow lay deep that winter, and the wolf's hind legs stuck many a time in its depths as he padded along to the village. From the forest behind, the moon lit up a dark path of tracks that led to the village, not straight, but in a line slightly curving towards the thicket, as though the wolf were involuntarily drawn to its shadows.

The road across the bridge was in use, although not even the bridge could be seen now in winter. The snow lay piled up high over the stream, and had levelled the banks with the fields. Only the willow twigs darkened the riverside.

The wolf sat down by the edge of the road and gave a deep, muffled howl. Reluctant, the dog's answer came from afar. And the wolf slunk on sideways, his tail between his legs.

The second hut on the skirts of the village belonged to Kolchagin – Andrey's and Dunyasha's father. It was a large hut. In the left half, surrounded by the garden, lived Dunyasha's elder sister, with her husband and child.

The wolves had grown fearless that winter because the menfolk had left the village. Some had been killed in the war; others shot in the towns. There was no powder, either, to waste on the wolves; far more people than wolves were being shot those days. And it was becoming increasingly difficult to feed the dogs.

Dunyasha's mother was still young at forty-five. She was called Anna, and Dunyasha's sister was called Annyuta also. The family lived in a very humble way, and when Dunyasha arrived from town it felt the extra burden in spite of the various things and the small sum of money she had brought. Of Andrey there was not a sign or a rumour.

Someone had given the Kolchagins' dog the odd name of Pryska. Pryska was of medium size, oldish and dirty. He scented wolves badly – but then, what was there for him to guard? The sheep were under lock and key, and the cow was in the stall on the other side of the old folks' wall. So there was nothing whatever to guard – unless, of course, he were to guard from a feeling of solidarity towards the other dogs. Pryska crouched close to the warm wall and tried to sleep, though he got his principal sleep during the day in the hut.

The wolf, too, knew perfectly well that everything was locked up. But the village drew him with its odour of stalls and sheep-cots. He was gaunt and ravenous, painfully ravenous. There might, perhaps, be frozen guts or bones in the rubbish-heaps. Just to breathe the rich, savoury air would be something.

He approached the huts, not by the road, but through the kitchen gardens. And not a dog yelped: all were asleep.

The wolf's nostrils dilated as he drew in the cold air. His muzzle was covered with hoarfrost. He crept up to one of the rubbish-heaps round which there were a number of dog-tracks: the dogs, too, were hungry.

Wherever the dogs had dug at the surface, the wolf gnawed down, aiding himself with his claws. He had hardly begun, however, when Pryska broke out into a bark, all the dogs of the village joining in after him.

Pryska led the chorus; he whined and howled, running up and down the yard and taking flying leaps up at the porch in his efforts to scare the wolf. Frightened himself, he fussed and he snarled, quivering with indignation that the wolf had come. But as for showing fight – well, but what could he, Pryska, do against a wolf! So he just sprang up at the gate and howled till he was hoarse.

Not a soul in the village stirred. The peasants woke up for a moment and knew that wolves were near. But that was a nightly occurrence. There was nothing for them to get up for: everything was locked up.

The wolf ran on from one rubbish-heap to another, scratching and gnawing. At one spot he scented his way straight up to a sheep-cot, right in the teeth of the dog's commotion. The cot with its warm sheep lured him on irresistibly, and saliva dribbled from his jaws, freezing as it fell to an icicle.

His ears ached from the dog's barking. Yet the village slept.

The village slept.

Round it, describing two whole circles, from hut to hut, from one rubbish-heap to another, ran the famished wolf, dripping in his hunger a trail of noxious saliva. Then, trotting out into the paddock, he sat down, licked himself and howled at the village:

CURSED IT FOR ITS FAMINE.

Beside Kolchagin's hut, Pryska cowered from the curse, and the hair of his coat stood on end. Man did not understand, but Pryska understood it. Something would surely happen.

There was a pole in the middle of the village, and on the pole, beneath the starling-cot, there was a bell. Oh, to strike that bell, that all might know:

HE, THE WOLF, CURSED THE VILLAGE, CURSED IT FOR ITS FAMINE!

May man, too, be reduced to burrowing in rubbish-heaps and tearing his dogs to pieces.

May he, too, be drawn by the rich warmth of sheep-cots.

May he howl at the moon as wolves and wish his neighbour all manner of ill, be scared of his own shadow, put his tail between his legs and become a mere shadow himself.

May he have nothing to keep under lock and key, to hide from the wolf's famished fangs.

AND MAY MAN'S HUNGER BE WORSE THAN THE WOLVES'!

If only the bell could have rung out the alarm of the pangs that stared man in the face, that he might be cowed with dread, gnash his teeth and dribble the saliva of hunger.

The moon, as it listened to the wolf cursing the village, smiled with incredulity. Or, if it did have any faith in those curses, it felt neither for wolf nor man.

When, however, the wolf caught sight of a hare bounding swiftly away from the kitchen gardens he suddenly felt a new lease of life, and dashed off in pursuit. The hare leaped lightly in a straight line across the frozen crust of snow. The wolf floundered on with laboured breath, biting his dripping tongue; but it had occurred to him to run in a curve to the forest to cut off the hare's escape.

The wolf devoured his prey with his eyes, whining with excitement and frightening it with those blazing eyes. Rounding the corners, they reached the skirt of the forest. There was a moment when his yellow fangs had almost nipped the bobtail. But the hare took refuge in a clump of bushes where he could be seen but not reached. And when, lifting high his head to see above the snow-laden twigs, the wolf advanced upon its cover, the white ball flew out unseen and sped on farther, out of reach.

Hopeless, the wolf went slowly on to a hollow in the depths of the forest, to smother his hunger in sleep and in hungry dreams of the warmth of sheep and the greed of man.

It was morning. The peasants were getting up in the village. Wagging his tail, Pryska pushed his way into the kitchen to get some sleep in the warmth. Its dog's work was ended.

The night was over. Day had begun.

– LXXIII –

FRIENDS OF CHILDHOOD

Vassya's heart beat wildly as he turned down Sivtzer Vrazhek and went up to knock at the door of the little house he knew so well

He was wearing a short winter coat, a scarf, felt boots with a pattern in red – Kazan work, probably – and a warm cap with earflaps. He had remained in bed for almost a month after the typhus, as the doctor had feared complications might follow. After the critical stage of his illness, Tanyusha had been to see him less often. It was difficult for her to get away, for she had the burden of all the housework on her shoulders. She did all the cooking and washing herself, and occasionally went to sell various trifles at the Smolensky marketplace. Most of her evenings – and on holiday afternoons too – were taken up playing at concerts. The general poverty had affected the clubs as well, and they were paying their performers less than before. It was impossible to get lessons either, especially in winter, when education almost everywhere came to a standstill owing to the fact that schools were not heated, and children and young people as busy as adults getting food.

There was another reason, too, why Tanyusha came to see Vassya less often. There seemed somehow nothing to talk about now. She had tried telling him bits of news, but events and rumours were all so confused and depressing that news was in no way suited to divert an invalid. She had sometimes come alone to see him, and sometimes Protassov had come with her, but more often they just happened to meet at his bedside. Alyonushka still came every day, although as a matter of fact he no longer needed nursing. She, however, could only keep up a conversation on the high cost of living. Both Tanyusha and Vassya felt ill at ease somehow in each other's presence, as though there were something that had been left unsaid. And so Tanyusha's visits grew rare.

Vassya rose from his sickbed when the streets of Moscow had long since been covered with snow. There was no one responsible now for cleaning the streets, so the snowdrifts remained in the roads, churned up by hoofs and flattened by sledge-slides. Even the pavements lay buried out of sight. In some places the snow had been scraped and piled up in a heap to clear a path to gates and entrances. In Sivtsev Vrazhek there had been no one to clear the pavement in front of the professor's little house since the dvornik's departure for the village late that autumn.

'What's the good of my staying on here? I'm only a burden!' Nicolai had said. 'Maybe things will be better by the spring. If not, I'll come back some time next year. It can't go on like this forever.'

His watch-box had been pulled to pieces for fuel. That had been the fate of the bathhouse long before, in his time even. But that, at any rate, had supplied them with firewood for the winter.

This was Vassya's first visit to Sivtsev Vrazhek since his illness, although he had been out for over a week. At first he thought of calling at an hour when he would be sure to find only the old professor at home. Then he decided that in any case he would have to bring himself sometime or other to see Tanyusha in her home, in those familiar surroundings... And, after all, nothing had actually happened. It had all turned out perfectly all right; and everything was as it should be.

He found only Tanyusha at home. The professor had gone for a walk, taking with him his portfolio full of books.

Tanyusha was glad that Vassya had come, but at the same time felt somewhat ill at ease. She noticed that he was not quite himself, and that he behaved as though he were in a strange house and not in the one he had known from boyhood. And Tanyusha knew that the cause was in herself. But was that her fault? Had she ever promised him anything?

Vassya had imagined that to have things out with Tanyusha would be difficult, and dreaded broaching the subject. And yet he felt he ought to speak out. He ought to tell her that he understood everything and that he wished her every possible happiness. After that, seeing each other would be easier, natural, and as it used to be – well, if not exactly as it used to be, it would at any rate be possible to talk again like friends. Anything to get rid of that embarrassment! But it turned out to be easier than he thought.

'Who is now living upstairs, in your room?'

'There's nobody at all for the moment. Dunyasha has gone, and that brother of hers, the Commissar, disappeared some time before she left. The rooms have been somehow forgotten, so the authorities haven't done anything about them. They just go on remaining empty. But it's possible that someone may be moving into them soon.'

'An acquaintance?'

'Yes. It's not quite certain yet, but Pyotr Pavlovitch may come. He has a flat of his own, it's true, with a bathroom too, but what is the good of a bathroom when the pipes are frozen everywhere? So grandfather suggested that...'

She went into a lengthy explanation why it would be a good thing for Protassov to move. Their house, she pointed out, was much nearer his work; also, his moving into the rooms upstairs would save them from being requisitioned, as he had a right to an extra room for his work. But she felt that her explanation was unnecessary and that Vassya was not even listening.

For a while they sat on in silence, then Vassya asked suddenly:

'Are you going to marry him?'

Tanyusha gave no sign of surprise at the question; indeed, it was almost as though she had been expecting it.

'I don't know,' she replied. 'I like Pyotr Pavlovitch very much. We've become great friends.'

And she added in the same tone:

'Don't you approve, Vassya?'

She glanced at him. He was sitting motionless, looking at the bright patch of the window; and his eyes were full of tears.

'Vassya, you aren't – you don't mean to say you're crying, Vassya?'

Without turning his eyes away from the window, he dived his hands into all his pockets in a frantic search for the handkerchief he had left, as though on purpose, at home.

'Well, really, Vassya!'

He turned away, and in a quivering voice that sounded strangely like a child's said:

'It's nothing. It's my illness, you know, Tanyusha, that has made me feel such an awful weanling – weakling, I mean.'

And having said something ridiculous, Vassya burst into tears.

Tanyusha comforted him like a mother comforting her child. She wiped his eyes with her own handkerchief, stroked his cropped, round head, and held her hand over his forehead, when he pressed against it. This was the first time, she reflected, he had ever pressed close to her like that; though he might often, perhaps, have wanted to before. That it should have become possible just then!

Vassya could not bring himself to raise his head. He was very much ashamed of his weakness for one thing; besides, it was absolutely essential that he should wipe his nose, and there was nothing for him to wipe it with. He must have grown dreadfully weak during his illness, he thought, for otherwise, of course, that would never have happened.

'You must hurry up and get quite well again, Vassya. You have grown so thin.'

'Do forgive me, Tanyusha, for this stupid exhibition.'

'Why, of course!'

'It wasn't as if I didn't know it all before. I guessed, of course... Only... but I wish you every possible happiness, Tanyusha. That's really why I came – to tell you.'

'Thank you, Vassya. I know. You are my dear friend, and always have been, ever since childhood. Only let's now talk of something else.'

'Let's by all means. I'll take this handkerchief, if I may. I'll wash and return it,' he added hurriedly. 'Will the professor be home soon? I'm sorry not to have seen him.'

'Aren't you staying?'

'Not long; I've got to get home.'

'Have you anyone coming?'

Tanyusha said 'anyone,' but she knew perfectly well that it could only be Alyonushka, who still came every day. And she looked for some sign of new confusion in Vassya's face. He answered, however, quite naturally:

'Elena Ivanovna is coming. She comes every day, you know.'

'What a nice person she is, and so thoughtful! It's she who pulled you through, Vassya. You would have been lost without her.'

'I know. She's wonderful! And so disinterested, although life isn't easy for her either. The time she has devoted to me!'

Tanyusha smiled to herself:

'You have probably grown very used to Alyonushka, haven't you?'

Vassya answered:

'I should think so!' but thought: 'She needn't have said that!' He realized that Tanyusha found it very convenient that he should be used to Alyonushka and go on needing her; Tanyusha would feel somehow freer – although he could not stand in her way, nor had any desire to. Let her love Protassov; let her marry him if she wanted to. It was stupid and absurd of him to have howled like a schoolboy. But there was no need for her to have talked of Alyonushka just now, and in a way that sounded exactly as though she were consoling him.

Vassya felt hurt on behalf of Alyonushka, too. She really had pulled him through, and hadn't stopped looking after him yet. Of course she wasn't like Tanyusha; she was much simpler and not very educated, and gave a funny little snort when she laughed. Still she was sincerity itself and very kind-hearted. Being with her wasn't the least bit of a strain. Why insinuate that here was a consolation for Tanyusha's not loving him, and for her marrying Protassov?

'Elena Ivanovna is quite a simple person,' he said, 'and she is very good to me. I have the greatest respect for her. She has been through a great deal in her life. I am greatly indebted to her.'

Tanyusha realized that Vassya could not have spoken otherwise. And she interpreted him in her own way, her woman's way, saying to herself: 'Well, I've no doubt he'll manage to pay her back somehow.'

And she brightened up considerably.

* * *

The professor came home tired, but in high spirits.

For one thing, though cold, the day was sunny and pleasant. Secondly, he had been shown, in the Writers' Bookshop, an English ornithological journal of the previous year which had somehow or other reached Moscow. On looking through it, he had discovered extracts from his own book on the migration of birds, and in a foreign tone of courtesy a few lines of homage to the author, 'the famous Russian scholar and indefatigable observer of our feathered friends.'

The professor had often read such expressions of tribute before, not indeed without pleasure, but with equanimity. Now, in such hard times, when he felt utterly cut off from the European world of learning, they moved him deeply. And as he went home along the Tverskoy Boulevard, hugging the portfolio with the journal which had been presented to him, he felt a warmth in his eyes, followed by the chill of a tiny frozen lump on his eyelashes. He felt a trifle ashamed, but deeply contented.

So they haven't forgotten the old man yet over there!

'If only I were a little younger,' he thought, 'and could wait for better times to go off abroad with Tanyusha – to Paris, London! I might even give a lecture in English to the Ornithological Society! ...Oh, but I don't possess a frock coat,' he remembered with anxiety. 'It had to be exchanged for potatoes. But I still have the dress-coat, which nobody will take because it is swallow-tailed and cannot be converted into a simple, practical jacket. And it is precisely the dress-coat I need in England if I am to lecture in the evening.'

And his thoughts ran on:

'If only I could have the book published! It is quite ready in rough; there is merely the copying out to be done. Ten years now that I have been working at it. But it is no good even thinking of having it published. It is only raw youngsters who manage somehow to get verse in print these days. And what amazing titles they do find for their volumes! *The Horse as a Horse* – heaven knows what that means, if it is not just impudence!'

But not even that could cast a shadow on the professor's mood. He was delighted to see Vassya again.

'Oh, but aren't you shorn! It makes your head look as round as a bullet. Well, good lad to recover as you have done! Come and see us now as often as you can.'

He pottered about, smiling; but, for all his embarrassment, could not resist drawing the English journal out of his portfolio and showing it to Vassya.

'Look what a rare thing has come into my possession! A new number – last year's, I know, but still... Not even the University receives anything from abroad, you know. They haven't forgotten me, an old man, in this number either. Nice, isn't it?'

Vassya glanced through the journal and looked at the illustrations.

'Yes, very nice,' he said. 'And how wonderfully the journal has been produced.'

'Well, that is hardly to be wondered at. They are experts. Besides, they have plenty of money.'

Tanyusha had prepared lunch, but Vassya was in a hurry to go.

'I really must be off.'

'But won't you have lunch with us, Vassya?'

'Can't, I'm afraid. I promised to be home by two o'clock.'

'Well, then, do come and see us soon.'

'I will. Goodbye, professor.'

'Why in such a hurry?'

'I really must be off.'

'Well, you know best. I have been so glad to see you, so very glad.'

When Vassya was gone, the old man called Tanyusha to him and stroked her head:

'Well, and how did you find Vassya? How quiet he is now.' 'But, you know, I have been seeing him quite often, grandfather.'

'I know, but is he not feeling rather depressed?'

'Why should he be feeling depressed, grandfather?'

'Well, on account of affairs of the heart. Be merciful to him, Tanyusha. He is so devoted, and he must be feeling it.' Tanyusha nestled up to her grandfather:

'I believe that Vassya will soon get over it, grandfather. In fact, things promise to be even better for him.'

– LXXIV –

THE TWO SIDES

Although the centre of the universe was, of course, the little house in Sivtzev Vrazhek, there was life apart from it, radiating out into far distances. Every human being clung on to life and each thought of himself as its centre, which indeed he was.

Andrey Kolchagin, too, was the centre of his own world – Andrey, a deserter in the Great War, as it was formerly called – or the Imperial War, as the same people now called it – formerly Commandant of the Hamovniky Sovdep and now commander of a scratch regiment in the civil war. Again a life of semi-starvation, again the cold and the lice; but with a difference. He had, in the first war, been nothing but a dumb slave, nothing but cannon fodder; whereas in the second he was a warrior fighting for the happiness of all mankind.

True, Kolchagin had no idea what should constitute this happiness; nevertheless, hunger and cold and lice now stood clearly justified in his eyes. It was essential, at all costs, to crush the foe at home, for if he were not crushed, dreadful punishment and revenge awaited all the Kolchagins. This time the foe was real enough: no longer the German Hans, with whom he had nothing in common, but that same company commander whose fist had dealt him backhanders on his left cheek. It was, however, fear for the future, rather than rancour – which had long since cooled – that urged them on. But to acknowledge that fear, even to oneself, was impossible. Fear is no standard. And just as devices like 'For God, Tsar and Country' had been thought of for the Kolchagins of old, so now 'For Socialism and Soviet Rule' was written up in white upon red. The words were no more comprehensible or necessary now than before. And, just as before, every man put into them a meaning of his own, the Kolchagins understanding them to mean: 'Save yourself and yours.' And fear and conscience goaded them on.

During the years of his desertion Andrey Kolchagin had enjoyed a number of things – freedom from the obligations which had been imposed on him by force, power, and an easy life, that had seemed to him almost princely. He had learned to think, too, which had not been required of a soldier before. He came to love the beauty of sonorous words and learned to pronounce them himself, became imbued with the spirit of the professional soldier, understood the meaning of great deeds, realized how cheap the lives of others were and how tremendously valuable his own. He was in favour now, a man to whom all paths were open; no longer a simple private, one of thousands and millions, but a picked man, to whom his superiors spoke as a human being, and who was honoured by the name of 'Comrade.' The mere consciousness that he owed his epaulettes, not to some training school or exalted rank, but to his own personal valour – coolness and daring – was enough to single him out for promotion; and that mere consciousness decided for Andrey Kolchagin and for many other Andreys, on whose side their place was, and on whose side their hope and devotion. It may be that, if verified, things might not appear quite in this light; but there was certainly no need of any verification in the camp of the gold epaulettes, for Kolchagin's experience there had been a harsh one and his judgment of it unerring. Here, on the other hand, everything was new and everything possible.

Face to face stood two brother armies, each with its own standard of truth and honour. There was the truth of those who considered their country and the revolution dishonoured by the new despotism and a new reign of force merely painted a different colour from the last, and the truth of those who looked upon their country and the revolution in a different light, seeing their dishonour, not in a shameful peace with Germany, but in the frustration of the nation's hopes.

Dishonourable indeed would have been the nation if it had not brought forward defenders of the idea of a cultured motherland, the idea of a nation keeping faith, the idea of gradual progress and education of mankind.

Poor indeed would have been the nation, if in the hour of the conclusion of an age-long dispute, it had not tried a complete shattering of the old, hated idols, a reorganization of life, of ideas, of economic relationships and of the whole social order.

Heroes there were on both sides; and clean hearts too, self-sacrifice, lofty humanity and animal brutality, fear and disillusionment, and strength and weakness and dull despair.

It would have been altogether too simple, both for the living and for history, had truth been one single truth and had it fought against falsehood only. There were, however, two truths and two honours fighting each other. And the battlefield was strewn with the bravest and best.

* * *

In those days fell a young cadet, whom everyone called Alyosha, a grey-eyed lad, scarcely more than a schoolboy. He killed with the rest and was killed himself. He lay on his back, his sightless eyes staring up at the sky. Why so soon? Oh, to have lived just a little while longer! Already his breast is decorated with the ribbon of St. George – for heroism in the slaughter of brothers! Alyosha has perished!

In those days fell, too, the soldier-commander and hero of the Red Flag, Andrey Kolchagin. Severely wounded in the head, he stumbled against Alyosha's body and dropped down beside it.

Without inquiring their names, without weighing their merits and failings, eternal night drew one pall over both.

– LXXV –

ZAVALISHIN'S DOMAIN

During the intervals between 'operations', Zavalishin would saunter along the passages and rooms of wherever he happened to be working, sleepy, slack, with swollen eyes. Everyone knew him, but he had no real companions. There were some who avoided him, repelled by his gruesome handicraft, never shook hands with him and even tried not to notice him.

Occasionally Zavalishin would enter the Commandant's or the general office, sit down in silence on a bench and ask when the next distribution of stores would take place, when the register would be examined and he receive his due. He carefully filled in the register after each batch of cases in his clear, crooked writing, entering the date, the number of cases, the numbers of the orders and attaching the documents. In this he stood firm; nor would he, even when drunk, do his job unless he were given a signed and stamped warrant.

Zavalishin had taken up with a certain Anna Klimovna, whom he had formerly courted on Saturdays. He had settled her now in his flat, though it was seldom enough that he saw her, except in the dinner-hours. The woman was still young, though staid and economical. She knew exactly what Zavalishin's profession was, but did not seem particularly interested. When she discovered what it was she was surprised, but she accepted the fact at once. It was a source of considerable satisfaction to her that the man with whom she was living was earning so well. Difficult though it was to get him to speak of his work, she would try to find out whether there were likely to be many cases left and whether he would not get a rise per head on account of the increased cost of living and the fall of the rouble. She surveyed him with interest whenever he returned from his work in a new suit of clothes or pair of high boots, aware that he always received whatever clothes were left over after an execution. She would alter them to fit him, lengthen the sleeves if necessary, and wash the soiled linen he brought. And she would do it all with her usual care, like the good housewife she was, her composure unruffled. Whenever Zavalishin came home drunk she put him to bed without scolding him overmuch, realizing that his work was not easy and that it was hard to get through it unless one were drunk. With the chairman of the House Committee, Denissot, she was on excellent terms; it was even possible that she received him on the days when Zavalishin worked overtime – days when he seldom came home.

When, in August and September, the bandits were 'liquidated',[1] there were many occasions when Zavalishin was obliged to work overtime. Those days he refused outright to work sober. Vodka was always put aside for him; he had not even to bother to get it for himself. On one occasion he went with an order to the goods' depot in the

---

[1] See p.228.

Sretenka to receive a forage cap, but was sent for before he had time to select one that fitted him. He left unwillingly, got through the work, filled in the register and went back to the depot, only to discover that all the best leather caps had been taken. For a long time afterwards he grumbled and grieved over it.

As a greatly needed and important personage Zavalishin was admitted everywhere. But the place he liked best to go to was the wing in the yard of No. 14, where was the common basement cell, called the 'Ship of Death'. The place drew him because it was mostly bandits who were down there in the pit – cool fellows, the sort he understood, and with whom one knew where one was. Zavalishin did not trouble his head about politics, and could not make out why some folk were in quod, others at large, and some 'sent to have their accounts closed'.[2] All he knew was that with the fellows down there in the Ship of Death there was no doubt about one thing: either you'd do them in, or they you. He felt more at home with those fellows too... They all knew each other, knew a thing or two about swearing, and would go to death with a swagger, except that they would first ask for a fag.

The 'Commissar of Death', Ivanov, had known many of them at liberty, and he would tell Zavalishin stories about them. Zavalishin found it very convenient looking down at them from the gallery that surrounded their pit. Some had been there long enough for him to know them quite well by sight.

Zavalishin was known by sight too. Whenever he sauntered idly up to the Ship of Death, bored, dull and indifferent, there would fall a deep silence below, more deathly even than when Commissar Ivanov appeared to call out names from a list. Ivanov had been a bandit himself, which was the reason, perhaps, why many of those below looked upon him as one of themselves.

It was only in Zavalishin's free time, when he was not very drunk and was bored with having nothing to do, that he roamed about all these places. His own headquarters, the place where he usually worked, was a low dark cellar in the same building, but with a special entrance from the yard – the first door on the left from the gate on the Malaya Lubyanka side.

It sometimes happened that Zavalishin had to work in the garage in Varsonofievsky Street, near the Church of the Resurrection. There

---

[2] See page 228.

was much more light and space there; but somehow he did not feel at home in the garage. In the beginning, when 'operations' took place outside the town, he had sometimes had to go for a drive in the Petrovsky Park check by jowl with the rest, in the very same van, which had not been pleasant at all. But he had looked upon it as a new job, which it was only a matter of getting used to. Nor did he work alone those days. Later on it was usual to send, not people, but 'stiffeys' out of town, and not straight from the place of 'operation', but through the Lefortovsky mortuary.

In Zavalishin's own headquarters, the cellar, he worked alone, without any help; for, as he rightly remarked, what was the good of help in a job like his? it would only mean extra bother and talk. As had come to be the custom, the condemned was escorted as far as the little passage that led to the cellar, then given a push towards the open door. Whoever accompanied him went out and closed the outer door till it was all over. The rest lay in Zavalishin's own hands – though for that matter nothing ever went wrong; they all came of their own accord into the light out of the dark little passage. First of all, Zavalishin took the order, for it was only on their presentation of it that he received his clients. He did not stop to bother about names – just saw that the numbers tallied, to make sure he got neither more nor less.

It was seldom that Zavalishin entered his cellar in his spare time; he was not fond of his cellar. It did once or twice happen, however, that, feeling bored, he lurched in quite drunk, turned the key and dropped down on the bench facing the bullet-riddled wall He had then bellowed out some dismal song, or fired his revolver at random just so that there should be a smell of powder and not only the musty cellar smell in the place. But he had never slept here, for fear of ghosts. He always carried the key about with him, and gave it up only to the women who did the cleaning. The men loathed that job.

Among the higher authorities of the place, Zavalishin knew scarcely a soul, nor had he any ambition to get to know them. He never attended meetings or elections, took no interest in the prisoners' schedules or in their extradition, nor in anything whatsoever apart from his own work. Even in the register of employees he figured merely as a warder. But insignificant though he was, he was perfectly well aware that he was in some way a special being, the most needed of them all and the most independent, and that that was the reason why he was fed and feared and given so much. They could get along without anyone else in the place – the others could be replaced – but they could not get along without him, Zavalishin; and there was nobody either who could take his place – at any rate it would be very difficult to find one who would.

Consequently, in fits of boredom and on days of idleness Zavalishin permitted himself to be difficult, and more than once threatened to throw up his job. Each time that had happened, however, he was either offered more pay or simply won over to a better frame of mind with a bottle of choice spirits.

Strenuous days of overtime work came in October as well, after the explosion in Leontievsky Street. And those were real harvest days.

– LXXVI –

AN INTERVIEW WITH A DIGNITARY

It was very cold. Fortunately, Tanyusha still had her old pair of overshoes. When she had to go to her concerts in the workmen's quarters she put on high felt boots over her shoes and kept them on till she was due to appear on the platform. Then, when her item was over and she had played for the encore she would thrust her feet into them again with joy and wait till the van came to the door to take the evening performers back to their homes.

But to go to the Kremlin in felt boots was quite another matter; it was the Kremlin after all. And so her old pair of overshoes came in useful once more.

At the Troitsky Gate a soldier took her pass into his lodge and brought it back stamped. She then made her way carefully along a path bordered with a heap of clean snow that had been cleared beside the palace walls. At the gate of the former Law Courts she again had to show her pass; and yet again, for the last time, at the entrance. Inside the building she was directed upstairs, and told to take the first turning on the right.

She did not have to wait very long. The secretary glanced at the pass and took from her the letter of recommendation.

'Just a moment. Will you sit down? You will probably be seen at once,' he informed her.

The people who passed through the waiting-room were all warmly dressed, evidently belonging to the place. The rooms were cold, which was perhaps the reason why they appeared so unusually large and curiously empty. Tanyusha felt very small and lost in the huge Kremlin building. People passed, looking at her with curiosity.

Presently the secretary returned and said:

'This way, if you please, comrade.'

He said it very politely, and even let Tanyusha through first. She had never had to go to see powerful, important people before, and in the dirty Soviet offices she occasionally went to on trivial matters the atmosphere had always been one of fussy inefficiency, and the officials irritable and rude. Here, however, everything was different; different, too, from what she had expected, for she had imagined that it would be like entering a fortress where she would everywhere be met with bayonets and distrust.

She entered a large, almost empty room with a lofty ceiling. The only furniture consisted of a divan, three armchairs and a bare round table of a former period. On the table lay a telephone directory and a couple of newspapers. The telephone stood on the window-sill. On the wallpaper were marks of furniture which had been removed, and in a far corner stood a cupboard with broken glass. It was warm and clean in here, and Tanyusha rather wished she had not entered in overshoes.

The door opened, and a man wearing a 'French' and wide trousers entered. He was a stocky individual of a type not Russian, with scanty hair and high cheekbones.

'Good-day,' he said, coming full upon Tanyusha. 'It's you, is it, who came with that letter? Well, sit down here. What have you come about?'

'I wanted to ask about a certain prisoner.'

'Well, I know that, it's in the letter. What is Astafiev to you? What are your relations?'

'He is our friend.'

'Who – ours?'

'He is a friend of mine and my grandfather's.'

'The professor? Your grandfather has something to do with birds, hasn't he?'

'Yes, he is an ornithologist.'

'Well, what about this Astafiev?'

'He has been unjustly arrested.'

'What d'you mean? We don't ever arrest unjustly. He has been arrested in connection with a very serious matter.'

'Astafiev was not interested in politics. He is a philosopher, and has been acting lately in workmen's clubs. I performed with him at concerts.'

'You sing, do you?'

'No, I play the piano.'

'Passed the finishing exams of the Conservatoire?'

'Yes.'

'Well, supposing you were to play at our concerts? We pay well, give our performers provisions. Come and play to us sometime or other.'

'Where are these concerts given?' Tanyusha asked.

The man in the 'French' raised his whitish eyes to her in astonishment:

'Why, here! – in the Extraordinary Commission.[1] We do have concerts, you know. You aren't a socialist-revolutionary, are you?'

'I belong to no party.'

'Well, then, why form friendships with socialist-revolutionaries – with this Astafiev of yours?'

'But he is not a socialist-revolutionary. He has nothing to do with politics. I know him quite well.'

'Well, then, we know him better still. So what is it you want?'

'I thought he might be set free since he is not guilty of anything.'

'If he's not guilty he'll be set free without any soliciting on your part.'

'But he has been in prison for over a month now!'

'That won't do him any harm. He can quite well stay on there for a year: that may teach him possibly not to organize conspiracies. There's no need for you to worry about him. It's best to give such friends a wide berth. We look upon that Astafiev of yours as a dangerous foe to the Soviet Government. It would be better for you not to interfere. Is he your fiancé, by any chance?'

'No.'

'Then what are you worrying for?'

Wiping his forehead, he added:

'All right, I'll inquire into the matter. Where do you live?'

Tanyusha gave her address.

'All right. We don't imprison people unjustly. If he's innocent he'll be set free, if he's guilty he'll get what he deserves. Don't you worry. Do you know Savinkov?'

---

[1] Commonly known as the Tcheka.

'Savinkov? No.'

He rose.

'You'll be given a return pass.'

He took his hand out of his pocket, but Tanyusha recoiled.

'Thank you,' she said.

'Good-morning. Come and play sometime or other. We pay well.'

In the big waiting-room the secretary wrote out Tanyusha's address once more and gave her a pass:

'You go out through the Troitsky Gate.'

* * *

The Kremlin stood covered with snow that was clean and white; Ivan the Great towered above, a frozen pile; the little golden domes of the Uspensky Cathedral were glittering bright.

And as she followed the pathway bordered by the heaped-up snow, Tanyusha felt quite small again and out of place in this unfamiliar world. At the Troitsky Gate a soldier took her pass and stuck it on his bayonet.

* * *

When Tanyusha left the room the man in the 'French' went up to the telephone and called a number.

'About this Astafiev case. How do matters stand now, Comrade Brickmann?... Well, you ought to give him a good scaring... Well, all right, it's your business. All the same I do think it would be better to keep his case quite apart from the others. Yes. Don't throw him in with the common herd. We'll see later on. Yes... Well, but I'm not saying anything. Let him stay on, by all means. All right... No, his fiancée or something has been round inquiring about him; a pretty girl, by the way. Well, so long. See you this evening.'

– LXXVII –

THE LITTLE PIG

Anna Klimovna, with whom Zavalishin was now living, was not a greedy woman – nobody could have called her that – but she was a very careful and economical housewife. For a woman of her station she lived prosperously enough, judging not only by present but by pre-War standards. Zavalishin brought home all sorts of supplies in jars, in parcels and bags, large and small; not rubbish either, such as cranberry leaves or clay soap, but genuine articles of the sort included in the rations of only the most highly valued people – white flour, lime-honey, lump-sugar and various kinds of spirits. He would bring her material as well, and galoshes and shoes – even shoes of the right size; and would give her money, a lot of money sometimes, although money didn't count of course in those days, as it was always worth less on the morrow.

No one in the house in the Dolgorukovskaya had the things Zavalishin had. Not even Denissov, the chairman of the House Committee, could stand comparison, in spite of the presents he accepted from everyone – presents for entering extra persons on the register (which entailed getting extra ration-cards), for sanctioning dealing in various hoarded goods on the premises, and finally for the very good reason that Denissov was the chairman and, as such, might well prove useful.

In these excellent circumstances Anna Klimovna might have run a household on a large scale, which undoubtedly she would have done had Zavalishin possessed a cottage on the outskirts of Moscow, or at any rate a real flat, or at least two rooms with a kitchen and larder. As it was, the two of them were cooped up in one room, while both the other rooms that Astafiev had occupied remained sealed. It was not possible to partition off a room in the diminutive hall; and as for the kitchen, which was small too, Anna Klimovna had already entered into possession of it and filled it up with jars and bags.

At one time she had thought of keeping hens in the kitchen, as other people did; but she was afraid that their cackling would disturb her sleep, and there was also the dirt and the smell to think of. And after all, why should she? She could get as many eggs as she wanted for her money without all that bother. One day, however, hearing that an old friend of hers, who did market gardening, had fattened a large pig and had made a lot of money out of it, she decided to do the same. It wasn't for the money that she wanted a pig, but for the sake of having a real household of her own, and in order to have some ham boiled and smoked for Easter. She knew the neighbours would be willing enough to let her have scraps, leaves of vegetables and anything that not even a hungry man would eat; and there would be no scarcity of fattening food for it. When the little pig grew into a big fat pig it would amply repay her for the expense of its feeding. It would have to be kept in the kitchen at first; afterwards it could be kept in one of the light sheds in the yard that Denissov had agreed to place at her entire disposal. He had approved of her plan; and in any case the sheds stood empty.

Accordingly, Anna Klimovna set out one day to a village not far distant from Moscow, where in exchange for some sugar, salt and spirits – principally spirits – she got a fat little sucking-pig.

At first it caused her a good deal of anxiety. She was afraid it might waste away, fall ill or be bitten by rats. Then, when it grew bigger, all her care went to see that it was not stolen, that it should move as little as possible, eat without ceasing and accumulate fat. In all these particulars she was completely successful. Those of her neighbours to whom she showed her pig were struck by its size and congratulated her. If the chairman, Denissov, had not only been anxious to retain Anna's good will but had also taken a personal interest in the pig's welfare and safety – he had been promised his share of it – one or other of the envious neighbours would undoubtedly have found a means of testing the strength of Zavalishin's locks.

Zavalishin, who was always gloomy and half drunk at home, took very little interest in the pig. Some time before Easter, however, Anna Klimovna took him into the shed to have a look at it. She had washed it clean, and there it was, fresh and pink, rolling in fat, its legs scarcely supporting its weight. And a fortnight before Easter she said to him:

'It's time to stick that pig. Salting and smoking take some time.'

'Well, stick it then.'

'Oh, but not me. It would be easier for you to do it.'

'But what's it got to do with me?'

'With you? But you'll eat it, won't you?'

'Eat it yourself. I mustn't touch anything heavy; the doctor told me I mustn't.'

'Been to the doctor? Means you're bad again, eh?'

'Means I'm not right.'

'What did he say?'

'What did he say!' Zavalishin growled sombrely. 'Well, he said if it goes on like this there'll have to be an operation; my belly'll have to be carved. Just let him try being ripped open.'

'Don't you believe him. It may just pass off.'

THE LITTLE PIG

Zavalishin was silent. The word 'operation' alarmed him because that was the term applied to the work he did in the various places where his services were required, although the expressions 'settle their accounts' or 'send them into the town with their things' were more current. However agonizing his internal pains, he could not face an operation. The last time he had been to a doctor the latter had said to him:

'Your kidneys are in a very bad way. It's no joking matter. Better make up your mind to undergo an operation before it's too late.'

Anna Klimovna waited till Zavalishin had a day off to announce to him again that the pig had absolutely got to be stuck that very day.

'But you give me a hand. You're more used to such things, and you've got more strength too.'

Zavalishin got up and fixed the holster with the Colt to his belt.

'What are you taking that for? You aren't going to shoot it! It's got to be done with a knife. I've got some knives ready sharpened to cut out the fat afterwards. And there's a hatchet ready too.'

When they entered the shed Zavalishin saw that Anna had already converted a door into a table by placing it upon some wooden cases, had brought a pail and got ready the knives and clean rags – all that an operation of such a nature required. She had changed, and was wearing a cheap old dress to save her good clothes. She had also brought a couple of kitchen overalls.

'Put it on, or you'll get your things splashed.'

The shed had a window; but they closed the door so that inquisitive eyes should not witness their labours. After all, the task was a delicate one.

The young pig grunted while Anna Klimovna washed its side with loving care and bound its legs. It had grown so fat that it could scarcely move.

'Help me lift it on to the table.'

They raised it with difficulty, and Anna again wiped over the pink sides with a wet rag.

Next she washed her hands and wiped them dry.

'You can manage without me,' she said in a soft voice of entreaty.

'It's not a woman's job. Here are the knives.'

But seeing how Zavalishin's beard shook and his eyes went white, she drew back:

'What's the matter? What's scaring you?'

Zavalishin was trembling like a leaf. He retreated backwards to the door and his right hand went to the holster to draw out his Colt.

'Drop it, I tell you!' she exclaimed. 'One can't slaughter an animal with that – you'd spoil the head!'

Zavalishin withdrew his hand, felt suddenly weak and sat down on a case:

'Do it yourself. I couldn't stick a pig. Just listen to it squealing.'

'Soft-hearted, aren't you? Scared of an animal... A man, too.'

'Shut up, I tell you! I can't do it, Anna.'

'What have I got to shut up for? I'll manage quite well without you. See if I don't.'

She took up a large well-sharpened knife, seized the pink snout in one of the rags, turned up the neck and slit it downwards. But the stroke was unskilful and lacking in strength. Blood spurted forth; the pig gave a powerful jerk and began to squeal. Anna hastily prepared to strike again, but a strong hand seized her by the shoulder and swung her away from her victim.

Zavalishin, with eyes bloodshot and features distorted, brandished his Colt.

'Get away!' he shouted hoarsely. 'Don't touch it or I'll kill you!'

She squealed just as the pig had done, dashed out of reach, pushed open the door and fled. She heard the sheave creak as the door banged behind her, and, without turning round, she ran to the entrance of the yard, where the chairman of the House Committee lodged.

A few minutes later Denissov and Anna Klimovna went cautiously up to the shed. All was quiet within, save for subsiding squeals. Both stopped at the door.

'Hey, Zavalishin!' Denissov called out. 'Come out for a moment.'

There was no answer.

'You might just go in and see what he's up to in there.'

'You go in. Fancy shooting it! He must have gone raving mad. He can kill people all right, but when it comes to animals...'

Denissov made the round of the shed on tiptoe and peered in at the barred window. Just under the window lay the pink carcass, and beyond it, half hidden behind a case, Zavalishin was sitting on the floor, his eyes fixed on the window. His big Colt lay on a case before him.

Denissov leaped back and rejoined Anna Klimovna.

'Well, I don't know what to make of it. Maybe he's really gone raving mad, that Zavalishin of yours. Wouldn't it be better to lock him in and run for the police?'

'But the lock is on the inside.'

Just then a shot rang out. They both darted away from the door and ran.

After the first shot came a second and a third, then another and another. Zavalishin was emptying the whole chamber of his revolver. Denissov and Anna Klimovna hid in the porch, while several tenants banged their doors in alarm.

Then Zavalishin's heavy tread resounded along the asphalt yard. Without looking round, his head bowed and his hand on his holster, he made straight for the entrance, went in and closed the door behind him.

Anna Klimovna ventured into the shed, and gave a little cry as she entered: the table she had set up was covered with blood, and the pig's head – a wonderful head, which she had promised to the chairman for all the trouble and care he had taken – was riddled with large-calibre bullets from Zavalishin's Colt.

'Oh, what has he been doing! How could he go and shoot at it with bullets? Cruel, I call it! He's gone and spoiled the whole head!'

And she was so genuinely chagrined that she actually burst into tears.

– LXXVIII –

VASSYA'S UNFAITHFULNESS

In his landlady's room, on the other side of the wall, the clock struck seven. By Vassya's watch it was already ten past. True, his watch gained a little, which was really rather convenient, as one was sure then of never being late. Still, Alyonushka usually came at half-past six, though she might of course have called in somewhere on her way from the hospital.

Vassya slipped the embroidered bookmark, with 'In Remembrance' worked on it, into his book, carried the cigarette ash out into the kitchen, picked up the scraps of paper off the floor and set straight the armchair cover. Another five minutes went by. He might, of course, light the primus and make tea himself. Before his illness he had always done everything himself; but Alyonushka had spoiled him a little since. It rarely happened that she did not look in in the evening after her day's work. She lived in the neighbourhood and her own home was not very cosy. It had ended by becoming a habit that they should take their evening tea together, and for Alyonushka to stay on till just after ten. After tea they would talk, or Vassya would read aloud while Alyonushka knitted or sewed. It was by doing occasional needlework and making simple hats that Alyonushka eked out her living. She it was who had embroidered that bookmark for him and mended his linen. That, too, had become a habit, although he had made a stand against it at first.

'I can do it myself,' he had protested.

But Alyonushka had shown him a sock with one of his darns. 'Do you call that a darn, I ask you? You simply drew all the stitches together in a knot, with the result that it's not a darn at all, but a sort of cocoon.'

'And how ought it to be done?' he had asked.

Alyonushka had taken out the darn, produced a ball of wool from her bag, and a quarter of an hour later there had appeared in the place of the cocoon a new darn that had taken his breath away.

'The colour of the wool doesn't quite match,' she said, 'but that doesn't really matter. That's all I had with me.'

Vassya had gazed at it in wonder:

'Oh, but that's absolutely marvellous!'

Alyonushka had finally won the day when she converted a frayed cuff into a brand-new one by mending and turning it. Vassya had been so amazed that he had actually gaped at her speechless, while Alyonushka burst out laughing in her clear, bell-like way till she grunted and stopped in confusion.

But to come back – should he light the primus or wait?

He did not have to wait, for the bell rang three times. That meant there was a visitor for him. Every lodger had his own definite number of rings, so that no one should have to open the door to other people's visitors. There was even a notice stuck up on the door with directions as to the number of rings for each lodger.

Alyonushka arrived tired and a trifle out of sorts. She had been kept at the hospital because a number of typhus cases had been brought in.

'We have nowhere to put our own patients as it is, without all these extra cases, and yet they will go on bringing them in,' she complained.

And she had worries at home as well. Her room was a large one, larger than was allowed for the use of one person; and now the chairman of the House Committee proposed putting someone else in her room, so that it should be occupied by two people. As an alternative he suggested moving her into a tiny room about the size of a larder. And she did not know what to do. On the whole, the latter seemed less objectionable; she would be alone there anyhow.

'Now I'm not interfered with,' Vassya observed. 'And such a room, you know, is reckoned for two. And then, if it came to the worst, I could get special permission from the university to keep it.'

'It's all very well for you.'

But it was not in Alyonushka's nature to remain gloomy for long, and as soon as she had had her tea she cheered up at once:

'D'you know you've got an ink stain on your nose – a mauve one? When shall I get you to be really neat!'

'Where?' Vassya asked in alarm.

'Where! On your nose, I tell you. On the very tip. Just have a look at yourself in the glass.'

Vassya glanced into the diminutive glass on the wall.

'But there's nothing there; it's only a tiny spot. I've been writing today.'

He licked his finger and made a smudge of the spot.

'Well!' cried Alyonushka. 'Aren't you ashamed of yourself, and you a research student too! Come here.'

She took a bit of material out of her basket – was there anything she hadn't got! – moistened it in warm water and rubbed away the stain.

'There now, it's all gone. Now give it a wipe with a towel.'

'Never mind the towel,' Vassya returned with decision. 'It will dry without.'

The point was that Alyonushka's eyes seemed to him very lovely and peculiarly gentle – a fact he had overlooked until now. Or could they have been like that always? He did not in the least want to move away from Alyonushka; and while she rubbed his nose he held on to her hand, fearing that the bit of material might be too hot. And when she came to the end of her rubbing he did not want to let go her hand.

Alyonushka took the rag with her other hand and did not draw away the one he was holding. Her hand was warm and soft and small. This, too, Vassya found particularly pleasant that evening.

And so they remained till Alyonushka said:

'What are you thinking of? You are looking at me just as if you'd never seen me before! What are you staring at my hand for? A hand is a hand, and here's another just like it.'

Vassya took the other one too.

'And what if I were to take you by the ear?' Alyonushka said. 'By both ears, like this!'

And she drew nearer. The blouse she was wearing was low-necked, and her throat was fresh and white.

At this stage, Vassya decided to defend himself; a research student really could not allow himself to be pulled by the ears!

Nothing came of reading aloud that evening. They spent the greater part of the time sitting side-by-side, screening the reading-lamp with a large open book. It appeared that both of them had many interesting memories which they had never shared with each other before. Alyonushka found it extraordinary that when Vassya fell ill with typhus it should have been she and no other who came to nurse him. For the doctor might quite easily have found him another Sister of Mercy, quite a different one – some old woman, for instance.

'How awful!' Vassya interposed at this point. 'That would have been dull!'

'Then you're glad it was me?'

Growing very bold, Vassya showed that he was.

Then he, for his part, recalled how he had wakened one night, some days after the critical stage of his illness was over and he was fully conscious again, and had looked at Alyonushka as she dozed in her armchair, wondering what the colour of her eyes could be. For some reason or other he had decided that they could be no other colour but green.

'Me, with green eyes? What nonsense you did dream!'

'But I was awake.'

'I don't care. Why, my eyes are blue, real genuine blue!'

'So I see now.'

'You don't see anything. And altogether you're dreadfully unobservant, dreadfully. You simply don't understand anything. And then – what right had you to look at me while I was sleeping?'

'But you were sleeping sitting in the armchair.'

'Well, I never! And altogether you do say the most impossible things!'

Vassya felt almost embarrassed. Nevertheless, the exchange of memories proved so absorbingly interesting that Alyonushka stayed on later than usual. Nor did she move until the clock on the other side of the wall struck midnight.

'Heavens!' she cried, leaping up in dismay, 'I've got to be up before seven tomorrow.'

It was not with a mere handshake, as usual, that they wished one another good-night; and Vassya found that most strange and, at the same time, most pleasant.

As he went to bed he tugged too hard at his shirt and tore it at the collar. 'What a nuisance!' he thought; 'Alyonushka is sure to give me a scolding.'

He tried to think of something sad before going to sleep, as he was in the habit of doing – of how wretched he was and how happy other people. But nothing came of it this time. On the contrary, a smile hovered over his lips and his thoughts were the least bit sinful.

Sinful because he had been unfaithful that day, and the infidelity had seemed pleasant and sweet, and, above all, neither hurtful nor distressing to anyone.

– LXXIX –

THE EXPLOSION

On the 25th September, after a long interval, the ornithologist again called in at the Writers' Bookshop in Leontievsky Street. But this time, carrying a portfolio crammed full of books had exhausted the old professor.

'If you will allow me to get my breath back first. No, pray do not disturb yourselves. I will sit down for a moment on this case, if I may.'

'It's a long time since you were here, professor.'

'Yes, pretty long, pretty long. All sorts of matters have stood in the way of my coming.'

The matters that had stood in the old man's way were just this: his bookcase and shelves were almost emptied. The only books left were reference books he could not manage without, and one copy of each of his published works. He had given Tanyusha his word that he would not sell these books, however hard life should be.

'But is it worth keeping them, Tanyusha? Perhaps Alexey Dmitritch was right when he said that there is no longer any need of science.'

'No, grandfather, he doesn't believe that himself. That is only his way of talking.'

'And, besides, what can I give the world now that I am an old man?'

'Don't, grandfather! One shouldn't talk like that. You distress me.'

Very glad was the old man that his granddaughter believed both in science and in him, who was a real scholar – for all he was now an old man – and not one of that band of youths, almost schoolboys, who in these troublous times took advantage of the dearth of scholars to assume academic titles and shape careers for themselves.

'Well, well, we'll come through somehow, I have no doubt.'

However, on the fatal and terrible day of the 25th September the ornithologist again took a portfolio full of books to the shop.

'So you are interested in numismatics, are you, professor?'

'I know nothing about the subject.'

'You have a good many curious books here. Nothing in your own line, professor?'

'To be quite frank with you, these are not my own books. I took them, as it were, on commission. I am so used to coming to do business with you that I thought I might try to collect books from various people I know. Will you decide what they are worth, as you always do? I have perfect confidence in you.'

'Are you working for a percentage, professor?'

'I am. I will not conceal the fact from you.'

And again no one in the shop was in the least surprised that here was an old scholar, of European reputation, selling other people's books for a percentage. And the fact that no one was at all surprised made it all the easier and simpler. There could be nothing wrong then or unseemly about it. Other people were probably doing the same.

On leaving the bookshop with his empty portfolio under his arm, the ornithologist looked about him with a satisfied air; there would be something left over, anyhow, for Tanyusha's housekeeping expenses – not much, of course, as the books had not been his own; but precisely because they were not it had been less of a wrench to part with them. What he had earned was the merest trifle; but he had earned it nevertheless by his work and his old man's thoughtful care.

On duty at the gate of the house next door, which stood far back behind railings, was a young Red Army soldier with a rifle. The people who entered it presented a paper – the requisite pass.

Making an effort to hold himself more erect and to step out more confidently, the professor went along to the Great Nikitinskaya.

There was yet another façade to the house which was guarded by the Red Army soldier, a façade looking out on a small garden in Tchernyshevsky Street. In this garden, which was railed off from the road, were a number of tall trees whose yellowing leaves still clung to the branches. A flight of stone steps led up to the second storey. There was no gate on this side of the house; nobody ever entered that way.

When it grew dark, and the by-street was deserted, windows lit up in this façade at the back. An important meeting had been fixed for eight o'clock that night, and a great number of people walked and drove up to the main façade in Leontievsky Street.

But only one man went up to the façade at the back in the by-street, and he did not come till about ten. Glancing about him, and keeping a hand over one of his pockets, he swung lightly over the railing, crouched to the ground and froze to immobility.

From the by-street, beyond the trees, it was not possible to see how a dark form mounted the steps to the balcony and warily peered in at a window. On the lowered blind a wide back was silhouetted, while through the chink a corner of the table was visible and the serried ranks of people beyond.

Then the dark form leaped back from the window, and an arm swung.

The explosion was heard as far as the outskirts of Moscow. The windowpanes in the neighbouring street were broken; those in the streets farther off merely rattled.

And the citizens, who were long since used to night-firing in the streets, were quick to discern the difference between this crash and the crack of a rifle, the rattle of a machine-gun, or even – though they were not quite sure about it – the boom of a gun.

There was no longer a roof to the house with the two façades, and one of the walls was down.

* * *

Zavalishin had been sober and glum all that day since the morning. As it did not happen to be one of his working days he had left the Lubyanka towards evening. When he reached home he took off the new jacket he had acquired after a recent 'operation' and sat down on the bed. Anna Klimovna was in the kitchen putting on the samovar and preparing to have a snack before going to bed, pondering as she did so on the two empty rooms in the flat. Not that Anna Klimovna was a grasping woman; it was simply that she could not resign herself to the fact that the door into Astafiev's rooms still stood sealed.

'The time he's been away now and the rooms going begging! You never know, he may not come back. You ought to apply to have the seals removed; and nothing would happen to you if you took them off yourself.'

'What d'you want his rooms for?'

'Have we got to go on living always in one room and a kitchen?'

'Can't be done.'

'But why can't it be done?'

'Because I tell you it can't! He may come back any time and find his rooms taken. His things are in there.'

'Sorry for a bourgeois! You're too mighty thoughtful about him.'

'Leave off, Anna! Stop going on at me. You've never set eyes on him; but I have. I know him.'

'What a friend!'

'Maybe he really is! Maybe he has messed up my life, but I respect him all the same – sort as if he was my best pal.'

After a moment's silence he went on:

'We drank together. Well, and what about it? He's got such brains, I tell you, that he's mastered everything. It's nothing to go by, his being arrested. And it's not for you, silly fool of a woman, to judge him. He's a learned man and not on a level with us peasants.'

'Learned! And what did he learn you, that learned man of yours?'

'That's my business. He may be my worst enemy, but I tell you I respect him all the same and won't have a hair of his head touched. So there! He's got more learned books along in his room that you've got rags. And he's read them all and knows about everything. And don't you forget he drank spirits with me, a simple, uneducated man, like with an equal, he did. That needs some understanding, Anna. But it's not for you, with your woman's brains, to understand things like that.'

The samovar had scarcely come to the boil when Denissov, the chairman of the House Committee, knocked at the door and called through, without entering:

'Hey, Zavalishin, they've called for you!'

'Who?'

'The car's outside, waiting for you; they want you to come down at once.'

Somewhat flurried, Zavalishin put on his jacket and took the holster with his Colt off a nail.

'What can they want you for on a free day?'

'Lord knows. Our free days are always liable to be turned into working days.'

'You ought to have some tea first.'

'Well, but since they've sent for me – just give us half a glass of spirits; up there on the shelf.'

And flaring up suddenly at being disturbed, he shouted to the woman from the doorway.

'And don't you touch that door or the seals! D'you hear! Just you mind your own business. Not enough rooms for her! Too grand, that's what's the matter with her,'

And he slammed the door behind him.

– LXXX –

EMPTINESS

After the fourth, and last, examination, Astafiev was transferred to a separate cell.

The examination was brief. Comrade Brickmann, who was always highly feverish before the spring, sat muffled up in a fawn-coloured sweater under the 'French' he invariably wore, the collar of which was much too big for his neck.

As he entered, Astafiev thought with compassion:

'So that's what he has come to, poor devil. Yet he still goes on wheezing and hoping for something.'

'Citizen Astafiev, it appears that people have been taking steps to obtain your release. I decided, therefore, to have you up again. It may be that we shall reach an understanding this time.'

'An understanding about what?'

'You deny having taken a part in the conspiracy and to having given refuge to a deadly foe of the Soviet Government. Well, then, what is your own attitude towards the Government itself? Do you recognize it?'

'Surely it stands in no need of any recognition on my part. I am not a foreign power.'

'It's no good trying to joke away the matter. I advise you to give me a straight answer.'

'You can hardly suspect me of tender feelings towards the power that has kept me unjustly in prison for over six months, Comrade Brickmann?'

'Which means your attitude is a hostile one?'

Astafiev crossed his legs and lounged back in his chair:

'Hostile – no; I am of a disposition somewhat too placid for that. Contemptuous would be nearer the truth.'

'What! Contemptuous of the workmen's and peasants' Government?'

'Oh, come, Brickmann! What have peasants and workmen got to do with it? You ought to be ashamed of yourself for talking such rot.'

The examining magistrate started:

'Comrade Astafiev, I'll be quite open with you: there is little evidence against you – only an anonymous statement to the effect that such a person spent a night in your flat. But you are a clever and daring man, a danger to us, Citizen Astafiev. You are far more dangerous than our small, open foes. People are taking steps to obtain your release, but I don't mean to let you out.'

Astafiev felt fierce rage rising in him towards the man in whose hands his fate lay – a frenzied impulse to seize him by his lean throat and squeeze the life out of him.

'What you say is prompted by personal feelings, Brickmann,' he returned, scanning his words as usual – 'hatred towards a well and independent man. You are an underling of the Government, whereas I am a free man; you are at your last gasp, and I, thank God! am well. It's obvious you must destroy me although you know perfectly well that you have nothing to accuse me of.'

The examining magistrate again stirred uneasily on his chair. Going red, he replied in a voice that broke into a piping whisper:

'As you say, I'm at my last gasp. My chest was smashed in prison by the butt-ends of rifles and I have consumption. But you put it brutally

EMPTINESS

and, in my opinion, in a way that shows a lack of principles; though, it's not on account of that, that I hate you and the likes of you, but on account of... on account...'

Comrade Brickmann was seized with a fit of coughing. He took a little phial out of his pocket, spat into it, put it back again and gave Astafiev an under-look out of his small, feverish eyes.

'Well, there, you see,' Astafiev remarked. 'What sort of a fighter do you call yourself? You ought to go down south.'

Breathing heavily, the examining magistrate returned hoarsely:

'I need no medical advice from you.'

While Comrade Brickmann wiped away the sweat that had broken out on his face, Astafiev looked round the room despondently. The windowpanes evidently had not been cleaned for a very long time. In one corner lay a pile of papers and newspapers, and a tarnished mirror hung on the wall.

'What a setting for you! You might at least have the windows cleaned; you would get more light.'

When he had got back his breath again the examining magistrate said:

'You may think what you like about me, but I will tell you one thing, Citizen Astafiev: it is not yet certain which of us is nearer – ' He hesitated.

'You mean to say – the next world?'

Instead of replying, the examining magistrate announced in a sharp, markedly official tone:

'I could, for that matter, set you free, should you consent to work with us.'

Astafiev smiled:

'Trying to insult me, are you? What an indefatigable soul you are, Brickmann. But I have no intention of being offended with you.'

'Very well. You may go.'

He rang. Astafiev rose, straightened his creased suit, set in order his hair that had grown long, and, scanning him from head to foot, observed with a good-natured smile:

'Really, Brickmann, do go down south. Give up this environment and all this dirty work of yours. I'm not saying this from malice. You really do look awful.'

The armed escort entered.

* * *

In his separate cell, Astafiev would sit on his wooden couch in his usual attitude, back to the wall and hands clasped round his knees.

He had no books; the prisoners were not allowed to read. There was neither paper nor pencil, nor even homemade chessmen. He had been in the habit of doing exercises in the common cell, and had taught the others to do them too. Here, however, he no longer felt any wish to keep up the habit. He felt no hunger. The food was execrable: wretched fish soup, plain boiled millet and a quarter of a pound of bread. At liberty, with such fare, he might have been envied by many. The tea was carrot-tea and was referred to as coffee. Shag was given to the prisoners, which was something at any rate; much could be forgiven the Central Tcheka for that boon.

During the first months of his incarceration, Astafiev had often thought of the possibility of his 'account being settled'. Finally, however, the thought lost its sharp edge. The worst of all was the general weariness of body and soul. At the beginning he had seen the clearest pictures of life beyond the prison walls: his old room with its precious books, Moscow streets, evenings at Sivtzev Vrazhek, his curious declaration of love to Tanya, his performances at concerts; in the past, his university work; and in a past that was still more remote, his travels abroad. But it was all fast fading from his mind. He no longer felt his old longing for freedom, nor even his old hatred of prison walls.

Recalling the conversation he had had that day with the examining magistrate, he thought: 'I tormented him. Better to have struck him than have spoken as I did. It turned out most unsatisfactorily.'

He remembered the loathsome pocket-phial and frowned with the instinctive disgust of the healthy:

'Why is such a man alive!'

But why was he, Astafiev, alive?

What meaning was there in his life? What did it really matter whether Comrade Brickmann 'liquidated' him in the course of the next few days or allowed him to go on living?

'Enough of this wretched existence, enough of murmuring and apish tricks. Why art thou disturbed? Whether thou shalt think over these things for three or one hundred years is all one.

And Marcus Aurelius also:

'Though thou wert destined to live three thousand years and as many times ten thousand, yet remember that man can lose no other life than that which he lives now. Neither can he in any wise lose the past nor the future; for how shall he lose what he possessed not?'

And King Solomon:

'The thing that hath been, it is that which shall be; and that which is done is that which shall be done: and there is no new thing under the sun.'

'Strange,' thought Astafiev, 'there are so many bright, cheering books, so many brilliant and witty philosophic truths, and yet nothing more comforting than Ecclesiastes.'

From the passage came a loud thump, followed by the footsteps and voice of the warder:

'Hey, knock again! Go on knocking!'

The Lett could not make out at once from which cell door the knock came:

'Hey, knock again!'

A familiar cry to Astafiev. One of the prisoners was asking for special permission to leave his cell and go to the lavatory out of regulation hours. But apparently he was not being let out. The poor devil was probably suffering now.

'If suffering is intolerable it quickly kills. If it is drawn-out it must be bearable; the mind meanwhile preserves its calm by strength of the reasoning faculty and suffers nothing.'

Thus should the philosopher comfort himself. Yes, the man in the street had good enough cause for hating the philosopher.

'As a matter of fact I am very far from all thought of a counter-revolutionary nature. I should have despised the nation if it had not done what it did, if it had stopped half way and allowed learned prattlers to turn Russia out in English dress – Houses of Parliament, an obliging police and well-groomed lies. And yet Brickmann was right: I am his enemy and the enemy of all who are like him. For what does it matter who strangles freedom of thought – a barbarous hand or an enlightened one? For it will of course strangle in the name of liberty and of the people. But how boring all that is.'

If they had come at that moment and said: 'Into the town with your things,' his pulse would not have quickened.

And his thoughts ran on:

'All these events – revolution, executions, strife and hopes, all our life and being – why, all that is nothing more than... the visible trail left for an instant by a swallow winging its way through the air. But no more;

not more, not more. Well, what then is real? Only – emptiness. Squeezed-out thought, swallowing itself. Absolute nothingness, emptiness.

'Emptiness.'

Astafiev stretched out his legs, closed his eyes and fell into a light slumber.

– LXXXI –

THE MEETING

Late that evening many prisoners were brought from Butyrok, from various camps and other places of incarceration. Prisoners were hastily removed from the Ship of Death, both on trifling matters and to act as witnesses; and their places were taken by those who, as hostages and dangerous foes to the State, were to pay a speedy penalty for the explosion in Leontievsky Street. The lists had been drawn up in a hurry, according to the notes of the examining magistrates and the council's remarks. It was essential that the repressive measures should be immediate and terrifying. There was no thought of chance errors. Neither the name nor the individual mattered so long as the number of names entered tallied with the number of those due to be shot.

For the sake of speed several vans were sent to the Petrovsky Park, and a large batch was dispatched straight from Butyrok to the Varsonofievsky garage; and still there remained very many for the cellar in which Zavalishin was at work.

The prisoners knew why they had been transferred: rumours of the explosion had reached the prison. Besides, in the general haste and confusion the armed escort did not conceal the reason that day. Pale and wrought-up themselves, they drove on the prisoners and kept clutching nervously at their holsters.

It was quiet in the crowded pit of the Ship. Only one puny, feverish individual kept going from one plank seat to another, trying, in a hurried whisper, to prove that he had been taken by mistake and that he would not, of course, be sent anywhere. The others listened to him in silence, without attempting to offer him any consolation, absorbed in thoughts of themselves and listening to the steps up above.

Between two and three in the morning the Commissar, accompanied by three soldiers, ran bustling up to the rail of the gallery and called out in a sharp, businesslike voice:

'Hey, how many have you got down there?'

'Sixty-seven.'

'Sixty-seven? But they've sent six to dig a pit for ninety!'

He looked incredulous for a moment, then slapped his forehead:

'That's right. Another twenty-three will be sent from the Special Department. That makes up the ninety.'

His mind at ease, he walked off briskly.

On the nearest plank, leaning against the wall, sat an old general, grey-haired and ragged, busily polishing his nails on his cuff. There was no room for him to sit apart by himself. From time to time he took out a pocket-comb and made a fresh parting. One stocky individual had put a paper with slices of bacon on the polished table and was eating in silence, as though afraid that he would not have time to finish up the remains of what his wife had been able to save and bring to the prison. Another of the prisoners had buried his face in his hands and was rocking himself with a rhythmic motion. Sitting hunched up, a dark man was glancing rapidly from one fellow-prisoner to another, screwing up his eyes, and now and again flashing his teeth as though attempting to smile. Several men were lying stretched out on the planks, with their hands behind their heads. Not one of them undressed.

Shortly after three o'clock the 'Commissar of Death' ran up again, without any list this time, and shouted to the soldiers:

'Give us two.'

The men on the planks leaped up, the dark individual flashed his teeth, another rapidly waved his hands before his face, the old general bowed his head and went on slowly polishing his nails. Both he and the puny individual, who had run up to explain that he had been arrested by mistake, were taken. The soldiers led them quickly away, pushing them up the spiral staircase.

'Get along! straight on, and hurry up about it!'

Then Zavalishin would raise his hand.

* * *

At daybreak it was the prisoners from the Special Department who were led down to the cellar where Zavalishin was at work. Commissar Ivanov looked in a couple of times and shouted from behind the door, where he stood looking askance at the asphalt gutter that ran along by the wall:

'You there, Zavalishin?'

'I'm here all right. Any more coming?'

'Hang on a bit longer. There aren't many more. D'you want me to bring you a bottle?'

'No. Send on the last lot quick. I want to get through and be done with it.'

And soon would come the call again:

'Hey, ready there!'

'All right,' the drunken voice would reply from the cellar.

After every three, the bodies were removed.

* * *

'Hey, ready there!'

Trying to stand firmly on his legs, Zavalishin lurched up to the door and raised his Colt.

The clatter of footsteps ceased and one light, even step came up to the door of the cellar. Then, when a shirt appeared in the doorway, Zavalishin uttered a hoarse command:

'Turn to your right!'

The man who had entered raised his head at the shout and Zavalishin's hand dropped.

The footfalls in the little passage died away and the main door slammed. The doomed man and the executioner stood staring at one another. Zavalishin shook from head to foot and all but dropped his Colt.

Scanning his face, the doomed man smiled a ghastly smile:

'Ah, an old acquaintance, I see! Well, and how are you, Zavalishin?'

The other's white drunken lips mumbled:

'Alexey Dmitritch!'

'The same, your old neighbour.'

Both were silent.

Astafiev's eyes ranged over the cellar, then with a squeamish look he glanced down at the slippery floor.

'Well, after all, what does it matter? May as well finish me off.'

He shut his eyes and waited with clenched teeth. Close behind him he heard a muffled muttering.

Then, clenching his fist and turning sharply upon the drunken executioner, he called out:

'Hurry up, you wretch! Hurry up, I tell you, or I'll snatch the revolver from your hands and shoot you like a dog! Finish off, you damned coward!'

Zavalishin raised his arm and dropped it once more. His drunken eyes were full of horror.

Then in his normal voice, speaking out loud and distinctly, with a note of ironic derision, Astafiev said to him:

'There, Zavalishin, didn't I tell you you weren't good for anything? And you actually boasted! Can't even shoot a man! Well, what is to happen now? Am I to go to bed?'

Going past the executioner, he sat down on the bench and lowered his head, The moment, however, Zavalishin again raised his Colt he quickly looked him full in the face and laughed:

'Well, at last! Now then – one, two... now then, you blackguard, now then – fire!'

– LXXXII –

OPUS 37

Two primuses were roaring in the kitchen, vying with one another in fierceness. Two housewives had just quarrelled because the wire cleaner belonging to one of them had just been found broken. Now so determined were they not to look at each other that they did not even turn their heads when Edward Lvovitch entered the kitchen.

The torn, dirty duster that belonged to Edward Lvovitch was hanging between the door and the range. He took it squeamishly between his fingers, thought of shaking it out, but, feeling that that would not do, took it straight to his room.

Edward Lvovitch tried to keep his room clean and tidy, but he did not possess a broom; someone either had used it as firewood or had simply made off with it. And lacking the energy to carry out an investigation among all the lodgers of the flat, Edward Lvovitch had become resigned to the loss, and managed ever since with no more than the duster, which he had no idea how to wash.

It was with this rag then that he first dusted the top of his grand piano, proceeding next to the music shelves and the table, and finishing up by flourishing it over the floor in the direction of the stove. A little heap of dust and some threads collected near the stove, and these he gathered up on a stiff sheet of manuscript paper and tipped into the fire.

His cleaning was completed.

Edward Lvovitch never touched the keyboard with the dusty rag, only with his handkerchief, which he would afterwards shake out and return to his pocket. The keys were sacred.

Uncovering them, he placed a manuscript, entitled Opus 37, on the rest, and a little pencil beside it.

Opus 37 was Edward Lvovitch's last composition. Opus 37 was finished and it was hardly likely that the little pencil would come in useful. Opus 37 was a curious, tuneless thing, composed in three days in all; a thing utterly novel and startling, even to Edward Lvovitch himself.

Formerly he would have protested with indignation against such morbid, nerve-racking music; and now the strange thing was – he appeared to have composed it himself!

The introduction was comprehensible enough and quite in accordance with the rules of composition; many works began in just such a way. There was logic too, and an intrinsic justification of the work in the opening. But the theme, scarcely yet hinted at and only just beginning to develop, was suddenly cut through – how explain it – by a sort of musical scratch, that went on to rip it from top to bottom. The theme persisted in its efforts to develop in the normal way and through its successive stages; but the scratch cut deeper, snapped the taut threads of the musical yarn, frayed the ends and jumbled it all into a tangled skein of tragic confusion. A moment of despairing struggle, the issue of which was uncertain.

Then ensued the most distorted and terrible of sequels. The threads were unravelled, the ends drawn out of the skein, and already the authoritative and imperious command could be heard (the bass notes!), when suddenly – complete paralysis of logic: utter treachery taking shape in those imperious bass notes themselves! The command had been merely a clever stratagem, an attack from the rear.

When Edward Lvovitch played through that terrible page he felt his worn old heart fail, almost stop; felt the stirring of his scanty hair on the nape of his neck and the slight twitching of his arched eyebrows. It was a criminal page; impermissible. And yet it was truth, life itself! Nothing there could be altered, not even by a demi-semiquaver. The composer was a criminal, but a creator too. A listener to truth and its servant. The world might go to rack and ruin, everything perish – but there was no going back. Suddenly all the threads snap; the ends of the musical yarn drop with a distant echo and are all at once silent. The theme dies away – and something new is born, something which horrifies the composer more than all else: the meaning of chaos is born. The meaning of chaos! But can there be such a thing as meaning in chaos?

Whether that product of wild treason to the whole of his past, to the traditions of the classical school, and to himself as the disciple and successor of the great masters of old – whether those pages shall be torn out of the manuscript book, crumpled, trampled upon, torn to shreds, depends on Edward Lvovitch. But he has not the strength to do it. The criminal loves his crime. If at this moment the indignant shades of Bach, Haydn, Beethoven and Mozart were to appear round his piano and try to snatch his manuscript from him, reviling him and heaping curses on his head, he would beat them off with his arms, with his pencil, his dusty rag – would raise his manuscript above his head; but as long as he was alive he would not give it up to anyone, neither to the living nor to the shades of the dead, not even to his mother's shade. If she begged him with tears he would weep all the tears in his body and die; but he could not yield, not even to her entreaties. There it is – the tragedy of creation.

When he had played to the end, Edward Lvovitch leaped up from the stool, rubbed his hands together and looked about him in bewilderment. Then, in his agitation, he started to pace rapidly from one corner of the room to the other, catching, as he turned, his jacket on the corner of his music shelves. Considerably startled, he picked up the fallen manuscript; after which he was at a loss to know what to do next. There was no doubt about it, Opus 37 was an extraordinary composition.

Extraordinary – yes. But who had whispered it to him? The devil? Death? Not the bullet, was it, that had pierced his windowpane one night and embedded itself in the plaster under the wallpaper? – could it have been the bullet that had whistled to him that there might be meaning in chaos, that there actually was meaning in chaos? There is meaning in death! And meaning in nonsense. Folly saddling counterpoint, lashing it with a whip and compelling it to serve it! Could that possibly be!

A bit of white thread had been left on the floor by the stove. Edward Lvovitch stooped, scraped it up with the nail of a delicate, musical finger and dropped it into the open stove. He straightened himself, not without difficulty, for there was an ache in the region of his waist. And all of a sudden, casting his eyes on the music that stood open on the rest, he understood.

'The conception of a genius!'

The suddenness of the discovery caused him to open his mouth, blink, and pronounce quite distinctly:

'I'm a genius. Opus 37 is the work of a genius.'

Edward Lvovitch sat down on the chair by the wall and placed his hands on his knees. From the kitchen came the hissing of the primuses and the muttered grumbling of the women lodgers. But Edward Lvovitch heard nothing. He sat bowed by the sudden consciousness that Opus 37 was the conception of a musical genius. Could it be that the moment coincided with the coming of old age? And yet another thought troubled him: they would not understand his latest conception; he was sure of it; no one would understand.

Evening was drawing on when Edward Lvovitch, who had forgotten to lunch, drew his check-lined coat over his meagre shoulders – moving quietly, as though afraid of spilling the cup of his revelation and fullness – put on his wide-brimmed hat on one side and, glancing round the room with unseeing eyes, opened the door and went out.

Edward Lvovitch needed fresh air. Opus 37 remained on the rest.

– LXXXIII –

THE CUCKOO CLOCK

The sun rose, mounted dispassionately to the zenith and sank down towards the west. Summer merged into autumn – beautiful in the country, dreary in the town. Winter came and locked the waters, blocked up the roads and buried the fallen leaves. Then it grew warm, spring returning once more to lavish green tinsel on nature and deceive man with hopes.

The cuckoo counted the minutes and watched the slow, even movement of the two hands that left no trace as they passed over the face marked with the twelve time-signs.

THE CUCKOO CLOCK

Those whose hour was come sank into eternal rest; new lives came into being; new wounds opened, ached and scarred over; sighs died away and gave place to joy; new fears started up with the coming of dusk. Washed off the rafts they had hastily knocked together, men floundered in the stream of Life. The river of Time flowed on with its usual roar.

The cuckoo clock, the professor's old clock, went on ticking the seconds, went on unwinding the spring, steadily, dispassionately, in obedience to the weights. Every hour and half-hour the wooden cuckoo burst from its diminutive house, nodded its head and called as many times as was necessary. And the professor said:

'Don't you think, Tanyusha, that it is time for your grandfather to go to bed? I will read a little in my room before going to sleep.'

'Of course, grandfather, do go!'

'Is Pyotr Pavlovitch coming home late?'

'He has a committee meeting tonight, grandfather. It's sure not to be over before midnight.'

'Will you be all right – not bored?'

'Oh, no! I'll stay up a little longer and then go to bed also.'

'Well, well.'

The old ornithologist was less vigorous of late. But then he was far from being as young as he used to be. He no longer went out as often as before. That day, however, he had ventured out and had met with a small joy.

At the corner of the Arbat he had seen a woman holding a tray covered with a clean cloth. From beneath the cloth peeped a golden-brown roll – real bread, of white flour, as it used to be in the old days. The woman glanced about her apprehensively, to make sure that there was no policeman in sight. One never knew what a policeman would turn out to be like, any more than one knew whether selling rolls in the streets was permitted or not.

Then, feeling in his pocket for the wad of notes with huge figures – hundreds of thousands, millions – the professor had gone up to the woman and had timidly inquired the price. She had answered him no less timidly. And the professor had bought one roll, paying for it as much as she asked.

He had not gone any farther that day, but had hurried home as fast as his old legs would carry him. That was for Tanyusha, for his dear, thoughtful grandchild – the first white roll. Like a snowdrop! Not for the taste of it, but for the joy it brought; for was it not a real white roll, such as there used to be in the old days!

'Eat it, please, in my presence.'

'We'll go halves, grandfather.'

'I couldn't hear of it! It's all for you. You eat it, and drink a little milk with it.'

'Grandfather, that's spoiling; I'm not going to eat it all by myself. D'you know, I'm going to put on some coffee, and we'll eat it together. Do, grandfather – please!'

'Well, then, just a taste, no more. What a pity Pyotr Pavlovitch is not at home; he could have shared it with us.'

They ate up the roll as if it were the Host, collecting the crumbs in the palms of their hands and tipping them into their mouths.

'Well, anyhow, rolls have appeared once more, Tanyusha.'

'Life in general is easier nowadays. Everything can be got if one has the money.'

'Last year I believe we had some white flour – the flour Vassya brought – hadn't we?'

'Yes. I even baked some patties once.'

'I remember, I remember; patties. How is Vassya these days? He has not been to see us for some time now.'

'I believe he is very well off. Elena Ivanovna is looking after him. She is an excellent housewife.'

'Well, Vassya deserves it. He has sterling qualities. Elena Ivanovna too; she is good and kind. Life must be easier for them together.'

So Vassya was not lonely. Tanyusha, too, had someone to look after and care for if Aglaya Dmitrevna should call to him from the next world:

'Well, my dear old man, is it not time for you to come to your rest?'

The little door of the clock burst open and the cuckoo called how many more minutes had dropped into eternity.

Grandfather is asleep, his beard spread comfortably over the sheet. Tanyusha is not going to bed just yet; she is waiting up for Pyotr Pavlovitch.

She tried to remember: for what had she been preparing herself? Not just for the chance meeting, surely, with the being who always comes unexpectedly, although ever awaited? Well, but it would all return still – knowledge, music – it would all come again. It was only for the time being that she had to think of how grandfather was to have enough to eat and what he should eat tomorrow, and how she could make things pleasant for the dear, intimate friend when he came back tired from the works or after late committee meetings. But those concerts of hers at the workmen's clubs – were they not the fruits of her long years of study? Was that not real service? It was true that Edward Lvovitch frowned and grumbled:

'You are ruining your tarent. Music must not be treated like that.'

Oh, he was undoubtedly a great authority on music, her old master. But what did he understand of life? Had he even known the harmony of unexpected, illogical, casually born consonances? Had he ever loved, not 'in general,' not his musical creation, but some real live human being?

The cuckoo darts out of the door and counts the number of hours lived through that day. But the hours only of today. Of the days and years of Edward Lvovitch, now grown quite bald and beginning to stoop, the cuckoo knows nothing. Maybe there never was any mystery; yet it may be, too, that there had been one at some time or other in the life of the old composer.

How many mysteries there had been in Tanyusha's own childhood! And how simple everything was now! It had all become clear to her, perfectly ordinary. And she herself was quite ordinary too, like everyone else. Just a woman. Nor was that wounding to her pride; she would not have had it otherwise now. And she loved a man who was just as simple and ordinary as herself. There were hundreds like him probably – good, honourable, intelligent, capable; but many such men might have entered her life. Why was it that he, and no other, should have become so near and dear to her? Pure chance? No, it evidently was meant to be. And so – right through life?

The cuckoo can tell nothing of all that; it merely keeps count of the hours. It has already announced the advent of midnight and the beginning of another day. Now the minute hand is approaching the first half-hour.

But before the cuckoo has time to throw open the door of its house the English bolt clicks softly in the hall.

'There he is. Then all is well...'

– LXXXIV –

A SURGICAL CASE

A new patient was admitted into the surgical clinic in the Ostozhenka. He had been brought in a cab by a composed and officious woman – his wife, probably – who said to the hospital authorities, while particulars were being taken down in the office:

'Now, mind you do all you can for him, because we can pay, you know. If you like we could pay in provisions – flour or anything else. Although' we do come of simple people, he's got a good job; has responsible work to do.'

The patient, a massive, somewhat puffy, but powerfully built, bearded man, was bathed and put in a private room, No. 9. He was in great pain and groaned a good deal: it was an attack of renal colic, and an immediate operation was necessary. He barely answered when he was questioned, and watched the doctor from under his brows with a look of fear and distrust.

'Am I going to die, eh, doctor?' he asked, moaning, while he was being examined.

'There's no earthly reason why you should. We'll operate on you and you'll get better. You've got stones and pus in your kidneys; it's that that brought on your illness.'

'It means the knife?'

'Don't worry; you'll be under an anaesthetic, so you won't feel anything.'

The operation was a very difficult and complicated affair. When his massive body was laid on the table the patient's eyes ranged over doctors and nurses and looked askance at the mask.

'Maybe it would have gone off without anything, mightn't it?' he asked in a muffled tone. 'I'm not keen on dying.'

When the mask was put on he gave a roar and shook his head. He soon calmed down, however, mumbling inaudibly as he went under.

An hour and a half later he was carried back to his room on a stretcher.

When he awoke he lay without stirring, his bleary, drunken-looking eyes roving over his room.

That evening his wife was told that the operation had been successful, but that the patient was too weak to be disturbed.

'We'll see how he is tomorrow.'

'Well, but is there any danger? Any risk of his dying? You do all you can for him; we're in a position to pay well.'

'There is always danger, of course. It was a serious operation and he lost a lot of blood. Was he a hard drinker, by any chance?'

'Oh, yes, he did drink. He couldn't do without drink at his work.'

'What sort of work was it?'

'Oh, responsible work, mostly at night.'

'Unfortunate that he drank.'

'I know. I told him so too. Maybe it all came from that.'

The woman's address was taken down. She gave them the number of the house in the Dolgorukovskaya and told them to ask for Anna Klimovna: everyone knew her, she added, the chairman of the House Committee also; they were on friendly terms.

The patient was lying motionless in the spotless room, looking up at the ceiling. He felt no definite pain, but there was a dullness in his head that reacted on the whole of his body. He was loath to stir his numbed brain, and lay on with vacant mind. Whenever the nurse entered the room, and especially when the doctor appeared in a white coat and threw back the blanket, the same look of distrust would return to his face and the hairy skin over the cheekbones would twitch.

On the second day, at lunchtime, the patient, who was lying in a stupor, suddenly groaned out loud. He lay very pale, as white as a sheet, every little hair on his face clearly visible. The nurse called the surgeon on duty. Examination revealed that the bandages were stained with blood. The surgeon had him transferred as carefully as possible into the operating theatre. It appeared that the ligatures, which had been placed over the larger blood-vessels of the kidney, had got loose, and that the parenchymatous haemorrhage had not ceased.

With the greatest difficulty they succeeded in retying the ligatures over the larger blood-vessels and putting artery forceps on the remainder, as well as on the bleeding cellular tissues.

'Don't leave him,' the surgeon said to the nurse, 'and keep a sharp eye on him. He is in a critical condition – lost a lot of blood. In another twenty-four hours, when firm clots have formed, we can try removing the forceps and leaving the wound plugged.'

Zavalishin heard the voices and words he did not understand, but felt as though in a mist. The pain was a dull pain, but there was a buzzing in his ears and a continuous hammering in his temples; a sense of desolation, too, weighing upon him, gnawing at his heart and driving away sleep and rest.

Anna Klimovna called in again to inquire after him, but they could give her no definite or encouraging news.

The surgeons' hopes had not been justified. Twenty-four hours later, when they thought of removing the forceps, it appeared that no clot had formed, not even in the clipped blood-vessels. Where forceps had been placed the devitalized tissues and blood-vessels were plainly degenerating. And again the bandages were found soaked in Zavalishin's thin blood.

'A most extraordinary case!' said the surgeon. 'A hard drinker, I know, but still... What obstinate blood! Simply will not coagulate. We'll just have to rely on plugging.'

They did not conceal from Anna Klimovna that the patient was in a bad way. They even allowed her in to see him; on condition, however, that she should not speak, merely remain with him for a couple of minutes. Anna Klimovna seated herself on the edge of a chair, cautiously glanced at the face of her bread-winner, noticed the white line of the eyeballs beneath the half-closed lids, heaved a sigh, and at a sign from the sister went out.

'Is he realty going to die?' she asked.

'He is in a critical condition. He is a bleeder, and there's no way of stopping the haemorrhage.'

'That means he may bleed to death?'

'It may happen. But we'll hope for the best.'

Anna Klimovna heaved a deep sigh:

'Well, perhaps that's his fate. But what a strong man he used to be.'

After imparting the news to Denissov, the chairman of the House Committee, she went on to say:

'They operated, but it seems they didn't do it properly. I told him not to go. It might have passed off without.'

'The doctors know best.'

'Still, he would have gone on living if he hadn't been to hospital. He ought to have held out to the end of the month anyhow. He gets his pay and rations on the first.'

'But how could he wait when he had such pains? And it wouldn't have made any difference.'

'That's true, of course. That was his fate.'

It was night. Zavalishin was lying in a state of semi-consciousness under the shaded light. He felt no pain; indeed, he did not feel his body at all. Only now and again he had a sharp sensation of cold in his shoulders and feet; and, like a dry salt lump, his tongue felt huge in his mouth and got in the way. Whenever he opened his eyes, shadows scuttled across the ceiling and hid in the corners.

Once, closing his eyes, he imagined that he was lying at home and that someone was knocking, steadily, ceaselessly, and as though with a flabby fist. He wanted to call to Anna Klimovna, and bellowed. But when the nurse came up and quietly asked him something or other he remembered that he was lying in hospital. Anna, then, must be all by herself at home. She had plenty of space there now, with all three rooms free. Their flat had become large and no one had been put into it; all the books had been sent to the warehouse.

Then, suddenly, it was just as if a voice he did not know called out:
'Hey, ready there!'
And another voice, an unforgettable voice, pronounced in a tone of derision:
'Ah, an old acquaintance, I see! Well, and how are you, Zavalishin?'
He started, wanted to call out, and felt a sharp, unbearable pain in his side.

Summoned by the nurse, the surgeon hastened up to the bed and discovered Zavalishin's massive body lying in a pool of blood which had soaked through all the bandages and was oozing over the sheets. There was a lot of it, a terrible lot of the executioner's blood which would not coagulate.

Medical science is not familiar with blood vengeance. On the death certificate it was simply recorded as '*Dissolutio sanguinis.*'

* * *

Anna Klimovna called in early on the following morning and was informed that Zavalishin had died in the night.

She did not cry, nor even produce a handkerchief. She merely asked what was to happen now – whether it was she who had to see about having him buried or whether the hospital would see to it. Downstairs, however, to the woman who was acting as porter, she said in a plaintive tone, shaking her head:

'And he had such an important job too, such a special job, though he did come of working people and was a simple man himself. They paid him in wages and rations for each bit of work he did, by the job like. Sometimes he'd get a lot of money all in one go; and he'd get all sorts of clothes. And there was always white flour with the rations, and honey, and often material and galoshes and all. It wasn't work anyone would have done, I know; but they really did pay him properly for it. We've got a flat with three rooms and a kitchen, and all sorts of stores, and for Easter I reared a pig.'

At this point, remembering her pig, Anna Klimovna gave her first sob, took out a clean handkerchief and wiped her dry eyes.

– LXXXV –

THE SIVTZEV VRAZHEK PARTY

The wooden staircase creaked a welcome under familiar footsteps; the door opened wide with warm hospitality, the hallstand received hats and coats with courteous bearing, and the walls of the old house caught the sounds of familiar voices.

On the professor's birthday the little house had gathered together all those who still remembered its open-hearted hospitality of old. Even Lenotchka, the young girl with the surprised lift of the eyebrows, now the mother of two children, even she – a rare guest these days – came to see the old man and the friend of her schooldays.

The first to arrive was the professor of physics, Poplavsky, in a black frock-coat worn quite threadbare, but wearing a new pair of galoshes, acquired at the price of long hours of waiting in a queue. Poplavsky, who was overjoyed with his galoshes, was of the opinion that things were far easier, and that the only misfortune was that it was almost impossible to get new books from abroad, even through friends.

'We shall get so behind the times that it will take us more than ten years later on to catch up with the rest of Europe.'

'No great loss,' Protassov put in, by way of cheering him up. 'We have quite enough knowledge as it is for the moment. It would be something if we could apply properly what we do know.'

Uncle Borya backed his colleague:

'What is the good of talking of new books nowadays? If only we could get carbon paper and ribbon for the typewriters! In our Department of Industrial Research…'

Vassya and Alyonushka came too. Vassya had suddenly acquired a grown-up, manly air, although he wore no beard, Alyonushka having taken a liking to the little cleft in his chin. Not a button of his was missing; his collar was clean, his handkerchief hemmed and marked. The old embarrassment was gone too. He talked with Tanyusha with a courteous friendliness, and recalled with Protassov their journey together as bagmen. Alyonushka bore herself naturally, but was nervous lest she should laugh. Towards the end of the evening, however, the professor said something funny to her and she went off into peals of her bell-like laughter, grunted, and was overcome with confusion on seeing Lenotchka's brows – she was not acquainted with Lenotchka – lift with surprise. Alyonushka sat next to the professor, who talked with her the whole evening, gazing affectionately across at Vassya.

The only people not at the party were those who were no longer able to come, those whose names were pronounced with a grave expression and in a low voice. Among the absent was one with whom Poplavsky, with his incomprehension and dislike of idle paradoxes, had had many an argument in this very same room; one whose tragic departure from the world of the living was too recent, too fresh still, for it to have faded from the annals of family sorrows. In spite of all that Moscow life could do to inure men to loss and misfortune, those gathered together in the peaceful rooms of the little house tried not to pronounce Astafiev's name. In course of time his name would come to be joined in the death-roll to the names of Ehrberg, killed so young, of Stolnikov, that tragic figure, and of many other friends, both close and distant.

Punctually at nine o'clock, the hallstand received and hung on its outermost peg the check-lined coat.

Blinking in the light and rubbing his hands, Edward Lvovitch entered, shook hands with everyone and sat down in his usual place at the tea-table – formerly on Aglaya Dmitrevna's right, now on Tanyusha's.

In honour of the occasion real tea was served; and in the very middle of the table, on a large dish, lay a wonderful sweet cracknel, made of white flour. In one little bowl was sugar; in another, cheap sweets. And there was real butter too, and a whole plateful of smoked sausage, cut in thin slices. In grandfather's honour the table had been decked to look very special and festive.

There was something else too, something which Tanyusha had specially prepared for Edward Lvovitch, and which excited general wonder: nothing less than sweet white rusks, his favourite delicacy. In the old days neither Aglaya Dmitrevna nor Tanyusha had ever forgotten to put out sweet rusks for the composer. But it was two years now since Edward Lvovitch had forgotten their flavour; Tanyusha had not been able to do more than dry bits of black bread for him. Today, however, she had managed to get a whole plateful for grandfather and her dear music-master.

'They are only for Edward Lvovitch! You must eat them all up and not leave a single one.'

He was embarrassed; but not even these special attentions could rouse him from his despondency. It was a long time now since he had evinced a lively interest even in conversations on music, even before the keyboard of the familiar grand piano.

The ornithologist sat in an easy-chair next to Alyonushka, whom he was playfully teasing, assuring her that Vassya could not stir his tea without her assistance:

'And to think how independent he used to be! So independent that he and Pyotr Pavlovitch used to go together and barter with the wild tribes of Russia. It was he who exchanged my hunting-boots for gold sand and ivory. That was what he was like!'

Uncle Borya attempted to talk about the grandiose plans of his Department of Industrial Research, especially those concerned with electrification, but Protassov broke in with an ironic smile:

'Plans! What are plans? Now, if you'd just abstain from interfering with the real work that is being done, our simple factory work. Plans are all very well: no particular harm comes of them of course; in fact they may even come in useful after all your learned talk is over.'

Tanyusha performed the dudes of hostess. As she looked round the compact small circle of family friends she said to herself:

'Grandfather is pleased. He is happy that he has not been forgotten. Edward Lvovitch must absolutely consent to play tonight.'

And when the plate with the sausage was empty and there remained only sweet crumbs of the cracknel, Tanyusha lit the candles at the piano:

'You will play to us, won't you, Edward Lvovitch?'

To her surprise he consented at once:

'Yes, I should very much rike to. There is one thing I have never yet – '

'Your new one?'

'Wer, it's over a year since I finished it. But I have never yet prayed it anywhere. It is entitred – that is to say, it has no name, but it is my rast work. It is my Opus 37.'

He went up to the piano, blew out the candles and waited for everyone to settle down.

Grandfather's chair was drawn up nearer to the divan on which Alyonushka, Lenotchka and Vassya had seated themselves. Poplavsky sat on a chair in a dim corner as usual Uncle Borya and Protassov remained at the tea-table.

Tanyusha settled herself on the rug at grandfather's feet, with her head on his knees.

* * *

Only Tanyusha could realize what a sacrifice Edward Lvovitch had made in consenting to play his last work. She listened, not missing a sound, and suffered with her master – suffered for him perhaps.

She saw that there had come a breach in his creative powers, that a catastrophe had taken place; that, powerless to deny the musical conceptions he had served all his life, he had suddenly shaken the pillars and brought down upon himself the temple they had supported. And now he was struggling under the ruins. Parallel with his own life, something new had been born, something he wanted to understand, master and – it seemed – justify. But he lacked the right means of expression and blending of tones. It was a cry of pain – nothing else; a cry smothered by the voices of others hostile to him and unknown.

Tanyusha saw how Edward Lvovitch's long fingers dug into the keys, how he longed to convince himself, how his pale, thin face twitched, how he suffered.

Oh, why had she asked him to play!

He ended on a broken chord, leaped up at once from the stool, pulled down the cover with quivering fingers, dropped it, started nervously, and remained, in his bewilderment, motionless, with his back to them all.

Tanyusha realized that she must come to his aid. She went up and, without a word – and everyone else was silent too – gently stroked his sleeve.

Edward Lvovitch looked round and muttered:

'Yes, yes, that's my rast work, Opus 37.'

Then he rubbed his hands and, without taking leave of anyone, went hastily out into the hall.

Tanyusha followed him. But she sought in vain for the right words to say to him. And were there such words?

Pulling his coat off the peg, Edward Lvovitch rapidly thrust an arm into one sleeve and lengthily searched for the other. Tanyusha helped him. Then he turned round and produced from his pocket the manuscript, rolled up tight and wrapped round several times with a piece of fine thread. He thrust it towards her:

'That's for you. I have dedicated my Opus 37, my rast opus, to you. It's for you onry. Yes, it's right that it should be. Goodbye.'

'Thank you, Edward Lvovitch. But why are you in such a hurry to go?'

'It's right that I should go. I must.'

He went up to the front door, caught at the bolt and, turning round, looked into her face again:

'Opus 37 is the work of a genius. Goodbye.'

Tanyusha heard him stumble on the stairs and hurry away.

– LXXXVI –

WHEN THE SWALLOWS COME BACK

The party broke up early.

'You must be very tired, grandfather. Won't you go to bed a little earlier tonight?'

'I am a little tired, it's true, but not sleepy. I will stay up a bit longer with you young people before going to my room.'

Tanyusha cleared away the tea things, moved the chairs back to their usual places and put the cover over the grand piano. Pyotr Pavlovitch helped her. The professor lay back in his deep armchair, with half-closed eyes. When all was tidy, Tanyusha returned to her place on the rug at his feet.

Stroking his granddaughter's head, the old man continued:

'When it's quiet in here and we are sitting like this it always seems to me as if the walls were whispering. The house is old and there is so much for it to remember. This house, Pyotr Pavlovitch, was built by my mother, Tanyusha's great-grandmother. In those days it was considered to be a grand place, a really large house, fit for people of good family. There were various offices in the yard, and stables, an aviary too, and of course a bathhouse. It is only quite lately that we had the bathhouse pulled down for firewood. Here I have lived all my life and here I have come to the end of my journey. But the house has now come to belong to no one, and the people on the other side of the wall are strangers.'

'They are quiet people, grandfather, not at all troublesome.'

'Oh, I am not complaining. We have all got to live. I am merely recalling what it used to be like in the past. Times have changed so.'

And he went on:

'Now tell me, Pyotr Pavlovitch — what is life going to be like for the young? Better than it was in my day, or the same, or more difficult?'

'I think that life is going to be more complex for us, professor. And as for living all one's life in one house, that of course is impossible nowadays.'

'And, in general, is life going to be any better? Things are in a dreadful state now, I know. But these are very special times; this is an age of transition. One must suffer through it and come out into a new age. The suffering will have to go on many years, of course.'

'Enough to last our generation.'

'I think so too. Long years must pass before life can right itself. There is Poplavsky, ever complaining that we have cut ourselves off from the rest of Europe and that we shall never be able to catch up again. It is hard on a scholar like him.'

'In that particular respect we shall catch up Europe sooner than Poplavsky imagines. It's the economic situation that is so desperate; everything has been destroyed and our poverty is appalling. And there are still so few people of the right sort.'

'The right people will come all in good time; there are many of them in Russia.'

'They will come, I know,' said Protassov — 'quite new people, stronger, I've no doubt, than those before them.'

The old man was silent for a moment; then, stroking Tanyusha's head, went on:

'It is such a good thing that Pyotr Pavlovitch is hopeful, Tanyusha. You, too, should try to believe in the future.'

'But I do believe, grandfather.'

'People will come, new people, who will try to do everything in a new way, in their own way. Then, having tried and failed and thought it over, they will realize that nothing new can endure without old foundations, that without these foundations whatever they build must inevitably crumble. They will realize, too, that they cannot do without the culture of past ages, that they cannot afford to sweep it aside. And they will take up again the old books and learn what has been learned before them and seek the results of former experience. That will come; that must come. And then, Tanyusha, they will remember us old ones as well, your grandfather also, perhaps, and put back his books on the shelf. His science, too, may be of some use.'

'Why, of course it will, grandfather!'

'And birds will come in useful as well. They cannot fail to be of use, my little birds! We will give them a place in life, won't we, Tanyusha?'

'Spring is coming, grandfather, and our swallows will be coming back soon.'

'They will, of course they will. It is all the same to the swallows what people are quarrelling about, who is fighting against whom and who comes out top. One today, another tomorrow, and so all over again... Now the swallows have laws of their own, and their laws are eternal. And these laws are of much greater importance than any of our making. We still know very little about them; so much yet remains to be discovered.'

They sat on a long time in silence. And, true, the walls of the old house were whispering. Bending his head to Tanyusha's, so that the grey beard tickled her brow, the ornithologist said in a voice caressing and low:

'Make a note of it, Tanyusha. Write it down.'

'Write down what, grandfather?'

'When the swallows come back this spring – make a note of the day. I may not be there to do it myself. But you will, won't you? Be sure you do it.'

'Grandfather!...'

'Yes, yes, make a note of it, either in the calendar or else in the notebook where I always write it down. There will be one note more. That is very important, Tanyusha, more important perhaps than anything else. You will, girlie, won't you? It would make me happy.'

Grandfather's gentle hand stroked her head.

'Grandfather, dear grandfather, why, yes, of course I will, grandfather...'